"Sometimes people think they're making mistakes when they really aren't." Ray's voice was surprisingly soft compared to her expression.

"How do you know the difference?" Lee's own voice sounded strange to her ears.

"You don't until it's over." Ray stepped closer to her and lifted her hand to Lee's shoulder again. Lee felt her heart thudding in her chest. The two women studied each other for a moment longer, and then Lee closed her eyes as Ray leaned forward.

LEE'S AWAKENING

by

Rebecca Montague

Cape Winds Press
Daytona Beach, Florida
2013

Printed in the United States of America
First Edition

ISBN 978-1-58972-008-4

Published by Cape Winds Press
http://www.capewindspress.com

BOOKS BY REBECCA MONTAGUE

A Wild Sea

Barnfire

Erotic Interludes, volume 1 (contributor)

Dedicated to Mercedes
Thank you

I.

"Have you lost your mind, Lee?"

Lee Compton paused from scanning her closet. "Hello to you, too, Louise." She pulled two blouses out and compared them, tucking the phone between her shoulder and ear.

"You're giving up The Lion King to go to a lesbian bar. Do you know how long it took me to get these seats?" Louise's voice was reproving.

"I promised Stacy I'd go last month. It's her partner's birthday." Lee didn't know what she should wear to a lesbian bar; she couldn't quite believe she was going to one, but that's where Donna's party was being held and she had promised Stacy she would attend. "I only got your message yesterday, and I called you right back. It's just a show, Louise. I think I'll survive." She gave up on the blouses and went to find a more casual shirt.

"A touring Broadway show finally comes to Daytona and you're going to a birthday party. I don't get you sometimes, Lee."

"I promised," Lee repeated, getting a little annoyed.

"Well, watch yourself. I'm sure those women won't believe you aren't interested." Louise sounded somewhat imperious as she spoke. "You know how they are."

Lee rolled her eyes. "And how are they, Louise?" She settled on a white button-down and started searching for a belt to match.

"They're lesbians. All they think about is sex. I'm worried about you going."

"Oh, for God's sake." Lee lost her patience. "That is not all they think about. Lesbians are just like us except they don't sleep with men."

"Well, you'll see." Louise's voice spoke volumes about what she thought of Lee's statement, and what she thought was that Lee was naïve and in for trouble.

"I have to get dressed, Louise. Enjoy the show. I'm sure Caroline won't be broken up that I couldn't go; she got my seat, after all."

"Fine. Are we on for tennis on Tuesday?" Louise still sounded concerned.

"Of course. Have fun." Lee broke the connection and stared into her closet, fighting the annoyance that had flared. Louise had been her best friend since grade school, but sometimes she could be very narrow-minded.

The doorbell rang as she ironed her pants. A glance at her watch told her she was running late; she went to let Stacy in, apologized, and offered her a drink.

Stacy took a rum and coke and sat on the couch watching her. "Real people don't iron their jeans," she commented finally, her voice laughing around the edges.

"Robert liked his jeans pressed. I got into the habit." Five years of ironing jeans and doing whatever else was required of a pampered housewife to keep her husband happy. It was the 'whatever else' that had finally gotten so old. *Treating me like a ten year-old ... Controlling bastard!*

"Forget Robert. He was a jerk anyway."

"They look better this way." Lee finished with one leg and started the other.

"Are you getting nervous about going?"

"No." Lee felt a little embarrassed when Stacy gave her a stern look. "Ok, some."

Stacy leaned back against the couch and studied her. "You won't have to worry about getting hit on tonight, at least."

"By men," Lee returned with a somewhat weak laugh. "But I

have you to protect me, right?" She finished ironing and held the jeans up for inspection.

"Well, you are a long tall drink of water, my dear." Stacy grinned when Lee turned and shot out her tongue. "You're safe. Donna and I won't let anyone bother you."

"Good. I can't believe you talked me into this."

Stacy shrugged. "It's just a gay bar. It's not like we invited you to an orgy."

"Still." Lee went into the bedroom to get dressed. As she buttoned her shirt she called out, "I'm going to be the only straight one there, aren't I?"

"Maybe," Stacy returned. "What difference does it make? We'll have fun. I bet I can get you to do karaoke."

"Not damned likely!" Lee slipped her feet into her loafers and returning to the living room. "All right, I'm as ready as I'm going to be."

"Good. You take as long to get ready as Donna does, and that's saying a lot. I know you spent forty-five minutes in there before I got here, deciding what to wear."

Lee growled at her. "God, you're annoying."

"But you love me anyway."

Stacy got up and waited while Lee got her jacket from the hall closet, then the pair went out to Stacy's car.

As Lee got in the passenger seat, she asked, "You're sure I'll be able to get home?"

"Someone will give you a lift or I'll spring for a cab. Stop worrying! We're going to have a great time."

Lee nodded, not at all sure of the last statement but willing to do just about anything to put the thought of Robert out of her mind. Maybe a night surrounded by women, even if they were lesbians, would lift her spirits.

After checking that Lee had fastened her seatbelt, Stacy turned on the car and headed for Maddie's.

*   *   *

"How's work?" Joan asked by way of greeting.

Ray Elliot sank down onto a bar stool and pulled out her

wallet. "Pretty good. We're wiring some fancy new house on beachside. These people want speakers in every room, so we're dealing with the audio guys while we're running wire. They can be so pushy. But without electric those speakers won't be much good, so I guess we'll win."

"Go get 'em." Joan put a longneck bottle on the coaster in front of her. "Any word on the promotion?"

"I still don't know if Steve is actually leaving." Ray took a swig of her beer. "But hopefully if he does I'll get the job. I have seniority."

"And you're damned good, or so you keep telling me."

Ray shot her a dirty look before laughing. "Fuck you." She grinned.

"No thanks. I've got Lisa to do that for me," Joan returned.

"What's it like to sleep with the same woman every night for forty years?"

"You'll find out some day." Joan wiped the top of the bar with a towel.

Ray snorted. "Not bloody likely. I'm not going to get caught by anybody."

"What about Terry?"

"Terry's fun, but I'm not going to fall in love with her." Ray took another drink. "She's already trying to make more of it than it is. I don't think we'll be seeing each other for too much longer."

"You need to slow down on the women or there won't be any left." Joan turned when someone called her name. "That's my cue to actually work." She winked. "You'll get caught, Ray, one of these days. Mark my words."

Ray watched her walk off before letting Terry wander through her mind. The sex was pretty good but she was awfully annoying otherwise, and lately she'd been hinting about wanting to make more of the relationship than Ray was willing to give. Ray wasn't the sort to hook up with a woman for more than a good time, and she knew it.

She picked up her beer and turned to survey the room. It was fairly empty, but then it was only seven thirty. Donna's party wouldn't start until at least eight, when the birthday girl was supposed to arrive, but given dyke time, it would more likely be eight thirty or nine.

She'd brought a gift, but wasn't certain she'd join the party; though she had known both Donna and Stacy for a long time, she didn't know either very well. There was a woman across the bar she was far more interested in trying to spend the evening with. Joan's parting comment rose in her thoughts and she drained her beer in irritation. *Who needs love, anyway? Pain in the ass waste of time.* Ray gestured for another drink and rolled her neck. She wasn't about to get caught. *Not now, not ever.*

*   *   *

Stacy hadn't yet found a spot into the back parking lot of the bar before Lee felt the butterflies starting to dance in her stomach. *You're being silly.* It was just a bar after all, and Stacy was there to make things easier.

"Ready?" Stacy glanced at her. "Relax; there will be hardly anyone here this early. You'll have time to get acclimated before it fills up."

"I'm not nervous," Lee lied.

"Bullshit. Don't worry, a couple of glasses of wine and you'll forget it's a gay bar."

"Until two women start making out," Lee replied, feeling a little better that Stacy was trying to smooth her nervousness.

"Well, that's true. But there will be a couple of men there, so you'll have some eye candy to distract you."

"I'm not looking for eye candy."

Stacy sighed. "You'll find someone right for you eventually. Just get back on the horse."

"Eventually. For now I'm going to enjoy being single." *As single as I can be with Robert begging me to come back.* It had been two months and despite the legal paperwork giving her maintenance he still hadn't gotten the idea that she was serious about the separation. *I should stop stalling and file for divorce.*

"You're thinking about that jackass again." Stacy pursed her lips. "Don't let him ruin your evening."

Lee frowned at her. "I'm not letting him ruin anything."

"Don't. Come on; I want to make sure everything is set up

before Donna gets here."

"Fine." Lee tried to calm her nerves as they got out of the car.

For a moment, she wished she had driven herself, but knew she'd never have found the place. She was horrible with directions. Stacy started for the door. Pushing thoughts of Robert and her general disinterest in dating again out of her mind, Lee blew out a long sigh and followed her inside.

*   *   *

"Hey, who is that?" Ray leaned across the bar and batted at Joan's arm before pointing to the two women that had just entered the building.

"That's Stacy, you idiot," Joan returned lightly.

"I know who she is. I mean, who is that with her?"

Joan adjusted her glasses and studied the tall woman briefly. "I couldn't tell you. I've never seen her before."

Ray took in the lithe shape of the woman beside Stacy Matthews. She was tall, maybe five ten, with sandy blonde hair cut in a boyish fashion. She wore a button-down shirt and blue jeans and seemed somewhat ill at ease. Ray thought she was the cutest thing to walk through the back door of Maddie's in a very long time.

Stacy and the woman came to the bar, where Stacy plopped down on a bar stool. "Heya Joan; bourbon and water, please. What'll you have, Lee?"

"Wine, please. Blush if you have it."

As Joan bent to pour the drinks, Ray lifted her hand in greeting. "Hey, Stacy. Is Donna still in the dark?"

"As far as I know. Tracy's done a pretty good job of dragging out this wedding thing. Donna's in her element, picking out dresses."

"Ah, heaven for a femme." Ray took a long drink of her Amber Bock and studied the woman Stacy had referred to as Lee around the bottle. Up close, she looked to be in her late twenties or early thirties with chocolate eyes that sucked Ray in and made her sweat. *Damn, where has she been hiding?*

"Yeah." Stacy's eyes narrowed as her gaze darted across Ray's face. "Ray, this is Lee, a friend of mine; a straight friend."

Lee seemed a little taken aback at the comment, but then her gaze slid to Ray's face and she blushed.

"Well, nice to meet you Lee, Stacy's straight friend." Ray felt disappointment; Lee looked like she could be a lot of fun.

"Likewise." Lee's voice was smoky, almost sultry, and Ray wondered if she knew it.

"I bought Donna a gift card to Victoria's Secret. I hope that was ok." Ray turned her attention to Stacy, very aware that Lee was still studying her.

"She'll love it. So will I. Give it to her before she gets drunk though or she'll lose it. I'm sure she'll be pretty high before she leaves here." Stacy laughed. "Thank God she doesn't have to work tomorrow."

Ray laughed with her. "Deal. So, Lee, have you known Stacy long?"

Looking startled at being spoken to, Lee paused a moment before responding. "A few years; we used to work together."

"Is this your first time in a gay bar?" Ray raised her eyebrow and grinned just a little.

Lee blushed again. Ray was somewhat disconcerted to think that it made her look adorable. The blonde took a not-too-ladylike swig of the wine Joan had just set in front of her before answering. "Yes, it is."

"See anything you like?"

"I'm not in the market for anything." Lee's voice wavered slightly.

"That's too bad; there are some real lookers in here tonight." Ray fought a laugh.

"I'm sure there are. Do you consider yourself one of them?" Lee raised an eyebrow and looked at her archly.

"Of course; you must be straight if you can't see that." Ray made sure her expression didn't show her humor. She caught the dirty look Stacy was throwing her and relented, although she was very much enjoying tormenting Lee. "I'm just kidding. Other than me you'll find we're just as normal as your straight friends."

"I have no doubt," Lee replied, appearing to regain her

composure. "If you'll excuse me, I need to use the restroom."

Ray made a gesture toward the back of the bar and Lee walked off, leaving Stacy still glaring at Ray.

"Will you lay off her?" Stacy hissed.

"Christ, Stacy. I was just having a little fun." Ray took another swallow of beer. "She seems like a nice kid."

"I promised her she'd be safe here. She's tired of getting hit on."

Ray lifted her eyebrow again. "I wasn't hitting on her."

"Well, don't. I know you; you've got that look you get." Stacy lifted her glass. "I'll beat you senseless if you embarrass her any further while she's here."

"What do you mean she's tired of getting hit on? Man problems?" Ray laughed. "Maybe she'd welcome getting hit on by a woman for a change."

"I mean it Ray."

Ray made a show of pouting. "Fine, don't let me have any fun." She turned the conversation to Donna, all the while her mind running over an image of Lee standing naked before her.

She'd never even thought about seducing a straight woman. She wasn't up for the trouble it could cause. Yet, even though she hadn't been flirting, she hadn't been entirely joking either. Something about Lee drew her in a way that no woman had in a long time, something intriguing and strangely arousing. Shaking herself, Ray drowned the thought with a long drink from her bottle.

*   *   *

Lee closed the door to the stall and leaned against it, trying to calm the pounding of her heart that had started when the brunette first spoke to her. Something about that woman made her nervous—nervous, but not afraid. The thought confused her.

It's just feeling out of place, she told herself sternly. She was uncomfortable enough without making herself totally nuts over a comment clearly designed to embarrass her. She'd been there three minutes and already the woman next to her at the bar had gotten under her skin.

Despite claiming not to notice, Lee thought the woman—*what was her name, Ray?*—*was* attractive. Her dark hair was cut even shorter than Lee's own and spiked up on top, where Lee's lay softly over her head. She looked to be in her mid-thirties but it was hard to tell underneath the deep tan, tattoos, and Margaritaville t-shirt the woman wore.

She had an open, honest face and a ready smile. Her grey-blue eyes snapped when she spoke and when she turned her gaze on Lee, they seemed to bore through Lee's own like a drill on high speed, leaving her feeling shaky and confused.

She certainly hadn't been flirting, of that much Lee was certain. If anything, she was making fun of her, and Lee had made it easy by blushing so quickly. For a moment, she cursed this habit of hers; it was apparent it had only served to egg Ray on.

Even so, she knew that her blush hadn't been the result of only Ray's words. The sound of the woman's voice, gravelly and low, sent a shiver down Lee's spine. It was a voice that managed to sound intimate in the most innocent of comments. When used intentionally, Lee was certain it could melt anyone's reserves.

Despite her forwardness, Lee sensed somehow that Ray had a good heart. She obviously had a sense of humor, even if it was a bit twisted. Lee felt that, given the chance, they could become friends. She didn't have many true friends, male or female; men always seemed to want one thing and one thing only, and Lee found most women too flighty to hang around with. Ray struck her as anything but flighty.

"It's probably good Stacy said what she did," she muttered. She would rather be introduced as straight than have to explain it herself in a more awkward situation, and she suspected the introduction was intended to head off just such an occurrence.

I can't stay in here all night. Even though Ray had thrown her, she had to get back out and pretend not to be nervous; otherwise, Stacy would never let her live it down. She quickly used the bathroom, washed her hands, and walked back out to the bar prepared to go toe-to-toe again with Ray if it came to it.

Stacy had moved to a table when Lee came back from the bathroom, while Ray still sat at the bar, deep in conversation with the bartender. Lee sat down across from her friend and reached for her wine.

"Never mind Ray," Stacy said. "She can be a pain in the ass. Don't let her bug you."

"She didn't bother me," Lee replied, although she knew Ray had bothered her, and not in the way Stacy was talking about. It was an unsettling thought.

"The others should be showing up soon. Tracy will bring Donna by around eight."

"I'm not really going to be the only —" Lee cut herself off and looked away. She caught sight of Ray, leaning over with a wry grin on her face, speaking to a blonde who had just joined her at the bar. Ray looked around, caught her eye, and winked. Lee pulled her attention back to Stacy and finished, "The only straight person here?"

"No. Some of Donna's co-workers will be here. There are a couple of nice single men, if you're interested." Stacy poked at her ice with her straw.

Lee managed to laugh. "Not interested. I'm through with men, at least for a while."

"Robert didn't hurt you that badly, did he?"

"He didn't hurt me, Stacy." Lee frowned. "He was just ..." she trailed off.

"He was just what?" Stacy cocked her head and looked at Lee curiously.

Lee sighed. "I don't know. I don't want to lose myself in someone again. My life can be complete enough without that. Robert wanted me to need him in order to breathe. I was stupid to buy into it, and I don't want to be sucked in like that again."

"You have been pretty damned independent since you left him," Stacy agreed with a laugh. "I can imagine you're going to be a handful."

"I refuse to settle this time. If that means staying single the rest of my life, so be it. There has to be someone out there, but if I don't find him, I'm not going to cry myself to sleep over it." Lee glanced over toward Ray once more, and found her watching them. Their eyes met yet again and Ray turned back to the bar.

Stacy waved at someone behind her. "Jo and Theresa are here. That means the others will be trailing in soon. Let me get us two more drinks and I'll introduce you."

"I'll get them." Lee wasn't sure why she offered so quickly, but Stacy shrugged and sat back down.

There was plenty of space for Lee to stand and get the bartender's attention, but she walked up beside Ray and put a twenty down on the bar.

"Two of the same?" the bartender asked.

"Yes, please." The bartender went to get the wine and Lee turned to Ray. "Will you be joining the party?"

Ray studied her from underneath her eyelids. "Maybe. Why?"

"I was just wondering. You and Stacy seem to know each other."

"We do. I know a lot of people. Now I know you." Ray grinned. "Maybe I will join y'all, but only if you let me buy you a drink."

Lee looked at her for a long moment, trying to decide what exactly she meant and whether she was joking or serious. "I won't turn down a free drink," she finally replied, refusing to let Ray put her off balance again.

"Good." Ray took a swig of her beer. "I'll be over in a few."

"Good." Lee took her drinks and turned to walk back to the table, where four women had joined Stacy; something made her turn back. "Of course, you'll have to let me buy *you* a drink."

Ray's smile was brilliant. "I won't turn down a free drink," she said in a laughing tone. Lee nodded and returned to the table, uncomfortably aware that she found Ray's voice even more intriguing. As she got settled, she glanced back and found the older woman watching her. A moment later, Ray dropped her gaze back to the bottle in front of her.

Twenty minutes later, the group had grown to nine. Three men had joined them, looking even more out of place than Lee had initially felt. Surprisingly, she started to feel uncomfortable once again when they apparently picked her out as possibly available and started trying to talk to her.

Instead of turning to Stacy, however, she found herself

looking in Ray's direction more often, though why she would wish for the woman's presence baffled her. After a few more minutes, Ray got another beer and came over to the table.

"Decided to join us?" Stacy raised an eyebrow at her.

"Yes." Ray glanced at Lee and took an empty chair a few seats down from her. "Might as well be sociable."

Lee tried to study Ray surreptitiously, but it seemed she was unsuccessful as Ray caught her gaze and grinned. Blushing, she looked down at her wine. *She has a great smile.* Even though she had asked if the woman would be coming over, she wasn't certain what she should do if Ray singled her out. *I'd rather talk to her than Tom, Dick and Harry over there, but ... Don't get paranoid, Lee. She's just another person at the table.*

During the next hour, Lee tried to keep up with the conversation, succeeding only about half the time. The mood was jovial and there was a great deal of flirting going on between the women. It seemed to Lee that flirting was second nature to lesbians. Ray was consummate at it, even throwing a few comments at Lee that were hard to interpret in any other way; they were certainly not meant as teasing.

Somewhere in the back of her mind, she realized that she wasn't embarrassed by the attention. In fact, she found it rather refreshing. Ray's personality shown in the crowd and to her surprise Lee found that she kept picking out the woman's gravelly voice among the chatter.

Ray was witty, had a bawdy sense of humor, and in general made Lee want to get to know her better. She wasn't sure why, because the older woman was far away from the type of person she normally counted as a friend, but the desire was there nonetheless.

Lee wasn't much of a drinker, and so she sat out of the game of quarters that sprang up after the first hour. When the smoke in the air started making her eyes water, she got up and excused herself to go outside for a few minutes. She stood on the back steps breathing deeply, listening to the music thumping from the building behind her, her thoughts unexpectedly on Ray.

"Gets kind of close in there, doesn't it?" Ray's voice was like an unexpected caress down her back.

"Smoky; and loud." Lee turned and saw her lighting a small

cigarillo. "Donna has a lot of friends."

"Yes, she does." Ray walked down the steps and stood on the gravel in front of her. "I hope I didn't make you nervous at first. I was trying to get a rise out of you and I shouldn't have."

"I wasn't nervous," Lee replied, watching the curve of Ray's lips as she drew on the cigar. The end glowed bright red as she sucked in and then Lee watched her blow smoke rings into the air.

She became painfully aware that she was starting to wonder what a woman's lips would feel like, at least what Ray's would feel like, and decided she'd better slow down on the wine for the rest of the evening.

"It's not quite like a straight bar, is it?" Ray cocked her head and looked up at Lee.

"No. It's a lot more laid back."

"We have our share of drama." Ray's voice was quiet. "But you're a lot safer here than your average place."

Lee hesitated before speaking again. "How did you know ... I mean, when did you know ... I'm sorry, I'm being rude." *Why in the name of God did I ask her that?*

Ray laughed. "You mean when did I come out? I was nineteen and my best friend kissed me on a dare. She was mortified and I loved it; didn't take much figuring out after that."

"Oh. You make it sound like it was easy. Stacy said she had a hard time of it."

"Some people do. For me it was like waking up and finding that I'd been living half a life." Ray drew on the cigar again. "I never looked back. Dropped my boyfriend like a rock, I did."

"You had a boyfriend?"

"Well, yeah." Ray gave her a wry grin. "Not that we were doing anything. That part was always gross to me. I tried it once and said 'no thanks'. I suppose that should have been a clue."

"Well, maybe you're lucky. It doesn't get a whole lot better when you get older." Lee's eyes widened as she realized what she'd said.

Ray studied her seriously. "You sound like someone who just got dumped — or did the dumping. Which was it?"

Lee blushed. "I recently left my husband. He's a jerk."

"Then you're better off without him." Ray drew on the cigar one more time and flicked it out into the darkness. "So, you seem to have settled in pretty quickly. Finding us lesbians a little less dangerous than you'd been told?"

"I never thought lesbians were dangerous." Something in the back of Lee's mind told her that Ray could be dangerous; very dangerous, but in a way that she didn't want to think any more deeply about. *What am I doing? I've never been attracted to a woman in my life.*

Ray laughed. "That's refreshing, an open minded straight girl. Or is it something else?" She cocked her head again and gave Lee a look that sent a shiver through her.

"What else could there be?" Lee kept her voice light, certain that Ray was picking on her again.

"Yeah, what else could there be?" Ray echoed, looking unconvinced.

"I'd better get back inside," Lee said weakly, not wanting to continue the conversation lest she find out that Ray was serious and not sure how she'd react if she were.

Ray shrugged. "Go ahead."

For a moment, Lee hesitated, then turned and walked back into the bar.

Ray watched Lee go through the door and reached into her back pocket for the tin that held her cigarillos. She pulled another one out, then lit it and drew in deeply. There was something about Lee that held her attention; she was obviously intelligent, outgoing—charming even. She was like a breath of fresh air among the chatter of the others. She was most certainly not a working class stiff like Ray herself.

Ray was certain that Lee found her attractive, consciously or subconsciously. She had responded to the flirtatious comments Ray made with her own, meeting her comment for comment; she hadn't reacted to anyone else that way.

She was certainly a good looking woman and Ray had seen that she wasn't the only one who had noticed that. Before she could ponder on it any further, the door opened and Donna and Janet came out.

Donna grinned at Ray as she pulled a joint out of her cigarette box. "Taking in the air, or the sights?" she asked coyly.

"Smoking," Ray growled back.

"I plan on doing that too. Want a hit?" When Ray shook her head, she pulled out a lighter, put the joint to her lips, lit it and inhaled. After holding the smoke in for a moment, she blew it out and handed the joint to Janet. "You do know Lee is straight."

"Yes. What does that have to do with anything?"

Donna laughed. "Because you haven't been able to keep your eyes off her since I got here."

"That's bullshit." Ray knew she *had* been looking in Lee's direction an awful lot; not that she was going to tell that to Donna, or to anyone else.

"She's good looking, though. You have to admit."

"Yes, she's good looking. And I'm not looking." Ray shifted and drew heavily on her cigar, almost choking on the smoke. "I don't need the hassle."

Janet passed the joint back to Donna, who inhaled deeply before speaking again. "Personally, I think she's just deluding herself about being straight. If it walks like a duck ..."

"My gaydar did register a blip when she walked in," Ray admitted slowly. "But it could have just been the way she looks."

"I think she's gay," Janet interjected. "She's just in denial. She was certainly trading come-ons with you like a pro; more easily than I would expect a straight girl to."

"Whatever. I don't plan on finding out." Ray realized that given the chance, she would be very tempted to find out. It was an unsettling thought. She dropped the cigar and ground it out with the toe of her boot. "I'm going back inside. I need another beer."

Donna made a dismissive gesture with her hand as she took another hit off the joint and Ray stomped up the stairs and pulled the door open.

Her original seat had been taken and the only available chair was next to Lee. With a sigh, Ray got a beer and went to grab it before someone else did. Lee turned and smiled tentatively at her as she sat down. Ray smiled back. She had a distinct feeling that it was going to be a long night.

Sometime later in the evening, Lee was glad she hadn't driven. She'd had far more wine than she was used to and things were looking a little uneven. Ray had stayed beside her, and the flirting had gotten to the point that one of the men, who had been trying to strike up a conversation with her all night, finally gave up and went back to his friends. *If nothing else, I should thank her for that!* They sat whispering between themselves for a few moments, gave Lee a look, and went back to their drinks.

"We play volleyball at some friends' house on Sundays. You should come out and join us," Ray said to her unexpectedly, emptying her beer.

"That sounds like fun," Lee replied, drawing her attention back from a consideration of why she found Ray's flirtations far more enjoyable than the man's had been.

"Get the directions from Stacy or Donna. They come every Sunday. Maybe you could ride with them."

Lee frowned slightly. "I rode with Stacy tonight. It makes me nervous not being able to leave when I want."

Ray caught her gaze. "Do you want to leave?"

"Not really." Lee searched Ray's face, desperate to know why she felt such a strong attraction for the woman. It was nothing like she had ever experienced. It wasn't sexual — *at least I don't think it is ... of course it isn't!* — rather a deep desire to get to know what lay past the social facade and into the soul.

"Are you riding home with them?"

"No. Stacy said she'd find me a ride or call me a cab." Lee paused. "I probably should have driven myself but I was afraid I couldn't find the place."

"I can drive you home." Ray's voice was soft again, almost tentative.

Lee recognized she had been hoping Ray would offer, and pushed away the questions that realization raised within her. "When did you plan on leaving?"

"Whenever you're ready." Ray glanced away and then back.

Lee looked at her watch. It was going on ten-thirty. "I should be getting home soon. Maybe at eleven?"

"Sounds good to me."

The pair spent the next half hour chatting with each other, so much so that the others started ribbing them. Lee fended off the comments with more humor than she felt; Ray wasn't flirting anymore, but the heightened awareness of her presence persisted. *I'm glad to be going soon; I'm getting really tipsy.*

When it came time to leave, Stacy caught Lee by the door and pulled her aside. "Are you sure you want to have Ray drive you home? I can get someone else."

"Why wouldn't I want Ray to?"

"Well, she's been laying it on pretty thick. She might take your accepting a ride to mean something you don't want it to."

Lee laughed, realizing she was more than just tipsy. "Don't worry. She's well aware that I'm not looking for that kind of a ride." *At least I hope she's aware of that.*

"OK." Stacy looked unconvinced.

"Tell Donna I love her and you two drive safely getting home." Lee kissed Stacy's cheek and walked out the door, finding Ray standing outside lighting another cigarillo.

"Warned you off about me, did she?" Ray asked as she took Lee's elbow and guided her into the parking lot.

"I think I can handle myself. I'm a big girl."

Ray laughed. "Don't worry; I'm not going to attack you."

They stopped in front of a large black pickup truck. Ray pulled out her keys and unlocked the doors, then went around and opened the passenger side for Lee, who climbed in wondering just how big a truck needed to be.

Ray got into the driver's seat and started the ignition. She muttered an apology as she turned down the radio when it came on at high volume, and backed out of the spot. Once they were on the road, she finally spoke. "You'd have a lot of fun at volleyball."

"I'm sure I would. I'll call Stacy tomorrow for directions. I assume it's not too competitive."

"It's an excuse to get together and drink," Ray replied. "But we play hard, despite having no skill at it at all."

"Sounds like fun." Lee smiled. "I need to get out more anyway." She wasn't sure why she was agreeing so readily to spending an afternoon with the same group of lesbians she had been so nervous about meeting earlier in the evening, but she was drunk enough that she didn't ponder it too long.

They rode in silence until Ray pulled up in front of Lee's building and whistled. "Nice digs. Does your condo face the river?"

"Yes. I'm only renting though." Ray had told her she was an electrician, and she wasn't sure why, but she didn't want Ray to think she had more money than she did.

"You don't work and you can afford this? What did you do, win the lottery?"

Lee blushed. "My husband is a doctor. He's paying me some maintenance. "

"Must be nice. Not the separation, I mean, the rest of it." Ray blushed too.

"The separation is damned nice," Lee returned. "It would be nicer if I could just work up the nerve to file for divorce. He's not paying me that much and I'm living off my savings right now."

"Well, I won't invite you to my apartment then. It isn't nearly as nice as yours must be."

"I'm sure I'd love it." Lee wasn't certain why she said it. She was fairly certain she wouldn't love it. She had a feeling Ray's idea of decorating involved posters and early American throw-away furniture.

"I doubt it."

The two women studied each other for a long moment and for some reason Lee's heart started pounding. "I should go." She cursed her state of inebriation for letting her mind run away with her. "Thanks for the lift."

Ray grinned. "My pleasure."

They looked at each other again, and then Ray leaned over. Lee froze. *Oh my God, she's going to kiss me.*

II.

Lee's mind spun as Ray leaned over. But instead of kissing her, Ray reached for the door handle and popped the door open.

"I try to be a gentleman," she said with a grin.

Relieved, Lee unfastened her seatbelt. "Thank you."

"Have a good evening. Hopefully I'll see you at volleyball tomorrow."

"I'm sure you will." Lee got out of the truck. She closed the door and waved as Ray pulled out.

As soon as she was safely inside her condo, she sagged against the wall and put her hand to her face. "What the hell was that?" she asked the empty room. She had been certain Ray was going to kiss her. *I am drunk.* She pushed off from the wall and went to pour herself one more glass of wine; at that point, she was fairly certain it wouldn't hurt anything, at least not until morning. Sipping from the glass, she paced the living room.

What would she have done had Ray actually kissed her? How would she have reacted? She couldn't for the life of her figure out why Ray had her so off-balance. True, Ray had been flirting with her all night, but then Ray had been flirting with everybody all night. She'd mentioned she was seeing a woman, and she hadn't been leaning into Lee's space the way men usually did when they wanted to get to know her better.

... and I've never been attracted to a woman in my life. That she

19

had reminded herself of the fact several times during the evening did not help matters.

Despite her confusion, Lee knew she wanted to get to know Ray better. Volleyball seemed a safe place to do that. It was that time of year when the nights were still cool but the days could quickly get hot, and Lee couldn't drink much in the heat. She told herself that it was the alcohol that had caused her to start imagining things, although she knew that when Ray had leaned over there wasn't much else to think but she was about to get kissed.

Her mind touched on what it would be like to kiss another woman. She had kissed women on the lips before, certainly. She had kissed Louise on the lips. They were brief brushes to say hello. She wondered what it would be like to kiss a woman the way she once kissed Robert, what it would be like to kiss Ray that way. The thought set her heart to beating irregularly.

"Oh, for God's sake," she grumbled aloud.

She finished her wine and put the glass in the sink. She needed to go to sleep before her mind could take its current train of thought any further. With a sigh, she headed to the bedroom.

*   *   *

Ray stopped at the Quick Mart and picked up a couple of tallboys. She drove down to the beach, got out and walked a little way, stopping finally and sitting at the foot of a seawall. She cracked the first beer and took a long swallow.

"You're a total dumbass," she muttered.

She had almost kissed Lee. There was no doubt she wanted to. She hoped Lee hadn't noticed how she quickly moved to open the door when she got close. Of course, Lee had closed her eyes and started to lean into her, but Lee was also obviously drunk. It would have been a terribly wrong thing to do to take advantage of that.

It wasn't that she had any qualms about seducing a woman she had just met. She'd done it plenty of times before. But she couldn't think of the blonde as just another conquest. There was something about Lee that drew Ray in and made it hard for her to breathe, something about Lee that scared her.

"She's not even gay. Jesus." *At least, she isn't admitting it to herself, if she is.* There was no denying that she wanted Lee, but Ray didn't want to lead her into something she'd regret.

She'd found during the evening that she liked the woman. Ray knew a lot of people, but she didn't have a lot of true friends, and she felt that Lee could grow into a true friend. She didn't want to risk that just to satisfy her libido.

"Just rein yourself in, Ray. Get hold of yourself before you do something stupid."

Ray wasn't used to being honorable when it came to women, but she knew in this case it was the only way to be. She sat for a long time more, staring out over the darkness of the ocean and drinking her beer, and brooding.

*   *   *

Lee met Louise for lunch after tennis the next Tuesday. They chose a café near the river and sat on the patio so Louise could smoke. After the general pleasantries were out of the way, Lee decided to tell her friend about Donna's party.

"It was a lot of fun." Louise looked at her skeptically. "I really enjoyed myself."

"I can't for the life of me understand why you would want to go," Louise replied, stirring her iced tea with her straw. "What could you possibly have in common with a bunch of lesbians?"

"For God's sake, Louise, stop being so narrow-minded. As a matter of fact, I met a very nice woman there." She wasn't sure why she mentioned Ray. She hadn't planned to, knowing how Louise would react. She was right on target.

Louise's eyebrows went up. "You met a woman? What's that supposed to mean?"

Lee frowned, regretting bringing it up. "I mean I met a woman. She's very nice; she invited me to play volleyball on Sunday. I had a great time."

"You played volleyball? I didn't know you still played volleyball. Where did you go?"

21

"Some friends of Ray's. Stacy and Donna were there too." Lee took a sip of her wine and toyed with her salad. "I'm going next Sunday too."

"Am I to guess that this is a crowd from the bar you went to? I still don't understand why you and Stacy are such good friends. She's not the type of woman you should be hanging around with." Louise leaned forward. "Be careful, Lee. If people find out you're spending so much time with a bunch of lesbians they're liable to start making assumptions about you."

Lee got annoyed. "So what if they do? I'm not going to choose my friends based on what other people will think of me."

"What about this woman? Does she think you're just going to be friends? It's more likely she's trying to get you into bed."

"Jesus Christ, Louise! Listen to yourself; just because Ray is gay doesn't mean she's trying to seduce me." Lee dropped her fork onto her salad plate and pushed it away. "That's like saying just because a man wants to be friends he's trying to get me into bed." As soon as she spoke, she realized she'd drawn the wrong analogy.

Louise nodded vigorously. "I rest my case." She pursed her lips. "I just don't understand this sudden fascination you have with gay women. The past few months you've really drifted away from the group. We've missed you."

Lee assumed the group she was referring to was the social set she was accustomed to moving amongst. Now that she was separated and not spending so much time with them, she could see that the 'group', as Louise called it, was nothing more than a clique. Lee had never been fond of cliques, and wasn't about to change her plans to satisfy one.

"It isn't a fascination. I've just met some new people, that's all. Our group"—she made italics in the air—"is too busy lunching at the club to play volleyball. Or go out for a night on the town. I'm only twenty-nine. I'm bored with the group."

The pair paused while their lunches were served and Lee cut into her chicken to hide her annoyance with Louise. She realized she'd been getting annoyed with Louise a lot lately.

"Are you sure you want to go through with this divorce? Robert misses you terribly. I'm sure he's willing to make changes to please you."

Lee put her fork down forcefully. "I don't give a fuck what Robert is willing to do." She ignored the shocked expression on Louise's face. "I should never have married him in the first place. He always treated me like a child." Robert was twelve years older than she was and never let her forget it.

"Well. He still wants to talk to you, to try and reason this out. Surely you still love him?" Louise reached for her tea.

"I do *not* still love him. I thought you were my friend, not his."

Louise gave her a strange look. "I am. But I'm fond of him too."

"Then you marry him." Lee drained her wine and signaled for another glass.

Louise laughed, albeit a bit falsely. "I'm already married, silly."

Lee picked her fork back up and changed the subject, not willing to have her lunch ruined by thoughts of Robert or arguments about her associating with lesbians.

She escaped from the restaurant as quickly as possible after dessert and drove home in a foul humor. Opening a soda, she wandered out onto the balcony to drink it, staring over the river and pondering why Louise was getting on her nerves so much of late.

One of the obvious reasons was that she seemed to be on Robert's side a lot more than Lee would have expected her best friend to be. Louise and Robert had hit it off when Lee first met him, and for a while, Lee thought it might be Louise who ended up dating him. She sometimes wished it had been, but then she wouldn't wish what she went through for five years on anyone, least of all Louise.

More annoying, and frustrating because of it, was how Louise treated Stacy. Lee had long ago given up trying to get the two of them together for outings. They were like oil and water. Stacy was very firm in her beliefs, as was Louise, and they clashed about almost everything. It was a very red state/blue state sort of situation when the two were together.

Lee liked both of them equally, which had surprised her in the beginning. Stacy seemed a lot more real than Louise, who had always been a bit of a snob. Donna was very real as well, and Ray … well, Ray was about as real as they got. All of the women Lee had met at volleyball seemed real. There was no pretense among them. They drank, smoked, cussed, and had a good time doing it.

It had finally dawned on Lee after a few hours at volleyball that flirting was a way for these women to express their camaraderie. It seemed natural and good-natured. Even Lee had been able to throw a few comments of her own, mostly at Ray, and it made her feel more a part of the group. Only this group wasn't a clique. It was a gathering of women.

Lee finished her soda and continued staring out over the water, contemplating Louise's narrow-mindedness as opposed to Ray's open acceptance. It was like night and day, and of the two, Lee preferred Ray's outlook. She sat for a long time, wondering what that meant for her.

*   *   *

Ray cast her line and leaned back to snag her beer.

Jackie glanced over and grinned. "Think we're going to catch anything?"

"A buzz," Ray replied. "Probably a couple of crabs; maybe something for dinner if we're lucky."

"Is there any better way to spend a Saturday?" Jackie took a swig of her own beer and reeled in her line slowly, tugging at the rod as she did so to encourage the fish to bite.

"I don't think so." The two were fishing near the drawbridge north of Ormond Beach. They had a cooler of beer, which was technically not allowed in the park they were at, and an arsenal of lures and baits with which to tempt the denizens of the Halifax River.

"So, what did Steve say about the job?"

Ray shrugged and tugged on her line. "He's definitely leaving and I do have seniority. I can't see why I wouldn't get it."

"Is it a big raise?" Jackie pulled back hard on the rod and started to reel in, then slowed. "Damn, missed it."

"Four bucks an hour," Ray answered. "It couldn't come at a better time, either. I'm closing on my house next week."

"Yeah, congrats on that. When's the house warming party?"

Ray shrugged again. "Pretty soon, I guess."

"Will Terry be there?"

Ray thought this a not too subtle way of asking if they were still seeing each other. "I doubt it."

Jackie shook her head. "What went wrong this time?"

"Nothing went wrong. She just wanted more than I was willing to give."

"How long did it last, three weeks? That's almost a new record." Jackie reeled in her line and recast.

"Fuck you." Ray stuck out her tongue as Jackie laughed. "She was better in bed than most."

"Someday, you're going to get caught by a woman, and I hope I'm around to see your face when you realize it."

Ray screwed up her face. "That'll be the day. Ray Elliot doesn't get caught. I'm enjoying being footloose and fancy free too much."

"In other words, committing to someone scares the crap out of you." Jackie finished her beer and dumped the can back into the cooler. She tossed Ray another one before popping the top on her own.

"I see no point in getting tied down. Who wants to wake up next to the same woman every day for the rest of their lives?"

"It seems to be working for Joan and Lisa," Jackie pointed out. "And Stacy and Donna have been together for ten years."

Ray snorted. "And I can name a dozen women who lasted less than two and got their hearts stomped all over. No thanks."

She had made the mistake of saying 'I love you' once. It had gotten her nothing but a broken heart, when the woman she'd said it to decided Ray's supposed best friend was a better catch than Ray was. That was when Ray was twenty-three and she'd kept the vow that sprang from it, never to let it happen again.

"You're awfully gun shy for someone who's never had a serious relationship," Jackie commented.

Ray almost told her about Tina, but stopped herself. It was another town and another time. *Why dredge up the past?* She'd known Jackie for six years and hadn't mentioned it before; she wasn't about to do it now. "Never plan to, either. I'll die a horny old lady chasing the sixty-something's around."

"God, I can almost see that. So, what's up with Lee? I haven't seen you flirting so horribly in a long time. Trying to trip the straight girl?" Jackie quirked her lips and leered over at Ray.

"I just like antagonizing her," Ray replied, feeling a little guilty at the white lie. "She's so cute when she blushes."

"Hell, admit it, Ray. You've got the hots for her."

Speaking of blushes ... Ray fought the heat rising in her face. "So what if I do? Nothing's going to come of it. Even I'm not stupid enough to mess around with a straight woman."

"Thank God you've still got your wits about you. I was starting to worry." Jackie's face showed her relief. "I was afraid Lee was the reason things went south between you and Terry."

Ray laughed. "Don't be silly. Terry is the reason things went south." She was many things, but she never slept with more than one woman at a time.

"Still, she is really cute."

"I suppose she is," Ray admitted slowly, not wanting to let on just how cute she thought Lee was. "In a straight girl sort of way."

"Anyway, when do you find out about the promotion?" Jackie paused to re-bait her hook and then cast into the river. "Four bucks an hour is pretty damned good for a raise."

"Steve said they'll make a decision in a week or so. He promised to put in a good word for me." Steve had often said Ray was the hardest worker on his crew, and one of the most proficient. She'd been doing electrical work for seventeen years; she guessed she'd better be proficient by now.

"Well, I hope you get it."

"Me too."

The pair turned their attention to catching dinner.

*   *   *

"Get your tits out of the way!" Ray growled as she reached

down to offer her hand to Lee, who lay in the sand feeling somewhat foolish. She had made a diving try for the ball only to have it bounce off her chest. The result was that the ball was on the ground and so was she. She took Ray's hand and let her pull her to her feet.

"It's been a while since I played volleyball," Lee returned, brushing off her front. "I think my cup size has increased since high school." She decided that wearing a sports top might not have been the best move as she realized sand was working its way into uncomfortable places.

"Do I have to follow you around and hold them while you hit the ball?"

"Gee, thanks." Lee's voice wasn't as sarcastic as her words. Ray had been flirting with her since she arrived. Of course, it seemed that Ray flirted with everyone, all the time.

Ray had arrived with a woman in tow whom she introduced as Terry. The woman was short and a little stout, but with a pleasant face and voice to match. That the pair were a couple was fairly obvious, and Lee was relieved when the two set up their camp chairs on the other end of the playing court from where she sat with Stacy and Donna.

They ended up on the same team, and the comments had started almost immediately. Not willing to be embarrassed, Lee started throwing them back. She found it remarkably easy, easy enough that she was a little distressed. But she found it impossible to stop.

The teams got ready and the woman with the serve on the other side powered one over the net. Stacy set it and Ray pounded it back over. Two women dove for it, colliding with one another as the ball hit ground.

"Side out!"

"Hmm, that looks like fun. You want to tangle on the ground, Lee?" Ray raised an eyebrow and gave her a quick leer.

"Sounds like a blast. Is there a cute guy around for me to do it with?"

Ray laughed. "I'm butch, but I'm not that butch."

"You two knock it off and play, will you?" Donna called from the service line.

The pair went to their positions and got ready. Donna

lobbed the serve just over the net. It was returned and Stacy slapped at it, throwing it high enough for Lee to set. Ray tapped it over for a point.

"Nice set."

"Thank you." Lee grinned. She was having more fun than she'd had in a long time. A drink break was called and everyone went back to their chairs and coolers. Stacy pulled out a wine cooler and handed it to Lee, who opened it and took a long swallow, grateful for the cold liquid.

"You seem to be holding your own," Stacy commented as she sat down.

"It's been a while but I think I can handle it."

"I wasn't referring to the game." Stacy indicated Ray. "She can lay it on pretty thick."

"It's amusing. I'm not going to let her get the best of me, that's for sure." Lee sat down as well and fanned herself. "Damn, it's hot."

"It gets hotter," Stacy replied.

"Wait until August," Donna added, leaning around Stacy to grin at Lee. "You'll think you're going to melt."

"You should get Louise to come one Sunday." Stacy made the suggestion off-handedly and then grinned as Lee coughed. "What, she's too good for us blue collar types?"

"You and Louise in the same vicinity is never a good idea."

"Not my fault." Stacy shrugged and then looked over at Ray and Terry. "Looks like the bloom is coming off that rose."

Lee followed her gaze and saw the two talking seriously with one another, Terry's face angry. A few minutes later, she got up and left. Ray leaned back and stared off across the pasture, seemingly lost. She didn't even get up when the game resumed, until Donna yelled at her.

"Everything ok?" Lee asked as Ray joined them.

"Everything's fine," Ray responded. "Let's play."

She was strangely quiet for the rest of the game, and wandered off afterwards, lighting a cigar. Lee watched her go, and then took a beer from Donna, picked up her own wine cooler, and followed.

* * *

Ray was leaning against a tree with her back to the court when someone came up.

"I thought you might like a beer."

Ray turned to look at her, annoyed at being followed. When she saw Lee though, her expression softened.

"Thanks." She took the can and popped open the top. "Having fun?"

"Yes. You don't look like you are all of a sudden. Want to talk about it?"

Ray studied her. "Terry and I had a disagreement." What they'd had was a quiet argument about Ray's flirting with Lee, but Lee didn't need to know that. Terry's possessiveness had just about torn it between them.

"I'm sorry. Will it be ok?"

"Probably not." Ray shrugged. "Not a big deal. We've only been going out a few weeks."

Lee's eyes darted across her face, expressive in their curiosity. Behind the pair, someone yelled that the next game was starting. Neither woman moved, and the voice informed them that they would be replaced if they didn't get their asses back.

"You go ahead if you want. I think I'll stay over here for a while." Ray turned back around and stared toward the house. She sensed Lee shift and then out of the corner of her eye saw her lean against the tree herself.

"I think I'll sit out this one. It's nice and cool under here."

Ray felt strangely relieved that she was still there. She turned to face her and drew on her cigar. "You seem to have gotten used to us pretty quickly."

Lee shrugged. "What's there to get used to?"

"Not all straight women are so willing to jump into a crowd of lesbians."

"Stacy says I'm an honorary lesbian anyway." Lee laughed. "I'm certainly tired of men, that's for sure."

Ray stared at her for a long moment, wishing that the *honorary* wasn't necessary. She reminded herself that it was a dangerous game she was playing, flirting with Lee when she knew full well it wasn't all in jest. And yet, she couldn't help herself when she said, "Well, if you want to try a woman, give me a call."

Lee blushed deep red and Ray cursed herself for stepping over the line. *And that comment is stepping way over the line.* She lapsed into silence, trying to think of a way to take the words back.

"If I wanted to try a woman, I would." Lee laughed finally, but it sounded a little forced.

"I'm sorry, Lee. Sometimes I just don't know when to shut up."

Lee contemplated her, her face still pink. "It's ok. Flirting seems to be a requirement for playing ball around here."

"Yeah. I just got carried away. Tact isn't one of my strong points." Ray shifted uncomfortably, well aware that she hadn't been joking in the least.

"I suppose if you'd meant it I'd be flattered." Lee glanced away.

"If I meant it," Ray echoed, hearing the hollowness in her voice. She cringed.

"May I have a drag off that?"

It took Ray a moment to register the change in conversation. "You smoke cigars?"

Lee laughed, genuinely this time. "I've been known to. Thanks," she added when Ray passed her the cigar. She put it to her lips and drew in, blowing smoke rings out as she exhaled. "Nice. What brand is it?"

"Partagas. It's a nice medium smoke." Ray felt the tension between them ease. "I buy them by the box."

"I might try them." Lee took another drag and handed the cigar back.

Ray studied her as she let the smoke trail from her lips, curling up around her face and dissipating into the air. "What other quirks do you have?" She managed to smile.

"Tequila makes my clothes fall off," Lee said with a perfectly straight face. Ray burst out laughing. "I'm not kidding." Ray laughed more heartily. "What, tequila doesn't make you crazy?"

"Of course it does, but not like that. I'm more likely to start buying shots for the bar and blow through a paycheck in an hour."

"What about you? What quirks do you have?" Lee studied her, her eyes twinkling.

"I like caviar."

"That's not a quirk. So do I." Lee leaned toward her and Ray felt her heart start beating faster. "Come on, there has to be something."

Ray hesitated. Finally, she admitted, "I like reading poetry."

Lee frowned. "That's not a quirk either."

"In bed. To someone." Ray blushed. "It isn't very butch." Lee stared at her. "Hey, you asked."

"That's the most romantic thing I've ever heard of."

"That's me, romantic," Ray replied cynically.

"If you do that, you are." Lee's voice was soft, distant. She shook herself. "It beats champagne and caviar in bed."

"Now that's romantic." Ray finished her cigar. She stubbed it out against the tree, trying not to put the two images together with Lee naked.

"So why aren't you caught?"

Ray wasn't expecting the question and it took her a moment to formulate an answer. "I don't believe in love," she said quietly.

"You don't?" Lee's face was disbelieving.

"No."

"Why not?" Lee finished her wine cooler. "Love is wonderful, if you can find it."

"If," Ray responded. "It doesn't happen very often and usually isn't worth it."

"Nonsense; it happens every day."

Ray looked at her levelly. "Has it ever happened to you?"

Lee looked taken aback. "Of course ..." she trailed off and shifted her gaze into space. "At least, I thought that's what it was."

"But it wasn't." Lee shook her head. "I rest my case. Take relationships while they're fun, but don't let your emotions fuck things up. It makes it easier to move on."

"I don't see how you can be so romantic and so cynical at

the same time."

"It isn't that hard." Ray shrugged. She glanced toward the court, saw that more than one person was staring their way, and realized how close they were standing and that they were leaning toward one another in an unexpectedly intimate way. "We should wander back before everyone over there decides we're sleeping together."

"You can't talk to someone without everyone assuming that?" Ray shrugged again. "You must have quite the reputation."

"I guess I do." Ray wondered why she was suddenly embarrassed by the fact.

To her surprise, Lee laughed lightly. "Wouldn't that be something for them to talk about? I'm sure you're good, Ray, but I don't think you're good enough to seduce a straight woman."

"I wouldn't try." Ray choked on the words.

"Good to know." Lee grinned at her. "Wouldn't they just die if I kissed you?"

I'd die if you kissed me. "Probably."

Lee seemed to be seriously considering it. She studied Ray for a long silent moment, and then leaned over and brushed her lips across Ray's cheek. "I really like you," she whispered before straightening up. "There, that ought to do it." Her voice danced with amusement.

Ray fought the blush that threatened to overwhelm her. Had she imagined the want in Lee's whispered words? She must have. "It ought to," she managed. "I'm out of beer."

"Ok. Back to the crowd."

The pair walked back together, Ray's mind burning with images she tried desperately to block out. It was going to take some work to put aside the desire Lee's lips had lit in her. But she had to. There was no alternative.

*　*　*

Lee glanced at Ray as they walked, surprised that she seemed embarrassed by the kiss. Lee had only meant it in the good fun that the rest of the afternoon had been. Ray couldn't possibly have taken it any other way.

They each went to their own seats when they reached courtside. The game had broken up and everyone was drinking and chatting. A lot of the chatting stopped as they came up, pleasing Lee. She had wanted to shake things up a bit, though she wasn't sure why. Stacy gave her a startled look when she sank down into her chair and reached for a wine cooler.

"What the hell was that?"

"What the hell was what?" Lee responded innocently. "I've kissed you on the cheek plenty of times."

Stacy looked like she was going to start sputtering. "But I'm me. Ray is ... well, Ray."

"We were just talking, Stacy."

"Ray Elliot has never 'just talked' with someone that long in her life." Stacy and Donna exchanged glances.

"She has now. She's very pleasant to talk to." Lee grinned. "Of course, I won't say what we were talking *about*."

"I think you're taking this flirting thing too far, Lee. You're treading on dangerous ground with Ray doing that. She's going to start taking you seriously if you keep it up," Stacy said sternly.

"Who say's I'm not serious?" Lee tried to keep a straight face, although deep inside a little voice was telling her that she was serious, just a bit. She pushed the thought away as if it were a snake about to bite her.

"Because straight women don't just walk into a gay bar, meet a lesbian, and decide they're gay too." Stacy sounded like she was trying to convince herself more than Lee.

"I'm sure they do." Lee watched the expressions flash across Stacy's face and relented. "It just didn't happen to me. I like Ray, I do. But not that way, and she knows it."

"As long as you do."

Lee made a face. "Of course I do."

Ray pulled her aside as they were leaving and invited her to go karaoke the next Friday evening. Lee accepted and climbed into her car before watching Ray back out in her truck. *Of course, I don't like Ray that way. I'm certainly not gay.*

33

Lee's Awakening

It was silly for Stacy even to bring it up.

As she drove off she realized that despite the protestations to the contrary, somewhere deep inside her there was the barest shadow of a doubt.

III.

Lee stood on the walkway to her parents' house looking at the front door with trepidation. An invitation to dinner from her mother was never innocent, and lately the topic had been Robert. If only she'd had the nerve to decline, but she didn't. Steeling herself and praying that Robert himself wouldn't be there, she went and opened the door.

"Mom! I'm here!"

"Come out on the lanai, dear," her mother called back.

Knowing that her parents would be cocktailing, she stopped in the kitchen for a glass of wine and then moved through the den to the screened rear lanai. Her mother rose as she stepped through the sliding doors. Thankfully, Robert was nowhere in sight.

"Something smells good."

"Hickory," Jim Compton announced proudly from beside the charcoal grill, as if Lee didn't know that he used the wood for flavoring. "Makes the steaks taste better."

"Hi, Dad." Lee went over and kissed her parents on the cheek before sitting down at the patio table.

"I saw Louise at the club yesterday. She tells me you've made a new friend." Ellen Compton leaned forward with a look of curiosity. "Someone Stacy knows?"

Great. Louise can't keep her big mouth shut for five minutes. Lee sighed. "Yes."

"Does she play tennis?"

Trying to picture Ray wearing a tennis skirt brought a smile to Lee's lips. "I doubt it."

"Did Stacy introduce you?" Ellen sipped her wine and looked innocent, which Lee knew was just a cover for something dire to come. She was being too nosy for any good to come of it.

Her mother still didn't know that Stacy was a lesbian, or she wouldn't have been so kind in reference to her. That was one secret Louise had managed to keep.

"We met at Donna's birthday party."

"How nice."

Lee waited for what was to come, but her mother just launched into the usual newsy gossip from the club and her bridge group, apparently assuming Lee cared what her mother's friends were up to. Lee listened and nodded while her mind wandered to what she should wear to karaoke the next night.

Her mother waited until right before dessert, in fact, to bring up the real reason for her invitation. "Robert called me earlier in the week."

"Did he now? How nice for you." Lee didn't even try to disguise the distaste in her voice.

"He still doesn't understand what went wrong. He asked me to see if you would call him."

"I'll call him when I decide to go ahead with the divorce but that's it." Lee stabbed what was left of her steak and cut a piece, shoving it her mouth before she could say something about Robert that would set her mother off.

"I don't understand why this has happened so suddenly. You seemed very happy six months ago." Ellen rested her chin on her hand. "What could have possibly upset you so much?"

"I really don't want to talk about it, Mom. It's between me and him." It was worth a try to head off the discussion, but Lee knew it was futile even as she spoke.

"Honestly, Lee. The only reason people go from being that happy to filing for divorce is infidelity, and I can't imagine Robert doing that. He adores you."

"It wasn't infidelity, and I wasn't that happy. I haven't been for a long time." Lee glanced away, knowing what her mother's response would be.

It was her father who spoke. "I can't believe that," he said gruffly. "You were happy as lovebirds at Thanksgiving."

"Robert was happy. I was pretending to be." Lee pushed her plate away. "I've been pretending for a year." How could she explain to her parents what it was about Robert that had driven them apart? She'd tried before. This wasn't the first time this same discussion had occurred around the dinner table. But for some reason her parents stubbornly refused to listen.

"We think you should go to counseling before you make such a drastic decision, Lee. You have to try and work things out." Ellen leaned back and took a swallow of her wine. Lee noted that it was her fifth since she'd arrived.

"Counseling would do no good, Mother. My mind is made up. I don't want to go back."

"But why? He's a good provider, he's handsome, and he adores you." Ellen looked puzzled and Lee's patience snapped.

"I'm not putting up with the emotional abuse any more. I refuse." *There. I put it on the table. See how Mom handles that one.*

"What are you talking about?" Jim asked sternly.

"I mean I'm tired of being treated like a child who needs to be told what to do about everything." Lee folded her arms across her chest. "He's not as sweet at home as he is when he's here."

Ellen made a dismissive gesture. "It's just his personality. He wants the best for you and he tries to show it. You must be overreacting."

Lee counted to ten before responding. "After five years I can guarantee you it isn't overreacting. Why are you taking his side in this?"

"We aren't taking anyone's side, Lee." Her father splayed his hands. "We just don't want to see a good couple split up over something that can be fixed."

They went around the issue for a good ten minutes more before Lee reached her limit. She stood and dropped her napkin on the table.

"My mind is made up, and nothing you or Robert says is going to change that. I'm tired of being lectured about it. You're just as bad as he is. I'm twenty-nine, not sixteen."

"Be reasonable, Lee—" her mother started.

"Be reasonable?" Lee was sure the veins were popping out in her neck. "I am being reasonable. It's over. Done. Not coming back. I'm also not discussing it again. I think I'll skip dessert." She turned and stalked out of the house.

Her hands were shaking as she started the car. It was infuriating to hear her own parents praising the man she had come to despise. She put both hands on the steering wheel and stared into space for a long moment; she wanted a strong drink. Strangely, the first person she thought of calling to vent to wasn't Louise or Stacy. It was Ray. Only, she didn't have Ray's telephone number.

She wasn't really aware of driving to Maddie's until she pulled into the parking lot. As she had hoped, Ray's big black pickup was parked out front. Realizing that she was about to walk into a gay bar by herself, she paused with her hand on the handle of the door, but her desire to talk to someone overcame her reticence and she pulled it open with a jerk.

* * *

"Isn't that the girl who was at Donna's birthday party?" Joan nudged Ray as the door opened.

Ray turned and broke into a grin. "Well, look what the cat dragged in!"

"I was hoping you'd be here," Lee said with obvious relief. She sat down on the stool next to Ray and pulled out her wallet. "Could I get a whiskey? On the rocks?"

"Sure thing, kid." Joan reached for a glass after shooting Ray a questioning glance.

"That's pretty strong medicine," Ray commented. "You look like you're ready to punch somebody."

"I am. Only that would involve actually seeing him."

Ray studied her. "Care to fill me in? Or would you like to tell me what prompted you to come in here first."

Lee bit her lip. "I was hoping to talk to you. You seemed like the perfect person to vent to about that bastard and my idiot parents."

"O-k-a-y." Ray dragged the word out as her mind turned over that Lee had sought her out instead of calling one of her friends. "I think I'm going to need something stronger for this. Joan, give me a rum and coke."

Joan sat the drinks down and took their money, making change before going to the other end of the bar to talk to another woman.

"I hope I'm not imposing." Lee seemed uncomfortable. "If you were waiting for someone ..."

"Nope to both. You have my undivided attention."

Lee took a healthy swallow of whiskey and gasped, her eyes watering. After a moment, she sat the glass down and leaned forward. "I can't decide who I'm angrier with, Robert or my mother."

"What happened?" Ray sipped at her drink, curious at what could have Lee — who struck her as remarkably self-contained — in such a tizzy.

"I had dinner with my parents." Lee blew out her breath and ran a hand through her hair. "All they wanted to talk about was Robert and how much he adores me."

"Does he?"

"Unfortunately." Lee frowned. "It would be a lot easier if he didn't. But he's still trying to get me back. How can it be so hard to understand 'get the hell out of my life'?"

Ray smothered a smile. "And I'm guessing he's enlisted your parents' help in this?"

"Not that it took much convincing. My parents love him. They have since the first time I introduced him to them."

"How long have you been married?" Ray studied Lee's face, liking the way anger set it into sharp lines and angles. It was very becoming.

"Five years. I should have known better when he started making suggestions on my wedding gown." Lee put her face in her hands. "How could I have been so stupid?"

"People misjudge each other all the time. At least you've realized it relatively quickly." Ray fought the urge to run her hand across Lee's shoulder.

Lee made a noise from behind her hands and then dropped them and looked into Ray's eyes. "Why can't my parents understand what he put me through?"

"That I can't answer, Lee." Ray lifted her hand and put it on top of Lee's where it rested on the bar. "But as long as you're doing what's right for you, what they understand or don't isn't really relevant, is it?"

"Stacy would have taken half an hour to say what you just did."

Ray laughed. "The higher the degree, the more long-winded the explanation."

"I'm just so damned frustrated." Lee reached for her drink with her left hand, leaving her right underneath Ray's—a fact that did not escape Ray's notice. "I can't wait for this whole thing to be over. I want my life back."

"I can imagine. He's a prick, I take it?"

"That's being kind." Lee rolled her eyes. "He's a controlling bastard, is what he is."

Ray considered her statement. Finally, she found the words she was looking for. "I can't see you being controlled by anyone."

Lee smiled. "Thank you. I've always liked to think I was independent. This was just a five year mistake. To think it took four years to see that. Pretty dumb, huh?"

Ray shrugged. "Not necessarily. I was in a relationship once where I didn't see what she was doing to me until it was too late to walk away with my dignity intact." *What the hell am I doing admitting that?* Ray tried to stop herself but the words kept coming. "I thought she'd change but she didn't. I'd rather have admitted to a mistake and moved on instead of what actually happened."

"What happened?"

"I caught her cheating with my best friend. And everyone knew it but me." Ray couldn't believe she was talking about it. She'd sworn she'd never bring it up in conversation again.

To her surprise, Lee turned her hand over, slid her fingers between Ray's and squeezed. "That must have been rough."

"It was. So you see, I don't think it's too dumb to get out before things get out of hand." Ray blushed. "You're very easy to talk to."

Lee laughed. "You're the first person I've heard say that."

"Well, it's true."

"It's easy to talk to you too. You seem very honest and real. I expect you'd call me an idiot if I was being one." Lee's face lightened. "Hopefully, I'm not being one."

Ray shook her head. "No, you're not being one, and I probably would. I tend to speak my mind; there's no confusion when people know where you stand. Let me buy you this one," she added when Lee gestured to Joan with her empty glass.

Lee blushed slightly. "Alright, if you'd like. Thank you."

"I'm guessing you'll be getting out of here after that. It'll be getting pretty full in here in about half an hour."

Lee studied her. "I probably should. I'm sure you've got better things to do tonight than listen to me whine."

Ray drew in a breath to answer and then paused. She had come out hoping to hook up with a woman she'd met two nights earlier, but somehow that seemed less important than continuing her conversation with Lee. "You aren't whining, and no, I don't."

Joan wandered over. "Ready for two more?" She reached for fresh glasses when Ray nodded. Her gaze lit on their hands and she raised an eyebrow before looking back at Ray curiously. "So, do I get introduced or do I have to do it myself?"

Ray told Joan Lee's name. "This is Joan, the owner. She's a sweetheart."

"Sweetheart, my left ass-cheek. Don't be spreading vile rumors about me, Ray."

Lee laughed. "Nice to meet you, Joan. You run a very cozy place."

Joan studied her for a moment. "You were in here for Donna's party, weren't you?"

"Yes."

"I haven't seen you since. You must have a girlfriend who doesn't drink."

Lee blushed deeply. "I'm straight," she mumbled.

"Really?" Joan looked taken aback and glanced their still-entwined fingers again. "I could have sworn ... just my imagination running away with me. Well, welcome to Maddie's."

"Thank you. Excuse me, Ray; I'll be back in a minute." Lee

got up and headed toward the restroom.

The minute she was out of earshot, Joan leaned over to Ray. "Is she kidding about being straight?"

"No. Why?" Ray studied Joan's face.

"Because I would have sworn she was a lesbian. And I'm not often wrong."

Ray looked after Lee. "I thought she was too when I first met her. But trust me, she's straight."

"Damn shame, she's a looker." Joan straightened up. "Though why she'd hang around with a scamp like you is beyond me."

Ray stuck out her tongue. "I'm a rogue, not a scamp. There's a difference."

"Right. Still—I wonder ..." Joan trailed off as if contemplating something and then glanced toward the bathrooms. "I could have sworn," she repeated, and then shook herself. "Well, I suppose I'd better stock the cooler before the crowd hits." She patted Ray's hand. "Don't scare her too badly." Before Ray could answer, she was off toward the other end of the bar.

When Lee returned, the conversation turned to lighter things. Two hours passed before Lee finally said she needed to get home. Ray walked her out to her car and Lee kissed her on the cheek.

This time, Ray's face didn't flame. "What was that for?"

"For being so nice to me." Lee looked into her eyes. "I think we could be very good friends."

I'd rather be a different kind of friend. Oh, shut up, Ray. "Me too. Drive safely."

Lee smiled at her, got into her Mercedes, and left. Ray stared after her taillights until they disappeared, then slowly turned and walked into the bar. She didn't feel much like hooking up with anyone anymore. All she wanted to do was have another drink and try to forget the sensation of Lee's lips on her skin.

*   *   *

"What the hell do you think you're doing?" Lee barely kept

from screaming into the phone.

"I don't know what you're talking about, Lee."

"The hell you don't, Robert! I'm reading the paperwork right now. I know for a fact our accounts are worth more than this." Lee slammed the papers down on her desk. "And this appraisal is almost fifty thousand dollars off."

"It's been a rough year in the market, sweetheart—" Robert's voice was placating in the way that drove Lee insane.

"Don't call me sweetheart, damn it. Answer my question."

"I'm not hiding money, if that's what you're suggesting. You're being hysterical."

Lee took in a deep breath and forced herself to calm down. "I am not being hysterical and I don't believe you."

"Why would I hide money? This separation is silly in the first place." He sighed. "If you'd just come home we could work this out."

Lee paced across her office and stared into the living room. She could just see the river through the sliding glass doors that led to the balcony. The view calmed her slightly, but only slightly. "I'm not coming back."

"Maybe you should see someone. They can write you a prescription for this paranoia you seem to have developed. I mean, this came on so suddenly—" in the background, Lee could hear his beeper going off. "I have to go, Lee. Why don't you come over tomorrow and we can discuss this like adults."

"That would be a first!" Lee snarled. "I'll prove you're trying to short our assets. I'm not a financial idiot; I know that's what you're doing."

"We'll discuss this later." His tone changed to the one he used when he was cross with her, the tone that suggested she was a child.

"To hell with you." Lee hung up and slammed the phone down onto its charger.

She knew he was trying to hide his assets, she just knew it. But proving it wouldn't be easy, if she could at all. The why of it didn't make sense though, unless he was trying to force her to come back by showing her what divorce would be like. He should know she didn't need all the fancy trappings that came with their lifestyle, that she was perfectly content to live simply, just to get away from him.

She called Louise, who managed to calm her down slightly, although it seemed to Lee that she was taking Robert's side more than Lee's own, as usual. Then she called Stacy.

"What a bastard," Stacy growled when Lee had filled her in. "When you file for divorce, I hope you screw him to the wall."

"I'd love to, I just hope I can. I'm so pissed off right now I can hardly stand myself."

Stacy was silent for a moment. "Come out with us tonight. We're going to karaoke at Maddie's. Donna's going to sing," she added when Lee didn't reply right away.

"I don't know, Stacy." Lee sat down on the couch and sipped at the drink she had made for herself.

"It'll be fun. And you won't have to think about old what-an-ass. Ray will be there."

Lee started. "Why would I care that Ray will be there?"

"I thought you two were becoming friends." Stacy sounded embarrassed. "I thought it would be nice that we wouldn't be the only two people you know."

Lee chose not to mention that she had been at Maddie's the previous night. "As long as you don't try to get me to sing something."

"I won't," Stacy promised.

"Ok, then." The two agreed on a time and Stacy hung up.

Lee took another swallow of her drink and stared into space, wondering why she was so pleased that Ray would be at the bar.

In fact, when Stacy mentioned her, Lee's heart had skipped a beat. It was a strange feeling, her anger at Robert still pounding against her temples while her stomach fluttered with the anticipation of seeing Ray again.

She finished her drink and went to get dressed, choosing a casual outfit that wouldn't seem out of place with the attire she'd decided was the norm for Maddie's. She didn't own too many t-shirts, so she went with jeans and a silk blouse.

As she fastened her belt, she wondered why she was choosing her clothing so carefully. What difference did it make how she looked? She wasn't hoping someone would notice. In fact, if anyone did she'd probably die of embarrassment. After a moment's pause, she pulled off the blouse and put on a polo. Deciding this was much better, she grabbed her purse and headed for the door.

The bar was crowded when she walked in. It took her a few moments to spot Stacy's red hair near the stage across the room. She pushed her way to the bar and ordered a glass of wine before working through the crowd to the table where Stacy and Donna sat with Ray and another woman.

"I see you made it over here without getting hit on," Ray said in greeting.

"How do you know?" Lee responded lightly, surprisingly relieved at actually seeing her sitting there. "Or were you just hoping I hadn't?"

Stacy shot her a look, but Ray just laughed.

"Anytime, darlin'."

Lee pulled up a chair and sat between Ray and Donna. "So, when does this karaoke thing start?"

"An hour or so," Donna replied. "They give everyone enough time to get liquored up. Otherwise no one would sing."

"And I hear you plan on getting up there."

Donna nodded. "After a few more of these I should be ready." She indicated the tall drink in front of her.

"You look nice," Stacy commented. "Don't you think so, Ray?"

"Damn nice." Ray leered at her.

"Too nice for you." Lee shot her a wry grin, finding Ray's expression amusingly exaggerated, and the stricken look that followed was so obviously faked that she had to laugh aloud.

The group lapsed into conversation that centered mostly around who was going to sing and how bad they would be. Every once in a while, Ray would throw in a flirty comment aimed at Lee, who would respond with one of her own. She thought it was a fun game to play, and Ray apparently thought so too.

"Do you want to dance?"

Lee looked up from her wine and found Ray looking at her intently. The DJ had put on a thumping dance tune and couples were spilling onto the dance floor.

"With you?"

Ray laughed. "Of course with me. What have you got to lose?"

Lee weighed her options. One of the things that had always annoyed her about men was that they seldom wanted to dance. But if she agreed, what would Ray make of it? Ray raised an eyebrow and Lee decided she shouldn't be so paranoid.

"Sure."

They moved onto the dance floor together and started dancing. Lee reasoned that they weren't touching, so it was really a case of them dancing in the same area. She enjoyed herself until the song ended and a slow one started up. She turned to go back to her seat, but Ray touched her arm.

"Let's keep dancing."

"It's a slow dance," Lee said, somewhat weakly.

"I know." Ray smiled softly. "Come on. It's not like everyone is going to be staring at you." Lee hesitated. "Of course, if I scare you ..."

"You don't scare me," Lee responded archly, stepping forward. "If you want to keep dancing, we'll keep dancing."

Ray slid her arms around Lee's waist and pulled her closer. Lee tentatively did the same to Ray and rested her chin against Ray's shoulder. *It's strange being the taller one.* There was a softness overlying the obvious muscularity of Ray's body that teased her and she drew in a soft, somewhat hesitant, breath.

The two moved together slowly and Lee allowed herself to be lulled into a pleasant haze wherein she could almost forget that she had her arms around another woman.

But she couldn't deny that she was enjoying the feeling of Ray's body touching hers. She wondered what was happening to her; simply walking into a gay bar couldn't possibly make her so intrigued with another woman. *Could it?* The dance ended, and almost unwillingly, Lee stepped back.

Ray gave her a little half bow. "Thank you."

"Thank you," Lee returned, trying to ignore the warmth still radiating through her body.

Ray went up to the bar while she returned to her seat, ignoring the confused look Stacy was giving her as she tried to sort out her own reaction to the dance. Ray rejoined them a few minutes later with another beer and a glass of wine.

"I said I'd buy you a drink." She sat down.

Lee thought that she shouldn't have any more to drink, but her voice betrayed her and spoke. "I am a little thirsty after that."

"Are you sure wine is all you want?" When Lee looked at her with a shocked expression, Ray just laughed and winked.

She came out of the bathroom some time later to find Ray lounging against the wall. With a nod, she started to step past, but Ray put out a hand and touched her shoulder. In the background, Lee could hear Donna singing in a very off-key voice. There were hoots and yells as she did her own rendition of a Martina McBride song.

"I wanted to talk to you."

"We've been talking all night," Lee replied, confused.

Ray bit her lip. "I wanted to talk to you alone."

A warning bell went off in the back of Lee's brain. "About what?" She forced her voice to remain calm.

"I really enjoyed dancing with you."

"I enjoyed it too."

Ray shifted her weight and removed her hand. "How much did you enjoy it?"

Lee blushed. "More than I probably should have," she admitted. "It was probably a mistake to agree." She realized that she had backed into the alcove where the pay phone was and that Ray was blocking her escape.

There was a very serious look on Ray's face as she stared into Lee's with those penetrating grey-blue eyes of hers. "Sometimes people think they're making mistakes when they really aren't." Her voice was surprisingly soft compared to her expression.

"How do you know the difference?" Lee's own voice sounded strange to her ears.

"You don't until it's over." Ray stepped closer to her and lifted her hand to Lee's shoulder again. Lee felt her heart thudding in her chest. The two women studied each other for a moment longer, and then Lee closed her eyes as Ray leaned forward.

"Ray! Get out here and sing, damn it!" A woman's voice from the end of the hall broke the moment and Ray stepped back, her face unreadable.

"I think that would have been a mistake," Lee murmured, barely trusting her voice.

Ray lifted her lips into what could have been a smile. "But you wouldn't have known for sure until it was over."

Before Lee could respond, she turned and strode out into the main bar, leaving Lee to sag against the wall trying to sort out the spinning emotions running through her trembling body. When she was finally able to return to the table, Ray was onstage doing a very good rendition of a Melissa Etheridge song, complete with dance moves.

"Are you ok?" Stacy looked questioningly at her as she sank into her chair.

"I'm fine," Lee responded a little faintly.

Stacy glanced at Ray and then back at her. "What happened back there?"

"Nothing." Lee fought the blush that threatened to color her face.

"Bullshit." Stacy leaned forward. "Did Ray say something she shouldn't have?"

"No." Lee's thoughts weren't on Stacy's questions in the slightest.

Rather, she kept turning over her own reaction to what she knew would have ended up as a kiss. That she hadn't pushed Ray away or at least turned her head didn't bother her as much as she thought it should, and that *did* bother her.

"I don't believe you. I was afraid this flirting thing would go too far. I'm going to talk to Ray."

"Don't. Please." Lee could hear the strain in her own voice. "I can handle it myself."

"Are you sure?"

She quickly nodded her head and Stacy sat back as Ray returned to the table to loud clapping from the bar. "You were fabulous, Ray," Lee said, desperate to change the topic.

"Thanks. I have fun, but it's nice to sound decent too." Ray took a swig of her beer and made a face. "Yuck, warm. Lee, do you want another glass of wine?"

It was as if the incident in the hallway had never happened. Ray was waiting for her answer with a blank face.

"Sure." She reached for her purse.

"I've got it." Ray stood and worked her way into the crowd. Onstage, another brave soul was trying to do a hip-hop song, badly. A group in the corner was cheering her on, and Lee was trying to tune her out.

The next glass of wine did nothing to settle Lee's nerves. Every time she glanced at Ray, she felt butterflies in her stomach and remembered the look on Ray's face as she bent over. It had been so serious and yet so soft. It was a look she had never seen on anyone before.

Finally, she had to escape. "I'm going to step outside," she told Stacy. "I need some air." Stacy just nodded and Lee pushed back her chair.

Outside, the music was muted and the night was unpleasantly humid, but Lee didn't really notice as she stood on the steps leading down to the back parking lot and tried to sort out what was going on with her. It was several minutes later when the door opened behind her and she heard the click of a lighter. Turning, she found Ray lighting a cigarillo.

"I hate that I can't smoke these things inside." Ray smiled.

Lee forced her voice to be light. "I'm sure they smell the place up."

Ray shrugged. "No worse than some of the cologne the butches wear. It doesn't smell good on a man; I don't understand why they think it would smell good on them."

"I've never been much into cologne on a man," Lee replied, thinking it was a strangely normal conversation to have considering what had happened not twenty minutes earlier.

"I don't know what you wear, but it's nice." Ray shifted and glanced away.

"Thank you."

They lapsed into silence for a while, and then Ray drew in a breath. "Look, about what happened in the hallway —"

"Don't worry about it," Lee interrupted quickly.

"I'm not particularly worried. I was wondering if you were. You didn't seem in a mood to stop me."

Lee paused before answering. "It happened pretty fast, but no, I don't think I'd have stopped you."

Ray's eyebrows went up. "Just how much have you had to

drink?"

Either too much or not enough. "I'm not drunk, if that's what you're asking."

"I'm pretty sure you were straight when you walked in tonight."

"I still am." Lee tried to ignore the tingling in her stomach. "But I wouldn't have stopped you. "

"That's a confusing answer, Lee."

"To be honest, I'm a little confused myself."

Ray studied her for a long silent moment. "I didn't plan for it to happen," she finally said. "I really haven't meant anything by the flirting."

"I know." Lee bit her lip. "I'm not sure why I feel this way about it. Maybe it *is* the wine." *Of course it is. What else could it be?*

"Well, I'm sorry. It was a dumb-ass move and I shouldn't have."

Lee glanced away, her mind replaying the look on Ray's face as she bent towards her. It sent a shiver down her spine. She shook herself, willing the image to go away. "Let's just forget it happened."

"Deal." Ray drew one last time on her cigar and flicked it out into the parking lot. "I'm going to sing again. Sure I can't get you up there?"

"No thanks." Lee managed to smile. "I'm averse to making a fool of myself. But I can't wait to hear you. You did a great job on the first one."

Ray grinned. "Thanks. I'll see you inside." She pulled open the door and vanished inside, leaving Lee alone in the darkness with her thoughts.

It was too easy imagining now what it would be like to kiss Ray, to feel another woman's lips on her own. Lee wasn't an idiot; she knew how lesbians made love. It was distressing that she could imagine doing those things with Ray. It was more distressing that imagining them turned her on.

Lee wrapped her arms around herself and stared into the darkness. "What the hell is happening to me?" She asked the question aloud.

Maybe hanging out with Stacy and Ray and the others was

just too much. Maybe she was just grasping for a relationship totally unlike what she'd had with Robert. Maybe she was losing her mind.

She didn't realize how much longer she had been standing there until Stacy came looking for her.

"We were wondering if you'd left," Stacy said. "Except your purse was still inside. What are you doing out here?"

"Thinking."

Stacy gave her a strange look. "About what?"

Lee sighed. "About a lot of things. Robert. My life."

"And here I thought we'd lifted your spirits."

"You did." Lee smiled wanly. "But I've dragged them down again, I guess."

"Are you sure nothing happened with Ray? She sure was in a hurry to go smoke after you came out here." Stacy shifted her weight and leaned against the railing.

"Nothing happened." Lee tried to open up to Stacy, but found the words impossible to speak.

Stacy crossed her arms and studied Lee seriously for a long moment. "If you say so."

"Really, I'm fine." Lee walked up the stairs. "I guess my wine is warm by now."

"Probably. Ray's up next."

Lee followed Stacy inside, leaving her thoughts at the door.

IV.

Ray watched Lee walking toward the table and fought to keep her face impassive. Inside, she was ablaze with emotions. Lee wouldn't have stopped her. She hadn't meant to try and kiss her, not until she was standing there and Lee's face was so innocently confused, her lower lip quivering just a bit as they talked. And then, before she knew it, she was leaning in and Lee was closing her eyes.

Lee wouldn't have stopped her. Maybe deep inside Lee had meant the flirting, just a bit. Not consciously, perhaps, but still meant it. Maybe there was more to Lee than she let on, maybe more than she even knew. Maybe if Ray had kissed her she would have responded with a kiss of her own, maybe even realized that she wanted more.

And maybe she would have run like hell. Intellectually, Ray realized that this was the most likely outcome, despite what her insides wanted to be true. It was bad enough to have almost done it; actually doing it would probably have ruined what friendship they had built up.

Lee had taken the entire incident remarkably well, considering. At least, outwardly she had. She had spent an awfully long time outside after Ray came in, and now she was walking back to the table with a troubled look on her face. Stacy was with her, giving Ray a hard stare, and for just a moment

Ray was certain Lee had told her what happened. But then Stacy sat down and turned to Donna and Lee sank down next to Ray with a faint smile.

"Have you gone yet?" Lee's voice was soft, but its softness didn't make Ray feel better. It made her feel that Lee was suffering inside.

"Not yet," she replied, reaching for her beer. "I could get you another glass of wine if you like."

Lee paled slightly. "No. Thanks. I'll get it. You've already bought me two."

"Ok." Ray leaned back and took a long swallow from her bottle to hide her discomfort.

Jackie was looking between her and Lee with a confused expression while Stacy spoke to Donna in a low voice that Ray couldn't quite hear. The singer on stage finished to loud applause from a group behind them and the KJ called her up.

It should have been an easy song for her. She'd practiced it a hundred times at home. But when she got onstage and looked down at Lee, she felt her throat close up. It was a ballad and she somehow managed to get through it without her voice cracking but it was far from her best performance, and she was glad to be done with it.

She stopped at the bar to order another beer and a shot of tequila to ease the uncomfortable tumbling of her stomach. *Tequila makes my clothes fall off.* She could picture the playfully serious look on Lee's face as she spoke the words. She had looked beautiful, a light sheen of sweat glistening across her body, her hair highlighted by the sun filtering through the branches of the live oak.

As Joan reached for the bottle, Ray stopped her. "On second thought make it Jack Daniels. A double. Neat."

Joan sought her gaze. "Is everything OK?"

"Yeah."

Looking unconvinced, Joan poured the drink. Ray picked up the glass and studied it. *Here's to making an ass out of yourself.* She raised it to her lips and knocked it back in a single swallow. Her eyes watered as she sat the empty back on the bar.

"Awfully strong drink for OK," Joan commented as she picked the glass up.

"Maybe." Ray turned and looked over toward the table. Lee was standing, purse in hand. Ray sighed; she'd really done it this time. Lee didn't even look like she was going to say goodbye. She turned back to the bar, considering another shot. Joan was giving her a concerned look, so she just dropped her gaze to her bottle and waited for Lee to leave.

"Are you avoiding me?"

Ray turned to see Lee standing behind her. "No."

"I have a tennis date tomorrow. I hate to leave so early." Lee's gaze searched her face. Ray thought she saw distress behind it.

"I was going to leave soon myself. Jackie and I are going fishing in the morning."

Lee started to say something, but whatever it was never made it past the thought. "I'll see you at volleyball on Sunday?"

"Probably." Ray tried to regain her air of nonchalance, wanting nothing more than to beg for Lee's forgiveness.

"Great. Drive safely. And thanks for letting me hear you sing. You're really good."

"Thanks." Ray knew no kiss on the cheek would be coming, and she was right. Lee shouldered her bag and walked away.

"That's not a good look, Ray." Joan leaned on the counter and slid another shot toward her. "It bodes trouble."

"It's nothing," Ray lied, picking up the drink. She looked over at the table and saw that all three of her friends were staring at her. She blew out her breath and tilted the glass, letting the liquor slide down her throat like liquid fire. "I'll see you tomorrow, Joan."

"I'll be waiting." Joan cracked a lopsided grin and turned to help someone else.

With another sigh, Ray went back to the table. "I'm going to take off," she said quietly, trying to ignore the look Stacy was giving her. "I'll see you bright and early, Jackie." Jackie nodded. "See you guys later."

She had made it out the back door before Donna caught up with her. "Ray, stop."

Unwillingly, Ray turned to face her. "What, Donna?"

"What the hell happened?"

"I don't know what you're talking about." Ray hoped her

54

face was as blank as she was trying to make it.

"You must have said something to Lee earlier. She hasn't been right since she came back from the bathroom." Donna crossed her arms and glared at her. "If you made a pass at her I'm going to kill you; if I don't, Stacy will."

"Give me a break."

"Well then, what happened?"

Ray bit her lip. "Nothing happened. If I'd made a pass at her do you think she'd have stayed?"

"Probably not," Donna acknowledged, her expression softening a little. "But there is definitely something going on between you two. I don't know what it is, but it had better not go anywhere. Knock off the flirting."

"She's flirting right back," Ray responded defensively.

"She's straight."

Ray threw her arms up. "Oh, for fuck's sake, I know she's straight! I don't need to hear it every fucking time we're in the same room together."

"Maybe you do," Donna threw back. "I wouldn't put it past you to go after a straight woman."

Ray stared at her. "That's low."

"If the shoe fits ..."

"The shoe does *not* fit. I flirt; she flirts. It's all in fun and she knows it. I'm not out to convert anybody. I just fucking *like* her. Is that a crime?" Ray reached for her cigars and realized she was out. *Damn it!*

Donna stared at her for a long moment and then seemed to relax. "Fine, Ray. Just as long as you understand that everyone else can see where this could lead, even if Lee doesn't."

Ray almost snapped out something she would have instantly regretted. Instead, she pulled out her truck keys and hit the remote unlock. "Don't worry about your straight little Lee, Donna. She'll be straight long after she's forgotten I exist. I'm well aware she's just hanging out here because she's going through a divorce. She'll get through it and move on. But for now, she's here and I like her and I'm not going to screw that up by acting like a jerk." *Except I've already acted like a jerk.* Ray pushed the unsettling thought out of her mind.

"OK. It's not like she needs protecting anyway. We're just

concerned."

"Don't be." Ray walked down the steps. "She's safe." Donna didn't say anything else as Ray walked to her truck. When she looked up after putting the key in the ignition, Donna was gone. Ray blew out her breath and dropped her head against the steering wheel. "Jesus-fucking-Christ!"

Was it that obvious? She had to heel herself in, enough flirting. Donna was right; it was getting out of hand, especially if Lee really did only mean it in fun—which she had to. Ray vowed that from that moment on she would treat Lee like a friend—a straight one. No more flirting, no more hoping that something more could come of their friendship.

Wishing it could be that easy, she started the truck and headed home.

*   *   *

"Lee! Pay attention!" Lee shook herself and glanced around at Louise, who was standing on the service line with an annoyed look on her face. "Can we please finish the set now?"

"Sorry." Lee bent down and waited for Louise to serve, pushing away the thoughts about Ray that had plagued her for days. The ball was returned and the ensuing volley left Lee winded by the time Louise put the point away.

"Match," Louise called breathlessly. "Great game, guys."

"We'll even it up next time," Carol promised as she walked toward the bench on the sideline for her bag. "Are you two staying for lunch?"

"No, I have a hair appointment," Louise replied. "Lee? Are you staying?"

Lee shook her head, wanting nothing to do with lunch at the club. "I have some things to take care of at home." The four women all shook hands and traded air kisses, and then Lee and Louise walked toward their cars.

"You were distracted the entire match, Lee. What is going on with you lately?"

Lee glanced at her friend. "Nothing; I'm just—this thing with Robert has me pretty upset."

Louise sighed. "I just wish you two could work it out. I know," she added when Lee shot her a dirty look, "but I still wish. I barely see you anymore. I hope you aren't sitting in that apartment staring at the walls."

"I'm not. I'm trying new things. I've started playing volleyball every Sunday, for one."

"With Stacy? Aren't all those women lesbians?" Louise glanced curiously at her. "What could you possibly have in common with them?"

"We all hate men," Lee snapped out, feeling instantly childish about the comment. "I happen to like playing volleyball. I'd forgotten how much."

"What about the rest of the time?" Louise apparently didn't deem her first statement worth a comment.

"Well, I went to karaoke the other night to hear Ray sing. She's pretty good."

"Karaoke? You're kidding me, right?" Louise laughed. "I suppose this was at that gay bar. You sure are diving headfirst into it, aren't you?"

"I've been doing other things as well. I walk on the beach every day. I've been antique shopping. I've caught a few movies that Robert would never have gone to see. I'm filling my time quite well."

Actually, she was going a little stir crazy in the apartment by herself, but she couldn't work up much enthusiasm for the social rounds she once made. Tennis was fine, golf once in a while, but the constant barrage of wishful thinking when it came to her marriage had quickly grown old. She was sure her friends meant well, but no one seemed to understand that she wasn't changing her mind.

"And yet all I hear you talking about when I do talk to you is Stacy this, Ray that. What kind of a name for a woman is Ray, anyway? What could it possibly be short for?" Louise shifted her tennis bag to the other shoulder. "I'm worried about you. In your current state it would be far too easy for some lesbian to trick you into something."

"My current state? And what state would that be, Louise?" Lee wasn't even going to get started on Louise's conviction that all lesbians thought about was sex.

"You're in a very emotional state right now, with the separation and all."

Lee snorted. "My emotional state is fine. I'm certainly enough in control of my faculties to know that I'm not gay. Just because I'm hanging around with lesbians doesn't mean I'm going to jump into bed with one of them. And I'm not naïve enough to not be able to tell if one is trying; which they aren't." She had a momentary vision of Ray's face leaning towards her and pushed it away.

"It's just very strange to me, that's all. A group of us is going on a cruise next month. Why don't you come along?" They stopped by Louise's Jaguar.

"I don't know, Louise. Boats make me seasick."

"It's a big boat. You can't even feel it moving. It'll be fun; they have a fabulous spa." Louise threw her bag in the trunk and turned back to Lee. "Come on. It'll be a girls' week out."

"I'm not sure I can afford it. Robert isn't paying me much maintenance and my assets aren't liquid enough for a big expense like that." Lee felt a little embarrassed making the admission, but it was true. A cruise would cost at least two thousand dollars, cash that she couldn't spare at the moment.

"You're just making excuses. Promise me you'll at least think about it."

"I'll think about it." Lee had no intention of going, but it was easier to let Louise think she was considering it.

"Great. Call me later, ok?"

Lee nodded and stepped back as Louise got into her car. After she had pulled out, Lee walked over to her own car and climbed in. She drove to the beach instead of home and found a parking space, walked to the water's edge and stared out over the waves.

She needed something to do with her time. All she had been thinking about for the previous three days was Ray and the kiss that almost happened. She had analyzed it from every conceivable angle and always came up with the same result; she wouldn't have stopped her.

What she would have done afterwards, she didn't know. All she knew was that at that moment, she wanted Ray to kiss her. She wasn't sure she'd ever feel that way again and wasn't sure she wanted to. But for just a moment, the want was there.

All that thinking was driving her insane. Thinking about Robert and the financial statements was making matters worse. Lee sighed and walked a little way down the beach. What she needed was something to take her mind off things. Maybe she needed a job.

The idea stilled her. She hadn't worked in over five years; there hadn't been a need to. Now, with finances tight and looking as though they were going to stay tight for a while, a job wasn't just a novel idea, it was probably a necessity.

She didn't think she could go back into social work; she had almost burned out on it before she got married. Stacy may love her job, but Lee hadn't. She wasn't sure what else she could do with her degree and she had no interest in pursuing a masters.

Still, it would get her out of the house; give her something to do with her days. It didn't need to be a particularly taxing job, just something to fill her time and bring in some extra money. It felt as though a light had broken through the clouds and illuminated her face. A job would solve a lot of problems. A job would help rebuild her self-confidence. She'd start looking in the morning.

* * *

Ray pulled two beers out of the refrigerator and returned to the deck. Jackie sat at the patio table staring out over the yard toward the trees. She turned her attention to Ray and grinned.

"I was beginning to think you fell in."

"Nah." Ray held one of the bottles out and Jackie took it. Ray sank down into her chair and opened her own beer, tossing the cap into the coffee can in the middle of the table.

"I could get used to this view." Jackie gestured over the length of the backyard with her hand.

"It's one of the reasons I fell in love with the place."

The property consisted of six acres. The house itself sat on a half-acre of fenced in grass beyond which lay a pond and just over two acres of pasture. There was a small building toward the trees at the back of the pasture that held a tack room and stall for a horse. Ray didn't ride and planned on converting the structure to a workshop eventually, but for now, it sat empty.

The remainder of the property was wooded and backed up to a state forest. She had a neighbor to one side; on the other was another wooded six acre lot. Ray thought that with luck, she'd be able to buy that plot before someone built on it. Either way, the property was wonderful.

"You'll have to have a campout, you know." Jackie leaned her chair back on two legs and gave Ray a grin.

"I think I'll leave those to Mitch and Kalynn; I might have a bonfire though."

"Sounds good. By the way, I brought you something." Jackie set her chair upright and dug in her back pocket, pulling out a folded, rather wrinkled piece of green paper. She passed it to Ray, who unfolded it and turned it right side up.

"A karaoke contest? Come on, I'm not that good." Ray set the paper down on the table and reached for her beer.

"I think you are. First prize is a weekend cruise for two. What's it going to hurt?"

Ray contemplated her friend. True, she had been doing karaoke for several years. True, she spent more than a few hours every week practicing songs. But she hardly thought she was good enough to go up against the best in the area. "You're nuts."

"You're chicken." Jackie stuck out her tongue.

"Am not. Just realistic."

"It's free. Come on. It's an excuse to go drinking. It'll be fun."

Ray considered the paper again. There were cash prizes for each week the contest ran, enough to pay for her drinks for the evening. The winners moved on to a bar final with the cruise as top prize. Maybe she could place and grab some free cash.

"OK, why not."

"Good." Jackie grinned. "When is the housewarming party?"

"I haven't decided yet. I want to make sure the pool pump and the hot tub are working right first. And that pool needs a serious cleaning." Ray gestured at the large above ground pool abutting the edge of the deck. The house had sat empty for long time before Ray bought it, and the pool needed to be drained and cleaned of several months' worth of debris.

"Well, if it means a party, I'll help you with that." Jackie followed Ray's gesture and looked into the pool. "Although that's pretty scary."

"I bought the place as a fixer-upper."

"You've got your work cut out for you. Even so I think it's cute as hell." Jackie finished her beer.

Ray thought it was cute as hell too. It was just over fifteen hundred square feet with three bedrooms and an attached one car garage. The rear deck was spacious and boasted, in addition to a 34' pool, an eight person hot tub and a propane hookup for a gas grill.

Part of the deck was covered, and a rough outdoor kitchen had been built with a counter, sink and space for a refrigerator. One of Ray's projects would be to rip it out and rebuild it, turning it into a tiki bar. The deck had been a major selling point for her.

There were details inside the house that attracted her too, arched doorways and built in bookshelves that told of how old the house itself was. She had been told that it had been built in 1935.

"Once I'm done it'll be perfect," she said.

"Do you think Lee will be at volleyball tomorrow?"

Ray blinked rapidly at the sudden change in topic. "I don't know. Why?"

"I don't know. I just thought you'd care." Jackie grinned at her. "You can't deny you've still got the hots for her."

"She's straight."

"The very fact that you keep repeating that every time I mention her tells me you've got the major hots for her, dumb ass." Jackie nodded at her own comment. "She sure seems to like you."

"OK, so I've still got the hots for her. It can't come to anything. And even if it could I wouldn't do anything about it."

Jackie's forehead creased in puzzlement. "Why not?"

"She's not just some weekend fling and you know it. She's way too high class for that." Ray sighed. "You know how I operate."

"Yes, I do. And if your reputation is halfway true, she could do a lot worse for an intro into lesbian sex. I doubt she's looking to hook up with anyone anyway, what with this divorce thing she's going through."

"She's not looking for an intro to anything."

Jackie studied her. "Are you sure?"

"What's that supposed to mean?" Ray drained her beer.

"I mean, she keeps showing up, and she keeps flirting with you. She may not realize it, but I could swear she's gay."

"She's not," Ray growled. "Now drop it."

"Fine." Jackie shrugged. "But if she keeps hanging around, eventually she's going to start wondering."

"Drop it." Ray got up. "I'm getting more beer."

"Whatever you say. Bring me two."

With an inner curse that her libido wasn't paying any attention to the rational part of her, Ray strode into the house.

*   *   *

"Out!"

Ray drew up short as the volleyball bounced in the sand just past the line. A fine sheen of sweat coated her face and arms, and it was all Lee could do not to stare at her.

In the previous week, she had managed to get past her initial reaction to the near kiss that night, or so she thought. Ray hadn't been at volleyball the previous Sunday, and now that she was here, Lee realized that confused emotions still lurked in her body.

All she had been able to think about since arriving was what it would have felt like to have Ray's lips on her own. It was distracting, and she hadn't played her best, but Ray kept grinning at her and encouraging her to dive for the ball.

The teams reset and Donna served. A woman on the opposing team hit a line back and Lee followed Ray's advice and dove for it. The problem was Ray was diving for it too. They collided just above the sand and ended up with Ray on top of Lee while the ball bounced off Ray's back. Stacy put it in the net.

"Sorry," Ray muttered as she put her hands down to push up.

The motion pressed her hips against Lee's side, and the sensation sent a bolt of energy through her. She held her breath until Ray was on her knees and then tentatively allowed her to take her hand and help pull her to her feet. The two stared at one another for a moment before splitting and resuming their positions.

The game ended a few minutes later and the teams returned to their chairs for a drink break. Ray sat a few chairs down from Lee, and Lee tried hard not to keep looking at her. It was becoming frustrating, this intense desire to be near her.

Lee had managed all week to convince herself that everything was normal. As soon as she arrived at Mitch's, she knew that everything was most definitely *not* normal. From the way she was acting, Ray seemed to have taken to heart their agreement to forget what happened, but Lee knew that she herself had been changed by it. She wasn't sure how much, but she was changed.

"Hey, you want some water?" Stacy's voice broke into her thoughts. She was holding out a bottle, which Lee took gratefully. The day was hot and humid and she felt wilted through the sweat beading her brow. "Are you ok? You seem a thousand miles away."

"Just thinking how crazy I am for playing volleyball when it's eighty-five degrees outside."

"Wait until August." Stacy laughed. "We have to cut the points in half just to survive the game."

Lee took a long swallow of her drink and noticed that Ray was staring at her. She stared back and was a little surprised when Ray winked. She smiled and Ray, apparently satisfied, turned her attention to Janet, who was lighting up a joint. Lee watched her take a hit and pass the joint to Ray, who took a hit before passing it down the line. When it came to Lee, she politely declined and Stacy shrugged, took another hit, and passed it back.

"I have to run to the restroom before we start again," Lee said a few minutes later. She got up and headed toward the barn, where Mitch and Kalynn had installed a bathroom. When she was done, she came out into the welcome coolness of the workshop that Mitch had set up in the main area, and found Ray standing there.

"Hey, you." Ray's voice held a quiet hesitance.

"Hey yourself," Lee replied, a little confused as they had greeted one another when Lee first arrived.

Ray didn't move towards her, just stood there with her hands in her pockets. Finally she spoke. "Look, um, would you like to ... grab some dinner when we're done? Maybe down at the Crab Shack?" She looked tentative and Lee felt her heart flip over.

"Sure." She hadn't known she would say yes until the word came out of her mouth.

Ray looked relieved. "Great. They're getting ready to start. I just have to take a leak before we get going."

"OK." Lee watched her walk past before returning to the court.

After the game was finished, they sat around talking for a while and the Ray stood up and stretched. "I'm heading to dinner; anyone for the Crab Shack?"

Lee was startled; she had thought they would be going alone. She realized that she *wanted* them to go alone. No one took Ray up on the offer though, and so she took what was left of her wine coolers and headed to her car with Ray in tow.

When they got to the parking area, Ray looked down at her with a grin. "It's just going to be us. I like that."

"Then why did you bring it up in the first place?"

Ray shrugged. "Don't know. To be polite, I guess. You do know where it is, right?"

Lee nodded. "But I should go home and shower first."

"Why? We'll be sitting outside." Ray laughed.

"Because I'm sweaty and covered with sand. Can we meet in an hour or so?" Lee studied Ray, who seemed to be oblivious to the fact that she was sandy and her shirt was wet with perspiration. Lee pushed away the thought that she looked wonderful like that.

"Ok, I guess. Just don't get all dressed up and femmie on me."

"Femmie? What does that mean?" Lee frowned.

Ray grinned. "You know; a blouse, makeup, all that crap. I like you just like you are now, natural."

Lee blushed. She had been planning on just that, a blouse, nice shorts and some makeup. "Ok." It surprised her that Ray didn't want her to dress up. Men had always seemed to be disappointed if she didn't doll up for them. *Why am I comparing the two?*

"I'll meet you there, then." Ray climbed into her pickup and drove off, and Lee followed suit.

* * *

Dinner was a pleasant affair. Lee and Ray talked like old friends, learning much about one another. It turned out they had similar interests. After they finished demolishing several dozen oysters and a couple of pounds of steamed shrimp, Lee suggested they drive up and walk dinner off on the beach. It was growing dark and the moon had just started to rise over the water.

Ray agreed and they met at the nearest parking area. Locking their vehicles, they took off their shoes and walked down onto the sand, striking out towards the Main Street Pier. The conversation continued and Lee found it surprisingly easy to talk to Ray without embarrassment. The only unsettling thing was that her nearness ignited a small flame in her belly that made her want to take Ray's hand.

Ray seemed to be preoccupied after a while and finally Lee, who was having serious trouble herself concentrating on the conversation, stopped.

"Do you want to head back?" she asked, looking into Ray's face. To her surprise, Ray appeared to be struggling with her own emotions.

"Not really. But we probably should."

Lee studied Ray's eyes; her gaze darted everywhere but back at Lee. A sudden realization hit her. "You want to kiss me, don't you?" She didn't phrase it as a question.

Ray flushed and ducked her head. "I shouldn't, I know. It would be a huge mistake."

"Aren't you the one who told me you don't know it's a mistake until it's over?"

Ray looked at her oddly. "You were the one who wanted to forget the whole thing."

Lee bit her lip and examined her feelings. "At the time I wasn't sure. I'm still not sure."

"You're straight."

"As far as I know, yes. But I can't deny that I still wouldn't stop you if you kissed me." Lee was startled at her own words. She hadn't realized how true they were until she spoke them.

Ray stood there and studied her for a long time, emotions flashing across her face. Finally, she reached out and put her hands on Lee's shoulders. "I hope this isn't a mistake," she murmured as she bent over.

It was as though someone had doused Lee in gasoline and lit a match, so fierce was the fire that raced through her body. Rays lips were soft, softer than Lee could have imagined. She ran her tongue lightly around Lee's lips, pressed with gentle insistence against them until Lee opened her mouth and allowed Ray's tongue to dart in and touch against her own.

Lee realized in the back of her mind that Ray was waiting for permission to go further, and she gave it by reaching out to touch Ray's lips with her own tongue. Ray's hands came to her head and pulled her closer as their lips melted into one another's and their tongues danced in the flames that threatened to consume Lee's very being.

As quickly as it had started, it was over and when Lee opened her eyes, Ray was studying her from under heavy eyelids.

"Was it a mistake?"

"I'm not sure," Lee answered honestly, although her body still trembled.

Ray kissed her again. This time the flames exploded into an inferno. Ray's lips were a melting softness against Lee's own, her tongue like liquid fire. The kiss deepened, Lee allowing Ray further in, her tongue dancing against Ray's with a hunger she wasn't sure she had ever felt before.

Ray's hands slid to her neck, then her shoulders, pulling her closer. Lee's own hands found Ray's hips before moving to her waist and sliding around her. She felt the curve of Ray's lower back, found that she wanted to feel the skin underneath the t-shirt Ray wore, found herself pulling the shirt out of Ray's pants and slipping her hands underneath, her fingers touching skin that seemed as hot as coals.

Ray moved her lips from Lee's and touched against her neck, her teeth nipping lightly at the skin, then slightly harder. Lee groaned despite herself and Ray tightened her arms, holding Lee against her as she kissed down to the join of neck and shoulder.

Lee's lips were dry and hungry and she eagerly drew Ray in when her mouth returned to her own. Their tongues danced together with abandon and time seemed to slow to a crawl.

Finally, Ray lifted her head away. Lee gasped for breath, pulling back and wrapping her arms around herself to still the trembling of her body. Ray wore a faintly hazy expression, her eyes not quite focused on Lee's face.

After a minute, Lee found herself able to speak again. "I don't think that was a mistake."

Ray kissed her once more, and Lee abandoned herself to it. This time she felt the planes of Ray's back, sensed the softness of breasts pressed against her own chest, felt the slight rocking of Ray's hips against hers, and tried to stop from wanting more.

When they parted, Lee was panting. Ray's chest was heaving and they stood there, a few inches apart, trying to catch their breath.

Finally, Ray swallowed hard. "We shouldn't have done that."

"Why?" Lee asked herself the same question, but her brain wouldn't respond with an answer.

Ray looked at her strangely. "You're straight, remember?"

"I'm not so sure any more."

"One kiss doesn't make you gay, Lee." Ray paced away a few steps and turned back around. "Even two kisses. It's easy to kiss someone."

Was it easy for you? Lee studied the lines of Ray's body. They were stiff as though she were holding herself back. "That's true." Her brain finally clicked into gear and told her she was making a horrible mistake by letting the kiss get to her. She was straight, no matter how good Ray's lips felt against hers. "Maybe you're right. It's just been so long since I kissed someone like that."

"We shouldn't do anything about it." Ray's voice was strong. "It wouldn't be right."

The more Lee thought about it, the more distressed she became that she had enjoyed the moment so much. "No, it wouldn't be. I'm not sorry that it happened, but I don't want to do it again."

"I want to be friends, Lee. I don't want to run you off. You need to know that."

Lee drew in a breath. "I want to be friends too. Maybe we should just forget this ever happened." *Like I forgot that night at the bar?*

"Agreed." The two women studied each other again. "Let's head back."

They walked in tense silence. Ray was obviously lost in her thoughts and Lee was busy convincing herself that she had made a horrible mistake. That she had been turned on by the moment couldn't be denied, but it didn't have to mean anything. It didn't have to go anywhere. A kiss like that had to turn someone on, straight or not.

It was a great kiss.

Damn it; stop thinking like that.

What have I gotten myself into?

By the time they reached their vehicles again, Lee had descended into complete confusion. The pair stood awkwardly, and finally it was Ray who spoke.

"I need to get going."

"Me too."

Ray shifted. "We won't ever talk about this again."

"No, we won't."

"Still friends?" Ray lifted her gaze to Lee's. This time there was nothing in it other than conviction.

Lee reminded herself that she wasn't going to let one kiss destroy her life. "Still friends."

They got into their cars and drove away.

V.

Instead of going home, Ray went to Maddie's. It was almost empty, and Joan stood wiping down the bar top with a towel.

"Hey, Ray. What brings you in?" Joan adjusted her glasses and smiled.

Ray plopped down on a stool. "I need a drink. A Corona and a shot of tequila."

Joan eyed her as she reached into the cooler. "That's a pretty tall order for a Sunday night."

"Yeah, well." Ray downed the tequila and picked up her beer. "I've had a rough evening."

"Want to talk about it?"

Ray looked at Joan. She was the sort of older dyke that you were either afraid of or in love with. She was genuinely kind and compassionate but in an instant could turn into a mean bitch if the situation warranted. She had thrown more than one twenty-something troublemaker out on her ear. She was sixty if she was a day, short and stocky with salt and pepper hair cut as militantly as Ray's own. Ray loved her like a mother.

"I kissed someone. It was a mistake."

Joan made a noise. "I don't think I've ever heard you say that."

"I've never felt that way before." Ray took a swig of her beer. "But it was a huge mistake."

"Why?" Joan looked at her curiously.

Ray hesitated. Joan was about the only person she would ever admit what she'd done to; Joan would tell her she was being an idiot and validate her own feelings. "She's straight."

"Are you crazy?" Joan snorted. "What a bone-headed thing to do."

"Don't I know it? I just want to be friends with her but things got carried away." Ray dropped her head. "She said she wasn't angry, but I don't know."

"Did she kiss you back?"

"Yes; but she's just broken up with someone. I don't know — I feel like I took advantage of the situation. I feel like a schmuck."

Joan snorted again. "You are a schmuck. Aren't there enough single women around here to satisfy you? Or have you run through them all?"

"No, I haven't." Ray cringed at the way Joan said it. "I'm not sure why I did it. I just hope she'll speak to me again."

"Was it that girl — what was her name — Lee?"

"Why would you ask that?" Ray lifted her head and tried not to look guilty.

"If anyone didn't notice you falling all over her, they're blind. So, was it?" Miserably, Ray nodded. "Oh God, Ray. Sometimes you're such an idiot."

Ray sighed. "I know. Can I have another shot?"

"Drowning yourself won't solve anything." Joan looked stern as she picked up the tequila.

"I'm not going to drown myself. The problem is she turns me on."

"You really are an idiot. Don't you know better than to go messing around with straight girls?"

Ray bit her lip. "I thought I did. What am I going to do, Joan?"

"If you have any sense at all you're going to put this idea out of your head immediately." Joan leaned on the bar. "Find some other woman to take up with for a while. You're good at that. It isn't like you'd have a hard time. I can name half a dozen who'd love to hook up with you. I won't," she added quickly when Ray raised an eyebrow questioningly, "but I could."

Ray finished her beer and Joan brought her another one. "You're right, Joan. I'm just lusting after her because I know I can't have her. It's stupid and it's got to stop."

"Now you're talking sense." Joan reached for a glass and poured herself a double shot of bourbon, topping it off with water. "There's a pool tournament tomorrow night. Come down and see if anyone catches your fancy."

"I think I will. Thanks, Joan."

Joan smiled gently. "That's why I make the big bucks, kiddo."

Ray hung around for another hour and then went home, convinced that she could put away her desire and treat Lee like the friend she wanted her to be. As she crawled into bed, the thought flickered through her that Lee might change her mind, but she put the idea away and fell asleep.

*   *   *

Lee closed the door to her apartment and leaned against it. Ray had kissed her, and she had kissed Ray back; not only that, but she had enjoyed it thoroughly. She blew out her breath roughly. She could try to deny it but it would do no good. She had thoroughly enjoyed kissing Ray and would probably do it again given the chance.

"Have I lost my mind?" She spoke to the empty room. "What was I thinking?"

As there was no answer, she pushed off from the door and went to the kitchen, where she poured herself a glass of wine before going back to the living room and collapsing onto the couch.

She wasn't gay. She couldn't be. She was twenty-nine years old and had never thought about another woman the way she seemed to be thinking about Ray. She wasn't sure she had ever thought about *anyone* the way she seemed to be thinking about Ray.

There was nothing to do but ignore the feelings in her body. In the morning, she would wake up and everything would be as it had been before. It had to be. She wasn't prepared to deal with the alternative. She drained her wine glass and went to bed, trying not to imagine Ray there beside her. It took a while, but finally she fell into a fitful sleep.

*   *   *

Lee tried to pay attention to what Louise was saying. Her thoughts were distracted, as they had been for several days. Finally, she shook herself and forced her attention back to her friend.

"… and of course Marsha decided that it would be best if Eric took the promotion."

"Really." Lee searched her mind for the first part of the conversation. "So when are they moving?"

"Next month. I didn't really think you were paying attention, Lee." Louise sipped at her tea and studied Lee curiously. "You've been distracted all day. What's up?"

The two were eating lunch after a morning of shopping. Mostly Louise had been shopping; Lee wasn't in the mood to look for new clothes.

"Nothing really," Lee replied, not willing to admit where her thoughts were. "I've decided to get a job."

"A job?" Louise echoed. "Are you planning on going back to DCF?"

Lee shook her head. The Department of Children and Families had been a nightmare of paperwork and casework overload, and without a Master's degree, there was no chance for advancement. How Stacy thrived there was beyond Lee's comprehension. "I had burned out on that before I met Robert. I think I'll look for something a little less stressful."

"Well, just don't end up at Burger King."

Lee laughed. "That wouldn't be such a bad idea, Louise. I just need something to supplement my savings while I liquidate some of my assets. I'm so glad I kept my accounts separate from Robert's. The way he's handling our joint money is making me nuts."

"I'm sure you're overreacting, Lee. The assessment on David and my house was down this year too. Hurricane insurance makes waterfront property a little less appealing these days." Louise leaned back in her chair.

"Maybe I am; but not much." Lee poked at her salad. "How is David doing in the tournament?" Robert was playing in the club golf championship too, but Lee didn't really care how he was doing. She only asked about David to change the subject.

"He's up in his flight. Are you entering the ladies'?"

Lee tilted her head and considered. "I don't know. I haven't played much lately. I might sit out this year."

"And I was hoping we could play together. Really, Lee, you should come with us on Sundays rather than spending every one at that volleyball game of yours." Louise's voice carried her distaste for the women at the game very clearly.

"I enjoy it. It gets me out with some different people. I'm feeling a little like an outsider with the group these days anyway."

Louise snorted. "It's only you who's feeling that way. Just the other day Catherine asked me when we were going to see you at Junior League again. It's as if you've dropped off the face of the planet. If you weren't in this tennis league we'd never see you."

"I'm going through a lot," Lee replied, not wanting to remember just what she was going through besides Robert and the separation. "I just need a break from all the social brouhaha."

"If you miss Joe and Alicia's party they'll be heartbroken. Alicia wants all of her bridesmaids there." It was Joe and Alicia's fifth anniversary and they were throwing a bash to celebrate. Lee suspected it was an excuse to show off the new riverfront house they had built, but she didn't say so.

"I'll be there. I hope Robert won't be."

Louise shrugged. "I'm sure he was invited. Surely you can stand to be in the same room with him for a while."

"If I have to be," Lee said slowly. "I'd rather not, especially if he is going to try and act all apologetic."

"He does still love you." Louise's voice was stern. "I think he'd say anything to get you back."

"It's not the saying, it's the doing." Lee finished her wine. "And he's not going to change the doing. He's forty-one; I doubt he's going to stop being such an ass."

Louise sighed. "I still don't understand how you could go from being so smitten to hating him so much. Last year on your anniversary you were positively disgusting together."

"That was last year." Lee looked for the waitress. She needed another drink to keep from lashing out at Louise for apologizing for Robert. "Last year I still thought he was going to change." She wasn't about to bring up the incident that had finally torn it between them. She didn't want to think about it, much less admit it to anyone.

The argument had been typical, his displeasure with her desire to go back to work part time, but his final response had been anything but typical.

He had grabbed her by the throat, a crazed look in his eyes. He released her a moment later, but it was enough to make her realize just how possessive he had become. At the time, the action hadn't upset her as much as it did now, with the passing of time bringing the realization that their relationship had gone from strained to violent.

"Well, everyone is confused."

Lee gave her a hard look. "Let them be confused."

Louise screwed up her face for a minute and then changed the subject. "Where do you think you'll look for work?"

"I have to see what's available. I'm not sure I want to go back into social work, but I'm not sure what else I can do with my degree."

"Well, you could always finish up your masters and go into therapy." Louise didn't look like she meant her statement, but Lee gave her credit for at least trying to be supportive.

"I suppose. I need something now though." She laughed. "Maybe I'll become an electrician. Ray seems to like it well enough."

Louise looked stricken. "Tell me you're kidding. I didn't know this Ray was so blue collar. Really, why do you hang around with her?"

Lee fought a blush as she asked herself the same question and came up with an unsettling answer. "Because I like her; and I don't really hang around with her. We just see each other at volleyball."

"Well, from the amount of time you talk about her you'd think you spent every afternoon together." A strange look crossed Louise's face and then vanished.

"She's interesting."

"Hmph." Louise finished her tea. "It seems to me like you're just going 180 degrees from your old friends. You don't have to, you know."

Lee bit her lip. "I know." She couldn't really explain why she enjoyed her Sundays so much. Being around Stacy, Donna, Ray and the others just seemed more relaxing and fun than playing golf with Louise and her other friends.

They finished their meal and parted ways, Louise to go meet friends for a round of golf and Lee to go back to her apartment. As she drove away, she wondered why she felt so alienated from Louise lately. They had been best friends forever and yet lately she felt like Louise was drifting away.

Or maybe it was Lee herself who was drifting. She couldn't deny that given the choice between going out with Stacy and Donna to Maddie's, and going to a play with Louise, she'd rather go to the bar. Louise just seemed so shallow compared to Ray.

Lee felt a jolt as the thought ran through her mind. Why was she comparing the two? She'd known Louise most of her life. She'd known Ray for a few weeks. Just because she felt a connection with Ray that she didn't feel with Louise didn't mean they were or would be better friends.

In fact, what had happened the other night was enough to guarantee that they wouldn't be. Lee wasn't sure she could let herself open up to Ray the way that she could to Louise, not the way that made her feel.

Her mind dredged up the memory of the kiss and her heart started thudding in her chest as she remembered the feeling of Ray's mouth against hers.

Damn it; stop that! Lee couldn't believe that a memory could make her feel so lightheaded. She pushed it away firmly, willing her mind to think about something else.

James Wilson had invited her out. She hadn't given him an answer yet but she thought that maybe she should. He was a very nice man, divorced with one son. They had known each other since high school and had always gotten along. He'd never cared for Robert and had never made a secret of it. Now that she and Robert were on the rocks, he'd finally admitted that he'd always wanted to ask her out.

She'd tell him yes. It was time she started dating. That would put to rest the strange feelings she had for Ray. Not that she wanted to feel them for another man any time soon. She didn't want to feel them at all, not yet.

As she realized she had once again put her thoughts about Ray in the same context as those she might have for a man, her stomach turned. It wasn't possible for her to feel that way about another woman. She didn't know why she did, other than knowing that Ray obviously had some of the same feelings for her.

She wondered if things would ever be normal between them again. She didn't want to give up their friendship, didn't want to avoid her. But she knew that there would always be a hint of the past lingering around the edges of their time together.

"Oh, for God's sake, Lee. Get a grip on yourself!" She spoke to no one, and was glad no one was around to hear. She was certain that if there were, she would soon break and spill her guts. And she didn't want anyone to know about it, no one at all, least of all Stacy or Ray.

She got home and went upstairs, and pulled out the paper. Perhaps looking for a job would distract her from all the confusing thoughts running rampant through her brain. Something had to.

* * *

Ray leaned against the side of her truck and took a long drink of water. It was damn hot and the stifling closeness of the house served only to exacerbate her discomfort. She was glad it was nearing the end of the day and she could soon go home.

Her boss came around the corner of the building and waved at her. Steve Johnson was about ten years older than Ray and had taken her under his wing when she started at the company six years earlier. He hadn't ever had a problem having a woman on his crew, even having figured out she was gay early on in their relationship, and in fact went to her for difficult jobs more often than others.

"We're almost done, Ray. Let's just knock it out and be finished with it."

"I'm only taking a breather, Steve. I'll be back in a couple of minutes." Ray took another swig of water.

He came beside her and leaned against the truck. "You've been distracted. What's her name?"

Ray blushed. Steve knew her too well. "No one special. I'm just thinking a lot about the house."

"Yeah, the new house. How's that going?"

"Good. I've got a lot of work to do but I think it'll be worth it." Ray shifted. "It'd be nice to get that promotion and bring in some extra cash, that's for sure."

Steve shrugged. "I've put in my good word for you. If that's not worth anything then they're losing out. You're damned good and the crew likes you."

"It's a shame to lose you, though. You're ten times better than I'll ever be."

"Time to move on," Steve said off-handedly. "I'm ready to stop working every day dawn to dusk. I think I'll like being a handyman a lot better."

"You're giving up good pay though." Ray finished her water.

"I'll be fine. It's just me, after all." Steve's wife had died several years earlier and he'd never remarried. "I don't need much, just my beer and cigarettes. There's a lot more to life than how much you make, anyway."

"Those things'll kill you."

"Look who's talking, Miss Cigar Aficionado," Steve shot back with a grin. "You'll get cancer before I do."

"I don't inhale," Ray retorted.

"Seriously, Ray. I know you've been itching about not getting a raise in a while. Just hang on until I get out of here and I'm sure you'll be getting a whopper."

Ray considered him. "You're the only reason I'm sticking it out. Martin's is hiring for a dollar more than I'm making now."

"Martin's has a bunch of assholes working for them. They'll

put you doing the shit work and you know it." Steve pushed off the truck. "Come on, let's get this thing done."

Ray tossed the empty bottle into the back of the truck. "Ok. You want to get a beer after work?"

"Sounds good to me."

The two went together back into the house. As Ray bent to finish pulling the wire for the kitchen, her thoughts drifted to Lee. She had probably never done a day of manual labor in her life. She certainly wouldn't consider getting involved with someone who did. Even if she did turn out gay, she was more likely to hook up with one of the lawyers or businesswomen who occasionally came to the bar than with an electrician.

So why was it Ray she had kissed? Ray reminded herself that she was the one who initiated the kiss. *But she kissed me back.* That thought nagged at her. Lee had kissed her back with a passion that surprised Ray even as it turned her on. When they parted, Ray knew she had to put a strong halt to what she was feeling before she stepped beyond what Lee was ready for. Even so, it hurt her when Lee so obviously instantly regretted what had happened.

They hadn't spoken since. It tore at Ray to think she might have ruined their friendship. More than once, she had started to dial Lee's number, but she always cancelled the call before it could ring. What would she say? They had agreed to forget it ever happened, but then they had agreed to forget that night in the bar too.

It was Friday. Ray wondered if Lee would be at volleyball on Sunday. She wondered if *she* would have the nerve to go, in case Lee did show up. She wondered why Lee had her so off-balance to start with. She was just a woman, and a straight one at that. Joan had been right; Ray could probably pick any woman in the bar on any given night and make time with her.

Maybe that's what she needed to do, pick up someone and have a good time. Some nice wild meaningless sex would drive any thought of Lee from her mind. She'd go home after her beers with the crew, change, and go down to Maddie's. There were a couple of women she'd been flirting with on and off. One of them had to be there.

Ray felt a little better after her decision. The sooner she got

Lee out of her system the better. And bringing home Kathy or Shellie would certainly go a long way toward getting Lee out of her system. She bent to finish her task, ready to get going.

*   *   *

Lee sat in her car steeling herself. She had parked next to Ray's pickup and was looking across the volleyball court at where she sat. The only way to deal with what she had been going through was to pretend it didn't happen. She just hoped Ray wouldn't bring it up. She was determined not to give Ray the chance; she would make sure they weren't alone.

She greeted the women she knew as she came up with her cooler. In the back of her mind, she wondered how Louise would react if she saw the easy familiarity with which they greeted one another. Ray lifted her hand in greeting before turning back to talk to a woman next to her. Relieved, Lee put her chair next to Donna and sat down.

"How's tricks?" Donna leaned over and kissed her cheek.

Lee shrugged. "I'm still looking for a job."

"Patience, my dear."

"Where's Stacy?" Lee looked around for her.

Donna shrugged. "She went fishing this morning. I'm sure she'll drag her ass in here eventually. So how did the date go?"

"It went well. James is a sweetheart."

James had been quite the gentleman, in fact. They had gone to dinner and caught up with one another. After dinner, James drove her home and didn't even try to kiss her. He had opened the door for her and just grinned at her when she kissed his cheek goodnight.

"Good." Donna glanced over at Ray. "I hear Ray had a good time Friday night as well."

Lee surprised herself with the flicker of annoyance she felt. "Ray has a good time most Friday nights, doesn't she?"

"So I hear."

"Is that her?" Donna nodded and grinned. "She's good looking."

Her companion shrugged. "I suppose she is. Ray has good

taste."

Relieved that Ray had obviously taken their agreement to forget the kiss seriously, Lee leaned back and let her attention wander over the field. The game got started soon after, and Ray ended up on the opposing team with the woman Donna identified as Shellie McMasters.

Shellie left after the second game. Ray still didn't come over to talk to Lee, who started to feel a little concerned that a rift had developed between them, something she had hoped wouldn't happen. She carried this concern with her through the third game. Finally, she headed toward the bathroom with the conviction that Ray either was annoyed with her or had decided she didn't want to be talked to.

She came out of the bathroom to find Ray lounging against the table saw. "Hey you."

"Hey." Lee shifted; she had hoped they wouldn't be alone, and the fact that Ray's position and words were exactly the same as the week before didn't help her nervousness. "How've you been?"

"Pretty good. I hear you had a hot date the other night."

Lee blushed. "I'm not sure that's what I'd call it, but I did go out."

"Good." Ray was silent for a moment, studying her. Finally, she spoke again. "Are things better?"

"Better?"

"After last week. I am sorry about what happened." Ray shifted her gaze to a point over Lee's shoulder.

Memories flooded Lee's mind, bringing a blush to her cheeks. "Yes, things are better," she mumbled.

Ray's gaze shifted back to her face. "You aren't angry with me?"

"No, I'm not angry." Lee knew she was many things, but angry wasn't one of them. "Are you angry with me?"

"No. Like you said, it was just one of those things." There was something in Ray's voice that caught Lee's attention, but she couldn't quite decipher what it was. "Anyway, you're getting back into the dating thing, I guess."

"Yes." Lee was almost embarrassed to be talking about her date with James.

Ray stuffed her hands in her pockets. "That's good. You deserve to start looking for someone who'll be better to you than that asshole Robert."

Lee didn't respond and the two women stared at each other. Lee's heart started skittering strangely and she found her gaze focusing on Ray's mouth. Finally, she forced herself to speak. "James is a very nice man. I've known him since high school."

"Well, if he doesn't treat you right, let me know and I'll pound him for you."

It took a moment for Lee to realize that Ray was joking with her. She managed to laugh. "Deal."

There was another awkward silence. "I'm having a housewarming party next Saturday, if you'd like to come." Ray's voice was tentative.

"If you want me to."

Ray's smile was genuine. "I'd like you to."

Lee smiled back. "Then I'll come. Call me with your address sometime this week. I won't remember it if you tell me now. I'll need directions too. I'm not very good with them."

"It isn't too hard to find," Ray offered. "It's only about half a mile from here."

"You'd be surprised." Lee laughed, feeling much more at ease than she had a few minutes earlier.

"Ok, I'll call."

Lee smiled again. "I look forward to seeing where you're moving to."

"It isn't much." Ray shifted and looked vaguely uncomfortable. "But I think it's going to be really neat when I'm done with it."

"I'm sure it will be."

The two women studied each other. Once again, the unwelcome pounding of Lee's heart that being near Ray had been bringing for the previous weeks started up again. She began to say something and then stopped.

Ray's expression was blank but her gaze searched Lee's with an intentness that seemed to bore through her and into her soul. Finally, she looked away.

"I should get going." Ray turned. "I'm supposed to be meeting Shellie for dinner."

"She's very pretty."

"Yes, I suppose she is." Ray shrugged. "She's got a good personality too."

Lee felt suddenly uncomfortable again. "I should be going too," she said quickly.

"See you Saturday then."

The two parted ways and Lee returned to where Donna and Stacy sat while Ray gathered her cooler and gear together and loped off toward her truck.

"Is everything ok?" Stacy leaned forward and studied Lee's face.

"It's fine," Lee replied. "I'm going to take off. I need to get some laundry done."

Stacy and Donna exchanged glances. "You aren't going to dinner with Ray again, are you?"

"No." Lee's brow furrowed. "Why would you ask that?"

"No reason," Donna returned quickly. "It just seems you're always taking off whenever you and Ray end up alone together. If she's bugging you, please let us know. We'll take care of it."

Lee managed to laugh. "Ray isn't bugging me. She was inviting me to her housewarming party." She tried to forget how her body had reacted to being alone with Ray. Ray hadn't shown any hint that she was thinking about the kiss and Lee was intent on feeling the same way.

"Oh. We're going too. Want to ride with?" Stacy asked.

"Sure. That would keep me from getting lost," Lee responded gratefully.

They exchanged goodbyes and Lee got in her car and drove home.

* * *

Ray made sure the keg was set up in the cooler and waited for her guests to arrive. There would be about fifteen women, maybe twenty. Jackie was the first to arrive, bearing a gift of Goldschlager and a framed print of two women in an embrace.

To her surprise, Donna, Stacy and Lee arrived next. Donna and Stacy had brought candles and a bottle of tequila, and Lee presented her with a bottle of champagne and a gift wrapped box.

"You'd better go ahead and open it," she said with a grin.

Ray tore off the paper and gasped at what was inside. It was a silver caviar tray with a mother of pearl spoon. In the center was two ounces of Beluga caviar. Ray glanced at the champagne. It was Dom Perignon. For just a moment, she felt embarrassed by the cost of the gift, but Lee's smile quickly overcame her reticence.

Donna and Stacy exchanged glances as Ray sat the gift down and enveloped Lee in a bear hug. "Thank you!" Her voice gave away her excitement. "You'll have to share it with me."

"Oh, I'm sure you can think of someone better to have it with." Lee winked.

Ray felt momentarily unsettled and then decided that Lee had gotten past the kiss and that things were back to normal. She winked back. "Maybe, maybe not," she quipped.

Lee laughed, coloring ever so slightly. "So, give us the fifty-cent tour?"

Ray put the champagne and caviar in the refrigerator and led the trio through the house, noting out of the corner of her eye as they went room to room that Lee seemed to be quite taken with the details Ray pointed out.

Once they were on the deck—which Lee pronounced absolutely perfect—Stacy and Donna poured themselves beers. Lee hesitated and Ray stepped in.

"I didn't know if you were coming, but I bought some wine just in case. It's in the fridge."

Lee's eyes lit with a spark of something that quickly settled back into her normal expression. "Thank you!" She followed Ray back into the house and they stood in the kitchen while Ray opened the wine and got a plastic cup.

"Your gift was great, but you shouldn't have spent so much money," Ray told her as she poured.

"Nonsense; I knew you'd like it and it was the perfect gift for a new house." Lee accepted the cup. "You didn't have to go out of your way for me. I am capable of drinking beer."

"What, and ruin my impression of you as the sophisticated lady?"

Lee's Awakening

Lee laughed. "I'm not that sophisticated."

"You've got me beat." Ray tried to ignore that being so close to Lee was making her body tremble.

"Sophistication is overrated." Lee sipped at her wine. "Good vintage. What's the label?" Ray showed her. "You didn't get that at the grocery store. I'll have to write it down and get some for home."

"Hey, Ray, are you going to sit in there and ignore everybody?" Jackie came trotting into the kitchen and pulled up short. "Oh, hi, Lee." She shot Ray a questioning glance.

"Hi Jackie." Lee turned to Ray. "I shouldn't monopolize you. I'll just wander back outside and grab a chair before they're all gone."

"I'll be out in a minute." Ray waited until Lee had gone outside before speaking to Jackie. "What?"

"You bought wine? Jesus, Ray. I thought you were over that thing for her."

"I am," Ray responded gruffly. "I just wanted her to feel welcome."

Jackie studied her levelly. "Don't bullshit a bullshitter."

Ray sighed. "OK, so I was hoping she'd come. That doesn't mean I want anything to come of it."

"Good. I thought Shellie had taken your mind off it."

"She did," Ray lied. "And she's going to be here in a little while, so I don't see where you're concerned that I'm talking to Lee."

"I didn't say I was concerned. I'm just saying you've got that look. You'd better get rid of it before Shellie gets here or she's going to get mad." Jackie shrugged. "Of course, if you want a scene ..."

"I do not want a scene; besides, Shellie doesn't have any right to get mad about anything. It isn't like we're actually dating."

Jackie snorted. "You dating would stop the lesbian world in Daytona Beach."

"Oh, shut up," Ray growled good-naturedly. "Let's get outside."

Lee was deep in conversation with a woman from volleyball when the two got onto the back porch. She glanced up and smiled at Ray before returning to her discussion. Ray went to

84

greet those who had arrived while she was inside. It was about half an hour later that Shellie arrived.

"Hi, Ray." She dropped a kiss on Ray's lips. Ray noticed out of the corner of her eye that Lee's expression hardened for just a moment before returning to its normal smile.

"Hey, baby." Ray kissed her back, more to remind herself that she was over Lee than because she felt any emotion. "Grab a beer."

"I think I will." She wandered toward the keg. Ray watched as Lee's eyes followed her. There was appraisal on her face that turned to an expression suggesting she found Shellie lacking in some way.

Ray walked over to where Lee and Donna sat. "Are you guys going swimming?"

"I wore my suit," Lee answered lightly. "But I'm not sure I'm going to get in. It looks like it's going to be crowded."

"Aw, come on." Donna snickered. "Or are you scared we'll all be ogling you?"

Lee laughed. "Stuff it." She glanced at Ray as she spoke, her expression more serious than her voice.

"At least we won't be getting naked." Ray forced herself to sound as amused as the others. "That doesn't usually happen until after dark."

The thought of Lee in a bikini set off a rush of heat through her body. The thought of her naked, which too easily followed, brought a twinge to her groin that both frustrated and upset her.

"That's a relief." Lee grinned. "I'll get in if you do." She spoke to Ray, who nodded.

"I plan on it. It's going to get really hot on this deck."

"Are you going to introduce me, Ray?" Shellie came up holding a plastic cup of beer. She was looking at Lee with a sharp expression.

"This is Lee," Ray said, feeling a bit uncomfortable. "Lee, Shellie."

"A pleasure." Lee held out her hand. Shellie looked at it for a moment before taking it.

"Same here. Ray, I'm going inside to change." She pressed her lips against Ray's in what seemed to Ray like a possessive kiss. It unsettled her and she didn't respond like she probably should have, because Shellie pulled back with an annoyed expression. She didn't speak again, but turned and strode off into the house.

Ray looked at Lee and found her gazing in another direction, her face flat. She wondered why she was so embarrassed for Lee to see her kissing Shellie. It wasn't as though there was any chance of her and Lee getting together. Lee was straight, despite the ardor with which she had responded to their kiss. It was something that shouldn't have happened, and Ray knew she just needed to forget about it, as Lee obviously had done.

The problem was, she couldn't forget about it. Even while she was in bed with Shellie, part of her was thinking about what it would be like to have Lee there instead. She tried her damnedest to push Lee from her thoughts and concentrate on the woman underneath her, but all it did was cause the thoughts to push back harder.

Ray knew that it wouldn't last much longer with Shellie. Already, Shellie was starting to act in a way that told she wasn't taking Ray's statement that it was just for fun seriously. Ray hated it when women started to think that because she hadn't stopped things after the first couple of nights that they had started to work their way into her emotions. Shellie obviously had reached that point, and that told Ray it was time to end things.

Ray wandered from group to group for the next couple of hours not paying a whole lot of attention to anyone. She was aware that she could pinpoint Lee's location at any given moment, and that Lee had been glancing in her direction an awful lot.

Shellie had come back out and gotten into the pool and was now flirting with someone else. Ray was certain it was to make her jealous, but jealousy would have required an emotional attachment that didn't exist.

She finally got into the pool herself, and was pleased when Lee followed shortly after. They ended up together on one side facing each other.

"Quite the party," Lee commented.

"Yes." Ray fought the urge to reach out and run her hand down the curve of Lee's side. She was wearing a bikini with a skimpy bottom, and she looked positively edible to Ray. Ray had seen that others were noticing as well, especially since Lee was evenly tanned and well-muscled in an attractively feminine way.

"Your house is adorable. It's going to be wonderful once you've renovated it."

Ray forced her attention away from Lee's breasts to her face. "Thank you."

Lee was studying her with a slightly concerned expression, one that vanished when their gazes met. For the briefest of moments Ray imagined she saw hunger in Lee's eyes, but when she looked again there was nothing.

"Shellie seems like a nice girl."

"She is," Ray replied with a shrug. "But it isn't going to work out."

"Why not?" Lee asked curiously.

Ray blushed. "I don't … things don't usually last very long with me. I'm not looking for a relationship."

Lee pushed away from the wall and floated a few feet from Ray. "So you've told me. Seems like a lot of energy wasted in containing your emotions."

Ray blushed even more deeply. "The emotions just aren't there."

"That's too bad," Lee said seriously. "I'd think you'd be a great catch."

The two studied each other once again and Ray's heart started hammering at her ribcage. She forced herself not to show what she was feeling and laughed. "Hardly; I'm a pain in the ass."

"Hmph. I don't believe you."

Before Ray could respond, someone sent a wave of water at them, dousing them both. With a growl, Ray turned and saw Jackie standing a few feet away with an evil grin on her face.

"You're going to pay for that," Ray promised firmly. Jackie just grinned more broadly. Ray went after her, leaving Lee behind. After catching Jackie and dunking her, she turned and saw Lee climbing out of the pool.

Water streamed down her body, beading off her sunscreen. Ray felt a hot rush between her thighs. *Damn it! Get a grip on yourself. She's straight.* The words had become a mantra that Ray found herself forced to repeat with unsettling regularity.

"I'm telling you, Ray; get that look off your face before Lee or Shellie notice."

"What look?" Ray turned to Jackie, who rolled her eyes.

"The 'if I don't get you into bed I'm going to die' look." Jackie crossed her arms. "I thought you said you were over it."

Ray blushed. "I lied."

"Obviously." Jackie shook her head. "You're playing a dangerous game, Ray."

"I'm not playing a game." Ray gave her a dirty look. "I'm not about to let Lee know how I feel."

"It's not hard to see if you're looking for it," Jackie commented. "No wonder Shellie's in such a snit."

Ray dropped down until she was underwater to give herself a moment to think. She came up smoothing her hair to get the water out of it. "I can't help it if Shellie's in a snit. I'm not sure I can help how I feel about Lee, either; I can make sure nothing comes of it, though."

"Right. Just keep telling yourself that until it becomes true. Because if you do something about it it's not only going to ruin your friendship, it's going to make you look like a complete asshole."

Ray refrained from telling Jackie she already looked liked an ass because of kissing Lee. At least Lee had apparently forgiven her that slip up. She wasn't about to make another; she was certain she wouldn't be forgiven so easily. She just let it lie and changed the subject.

VI.

Lee studied herself in the mirror. She had agreed to go out to dinner with Ray and a couple of others after volleyball. They were to meet at the Crab Shack at six. It had come to be a habit to go there after volleyball for oysters and beer. The clock on her bedside table now read five-thirty and Lee couldn't decide what to wear.

She had settled on a pair of khaki shorts but couldn't put a shirt with it. There were four spread out on the bed. She wasn't sure why it made such a difference, but for some reason she wanted to look good. She finally settled on a light blue blouse and went to fix her hair.

Ray was there when she arrived, but no one else was. They got beers and sat at one of the picnic tables waiting.

"You had a couple of good points today," Ray said after a few minutes of silence.

"Thank you. You made some good saves."

They were silent for another minute. Finally, Lee had to break the silence. "How did you get to be an electrician?"

Ray laughed. "Completely by accident. I wanted to go into auto repair but the course was full at the college so I picked electrical. I figured I could apply it to the auto course when it came open. I just never quit."

"How long have you been doing it?"

"Since I was twenty; I've been with Baylight for six years now." Ray took a swig of her beer. "I might be getting a promotion to crew boss soon."

"Well, I hope you get it. I was in social services before I got married. I worked for DCF." Lee looked out across the river. "I hated it."

"You quit when you got married? Why?" Ray looked at her curiously.

Lee sighed. "Because Robert didn't want me to work. It was just an excuse really. I was so burned out I could barely make myself go in every morning."

"Why didn't you have children?" Ray shook herself. "Sorry, that was kind of a personal question."

"It's ok." Lee smiled. "I was just postponing it. I figured I'd start when I was thirty or so. I'm not so sure I want children now. What about you? Ever thought about children?"

Ray snickered. "Hell, no. The world doesn't need any mini-me's running around. One of me is bad enough."

"I don't think you're that bad."

"You don't know me very well." Ray grinned. "I'm the kind of woman you don't bring home to mother."

"Bringing you home to my mother would probably give her a stroke." Lee laughed. "Although it might be worth it just for that."

Ray gave her a startled look. "You don't get along with your parents?"

"Not really. They like to treat me like I'm sixteen."

"That sucks." Ray swigged off her beer. "My mother couldn't care less what I do. After the whole coming out experience I guess she figures the worst is over."

"What about your father?"

"He died a few years ago. But he felt pretty much the same as my mother." Ray shrugged. "I always was a tomboy."

"Was it hard for them?"

Ray shrugged. "A little bit. Mostly because they liked my boyfriend at the time and were hoping I'd get married."

"My parents love Robert. They're less than thrilled that I'm divorcing him. Sometimes I think they'd rather have him for a son than me for a daughter." Lee dropped her gaze to the table and tried not to blush. "They sure keep taking his side in things."

"Some parents." Ray snorted. "It's too bad we don't get to pick 'em."

Lee managed a smile. "I don't think I'd have picked mine. Where is everybody?"

"I don't know. You have to understand dyke time; six usually means six forty-five. You'll just have to deal with me until they get here."

"That's hardly a bad thing." Lee's heart skipped a beat at the thought of being alone with Ray for another half an hour.

Ray grinned at her. "Good to hear."

It seemed very easy to talk to her after that, like it had been before the kiss had thrown everything into turmoil. They discussed family and childhood in more detail than Lee had ever gone into with anyone before.

Ray was sympathetic about her dysfunctional relationship with her parents, and Lee was envious of Ray's open family life. By the time the others showed up, the two had learned more about each other than Lee had ever shared before.

After dinner, the group decided to walk on the beach. Lee was a little tentative considering what happened the last time but reasoned that in a group everything would be ok. Unfortunately, once there everyone paired up and wandered at their own pace, leaving Ray and Lee together. They walked a distance apart for a while, and then Lee found that they had narrowed the gap until they were almost touching.

They continued to talk and before Lee realized it, they had been walking for almost twenty minutes. The others had already turned back and the two stood together for a moment looking at the rising moon.

"It's a romantic night," Ray commented, glancing at Lee. "The sort of night you should be out with someone like that James of yours."

Lee nodded, although she surprised herself by thinking she would much rather be there with Ray than with James, who despite being sweet and gentle was something of a zero personality-wise. "Well, knowing that you're a romantic even though you deny it, I can't imagine that you wouldn't rather be here with someone other than me."

"I don't know about that." Ray's voice was soft.

"Don't be silly." Her response was light, but her heart had started pounding. "It's always better to share a romantic moment with someone you care about."

"I know." Ray fell silent for a long moment. Finally, she said, "We'd better head back before the others all leave."

"I suppose you're right." Lee didn't really want to leave, but she had a sneaking suspicion that if they didn't things might get out of hand. She knew that the kiss had stormed directly into the forefront of her thoughts as they stood together, and she wondered if the same thing had happened to Ray.

"I'm glad you weren't sorry it happened."

It took a second to register Ray's words. Lee turned to her and found the older woman gazing at her with a soft look that couldn't be mistaken as anything but longing.

As soon as their eyes met Ray shook herself and the look vanished, but Lee knew it had been there. Strangely, it made her feel warm all over and set free a flock of butterflies in her stomach.

"It shouldn't happen again," Lee said weakly, more to convince herself than Ray.

"I know." Ray's face took on a severe expression. "It won't."

Even more strangely, Ray's words disappointed Lee. She took a step forward, realizing that she could easily kiss Ray in the next moment, or the next. The realization confused and frightened her. She pulled up and stared at Ray, who was staring back.

"Let's go." Lee forced herself to turn around. They started walking in silence. After a time, Lee realized she hadn't left herself any choice where Ray was concerned. Her emotions were overwhelming her. She stopped, reached out, and took Ray's hand. Ray glanced at her, obviously startled, but didn't pull away. Lee stepped forward so that a breath was all that separated them. "I can't help it, Ray. I don't understand it, but I can't help it."

Their lips met in a tender touch that sent a wave of heat over Lee's body. Ray tentatively slid her arms around Lee's waist and pulled her closer, her mouth gently working against Lee's.

The kiss was soft, gentle and warm, and Lee felt her knees go weak.

Slowly, the passion built as their tongues met and danced together in warm darkness. Lee pressed herself against Ray's body, her arms tightening around Ray's shoulders. She felt the softness of Ray's breasts against her, felt Ray's chest rising and falling, and knew that she was surrendering more than her mouth to the kiss. She tried to be afraid, tried to stop, but she was beyond reason.

As the kiss deepened, Lee found her body responding in a way that she would never have imagined. Bolts of energy ran from her neck down across her breasts and met in her groin in an explosion of wetness. She groaned as Ray's hands cupped her buttocks and lightly squeezed. Ray's lips moved into her hair and down across her eyes before reclaiming her lips.

In all her life, Lee had never responded to a kiss the way she was responding then. Her mind refused to process the information, and she was left with only the raw want that swept over her body.

Finally, Ray lifted her head and looked down into Lee's face. "I don't think you should have done that."

"I don't care," Lee answered breathlessly. "If I hadn't I'd have died regretting it."

Ray stepped out of the embrace and crossed her arms, studying Lee levelly, although her own breath came raggedly. "Got it out of your system?"

Lee cringed at the tone in her voice. "I don't know."

"You know I want to kiss you again."

"I want you to."

There was nothing gentle about this second kiss. Ray's lips crushed against Lee's, her hands pulling Lee against her roughly. Lee tried to groan but couldn't even breathe. Every fiber of her being tingled with arousal as Ray moved her mouth to Lee's neck, biting down to her shoulder.

She lifted her face back to Lee's and sought her mouth again, her hands running up Lee's sides to slide across the curve of her breasts. As her fingers found the rapidly hardening buds of Lee's nipples, she abruptly dropped her hands and pulled away.

"I'm sorry," she gasped. "I'm so sorry."

Lee's Awakening

"Why?" Lee's voice was faint as she fought with the desire crashing through her body.

"I shouldn't have ... I swore I wouldn't."

Slowly, reason returned to Lee's brain and she felt a wash of embarrassment. Once again, she had allowed a romantic moment to suck her into something she normally would never even consider. She didn't understand why Ray made her want to do the things she did, but it had to stop.

"I shouldn't have either," she murmured. "I don't know what came over me."

"I wish you'd figure it out. You make it very hard to behave."

Lee blushed. "I'm sorry. I'm not being very fair to you, am I?"

"No," Ray responded bluntly. "I'm a lesbian, Lee. When you do things like that it makes me want to do more. That isn't fair to me, when I know you don't want anything of the sort."

"I don't understand it at all. I want to be friends with you, but sometimes I ... I can't explain it. You're right; I don't want anything more. It's unsettling enough that I enjoy kissing you this much."

"Well, it has to stop. Either that or we can't be around each other alone." Ray paced a few steps. "I'm not made out of stone, Lee. When you kiss me like that ... it has to stop."

Lee bit her lip. "I agree. It won't happen again."

"It can't. I can't take it again. It's going to go too far."

"I see that. I promise; it won't happen again." Lee wrapped her arms around her chest. "I don't want to lose your friendship, Ray. I've come to value it."

"And I don't want to lose yours. But we can't go on like this and have it survive." Ray sighed and ran her hand through her hair. "Let's just go back. If the others haven't left they're going to be wondering where the hell we are."

They didn't speak again until they were at their cars. Four of the group were left, and they all gave the pair confused looks when they came up. Lee tried her best not to look guilty and made her escape as quickly as possible. As she drove home, she fought the tremors of her body that came with remembering the kiss.

It couldn't really have happened. She couldn't have kissed Ray like that. She couldn't have wanted to breathe her in until they were one being, to kiss every inch of her body a thousand times until she knew it like the back of her hand.

She might have denied it to Ray, but there had been a long moment in the midst of things when she *had* wanted more; a lot more. It terrified her to think what that could mean.

How could she have gotten so entangled in this? Had her body turned traitor on her, wanting things that her mind couldn't accept? It made no sense for her to feel this way about Ray. She hadn't ever felt this way about Robert, not even in the beginning. *I've never felt this way about anyone.* There had to be a logical explanation for it.

If only there was someone she could talk to. She couldn't admit what had happened to Stacy; she'd only lecture and get mad at Ray. But there was no one else she would dare talk to. She would just have to deal with it on her own.

* * *

"Hand me that wrench, will you?" Ray held out her hand and waited for Jackie to put the tool in it before reaching back under the sink. "This damned thing just doesn't want to break loose."

"Hit it," Jackie offered. "If it breaks it needed fixing anyway."

"I'd like to be able to *use* the sink, Jackie." Ray tried one more time and managed to get the pipe loose. "There." She got up and held the piece of PVC in her hand. She could see a thin crack along the bottom. "Well, this should be easy enough to fix."

"Have you heard any more about the promotion?"

Ray rolled her eyes. "The scuttlebutt is that they're looking to hire someone from outside the company. I should start looking for another job."

"Isn't that risky?" Jackie reached into the fridge and pulled out a beer. She offered it to Ray, who took it and cracked it open. Jackie got out another one and rejoined her.

"Well, if they don't respect my work enough to promote me I don't know if I want to work there."

Jackie shrugged. "You do what you need to. I don't think I'd quit without knowing I had another job."

Lee tossed the broken pipe onto the counter and took a swig of her beer. "I don't plan to. Steve keeps telling me to hang on a little bit longer. I'm getting tired of hanging on."

"I can't really blame you. Say, how did dinner go the other night? I heard from Tracy that you and Lee were out on the beach forever."

Ray fought the blush that rose to her cheeks. "We were talking."

"For forty-five minutes?" Jackie laughed. "Since when do you two talk so much, or more specifically, since when do *you* talk so much?"

"Time just got away from us. What do you think happened?"

Jackie laughed. "I'd like to think the two of you made out, but knowing that's about as likely as me going straight I'll have to believe you."

Ray hid her face so the pained expression wouldn't show. "Yeah, we made out. Be real, Jackie." She drew in a deep breath. "Actually—"

"Actually what?"

Ray swallowed hard. "She kissed me."

"*She* kissed *you*? Are you sure it wasn't the other way around?" Jackie's eyebrows shot up.

"I'm sure. She was pretty freaked out about it." Ray glanced away. "I don't know what possessed her to do it."

"Did you kiss her back?"

"Yes."

Jackie made a noise. "I told you that you were playing a dangerous game, Ray."

"It isn't a game anymore. This is serious." Ray shifted uncomfortably. "I'm not sure what to make of it."

"Is this the first time it's happened?" Jackie studied her evenly.

"No, it's happened once before. Only then, I kissed her. But she wanted me to, at least wanted me to until I did it. We

96

agreed to forget about it, but obviously she didn't."

"Jesus, Ray." Jackie ran her hand through her hair. "You sure know how to get yourself in some messes."

"She says she doesn't want anything more to come of it. But I swear, the way she kissed me ..." Ray trailed off and stared at the wall uncomfortably.

Jackie looked sternly at her. "You should know better than to get involved with a straight woman going through a divorce. She's probably just hoping she can get some comfort from a woman since her man turned out to be a jerk."

"I don't know, Jackie. She seems really confused about what happened." Ray sighed. "Hell, I'm confused about what happened."

"You're nuts. You know that?"

"Maybe I am. All I know is that I don't want to lose her friendship, but if this doesn't stop, I'm going to have to stay away from her. It can only end badly." Ray fiddled with her wrench. "No matter how I might want it to be otherwise."

Jackie was silent for a moment. Finally, she chuckled softly. "Figures you'd fall for someone you can't have."

"I haven't fallen for her. I just have the world's worst case of lust going."

"Whatever." Jackie finished her beer. "Do you have the part to replace that?" She pointed at the broken pipe.

"No. I wasn't sure how bad it was. I'll have to run down to Lowe's. I might as well pick up the new faucet while I'm at it, and some more beer. You want to ride with me?"

Jackie shook her head. "No, I think I'll stay here. Your hot tub is calling my name."

Ray laughed. "It tends to do that. OK, I'll be back in a few."

As she backed out of the driveway, Ray wondered if her life would ever get back to normal, if the hungry want she felt for Lee would ever go away. It would have to. There was no other option.

*   *   *

Lee felt the water tugging at her ankles as she walked along the beach. The sun was just setting, casting a reddish glow across the waves. Her thoughts weren't on the beauty of the early evening, but rather on the same thing that had been chewing at her for two days—Ray.

Something had changed with their last kiss. Lee wasn't sure quite what it was, but something was definitely different. She had been in turmoil ever since, her mind fighting with her body over what it meant. She couldn't deny that Ray was an excellent kisser. She couldn't deny that the kiss had turned her on. But it was most likely the result of Ray's skillful use of her mouth instead of something more sinister. *It has to be.*

Lee bent and picked up a seashell. She examined it and then flung it across the waves. She was going out with James. She liked James. Just because she hadn't slept with him yet didn't mean she wasn't interested in doing so. He would be the first since Robert, and she was just a little nervous about taking that step. When the time was right, she had no doubts that it would happen.

She wondered if her attraction to Ray was just a reaction to Robert's treatment of her. Ray was about as opposite to Robert as a person could be. Knowing that Ray was a lesbian perhaps made her attractive in a rebound sort of way; it was possible that she was subconsciously hoping to find something better with a woman.

Lee hoped that wasn't the case. She thought it would be very shallow and petty of her to treat Ray as though she was just a convenient crutch for getting through a difficult time in her life. Ray deserved better than that, especially since she had admitted that it turned her on when they kissed. It was obvious that Ray was interested in her, and she hadn't helped matters by kissing her on the beach that night.

Whatever the reasons for it, Lee knew she had to get herself under control, and quickly. Ray wouldn't tolerate another repeat of that night and Lee didn't want her to withdraw. They had become friends; Lee had few honest friends to turn to already. Ray told her what she thought in no uncertain terms, a trait that Lee found refreshing.

Her musings were interrupted by the ringing of her cell phone. She glanced at the screen; it was her mother.

"Hi, Mom."

"Lee, dear. Have I caught you at a good time?" Her mother sounded suspiciously cheerful.

"I'm just taking a walk." Lee kicked at a wavelet.

"Good. Robert called me today."

Lee groaned. The last thing she wanted to deal with was her mother talking about Robert. "I don't particularly care, Mom."

"Hear me out. He says he's getting another appraisal on the house. He wanted you to know that he's doing everything to make sure you don't doubt his honesty. He just doesn't understand why you're being so money oriented all a sudden."

"Money oriented? We were together for five years and he wouldn't let me work during that time. I only want what's fair." Lee blew out her breath in annoyance.

"You *didn't* work during that time, Lee. How much do you think you're entitled to?" Her mother had the tone she got when she was ready to launch into a lecture.

Lee forced herself to remain calm. "He's the one who wanted me to quit my job in the first place. He's complaining about even paying the maintenance!"

Her mother made a noise. "I don't see why it has to come to this. You still haven't explained why you won't go to counseling."

"Because I don't want to. I don't want to save anything." Lee wanted to throw something. "Why do you constantly take his side in this? I'm your daughter, for God's sake!"

"Robert is the best thing that ever happened to you, Lee. He gave you everything you wanted; you'll have to look hard for someone who adores you as much as he does."

Lee rubbed her face. "I don't love him, Mom." And she didn't. She was beginning to realize that she probably never actually loved him.

"Your father and I went through something like this early in our marriage too. We weathered it, and realized we couldn't live without each other. If you'd just give it a chance I'm sure you'd get through this the same way."

"You just don't get it, do you? I don't *want* to get through this, at least not with him. I want out, and I'm getting out. I don't care if he thinks he's going to shrivel up and die with me gone; I'm gone." Lee stopped walking and stared out over the water, willing herself to remain calm.

"You need to stop being so selfish—" her mother started.

Lee lost her temper. "Selfish? God damn it, Mother; get it through your head! He was a controlling bastard and I'm not taking it any more. If that's selfish then I'm selfish. But I'm not going back and I'm not talking about it anymore!"

"Don't curse at me, Lee. It just shows how hysterical you are."

Lee hung up on her. The phone rang almost instantly, and she turned it off, shoving it back into its holster with a growl. Leave it to her mother to try and turn everything around and make it Lee's fault.

She walked a while longer, angry at the conversation, angry at her mother and angry at Robert for using her to get at Lee. Finally, she realized that by getting angry she was letting him still control her. She calmed herself down and turned to go back to her car.

Ray had invited her out to hear her sing at some karaoke contest she had entered. There would be a group of women there, Stacy and Donna included. It would be nice to get out and relax with friends. They wouldn't try to say that Robert was in the right. She might even be able to enjoy herself without bringing it up at all.

*   *   *

The contest was at a little bar that catered to bikers. Lee parked her car next to Ray's pickup, nervously locked it and activated the alarm. She'd never been in a place quite so rough looking. She spotted Donna's car and felt a little better, first because she would know more than one person there, and second because it meant she wouldn't be alone with Ray.

There were five women sitting at a booth in the corner of the bar. Lee recognized them all, including Ray's friend Jackie. The other two were the couple who owned the farm where they played volleyball, Kalynn and Mitch. Ray was up at the bar when she came in so she worked her way to join her and to order a drink. She had a sneaking suspicion that wine wasn't on the menu and was correct. She settled for an import beer and turned to Ray, who was smiling at her.

"I'm glad you came," Ray said. "You'll get to hear me scaring small animals."

"Well, you must be reasonably good. Isn't this the monthly finals?"

Ray nodded. "Though how I got here is beyond me."

Lee laughed. "It couldn't possibly be because you're good, could it?"

"I suppose someone thought so." Ray shrugged and grinned.

They made their way back to the table, where Lee greeted everyone and pulled up a chair to sit between Kalynn and Ray. She noticed Jackie giving her a strange look, but she said nothing and Lee dismissed it.

"Well, look who decided to come slumming." Donna winked at her. "Did you set the alarm on your car?"

Lee blushed. "Yes."

Everyone laughed and Donna leaned across the table and patted her hand. "It's ok, dear. Most everyone is here for the contest. You won't have to contend with the bikers."

"Oh, shut up." Lee stuck out her tongue and the table laughed even harder. She took a swig of her beer and glanced at Ray, startled to find her studying her out of the corner of her eye with a serious look on her face.

The conversation danced away and for a while, Lee listened as the group gossiped about other friends. She was a little surprised that she recognized a lot of the names, and realized she knew more people from volleyball than she'd thought. It was a loose group, and different women came on different days. In all there were probably twenty-five who showed up on a semi-regular basis, and between Stacy and Ray, she'd met them all.

Finally, there was a lull and Lee turned to Ray. "How did you get into doing this?"

Ray grinned at her. "Alcohol."

"Seriously."

"Alcohol," Ray affirmed. "I got drunk at Maddie's one night

and someone dared me to get up and sing. It was a lot of fun so I did it again. And came back the next week, and the one after that."

"So I guess you're pretty good. You must have a natural voice."

Ray shrugged. "My father made me take lessons in high school and I was in the chorus. I play piano too," she added when Lee raised an eyebrow. "And trumpet. I was in the band."

"You don't seem like the musical sort." Lee wondered why she couldn't imagine it.

"Well, what did you do in high school?"

"Drama club. And art club. I played a lot of sports — volleyball, in fact. And softball." Lee smiled. "Didn't expect that, did you?" She asked when Ray's face showed surprise.

"Drama and Art I can see. But you don't look like the jock type. What else did you play?"

"Soccer and tennis. I was on the field hockey team for a season but I got a concussion from a high stick and my mother wouldn't let me play anymore."

"I was in the rocket club and the science club," Jackie volunteered. "And I was in drama club too."

Everyone shared their high school extra-curricular activities, laughing at some and nodding at others, such as Donna's computer club experience. She was a web designer now and still a techno-geek.

"So do you practice at home?" Lee asked Ray after the discussion died down.

"A few hours a week. I have my own set up. Not as extensive as this." She gestured at the equipment on the stage. "Just a machine and some CD's. I record myself sometimes. It's fun."

"Obviously the practice is paying off. What happens if you win tonight?"

"Well, the top three places get a cash award and the winner goes to the finals in August. The top prize there is a cruise. I don't expect to win. But it pays five places and fifth prize is five hundred dollars." Ray grinned. "That's a night of caviar and champagne."

"Yeah, you're the caviar and champagne sort." Jackie snorted. "Next you'll tell me you like to scatter rose petals across the bed."

Ray blushed. "Can you see me doing that?" she asked lightly, though to Lee her face seemed a little secretive.

"No," Jackie replied with a wry grin. "Now, offering to change someone's oil; that I can see."

"That's more my speed." Ray laughed. "My idea of romantic is putting up a ceiling fan in the bedroom."

Everyone laughed with her, though Lee's laughter was a bit faked. She caught Ray's gaze and Ray winked at her. Lee blushed, not sure how to take the gesture.

It was finally time for the contest to start. Ray went third and belted out a country tune that brought cheers from the audience. Lee thought she had easily been best so far. Each singer had to do two songs of different tempos, and Ray waited to come up again with a grin on her face.

Conversation mostly centered on the performance of the other contestants with the group in agreement that Ray was the best thus far. Lee found it easy to participate, and noticed that her thoughts about Ray didn't dwell on their kiss. Rather, she enjoyed her company and didn't really think of it at all.

Ray's next performance brought even louder applause and she sank back down in her seat with a big grin. "I really knocked that one out of the ballpark," she said proudly.

"Yes, you did," Lee confirmed. "If you don't win, I'll be surprised."

"Well, we don't find out until next Wednesday."

"If you do, I'll buy you dinner," Lee promised.

Ray's expression changed ever so slightly. "I hope I win, then."

The two women studied each other for a moment and then Ray looked away. Lee found herself wondering how she would be rewarding Ray if they were lovers. The answer sent a chill through her, both because it was so intimate and because it made her wish for a moment that it could happen.

She shook herself. She had managed to avoid thinking like that for the entire evening and now all of a sudden it was in the forefront of her mind. It distressed her that she could so easily imagine a situation where they could be together in that way and that imagining it made her ache for Ray's lips.

Stop it, Lee. Just because Ray is a great kisser doesn't mean you have to start imagining things like that. Lee took a long swallow of her beer and forced her thoughts to something else.

They all walked out together when it was over. Ray and Lee stood at Ray's door; Lee shivered with her nearness. They studied each other and Lee's heart began thudding against her ribcage. She forced herself to remain calm as she bent over and kissed Ray's cheek.

Ray moved her head as Lee's lips touched her skin as if to capture her mouth with her own. Lee pulled back and forced a smile, although part of her had wanted to turn her own head to meet those lips.

"I hope you win." She prayed that her voice didn't betray what she was thinking.

"Me too," Ray replied. "Thanks for coming to cheer me on." Her eyes searched Lee's face.

"My pleasure." Lee was painfully aware that Jackie and Stacy stood not five feet away talking to each other. She stepped back and reached for her keys.

Ray shifted. "I'm having a painting party at my house this Saturday. Would you come?"

"Of course," Lee responded. "I'll wear my grubby clothes and try not to get more paint on myself than the walls."

Ray laughed. "I'm sure you won't be the only one. I'm having pizza and beer and there's always the pool."

"Sounds like a good time."

"I hope so." Ray shifted again. "I guess I should get going since I have to work tomorrow."

"I'm filling out more applications myself. I guess I'll see you Saturday." Lee hit the remote unlock on her car. Ray nodded and climbed into her truck while Lee went around to get into her own vehicle. Stacy caught her as she rounded the front bumper. She pulled Lee aside and gave her a stern look.

"You really should stop kissing Ray on the cheek, you know."

Lee was startled. Surely, Stacy hadn't figured out what had happened. "Why?" She kept her voice light. "I kiss you on the cheek too."

"Ray's—well, Ray's starting to get that look she gets when she's into someone." Stacy bit her lower lip. "I just don't want you to get into an awkward position."

If you only knew ... Lee forced a laugh. "I think I can handle myself."

"Okay." Stacy drew the word out. "I'm just giving you fair warning."

"Well, thank you, but I'm a big girl. I'm not worried about Ray misunderstanding me."

"As long as you know what you're doing. I guess I'll see you on Saturday?"

Lee nodded and got into her car. As she backed up, she blew out a breath at how nervous she had been to think that Stacy might know about what happened that night on the beach. She hadn't realized how concerned she was that someone else might find out until that moment.

I just hope Ray doesn't tell anyone. I know I won't. With a sigh, she headed for home.

VII.

Steve looked like he had bad news the moment Ray saw him. He came into the room with his head down, trying to avoid looking at her. She finished wiring the outlet and stood up.

"What's up, Steve?"

Steve shifted uncomfortably. "I've got bad news. But don't take it the wrong way."

Ray somehow knew what he was going to say. "I didn't get the promotion."

"No." Steve shook his head. "They hired someone from Martin's."

"Son-of-a-bitch!" Ray exclaimed angrily. "How could they do that?"

"I don't know."

Ray looked for something to throw. "That's it. I can't believe this!"

"Look, why don't you take the rest of the day off? Go have a few beers and be mad." Steve splayed his hands. "I know you won't be any good here."

"Damn straight! And maybe I won't come back in the morning."

"Don't go getting all irrational on me, Ray. You're the best electrician on this crew. And I can guarantee you that you won't get the same benefits somewhere else." Steve looked apologetic.

"There's more to life than benefits, Steve." Ray kicked at a roll of wire. "There's my dignity."

"Just stick it out. Maybe this new guy won't be so bad."

"Yeah, I'll stick it out; but just because you asked me to. And if he turns out to be a jerk I'm out of here." Ray ran her hand through her hair. "I don't believe this," she repeated.

"Go on, take off. Stop by the bar and have a few." He clapped her on the shoulder. "And buck up."

Ray had her cell phone to her ear before she was out of the house. After the briefest of conversations, Jackie agreed to meet her at Maddie's. Ray threw her equipment in the back of the truck and peeled out.

She beat Jackie to the bar and sat down on the stool with a foul look on her face. Joan sat two beers in front of her and waved away her money.

"You have that look." She leaned on the bar.

"I didn't get my promotion." Ray took a long swallow of the first beer, downing at least a quarter of it. "The sons-of-bitches hired someone from Martin's."

"I'm sorry to hear that. That's what you get from a bunch of testosterone-laden assholes."

"Like six years means nothing." Ray looked over her shoulder as Jackie entered the bar. She saw Ray and lifted her hand in greeting. "I may just sit here all night and drink."

"You do that and expect to get a ride to pick up your truck tomorrow, because I won't let you drive." Joan poured a rum and coke and sat it on a coaster as Jackie slid onto the stool next to Ray.

"Okay, what's the scoop?" Jackie asked as she paid for her drink.

Ray related the story. When she was finished, Jackie had a scowl on her face.

"You should quit," she said firmly.

"The problem is I was kind of counting on that promotion to do renovations at the house. I can't really quit. How would I afford my mortgage?"

Jackie considered her words. "That's true. But it sucks."

"Damn right it does. Now I have to deal with some yahoo

from Martin's who probably has an attitude toward women in the field." Ray took another long drink.

"So where does this leave you with the house?

Ray growled. "It means converting the garage will have to wait. And the workshop is on hold indefinitely."

"Bummer."

"Serious bummer." Ray finished her beer and reached for the second one. "Sometimes I wish I'd picked a different career."

Jackie snorted. "Bullshit. You love being an electrician and you know it."

Ray lapsed into contemplation. She did love being an electrician. She'd been doing it so long she couldn't imagine any other job.

"I suppose I shouldn't be so mad, but it's the principle of the thing."

"You have every right to be mad," Jackie replied. "You deserved to get promoted and they hired some asshole from outside instead."

"I really had my heart set on converting the garage, too. I'd already picked out the pool table I want to put in there." Ray sighed.

"Well, the kitchen is coming along nicely."

Ray thought about it. The bottom cabinets and countertops were already in, one of the first things she had done. Her next project was the upper cabinets and new appliances. That would take more time than she had planned too. "I'm pretty pleased with the countertop."

"Have you picked up the paint for this weekend?"

"Yeah; I think the chocolate for the den is going to look fabulous." It was a bold color choice, but the room had plenty of windows and Ray favored a more masculine feel for a room intended to be relaxed in.

"It's going to make it really cozy. I like that. A nice leather armchair with those built in bookshelves and it'll be perfect for you. I can just see you in there listening to your jazz, reading Shakespeare and smoking a cigar."

Ray laughed. "Since when do you think I read Shakespeare?"

"Well, it fit the image better than those smutty romance novels you read." Jackie grinned back at her.

Ray stuck out her tongue. "You read them too. You still have two of the ones I loaned you."

"*Erotic Interludes* warranted a second reading."

"And I'll bet you read it in bed."

"Damn straight." Jackie finished her drink. "You still planning on the Jacuzzi tub for the bathroom?"

"Yep. Johnnie's going to plumb it in for me." Ray smiled. "It pays to know a licensed plumber. He's going to do it for a case of beer."

Jackie nodded. "That's a cheap rate. I guess once we have the painting done we'll be having a furniture loading party."

"I still have two months on my lease. I'd like to get the floors done before I actually move in."

"Probably a wise move." Jackie signaled for another drink. "So, any more on the Lee front?"

"No. She's coming to help us paint, but something tells me she'll be one of the first ones to leave. I think I've scared her." Ray grimaced. "My libido sure gets the best of me sometimes, damn it." There was something a little more dangerous than libido going on where Lee was concerned, but Ray didn't particularly want to think about what.

Jackie took a swallow her new drink. "Considering what happened the other night I'd say she more likely scared herself."

Ray shrugged. "Same result."

"True." Jackie eyed her. "Feeling any better?"

"Yeah, actually. Thanks for taking my mind off it."

"Any time, pal o' mine." Jackie laughed. "So, the price of therapy today is another drink."

Ray laughed too. "You got it."

* * *

"I got a job today." Lee poured two more glasses of tea and walked back to the sofa.

Louise accepted her glass and smiled. "Congratulations. What will you be doing?"

"Office work; it's at an insurance agency. I'll be filing papers and answering the phone."

"Sounds easy enough. What does it pay?" She leaned forward as Lee sat down in the recliner.

"Enough to pay the bills, barely. But I've been looking for three weeks." Lee sighed. "I had no idea finding a job could be this hard." She'd been putting in applications almost every day with nothing even resembling a nibble. When the agency offered to hire her on the spot, she'd leapt at the opportunity.

"Well, I'm proud of you. If you're actually going through with this divorce it's good you're standing on your own two feet."

"Thanks. I could liquidate some of my assets, but I hate to do that. It's my retirement savings." Lee sipped at her drink. "I get benefits after ninety days."

"Nine to five?" Louise raised an eyebrow. "What about our tennis league?"

"Eight to three and I've already told them I need Wednesday mornings off until the end of the summer."

"That's good. I heard yesterday that Robert is putting the house up for sale." Louise nodded as if to herself. "I guess he's starting to take this thing seriously."

Lee grunted. "It's about damn time. I wondered how many months it would take before he got a clue that I wasn't kidding around."

"Well, he's still pretty miserable about the whole thing but he's been through this before, so I guess he knows when to give up." Louise leaned back and drank more of her tea. "I must admit I'm still sad that you two are splitting."

Lee got up and paced to the sliding glass doors, staring out over the river. "In a way I'm sad too. But I'm angrier than I am sad."

"How is it going between you and James?"

Lee thought about James. Things were going well, she guessed, in a platonic sort of way. He was apparently waiting for her to let him know she was ready for there to be more to their relationship. They were in a comfortable space, but Lee wasn't feeling the spark that told her anything long term could come of it.

"They're going well. We're going to the theatre next week." She turned back to Louise. "Has Robert heard?"

Louise shrugged. "I don't know. He's bound to sooner or later."

"I went to watch Ray do karaoke Tuesday night. It was a lot of fun. You and I should go sometime."

Louise laughed. "You can't be serious. Honestly, Lee, why are you slumming so much?"

"I'm not slumming," Lee responded sharply. "There's nothing wrong with being blue collar."

"Okay. But you aren't. Why this fascination with Ray? Are you collecting lesbian friends now?"

Lee refrained from telling her just how many lesbian friends she was picking up, although she was tempted to just to see the look on Louise's face. "Ray's a very nice person. You should meet her; you'd see."

Louise shrugged. "I'm sure I will, whether I want to or not. I swear; you're like a kid with a new puppy."

Lee changed the subject. "Do you know how much Robert is asking for the house?"

"Not off-hand. I would guess in the mid sixes. Ours was appraised this spring for five ninety and you have another bedroom and the dock." Louise threw the numbers around as if they weren't hundred-thousands.

Lee felt a momentary irritation with her. Louise came from more money than Lee; her parents were part owners of the largest real estate company in the county. Lee wondered if she could survive living as Lee herself was, without a maid and lawn service, landscapers and pool men.

She couldn't see Louise in a two bedroom apartment, overlooking the river or not. Louise had never lived in an apartment. Louise had never driven anything less expensive than a Volvo. She certainly had never had a job. She had married during her last year of college and never had to fend for herself.

"Well, the last appraisal I saw for the house had it at six hundred. I thought it was low then and I'm sure of it now."

"There is the hurricane insurance ... maybe your elevation is lower than ours." Louise looked contemplative.

111

"We're all on the flood plain. I'll have to find out. If I have to pay for an independent appraisal I will." Lee finished her drink. "Do you want a refill?"

"Why not? I don't understand why you distrust Robert so. He loves you too much to try and keep you from getting what's rightfully yours." Louise studied her evenly.

Lee had her own opinions about what Robert would try. "Divorce does strange things to people." She took Louise's glass and went back to the kitchen.

"I guess. Look at you."

"What's that supposed to mean?" Lee's irritation flared again.

"I mean, you've all but turned your back on your friends, you're spending all of your time with Stacy and her group, you're suspicious of Robert … if I didn't know you as well as I do I'd think you were having some sort of breakdown." Louise accepted the glass Lee thrust at her as though her words had no effect.

For a moment, Lee wondered if she *was* having some sort of breakdown. The way she was acting around Ray was certainly not normal for her, and she *had* been avoiding her old friends. She was certainly suspicious of Robert.

But hanging around with Stacy and her friends felt so much more real than what she had in her old social group. She enjoyed herself more than she ever had at the club. And despite how strange her feelings toward Ray were, they couldn't mean she was losing her mind. Desperate for a change, maybe, but not crazy.

"I'm not having a breakdown, just broadening my horizons."

Louise rolled her eyes. "Couldn't you broaden your horizons in a direction that didn't involve spending time in a gay bar? Really, Lee, can you imagine how Martha or Betty would react if they knew you were doing that?"

"I don't particularly care how Martha or Betty, or anyone else for that matter, would react. This is my life. I'm not a slave to some predetermined social path." She took a deep swallow of her tea before she could say something she might regret later.

"You didn't seem to mind it before this breakup started."

"I didn't really know any better then. I do now. I *enjoy* going to the bar, and karaoke, and playing volleyball. It doesn't matter whether I'm with lesbians or not."

"You always were stubborn." Louise lit another cigarette. "Let's go to Billy's for dinner."

Lee studied her. Sometimes there was no reasoning with Louise; this appeared to be one of those times. It was best just to let this dog lie. "Sounds good. I'll get dressed."

* * *

The living room and den were done and everyone was taking a break on the deck. Ray sat opposite Lee, puffing on yet another cigar. She was chatting with a woman Lee knew vaguely from volleyball, but who was apparently good friends with Ray. They were discussing baseball, a subject about which Lee cared little, so her attention was wandering.

"Hey, Lee!" Lee dragged herself from her thoughts and turned to Stacy. "We're going to take off."

"Ok. Are we still on for dinner?"

"You betcha." Stacy glanced at Ray. "Are you staying much later?"

Lee frowned, confused by the tone of Stacy's voice. "There are still two bedrooms to paint."

"There are plenty of people. Y'all are going to be getting in each other's way." Stacy glanced at Ray again. "We could always go to dinner early."

"I'm going to stay for a while."

Stacy shrugged. "Ok. Call me when you get home."

"Will do." Lee lifted her hand in a mock salute and Stacy nodded and spoke to Ray, whose face went flat as her gaze slid toward Lee. Lee watched Stacy walk off, wondering what the exchange had been all about.

"Where are you all going for dinner?" Ray's voice brought Lee's attention across the table.

"Houston's; want to come?"

"Maybe. It depends on when we get done." Ray leaned on her elbows. "I'm kind of surprised you're still here. I figured you'd have gotten bored by now."

"I'm having fun, actually." She was spattered with paint, as was Ray and just about everyone else still left on the deck. The original group had dwindled to a handful. "It's been years since I got to paint anything."

"Well, glad to have you," Ray responded. "Do you like the wine I bought?"

Lee looked at her glass. "Very much," she replied. "It's a very nice one. But you didn't have to go to the trouble. I brought wine coolers."

Ray shrugged. "Wasn't any trouble."

"Thank you anyway."

Ray grinned. "My pleasure." Her words sent an unexpected chill down Lee's spine. They sounded particularly intimate in the low, gravelly voice that Ray spoke with.

Finally, though Lee wasn't sure how it had happened, it was down to just her and Ray. They were almost finished with the second bedroom. Lee was painting the trim while Ray used the roller on the last wall to be done. They worked in silence until Lee playfully splattered paint across the front of Ray's t-shirt as she bent to reload her roller.

"Hey!" Ray looked down and then back up with a glint in her eye. "I'll get you for that."

"I'll warn you, I'm armed," Lee retorted, holding out her paintbrush.

Ray swatted at her with the roller, leaving a paint streak across her arm where she threw it up in defense. "Mine's bigger than yours."

It escalated from there into an all-out paint fight that ended when Ray tackled Lee around the waist and pulled her to the ground, straddling her hips while she caught Lee's wrist and wrestled the paintbrush from her hand.

"I win," Ray said breathlessly. Beneath her, Lee's chest heaved as she caught her own breath.

"I surrender." Lee looked up into Ray's face, spattered with white and pale yellow paint; she looked positively adorable.

As the moments passed, she became aware of Ray's weight on her thighs and of the closeness of her body as she knelt over her. Ray was looking down at her with a strange expression, not moving. Their gazes locked. Lee caught her breath and held it as a tremor of desire ran through her body. If Ray kissed her, she would just die. If she didn't kiss her, she would die anyway.

A heartbeat later, Ray bent her head. Their lips met in a kiss that grew deeper as Ray lowered her upper body onto Lee's. She released Lee's wrist and rested her elbows on either side of Lee's head, her fingers buried in Lee's hair.

Lee felt a crashing surge of electricity shoot through her body. Her nipples tingled into hardness against Ray's chest as her arms moved of their own accord to circle Ray's waist. She tightened them, drawing Ray closer against her as their tongues teased and danced in the warm wetness of their mouths.

Too soon, Ray lifted away, a startled look on her face. "Oh, Jesus — I'm sorry Lee." She tried to get up but Lee held her.

"Don't move." Her voice sounded strange to her ears.

"I shouldn't have ..."

Emotions and desires shot through Lee's body, bouncing off each other and exploding into a fire of want that shocked her with its force. "Kiss me again."

"But — "

Lee didn't wait. She moved her hands to the back of Ray's head and pulled her down, capturing her mouth with her own, knowing only that she had to feel the softness of Ray's lips again. Any sense of control she might have had melted away as they kissed. Lee was hungry, nibbling at Ray's lips when their tongues took a breath apart.

Ray groaned around the kiss, pulling away again. "Please, Lee. You're making it very hard for me to stop."

"I don't want you to stop," Lee replied, shocked at her own words. She felt the fullness of her groin and knew that only one thing could assuage it, one thing that only Ray could give her.

Ray lifted her head and looked deeply into Lee's eyes. Lee could see the turmoil of emotions behind them that finally settled into acceptance. They kissed again as Ray straightened her legs out and lay fully against Lee's body. Lee found herself lifting her hips against Ray's, her hands moving over Ray's back to pull her t-shirt up, to feel the skin beneath.

Ray maneuvered her legs so that she lay between Lee's and Lee bent her knees, raising herself against Ray's hips with even more hunger. Ray kissed down her neck to her shoulder and back up, biting along the way. Her lips moved along the line of Lee's jaw and reclaimed her mouth.

Her hands trailed up Lee's sides and slid between their bodies to cover her breasts. This time it was Lee who groaned as Ray lifted away and lightly squeezed, her fingers sliding across Lee's hardened nipples in an almost casual way.

Ray was breathing heavily as she lifted her head. "Are you sure?"

For a response, Lee moved to pull Ray's t-shirt up over her head. Ray shrugged out of it and tentatively reached to pull Lee's out of her jeans. Lee arched her back to allow Ray to slide the cotton up her ribcage and over her bra. Ray lifted it off her shoulders and the rest of the way off before dropping her head and kissing the point of Lee's neck, her tongue moving lazily down to the top of Lee's bra.

Her hands reclaimed Lee's breasts, this time capturing her nipples through the fabric with thumb and forefinger, gently rolling the hardness of them. Lee let out a long, hungry groan and arched her back again.

Ray slid her fingers underneath the bottom edge of the last vestige of clothing covering Lee's chest and pulled upward. She gazed down at her for a long moment as Lee lay there in anticipation of what might come next. Ray finally sat up again, straddling Lee's thighs, covering her breasts with her hands, running her fingers across the hardened tips of Lee's nipples. Lee couldn't believe the pulsing arousal that ran from them to her groin under Ray's touch. No man had ever made her feel this way.

Finally, Ray bent her head and captured a rigid bud with her mouth.

"Oh, God," Lee groaned. Ray captured the other nipple between her fingers and squeezed before rolling it as her mouth suckled at the first. Lee tangled her fingers in the top of Ray's hair, trying to pull her mouth closer to her breast.

Ray kissed a hot, wet line to the other breast, claiming the first one with her other hand. Lee's mind was thick with desire. She found herself incapable of coherent speech when she tried to beg Ray not to stop.

Incapable of speech until Ray's hands moved to the buckle of her belt. Something in the back of Lee's mind snapped into reality and she realized what she was doing. She tensed and Ray instantly sat back, her face a mask of confusion, desire and frustration.

"I—I can't do this," Lee stammered, pulling her bra back down. "I shouldn't ... I can't."

Ray reached for her t-shirt and pulled it back on. "I'm sorry, Lee. I'm very sorry." Her voice was thick with regret. She stood and walked out of the room, leaving Lee lying on the floor with her arms wrapped around her chest.

What did I almost do? Lee sat up, found her own shirt, and pulled it on. She was painfully aware of how aroused she was as she stood and ran a hand through her hair. *Ray must think I'm insane.* She had to go find her and explain. But what would she explain and how? She had drawn Ray in even as Ray tried to stop.

It was no one's fault but her own that she was in this situation. It didn't matter how it started or what had happened, nothing further could come of it. *I'm not gay. I'm not.* No matter how many times she repeated the words in her head, they still rang strangely hollow. *Am I?*

She roused herself and went out to the deck. Ray was standing against the rail with a cigar, staring across the pond. Lee sighed and went to try and apologize. Ray turned as she approached, her face unreadable.

"I'm sorry, Ray."

"Don't be." Ray's voice was gruff. "Let's just forget it happened."

Lee bit her lip. "I can't forget it happened. It's just ... I'm not ..."

"You're straight," Ray said dully. "I should have known better."

"I started it. It was—well, it was just too much too fast."

"But you *are* straight."

Lee paused, struggling with her emotions. "I think I am. I don't know anymore. I'm just very confused right now."

Ray took a drag off her cigar. "I guess you have a lot to think about then."

"Yes, I do. I don't—I don't think we should be alone together for a while." Lee forced the words out. "It isn't that I don't trust you...."

"Obviously I'm not very trustworthy." Ray dropped her head. "I can't say I'm sorry enough."

"Don't be sorry." Lee blew out her breath slowly. "Just be—understanding."

Ray looked at her again. "Understanding?"

Lee nodded. "I'm not telling you I never want to see you again. I just ... I need to deal with this without being so close to you. When I'm around you I don't—well, I don't think clearly."

Ray smiled wanly. "Coming from anyone else I'd be flattered." She glanced away. "I didn't want to drive you away."

"You didn't. But this throws my whole life into turmoil." Lee dropped her gaze. "I have to go."

"Then go. I won't stop you."

Sensing that any more talk would be futile, Lee turned and went back into the house. Retrieving her purse, she went out to her car. Once in the driver's seat, she stared at the house for a long time, struggling with her emotions. Part of her wanted to run back inside and into Ray's arms. The other part of her was terrified of the first part.

Blowing out her breath finally, she drove away.

Ray listened as Lee's car accelerated down the dirt driveway. She drew on her cigar and stared out across the pond again, her body trembling with hot aching want that pierced her in its intensity. Her mind whirled with the implications of what had happened. Lee would never speak to her again, of that much Ray was certain.

Lee had been so eager, so hungry, that her want had overridden Ray's own reticence at going further than the initial kiss. But obviously, Lee's hunger only went so far. There was no denying that Lee had been turned on by the encounter, but she had put a stop to it the moment it started to cross the waistline.

Ray cursed under her breath. She wasn't sure why she had kissed her in the first place, and now she knew that it had been yet another mistake and a horrible one at that. The only thing that could be done was to move past it and hope that the regret would fade one day.

VIII.

Lee wasn't even sure she wanted to go to the party. Helping her aunt and uncle celebrate their fortieth wedding anniversary at the club seemed like a dreadful bore when she could playing volleyball. But her mother had applied enough guilt that she had finally given in and so she got dressed and drove to the club, praying that she could make a quick escape.

It seemed that every cousin she had was there, and her plans of just staying an hour were almost immediately thrown out the window as she was forced to catch up with relative after relative, many of whom she hadn't seen since childhood.

That was enjoyable compared to what happened next. As Lee made her way to the bar table for another glass of wine, she spotted Robert standing off to the side scanning the crowd. His eyes found her and he smiled. Lee felt her stomach sink. *God damn it. What's he doing here?* She thought of vanishing immediately, but just then a great-aunt took hold of her arm and began to regale her with a story about her father's childhood. By the time she had escaped, Robert was close enough to reach out and touch her.

"Lee. You're looking good." His smile was oily.

"Robert." Lee set her face to avoid showing any emotion.

"Can I get you a glass of wine? I'm sure that's what you're having." He gestured toward the bar.

Lee shook her head. "I can get it myself, thank you. I hear you have the house up for sale."

"Yes." Robert looked mournful. "If you really aren't coming back there's no point in having such a big place. I can get by in a condo closer to the hospital."

"Yes, I suppose you could," Lee replied, not really caring about it. "What's your asking price?"

"Six seventy-nine. I'm hoping to get an offer in the low sixes. After all, the appraisal was only five ninety."

Lee counted to ten. "That appraisal is low and you know it."

Robert splayed his hands. "You can get your own done if you like."

"I just might."

"I hear you and James Mitchell are going out." Robert's face twisted with anger for just a moment, and then his expression settled back into its mournful look.

"Yes." Lee sucked in her cheeks and bit down on the insides to stop her from making a comment that would simply infuriate him. "We've been separated for four months, Robert. I'm free to see other men."

"But we are still married." He studied her seriously.

Lee drew in a deep breath. "We haven't been close enough to call it a marriage in so long I don't care. I'll do as I please."

"Well, get it out of your system then. Maybe it'll make you see how much I love you if you see how someone else treats you."

"Don't tell me you love me, Robert. I don't want to hear it." Lee shifted her gaze over his shoulder and saw her mother studying them with a smile on her face.

"But I do. And I just know somewhere inside you still love me too, otherwise you'd be asking for more maintenance. Not that I think you should get any." He crossed his arms. "It'd be easier for both of us if you'd just come home."

Lee cleared her throat. "I'm not coming home. I'm not in love with you and I don't even want to be talking to you. Why are you here, anyway?"

Robert gestured widely with his hands. "Ellen invited me."

Lee shot a dirty glare in her mother's direction, and was rewarded with a bigger smile and a wave that suggested her mother was pleased that the two were talking. "She had no right. You aren't family."

"She thought I was, so here I am. I'm glad to see you, Lee. What's so bad about that?"

"You aren't going to win me back with this pitiful puppy routine. I'm through being controlled by you." Lee crossed her arms as well and gave him the same dirty look she had given her mother.

Robert looked pained. "I never tried to control you."

"The hell you didn't. What do you call telling me when I could go out with my friends and where I could go?"

"I was concerned about you. When you and some of your friends go out, you sometimes have too much to drink. I'm worried that you might hurt yourself driving home." He studied her as though he were chastising a child.

Lee felt her temples start to throb with anger. "I've never driven drunk in my life, Robert."

"If not you then one of your friends. Betty likes to pack away the martinis. Remember her at the Dupree's Christmas party last year?"

"I'm not getting into an argument over my friends with you. I'm through with getting into arguments with you. You can't justify or explain away how you treated me. It's not going to happen. Now, I'm going to walk away and you'd better not follow me." She uncrossed her arms and stepped past him before he could speak again. As she moved into the crowd, she heard him speak one more time.

"You'll come home, Lee. It might take some time, but you'll come home."

Lee got another glass of wine and sought out her mother. Taking her by the elbow, she guided her out onto the balcony and away from other people. Her mother had a pleased look on her face.

"How could you do this to me, Mother?"

"Do what?" Ellen blinked innocently.

Lee pointed back inside. "Robert told me you invited him. He's not even family!"

"As far as I'm concerned, he is." Ellen crossed her arms and gave her daughter a stern look.

"You invited him specifically so he would run into me. When will you stop meddling?"

Ellen shrugged. "Is it meddling to not want my daughter to make the worst mistake of her life?"

"Oh, my God." Lee threw up her hands. "It is not a mistake. And even if it were, it's none of your business."

"You're my daughter—"

Lee lost her temper. In a very quiet voice that trembled with anger, she said, "I am twenty-nine years old. I'm not some child to be protected. Now, stay out of my business!" She turned and stormed back into the room. She caught sight of Robert once more as she strode out the front doors and it only served to make her even angrier.

She slammed the car door shut and pulled out her cell phone. Stacy didn't answer, and neither did Louise. For a scant second, she considered calling Ray, but thought better of it. The last thing she needed to do was talk to her when she was so emotional.

She wanted a drink, and a stiff one. Ray had mentioned that Joan at Maddie's was a good listener. Maybe she could calm down there. It was better than going home and sitting alone in her apartment stewing. She put the car into gear and took off.

There were only a few cars in the back parking lot when Lee pulled in, which suited her fine. She parked and got out, heaved a sigh and went up the stairs to the back door, pulling it open with a determined tug.

There were six women at the bar. The jukebox was silent, and Lee slid onto a stool thinking how much different it was from the other times she had been there.

Joan came up and set down a coaster. "What brings you in here?" she queried with a somewhat startled expression.

"I needed a drink," Lee replied. "This seemed like the perfect place. I'll take a bourbon and water, please." She was aware that she was being studied by the other women in the room, but it only made her slightly uncomfortable. She was probably overdressed in her suit but she didn't care.

Joan set the glass on the counter in front of her. "Will Ray be wandering in?"

"I couldn't tell you. I haven't talked to her in a few days."

"Really. So you came in here all on your own?" Joan raised her eyebrows.

"Yes." Lee sighed. "I just came from a party for my aunt and uncle. My husband showed up and things went to hell from there. I need a break from thinking about it."

"I take it there was a confrontation." Joan wiped down the top of the bar with a towel.

Lee nodded. "And not only with him. My mother and I got into it too. She keeps trying to run my life for me, and I'm getting sick of it."

Joan cocked her head. "How old are you?" Lee told her. "It's been my experience that parents don't give that up until you're at least thirty-five."

"That makes me feel better," Lee growled sarcastically. "She'll have driven me insane by then."

"At least your parents still speak to you. A lot of women who come in here can't say the same."

Lee made a noise. "I sometimes wish they didn't. It would make my life a lot easier."

Joan studied her. "Be careful what you wish for."

Lee was silent, toying with her stir stick. What would she do if her mother never spoke to her again? What could cause such a thing to happen? Lee had a sudden vision of kissing Ray; that would set her mother off like nothing else.

Thinking about Ray set off a slow explosion of heat in her stomach. Sitting where she was, it was too easy to remember the sensation of Ray's body on top of hers, of Ray's mouth on her breasts. She closed her eyes, willing the memory to go away, but it stubbornly clung to the edges of her thoughts even as she forced herself to think about something else.

"Are you ok?" Joan sounded concerned.

Lee opened her eyes and found Joan looking at her strangely. "I'm fine. I'm just so damned angry. Do lesbians have the same problems with their partners?"

"Hell yes; and worse. Two women in the same household can make for some volatile situations."

"How did you know ...?" Lee trailed off, embarrassed.

Joan laughed. "What, that I was gay? I sort of knew it all along. It terrified me, too, until I met Lisa. I was twenty-five and she was nineteen. Neither one of us had a clue what we were doing, but it just all happened naturally. Been together forty years now."

"That's a long time," Lee said in awe. "It would scare me too, thinking that I was." She wasn't sure why she said it, because she had thought about it and she *was* scared.

Joan shrugged. "It scares the hell out of most women. We're all trained to get married and have children. When you realize you aren't interested in putting a man into that equation it can be very emotionally distressing."

"How do people get through it?"

"At some point you just do." Joan picked up Lee's glass and made another drink. "If you really are gay there comes a certain situation, with a certain person, when you can't deny it any longer. You may not ever do anything about it, but you'll always know you could have. Even if you pretend you're not for the rest of your life, part of you will always know you're pretending."

Lee digested her words. She had come very close to that moment with Ray just the day before. Her fear had stopped her. She realized that it was only her fear, not that she thought it was wrong. She was afraid she would find herself forever changed by the experience; that the Lee she had become comfortable with would be gone and a new Lee would emerge who would be foreign to everything she'd known to that time.

"I would think it would be a hard thing to adjust to," Lee commented, paying for her drink.

Joan made her change and leaned against the bar. "Depends on the person. Some take to it like a fish to water. Others— well— others go through an extended period of self-hatred. But for the most part adjusting isn't too terribly difficult, especially if you've found someone who makes you happy. Why all the questions?" She leaned on her arm and gave Lee a solemn look. "Thinking about climbing the fence?"

"Not at all," Lee lied. "I'm just curious."

"Curiosity killed the cat."

"I suppose it did," Lee admitted. "But I'm curious all the same. Maybe I've been hanging around with Ray too much."

Joan laughed. "That'll do it. She flirts enough to make just about any woman doubt her sexuality."

"I don't doubt my sexuality," Lee returned quickly.

"I didn't say that you did."

Lee finished her drink. When bar started to fill up, she realized that she wanted to be gone if and when Ray made an appearance. She said goodbye to Joan and left. As she was sitting at the stoplight waiting to turn onto the main road, Ray's pickup turned in front of her.

For just a moment she thought about going back, but then the light changed and she continued on, fighting the feelings in her chest that told her she had made a big mistake by stopping what was happening between her and Ray.

*   *   *

"I don't understand what the fucking problem is." Ray slammed her tester down and ran a hand through her hair. Jackie leaned against the counter and crossed her arms.

"Come on, Miss electrical genius. You can figure anything out."

Ray shot her a dirty look. "I tested all these outlets before I bought the house. They worked fine. Now they don't. I don't get it."

"There's got to be a short somewhere, right?" Jackie shrugged.

"Yeah, but where? Half the time they work, half the time they don't, and it's never the same ones."

Jackie laughed. "Maybe the place is haunted."

"Very funny." Ray turned to her tool chest and contemplated what to try next.

"So, do you know why Lee wasn't at volleyball on Sunday?"

Ray hoped her face didn't betray the emotions that rampaged through her at the thought of Lee. When she hadn't shown up to play for a second week, Ray was certain she wouldn't be coming back for a long while. If she ever did. She cursed herself once again for letting things get out of hand.

"No." She stood and went to the refrigerator for a beer. "God damn it. Now the fridge is out."

"It was on last time I was in there. Seems kind of strange, her just dropping out of sight like that." Jackie picked up her bottle and tipped it back.

"Maybe she's gotten serious with her boyfriend."

Jackie considered her words. "Maybe. Did she say anything about it at the party last Saturday? She was still here when I left, so I figured the two of you did some chatting."

"She didn't mention it."

"And you've barely mentioned her all week." Jackie gave Ray a concerned look. "What happened after I left?"

Ray blew out her breath. "Nothing happened. I have to check the breakers."

As she walked out to the garage to check the breaker box, Ray considered, for perhaps the hundredth time what really *had* happened and how it could have escalated into something that went so horribly wrong.

That Lee was really upset over it seemed obvious, even though she had been the one to instigate it. *I must have scared the ever-loving crap out of her.* She was surprised at how much she missed Lee. It wasn't as though they spent a lot of time together, just Sundays and a few Saturdays, but not seeing her had been a hard thing to swallow.

She and Jackie had been out to the bar the previous night, and there had been several unattached women there that fit Ray's tastes perfectly. But she hadn't been in the mood for flirting. She blamed it on work at the time, but now she wondered if it was because of something else, because of Lee.

I can't possibly be falling for her. The thought seemed ridiculous and frightening at the same time. She hadn't been emotionally attracted to a woman in a very long time, and wasn't particularly interested in being so now.

That she missed Lee must mean nothing more than she missed a friend. And Lee had become a pretty good friend over the preceding months. Maybe not on the same level as, say, Jackie, but pretty good nonetheless. She could talk to Lee about things she wouldn't even talk to Jackie about, different things than she and Jackie discussed.

Reaching the breaker box, Ray put Lee firmly out of her thoughts and looked for the breaker to the refrigerator. It was

127

tripped. With an inward curse, she flipped it back on and returned to the kitchen. Jackie had gone into the living room and was staring out the window at the pond.

"I'm tired of fucking around with this," Ray growled as she came up next to her friend. "You want to go down to Maddie's for a couple of beers and a game of pool?"

"Sure." Jackie turned to her. "You know, I kind of miss Lee being around. She sure brightens a room."

"Yeah, I guess she does," Ray replied, even more tired of thinking about Lee. "I have to go back to the apartment and change. Meet you there in an hour?"

"Okay."

As usual, Ray beat Jackie to the bar. Knowing that it would be at least a half hour before she would show up, Ray slid onto a bar stool and motioned Joan over from a conversation with her partner. Lisa waved at her and turned her attention to the video game sitting at the end of the bar.

"Hey, kiddo; the usual?" Joan grinned at her and Ray nodded. "How're things going?"

"Work sucks." Joan hadn't been there the previous night and so hadn't heard about the argument Ray and her new boss had gotten into. "Jimmy is a complete jerk."

"Sorry to hear that." Joan sat a beer on the bar and waved away Ray's money. "I'll add it to your tab. I don't want to be making change for you all night. Any particular reason he's a jerk?"

Ray took a swig of her beer. "He doesn't know half as much as I do, and he gets all defensive when I'm right and he's not. We got into an argument yesterday. I finally gave up trying to tell him I was doing the job the right way. Let him think he knows it all. I don't give a fuck at this point."

"Must be tough dealing with a new boss. You and Steve got along so well together. He seemed like an OK Joe."

"He is." She'd brought Steve to the bar a couple of times. He and Joan hit it off, which was odd since Joan was the original man-hating feminist. For Joan to call him OK was high praise.

"You shouldn't be getting into arguments though. I mean, he may be a jerk but he still outranks you, right?" Joan leaned on the bar and raised an eyebrow at her.

"I suppose you're right. I just know we're going to butt heads more than once."

Joan sucked on her upper lip for a moment. "Don't let your temper get you into trouble."

"Yes, Mother." Ray cracked a grin.

"Oh, I didn't tell you. Lee was in here Sunday night."

Lee's name sent an unwelcome pain through Ray's chest. "With Stacy I presume."

"No." Joan looked a little confused. "She was by herself. Had some interesting questions."

"Interesting how?"

Joan gave her an even look. "Questions that make me wonder whether she's reconsidering certain things. You wouldn't have anything to do with that, would you?"

For just a moment, Ray's heart leapt. But then reality settled in and she realized Lee was probably just curious about what had possessed her to start something with Ray.

She made sure her tone was light when she answered. "Not me. I don't do initiations. Not that I think she's looking for one. She's just been hanging around Stacy and me too much. That's got to make a girl curious."

"Mm-hmm. I've been around long enough to know when you're lying, Ray. And if you were Pinocchio some gay guy would be seriously in love with you."

Ray coughed. "Ok, she kissed me again."

"I thought as much, though to be honest I figured you'd be the one to start it this time. Was it just a kiss?" Joan crossed her arms and got the 'I'm about to lecture' look that Ray hated. She hung her head.

"Not exactly."

"Damn it, Ray! You should know better." Joan threw her hands up. "I thought you were an idiot when you kissed her back. Now I know you're an idiot. Just how far did it go?"

"That's none of your business, Joan." Joan just glared at her. "Okay, far enough to scare the crap out of her. Far enough she's probably never going to speak to me again. But it never crossed the waistline."

Joan shook her head. "Leave it to you to let your libido ruin a perfectly good friendship."

"I'm kicking myself enough without you helping me."

Joan snorted. "You deserve it, Ray. I ought to be kicking you in the ass. Literally."

"I don't know how to apologize. I'm afraid she'd hang up on me." Ray tried not to let on how miserable she was thinking about it.

"You should at least try. She's obviously having at least some doubts about herself, and it isn't at all fair for you to ignore her instead of being up front and apologizing."

Ray sighed. "I know you're right. But it's just so damned hard. Maybe she'll show up at the cookout this weekend."

"Call her." Joan crossed her arms again. "Call her tomorrow."

"Alright, I will." Ray glanced over as Jackie walked in the door. "Do me a favor; don't mention this with Jackie around. I don't want her to know what a schmuck I've been."

"I ought to. You deserve some embarrassment. But I won't. Just take care of it."

Ray nodded and turned to greet Jackie, her thoughts anywhere but at the bar.

*   *   *

Lee sat on Stacy's patio waiting for her to bring out two glasses of wine. She stared over the landscaped yard and wondered how she would approach the subject she was about to bring up. Stacy returned and sank down in the chair opposite her, holding out a wine glass.

"Okay, Lee. What has you so flustered?"

"Did I sound that flustered on the phone?" Lee sipped at her wine and fought the butterflies in her stomach. She thought that this would probably be the most difficult discussion of her life. But she knew she had to talk to someone before she went insane.

"Like you were either going to pass out or scream, one or the other. So what's up?" Stacy leaned forward.

Lee bit her lip. "I'm very confused right now, and you're the only person I could think of that I can talk to about it."

"What's the problem?" Stacy sounded slightly concerned. "Is Robert being more of an ass than usual?"

"No. It has nothing to do with Robert. It's—it's about Ray."

Stacy gave her a look that suggested she had an inkling of what was to come. "What about her?"

"Do you remember telling me that straight women don't walk into gay bars, meet a lesbian, and decide they want to be one too? And I said that hadn't happened to me?"

"Yes," Stacy responded slowly.

"I might have been mistaken."

"What?"

"Ray. I've kissed her. More than once." Lee blushed when Stacy's eyes widened.

"You didn't! When did this happen?"

Lee bit her upper lip. "The first time was several weeks ago. And again that night we all went out to the Crab Shack. And last week, after the party."

"What did she do? She didn't push things, did she?" Stacy's voice grew rough. "I'll kill her if she did. She should know better, especially with you and the divorce." Almost as an afterthought, she said, "You really kissed her?"

"Yes." Lee nodded miserably. "And I—I enjoyed it. A lot."

Stacy gave her a confused look. "What do you mean, you enjoyed it? Ray's supposed to be a great kisser; it doesn't surprise me that you'd enjoy it some."

Lee's face grew a deeper red. "I mean I really enjoyed it. Like, I'd do it again in a heartbeat enjoyed it."

She was beginning to think she'd do far more than kiss given the chance. More than she had that afternoon. Perhaps she already knew it and was just deluding herself that there was some kind of choice.

"Oh." Stacy's face grew serious. "Oh, boy. What do you think's going on?"

"I think ..." Lee trailed off and took a deep swallow of wine. "I want to do more than just kiss her."

Emotions flashed across Stacy's face. "You can't be serious. Please tell me you aren't serious."

"I've never been more serious in my life. What am I going to do, Stacy? This is all so confusing."

Stacy got up and paced across the patio, staring off across the yard for a long, silent moment. Finally, she turned back around. "You don't suppose this is because of Robert, do you?"

"No." Lee flushed in embarrassment. "I slept with James last night."

Stacy's face registered complete confusion. "What does that have to do with anything? You're straight; you're supposed to sleep with your boyfriend."

"I hated it. I always thought Robert and I had such a nonexistent sex life because he worked all the time. Now I know it's because I didn't want to have sex with him. I don't think I've ever been turned on by a man, not really turned on."

"How do you know? I mean, what have you got to compare it to?" Stacy studied Lee's face intently. "You and Ray didn't …?"

"No, but … well, it did go further than just a kiss last week. I've never felt like that in my entire life. I didn't know you could feel that way." Lee closed her eyes. "I don't know what to do, Stacy."

Stacy didn't answer her, and Lee opened her eyes to find her with one hand over her face. Finally, she lifted her head and met Lee's gaze with a sympathetic one of her own. "Robert is a jerk and James wasn't good in bed. Two men are hardly enough to base your entire sexual identity on. Right?" Her voice didn't hold much conviction.

"Stacy, I want to sleep with Ray. I don't think my history with men has much to do with that."

Stacy sighed. "So you think you're gay?"

Lee drank more wine. "I don't know what I am. All I know is that Ray touches me and I want to fall down. I look at her and all I can think about is kissing her."

"Oh, God. This is really out of left field, Lee. I mean, I knew the two of you were flirting like there was no tomorrow, but I never thought there was anything to it."

"There wasn't, at first. Or I didn't think there was. Now … I kind of freaked out on her. She hasn't called me since. I'm afraid I've really screwed things up." Lee chewed on her lip.

"You haven't fallen in love with her, have you? Because Ray is the last person you want to fall in love with. She doesn't believe in the word." Stacy turned toward the house. "I'm bringing out the bottle. I need more wine for this."

Lee stared at her hands until Stacy returned. After Stacy refilled both their glasses, Lee looked at her and heaved a sigh. "I haven't fallen in love with her. I know how she feels about it. But I do want to sleep with her. What am I going to do?"

"Well, as much as I hate to admit it, there's only one real way to figure out whether what you're feeling is true or if it's just you thinking your life would be better with a woman."

Lee looked inward. She had spent a sleepless night after coming home from James's apartment, her mind refusing to stop thinking about what her reaction to the sex had been. She had tried a dozen ways to come up with a different conclusion than the one she had finally been forced to accept.

She'd finally had to accept that she wanted nothing more than to feel Ray's skin against hers again the way James's had been. Only Ray's had felt much softer and warmer than James's. Touching him made her shudder, and not in a good way. Touching Ray felt like stroking herself.

Stacy was looking at her. "I don't even know if she's speaking to me. She hasn't called," Lee said quietly.

"Well, the cookout is this Saturday. You already agreed to come. I'm sure she'll be there." Stacy looked up as Donna came out the sliders onto the patio. "Hey, honey."

"You two look like you're discussing something serious." Donna dropped a kiss onto Stacy's lips. "What's going on?"

"You'd better get a drink for this, sweetheart." Stacy tilted her head toward the door.

"That bad, huh? I'll be right back." She returned with a tall glass and sank down into one of the deck chairs. "All right, who died?"

"Nobody died." Lee managed to laugh. "At least, not yet."

"Then what?"

Stacy glanced at Lee, who nodded. "Lee thinks she's gay."

"I could have told you that," Donna responded. "I'm surprised you didn't see it too, Stacy."

"I'm sorry?" Lee cocked her head and looked at Donna quizzically. "How could you know? I'm only just starting to think it myself."

Donna giggled. "Gaydar, Lee. You've set mine off ever since I met you."

"Nice of you to clue me in," Lee told her stiffly, not sure how to take the comment.

"Relax. I figured if you were meant to come out, you would eventually. Although if I'd thought you would listen to me, I'd have told you before you married that bastard Robert. So I'm guessing Ray's the one who finally turned on the light switch?" Lee nodded. "Could do worse, I suppose. At least you don't have to worry about hooking up with the first woman you meet. There's lots of fish in the sea, it's best to follow a catch and release policy for a while. Is she as good as her reputation?"

"Oh, for God's sake, Donna. It isn't like I've slept with her." Lee turned bright red.

"Donna!" Stacy's voice was reproving. "Stop picking on her."

"Who's picking?" Donna grinned evilly. "See, I've lifted the mood already."

Lee stuck out her tongue. "You're an ass, Donna."

"So what are you going to do about James?" Stacy queried, as if she had just remembered who had caused the entire conversation.

Lee shrugged. "He's a nice guy, but ... I guess I'll have to tell him straight out that I'm not interested."

"Straight is apparently something you're going to have a hard time with," Donna giggled, ignoring the glare Stacy shot at her.

"This is not funny," Stacy growled.

"Yes, it is. Or it should be. Coming out should be funny like you've just gotten the punch line to a good joke, not depressing like you've found out you have some horrible disease."

"I suppose you're right," Lee admitted slowly. "So why do I feel like this? Hell, I don't even know if I *am* gay."

"There's only one way to find out," Donna replied. "Does Ray know how you feel?"

"I'm not sure. I've been sending pretty mixed signals lately."

Donna sobered. "Did something happen? Is that why you haven't been at volleyball the last two Sundays?"

"Something like that." Lee shifted uncomfortably. "I freaked out on her and she hasn't called me since. I haven't had the nerve to call her either."

"Listen, kiddo. I don't care who you are, the first time things start to get hot and heavy with another woman, you freak out." Donna smiled gently. "I remember how freaked out I got, and I already had a pretty good idea I was gay."

"I freaked out for six months," Stacy added. "Every time I went home with someone I was sure something horrible was going to happen like my parents finding out."

"Oh, shit. My parents," Lee groaned. "I forgot about them."

Donna reached over and patted her on the knee. "Trust me, honey. Your parents are the last thing you need to be thinking about right now."

"What if I'm wrong? What if it happens and it's a horrible mistake?"

Stacy shrugged. "At least you'll know. Ray — or whoever — won't take it that hard."

Lee remembered Ray's face that night in the bar when she'd said that Lee wouldn't know if it was a mistake until it was over. Now, more than ever, that seemed to be true. "I suppose I should talk to her."

"That would be a good idea," Donna counseled. "If you don't want to call her, meet up with her at the cookout. She's bound to be there."

"I will." Lee finished her wine. "Can I have another glass? And then I should get going. I'm supposed to be meeting Louise for dinner. I can imagine how she'd react to this whole situation."

"Don't worry about her." Stacy poured another glass for her. "Just worry about Ray. There'll be time for everyone else later. Just don't back out. You'll regret it down the road."

Lee took a swallow of her wine, feeling much more relieved than when she had arrived. Talking to Ray might lead to something else, but she finally felt she was ready to face that head on. "Deal."

IX.

As soon as Lee saw Ray, her determination wavered. The older woman was wearing a t-shirt and denim shorts and Lee thought she looked absolutely wonderful. The sight of her left Lee so breathless that she was afraid she wouldn't be able to speak even if she had the chance. Her body reacted with a tingling in places that only Ray had ever made her tingle.

Ray didn't spot Lee right away, and when she did turn and meet her eyes, she blushed a deep red and dropped her gaze, turning back around.

For a moment, Lee was distressed. Surely, Ray couldn't be that upset about what had happened. Maybe she was embarrassed. Whatever the cause of Ray's reaction, it was two hours later before Lee got the chance to talk to her.

They met up at the pavilion, where everyone was depositing their culinary contributions to the pot luck. Lee was looking for Stacy, and Ray was apparently looking to snag something to eat a bit early. Whatever the reason, they were suddenly within a few feet of each other; too close for either to make a graceful getaway.

"Hi, Ray." Lee prayed her face didn't betray how nervous she was.

"Lee." Ray shifted from one foot to the other.

They didn't speak for about a minute. Finally, Lee forced the words out. "I apologize for the other Saturday. I reacted badly."

"No need." Ray's voice was gruff. "I was out of line."

Lee swallowed. "No, you weren't. I—I think we need to talk."

"We are talking." Ray gave her a curious glance.

"Not here, somewhere private. I should have called, but ..."

"But you didn't," Ray finished quietly. "I really thought you were never going to speak to me again."

Lee was startled. It had never occurred to her that Ray might have taken her hasty departure to mean she was angry. "Of course I was going to speak to you. I was as much a party to what happened as you were. I just ... I had a lot to think about. Please—I really don't want to talk about this here."

"Why not? Oh, okay." Ray relented when Lee gave her an almost pleading look. "How private do you want to be?"

"Just not where anyone can walk up on us."

"Some of us are going out in the canoes. Ride with me. No one will be able to hear us then." Ray shrugged. "If you want to."

"I want to." Lee shifted. "This isn't going to be a bad conversation, Ray. I'm not going to lay into you."

They walked toward the bank of the river, where several canoes were beached, Ray in front with Lee following. Ray was silent until they were almost to the little group that had gathered with paddles in hand.

"I'm glad you're still speaking to me," she said softly, glancing back with an expression that made Lee's heart pound.

"I'm glad you'll talk to me."

They launched their canoe along with four others and began to paddle out into the marsh across the river from them. There wasn't much current, and once in a while, a fish would jump nearby. They were silent until they had managed to separate themselves from the group and were drifting alone, the rest having chosen a different path through the reeds. Even the sounds of their laughter were fading.

They came to a dredge island and beached, and got out to sit in the sand facing each other.

"What did you want to talk about," Ray asked, skipping a

shell out across the water.

"About what happened."

"I'd rather just forget what happened." Ray's voice was hard.

Lee swallowed, a feeling surfacing that this wasn't going to go as well as she had hoped. "I can't forget it. If it was something you didn't want to, well … there's nothing I can do about that."

"You sure seemed to want to forget it after it happened."

"I was scared." Lee paused. "I've never felt quite like that before."

Ray gave her a curious look. "Felt like what?"

"When you touched me, I—I couldn't breathe." Lee averted her eyes. "Nothing had prepared me for that."

"When you stopped me I was sure it was because I had gone too far. I never intended to push you to do something you didn't want to." Ray coughed. "I never intended to start anything in the first place."

"What happened, happened. That's not what I really wanted to talk to you about." Lee chewed on her lower lip for a moment. "I wanted to talk to you about what could happen."

Ray's eyebrows drew together. "What do you mean?"

"I mean—" Lee paused, not sure she could actually say the words. When she saw the expression on Ray's face, she knew she had to. "You really turn me on, Ray."

"I kind of guessed that." Ray sighed. "I'm sorry. I don't do it on purpose."

Lee puzzled over this statement for a moment. "Why would you be sorry?"

"Because it's got to be confusing for you. I mean, you're straight and there I was trying to make you want me. Not that I was doing it intentionally," she added hastily when Lee started to speak.

"Intentionally or not, you succeeded. And you don't need to be sorry about that. In fact, I'm glad it happened."

"Why?"

Lee smiled. "Because it made me realize I've never known what true want was before you."

"What do you mean?" Ray seemed to be having trouble

comprehending Lee's words.

"I want you and I won't know if that's a mistake until it's over."

It took a moment for recognition to register in Ray's eyes. When it did, they widened and she looked at Lee in a new light. "Are you saying what I think you're saying?"

Realizing that the time for talking had long since passed, Lee moved onto her knees and leaned over to Ray, taking her face in her hands. "This is what I'm saying," she whispered, her heart thudding wildly as she pressed her lips against Ray's mouth.

At first, Ray was rigid beneath her, but then as the seconds passed, her mouth softened and her lips parted. Her tongue ventured out to find Lee's and her arms came up around Lee's shoulders, pulling her closer. The kiss deepened and intensified as their bodies came together and Ray pulled Lee down onto the sand.

Finally, Lee had to breathe. She pulled back and drew in a gasping breath. Ray's chest heaved as she looked over into Lee's eyes, her own wide and surprised.

"I'm sorry I've been so confused." Lee trailed her fingers along the side of Ray's face. "I'm still confused. And part of me is terrified. But I know what I want now and I'm not going to let fear stop me. I'm not going to stop you."

"You said you were sure before." Ray's voice was tight, as though she were having trouble talking.

"This time I *am* sure." Lee let her fingers trail down Ray's chin to her chest, resting her hand at last on the upper curve of Ray's breast, her little finger just touching the nipple. She felt Ray's sharp intake of breath and smiled. "I've never been so sure."

"Here? In the open?"

"Why not?" Lee was surprised at the risk she was taking, of them being found in a situation that would be embarrassing— *no, utterly mortifying.* Even so, Ray was beside her, giving her a look that echoed her own hunger, and her desire to feel that woman's touch as she had before quickly overwhelmed any reticence she might have had.

Ray studied her for a scant moment before moving to press her into the sand with her body. They kissed again before Ray pulled Lee's shirt out of her shorts. She bent to kiss her belly, working her tongue up to the bottom edge of her bra. Her fingers slid across Lee's breasts, circling over her nipples with the palms of her hands.

Lee felt them tingling into hardness and ran her hands down the planes of Ray's back to pull her shirt up as well. She lifted her shoulders to allow Ray to pull her shirt the rest of the way off before pulling Ray's over her head. Ray wore a bikini top under her shirt, and Lee found herself startlingly eager to untie the top string.

Ray stopped her and instead slid her fingers under Lee's bra, lifting upward and freeing her breasts. She slipped her free arm under Lee's shoulders and lifted her up, pulling the bra up even more. Lee helped her by shrugging out of it, leaving her topless. Ray smoothed Lee's shirt out on the sand and moved her so that her back lay on it before pressing her down with the weight of her body as her mouth sought out Lee's lips.

Lee felt Ray slip between her thighs, felt the pressure of her hips spreading her legs further apart. Ray's tongue traced a line to her ear and she bit gently against her earlobe before scraping her teeth down Lee's neck to her shoulder. She bit against the muscle and began to move her hips against Lee's groin.

Lee let out a long groan, her arms coming up to hold Ray against her. She found herself tilting her own hips so that Ray's movements hit her dead center of her heat and felt the bolts of energy that shot through her body with each gentle thrust.

Ray kissed across her throat to the other shoulder and back up her neck to her mouth. Her tongue danced against Lee's with quiet passion as one hand came up to run through Lee's hair, grasping the short strands at the back of her head while her hips moved in a slowly gyrating motion.

Lee untied the back of Ray's bikini top and pulled impatiently at the top string until it came loose. Ray lifted her body for Lee to move the fabric off her chest and then lay back down, pressing her breasts against Lee's. Her nipples were two points of white heat. Lee ran her hands along the length of Ray's back, unhindered by clothing, slid across her buttocks and tightened to pull Ray's hips more firmly against her.

Ray kissed down Lee's body again until her mouth found a

nipple. Lee's breath hissed between her teeth as her back arched. Ray sucked the nub in and let it slip between her teeth with a gentle scraping motion.

She sucked it back in and vibrated her tongue against it. Lee closed her eyes and pressed up against Ray's lips. Ray shook a hand free of sand and closed her fingers around the second nipple, squeezing ever so lightly, and then a little harder. She lifted, pulling the bud up with her, and then let it fall back between her fingers. Reclaiming it she began to roll it between thumb and forefinger.

It took all Lee had not to cry out with the sensations that crashed through her body, pleasure circling out from where Ray touched her, meeting and exploding in her stomach. Ray released her nipple and kissed over to the second, covering the first with her other hand. Lee found her own hips moving against Ray's, lifting upwards to meet her. Finally, she found the breath to speak.

"Please, Ray, please."

Ray lifted up onto her knees and gazed down at her. "You're beautiful." She spoke in a low voice that sent shivers down Lee's spine. She now knew how intimate Ray's voice could sound.

Ray retrieved her own shirt and reached down to grasp Lee's shorts at the top. She lifted up and worked the shirt underneath Lee's bottom, then unbuttoned Lee's shorts and slid the zipper down. Lee held her breath as Ray moved beside her and slipped her shorts and underwear down to her knees. She kicked out of them, lying naked under Ray's soft gaze.

"Beautiful," Ray repeated, tracing her hand all the way from Lee's throat to the top of her blonde curls. She flattened her hand and pressed the palm against Lee's belly for a moment, and then slipped her fingers down into Lee's hair. Her middle finger found the slick wetness at the center of Lee's triangle and pressed in against it. Lee's hips jerked upward and a long groan escaped her lips.

She could barely think with the thundering jolts of pleasure that exploded outward from Ray's fingers. She knew she had never been so wet in her entire life, had never wanted someone's touch so badly.

Lee's Awakening

Ray moved slowly, wetting her finger as it worked between Lee's lips and to the core of her hunger. She made long upward strokes, pressing with increasing firmness against the hardened bud of Lee's clitoris, eliciting upward thrusts from her hips and groans from deep in her throat.

Lee spread her legs further apart, willing Ray to slide into her. Ray knelt once again between her thighs and continued to move against her until she felt she could take no more.

"Inside," she pleaded. Ray grinned down at her and pressed into the hot grasping well of Lee's center with two fingers. Lee thought she was going to come right there, but Ray buried her fingers and left them still.

"Do you like that?" Ray asked, pressing her thumb against Lee's clit. Lee couldn't speak, could only nod. Ray began to move slowly in and out, gaining speed and intensity as Lee's hips caught the motion of her hand. Lee bent her legs up and offered herself more fully to Ray's hand.

Ray paused and questioningly pressed against her with a third finger. Lee nodded and dropped her head back as Ray filled her again. The sensation of her fingers was only heightened when Ray leaned forward and claimed one of her nipples with her free hand, pinching at it, rolling it between her fingers while her other hand continued to plunge into Lee's hungry well.

Finally, Lee sensed the orgasm gathering and abandoned herself to it, biting back a scream as the walls of her center contracted in spasms against Ray's fingers. Ray brought her back down after what seemed an eternity by slowing her hand, finally stopping and withdrawing her fingers. Lee could only watch as she lifted her hand to her lips and licked Lee's juices from her fingers. The sight sent another spasm of pleasure through her.

Lee tried to speak and found her throat dry. Ray lay back down and kissed her tenderly, stroking her hair. After a minute or two, Lee was able to move and she brought her hands to Ray's waist. Ray allowed her to roll her over, sliding her body onto the shirts that lay in the sand. Lee looked down at her body and felt a surge of desire that ignited something inside her that she couldn't quite identify.

Tentatively, she lifted her hand and ran light fingers across one of Ray's nipples. Ray arched her back and groaned. Emboldened, Lee bent down and touched her tongue to it, slowly circling the hardened tip, tasting the sweat and salt of Ray's body. Ray's hand came to the back of her head, trying to pull her closer. Lee swallowed and fastened her lips around the nipple, drawing it into her mouth. Ray made a guttural sound and tightened her fingers in the back of Lee's hair.

The taste of Ray's skin and the feeling of the nipple in her mouth brought a fresh rush of wetness and Lee wondered if she would ever be dry again. After several minutes spent acquainting herself with Ray's breasts, she came to the top of Ray's shorts and pulled them down. When her fingers came to the wetness between Ray's thighs, her eyes widened.

This is what a woman feels like. She had felt herself before, certainly, but the sensation of Ray's wetness on her fingers her made her feel as if she'd never touched a woman's arousal before. Ray's clit was swollen and hard and Lee explored it with her fingers, bringing jerks from Ray's hips with each stroke.

"God, yes," Ray hissed. When Lee went to go further down, Ray stopped her and guided her fingers back to her hardened nub. "Rub there," she instructed, pulling Lee's head back to her breast.

Lee fastened her lips around a nipple again and did as Ray asked. She felt clumsy and inept, but Ray's groans gave her confidence and finally she felt Ray's body still for a moment and then she let out a cry as her back arched off the sand. Lee was surprised that she could feel the orgasm so strongly through Ray's clit alone, and when it was over Ray reached down and stopped her hand.

"Please, no more," she gasped. Lee moved up beside her and Ray pulled her into her arms. They lay like that for a long time before Ray spoke again. "Was it a mistake?"

"No," Lee answered. And then she started to cry.

* * *

It took a few moments for Ray to realize there were tears in Lee's eyes, and when she did, confusion set in. *Why is she crying?* Aloud, she asked, "Are you alright?"

Lee nodded, apparently unable to speak. Ray tightened her arms and pulled the woman closer. Lee buried her face against Ray's shoulder and kept crying. Concerned, Ray stroked her back and murmured into her hair.

Finally, Lee lifted her head, her cheeks streaked with wetness, and looked into Ray's eyes. "I'm sorry." Her voice betrayed deep emotion.

"Don't be. Are you having second thoughts?"

"No." Lee sniffled. "But I'm feeling a little overwhelmed. I didn't expect ..." she trailed off and buried her face again. Ray waited patiently for her to speak, her voice coming muffled by Ray's skin. "I didn't know it could be like that."

"Now you do." Ray smiled into Lee's hair. "It can be that and more."

Lee rolled away and sat up, apparently mindless of the fact that she was now sitting naked in the sand. She pulled her knees up, wrapped her arms around them, and stared off over the water. "I waited twenty-nine years to feel like this. Now that I do ... I'm not sure I can handle it."

Ray propped herself up on one elbow and studied Lee quietly. Lee met her gaze for a short moment before looking away with a blush coloring her cheeks. Ray was somewhat disconcerted to think that she had never seen so beautiful a sight as Lee sitting there before her.

"I'm sure it's a big shock to realize you've become something you never expected to be," Ray said finally.

Lee's laugh was tinted with just a hint of pain. "That's one way to put it."

"How do you feel about it now that it's happened?"

Lee's eyes lost their focus for a minute and then she shook herself and looked at Ray levelly. "I don't regret it in the least."

"Well, that's a start." Ray smiled. "You haven't run screaming yet."

Lee sighed. "I'm not going to either. But that doesn't mean I'm ready to announce to the world that I'm a lesbian."

"It doesn't have to." Ray sat up as well, aware of the fact that she was also covered in sand. "It doesn't even have to mean that you *are* a lesbian. It just means you enjoyed it and you might do it again. Would you?"

"Do it again? I sure hope to." Lee laughed again, this time naturally. "I just don't necessarily want all my friends to know that."

"It's not like you have to take out a billboard on the highway, Lee. You don't have to tell another living soul. It might make it difficult to find dates ..." she ducked the shell Lee pitched at her. "Seriously; I'm not about to hand out bulletins that we had sex."

Lee leaned back on her hands. "I hadn't really thought past the want of you," she responded seriously.

"And?"

"And I'm not sure what to do next."

Ray studied her. "You don't have to plan out the rest of your life right now. You did it, you liked it, you want to do it again. That's really all you need to think about."

"Thank you." Lee gave her a grateful look.

Ray was startled. "For what?"

"For being you. For being gentle enough not to scare me. For not expecting me to be perfect."

"Nobody's perfect." Ray laughed.

"I've had enough people in my life think I should be. I'm glad you aren't one of them." Lee shrugged. "So now what?"

Ray considered her question. As simple as it was, it held a depth of possible answers and raised myriad questions. There was what to do in the immediate sense, and what to do in the greater sense. What to do between them and what Lee should do apart. She wondered which question Lee meant.

"Well, for right now we need to figure out how to explain the fact that we and our clothes are covered in sand. And I want to wash off ... this stuff is getting into some uncomfortable places."

Lee studied her, emotions flashing across her face. Finally, she sighed again. "I suppose you're right. What about ... us?"

Uh-oh. "You know how I feel about relationships."

"Don't worry; I'm not looking for one." Lee replied soberly. "But is this going to affect our friendship?"

"I don't see why it should. We can just be closer friends than most. I'm sure once you get used to the idea you'll find someone else to play tag with." Ray lifted her shoulders and shrugged.

"So you wouldn't rule out ...?"

"Doing it again? I'd love to. I've had the hots for you since the first night I met you." Ray grinned. "It takes more than one time to put out a flame like that."

Lee smiled back at her. "Good, because I've developed quite the case of hots for you too."

They sat grinning at each other for a minute. Finally, Ray forced her attention away from Lee's breasts and back to reality. "We do need to get cleaned up and head back."

"Into the river?"

Ray eyed the water dubiously. "There's got to be tons of oyster shells in there. That could do some serious damage."

Lee tilted her head and looked across the marsh. "I suppose you're right. We'll just wash off as best we can. A jump into the water at the swimming area won't harm anything."

"Can you pretend nothing happened?" Ray raised an eyebrow at her as she stood up.

"I've been pretending nothing's happened for weeks. The only people who know how I feel are Stacy and Donna."

"Alright then."

They got dressed and re-launched the canoe, paddling back to the landing area in silence. The others had already returned, and of course, there was good natured ribbing about what could have taken the pair so long. Ray played along with greater humor than she felt; despite her promise not to say anything, she felt like she was going to burst if she didn't. Not to boast about a conquest, but to express her awe that she'd been chosen to be first.

They both went to the swimming area and jumped in. Ray eagerly worked the sand out of the most uncomfortable areas, not caring that she would be dripping wet when she got out. Lee went so far as to take off her shorts while standing next to Ray, who ran a quick hand down her thigh and grinned when Lee giggled.

"Remind me not to do that again without a proper blanket," Lee commented with a sideways glance as she rubbed her shorts

146

between her hands.

"Tell me about it; romantic in theory, somewhat less so in practice."

Lee laughed. "I wonder what they would have thought if they had come up on us."

"I'm glad they didn't," Ray replied gruffly. "That was one mood I really didn't want ruined."

"Me either."

They grinned at each other and Lee slid her shorts back on before splashing at Ray, who splashed back. A few minutes later, the pair waded to shore and dripped their way to Ray's truck for a couple of beers.

"We'd better not spend the rest of the day together, or people will get suspicious." Ray didn't want to be apart from Lee just yet but was realistic about how people would perceive the sudden reconciliation.

"Can we get together after volleyball tomorrow? I was thinking we could go to dinner somewhere and talk."

"Talking would be the last thing on my mind," Ray admitted in a low voice that she was sure betrayed how much she still wanted Lee's body.

"Why not make it my condo and we can have dinner in bed?" Lee gave her a grin that could only be interpreted as an invitation.

"You've got a deal." A shadow of doubt raised itself. "Assuming you don't change your mind about what happened when you wake up tomorrow."

"I won't." Lee leaned over and kissed her on the cheek. "I'm sure we'll run into each other later. I'm going to go find Stacy."

"I'll be waiting."

After watching Lee saunter away, Ray leaned against the truck and drank her beer, her thoughts turning over the encounter. Lee's response to her had erased any doubts that she might just be experimenting. Her orgasm had been intense and prolonged, her muscles clamping down on Ray's fingers like a vise.

Ray had never suspected Lee was capable of such passion; outwardly, she was very self-contained. Still waters ran very deep in her case. She was certainly an eager lover, inexperienced but obviously willing to learn. Even though Ray had always been the sort to leave that sort of thing to others she found herself strangely eager to see how Lee would blossom with the passing of time.

Everything about Lee seemed to attract her in ways that were contrary to how she had interacted with other women. The thought was faintly discomforting, and she finished her beer with a firm resolution not to think about it anymore. Their attraction was purely physical, and she intended to keep it that way.

* * *

"I see you and Ray talked." Stacy motioned toward Ray's truck with her beer. "How did it go?"

"It went well," Lee replied, hoping not to blush. "We worked things out."

Stacy studied her. "I guess so. No details, please; I can see what happened in your eyes."

Lee's face flamed. "Is it that obvious?"

"Only if you were expecting something like that to happen in the first place," Stacy said, shrugging. "Did it answer your questions?"

"Yes." Lee took a swig of her beer to cover her embarrassment. "I'd really prefer if no one else knew about this."

"Fine with me," Stacy responded. "It's not my style to out people."

Lee looked away. "I'm not saying I'm a lesbian. Just that ... well, I might be."

"It's just a word, Lee. You don't have to say you're anything if you aren't comfortable with it. It might take some time before you are."

"I feel like I should be freaking out." Lee chewed on her lower lip. "I'm surprised at how calm I am." She was calm only insofar as not running as fast as she could in the opposite direction.

The thought of Ray's fingers between her legs was enough to

drive her insane with hunger. She'd never before been aroused by the mere thought of sex. Ray had been alternately gentle and rough, drawing an orgasm from her that was unlike any she had ever experienced.

"Well, it could be shock," Stacy offered.

"It's not shock." Lee managed to laugh. "Amazement, maybe."

Stacy laughed with her. "I've heard Ray is pretty amazing." She suddenly sobered. "You do know she isn't going to get caught."

"I'm not looking to catch anyone. It doesn't matter who it is; I'm avoiding relationships for a long while." Lee was disconcerted to think that a relationship with Ray might not be the worst thing in the world.

"That's a wise decision," Stacy answered, "especially now."

"Especially now," Lee echoed, looking away. "This does throw my whole life into disarray, doesn't it?"

"Only if you want it to," her friend said quietly. "Is it something you didn't want to happen?"

"Not at all," Lee answered quickly. "I just meant that I've been living my life based on a set of assumptions that no longer apply. I have to sort all this out in my head before I can start moving forward again."

"I guess so." Stacy smiled softly. "I guess this isn't something that's as easy to wrap your mind around at thirty as it is at eighteen."

"No, I guess not. I'm going for a walk; I'm all flustered and I don't want to be around anybody until I can get myself calmed down."

"I don't blame you." Stacy reached out and touched Lee's shoulder. "If you need to talk later ..."

"I know who to call," Lee replied. "Thanks."

She got a soda out of the cooler and wandered toward the entrance to the nature trail that led out from the picnic area. It was cool under the trees, and she walked slowly, her mind replaying the earlier events of the day.

There could be no denying that everything had changed when Ray's fingers drew from her the most intense orgasm she'd ever experienced. Although she didn't have extensive experience with men, she had enough to know that not one had ever made her feel the way Ray did.

Am I a lesbian? The thought was mildly unsettling. She had known Stacy long enough to know that being gay held its own unique set of challenges. Lee wasn't certain she was ready to add those difficulties to her life. At the same time, all she had to do was think about Ray's face above her, framed by sunlight, and she started shaking with hunger.

Stacy's right; it's just a word. A word with life-changing implications, Lee realized; but her life was already changed irrevocably. She had shared something with Ray that she had never thought possible. She had experienced passion in a way that made her weak in the knees to think about; she couldn't easily pass that off as experimentation.

She walked and thought for a long time, and when she returned to the picnic area, the only resolution she had come to was the knowledge that if wanting to be with Ray again made her a lesbian then she was one. Her tongue might trip over the word, but her body didn't. As for the rest, only time would tell.

X.

Despite what she had told Ray and what she had told herself as well, Lee woke up the next morning wondering just what in the hell she had done. She still didn't regret it, but she was having serious doubts as to whether she could handle the implications of doing it again. She sat at the kitchen table with a cup of rapidly cooling coffee and stared out the sliding glass doors as her mind turned over what she should do next.

She had invited Ray over for dinner, with the unmistakable understanding that it would involve more than eating. Should she continue with that plan and if not, how would she explain it to Ray? As she sat there, the phone rang. With a long sigh, she went to grab the handset.

"Good morning." Ray's voice was tinged with apprehension.

Lee answered with a greeting of her own. "I was just thinking about you."

"I figured if you were awake yet you would be."

Lee bit her lower lip. "I have a lot to consider."

"I figured that too. We should talk."

"That would probably be a good idea." Lee cringed as she spoke the words, part of her wanting nothing more than to feel Ray's arms around her again, though part of her wanted to run as fast as she could in the opposite direction. "Do you want to do it after volleyball?"

"Probably before. Look, Lee ... I'm not sure it's a good idea for us to jump into this without some serious discussion." Ray paused. "Can I come over?"

"Yes. I can make some breakfast if you like."

Ray agreed and they broke the connection. Lee scanned the room, desperate to understand why she was in such turmoil. On the face of it, it was obvious, but there was something deeper than she just couldn't drag to the surface.

By the time Ray arrived, she was dressed and on her fourth cup of coffee. When she let Ray in, she could tell that the older woman hadn't slept well either. After closing the door, the two looked at each other uncomfortably. Finally, Ray stepped forward and kissed Lee gently on the lips.

"How are you doing?" she asked in a quiet voice.

Lee shrugged. "Would you like some coffee?" She didn't want to answer the question, because she wasn't sure of the answer.

Ray studied her for a long moment. Finally, she looked away. "Sure."

When they were sitting down at the table, and having declined breakfast, Ray looked down at her hands for a very long time before speaking again. "I did a lot of thinking last night."

"I've been doing a lot of it this morning," Lee responded. "I'll be honest, Ray, I'm very confused right now."

"I'm not surprised." She heaved a sigh. "Do you regret what happened?"

"No. But I'm not sure if I'm ready for the repercussions."

Ray looked at her with something akin to sympathy. "I can understand that. But you do know there are going to be repercussions no matter what you decide."

"I know." Lee took a drink of her coffee and wished she wasn't so confused. "I wasn't thinking very clearly afterwards. It was unexpected. Not that it happened, because I was hoping it would; how I felt after ... that wasn't completely rational."

Ray shifted in her chair. "I don't want you to feel pressured, Lee. I don't think it's a good idea for us to keep our relationship on that level right now."

Lee felt a wash of relief. "I agree with you. It isn't that I don't want you, Ray. It's just that I'm not sure I can deal with what doing something about it would mean for me."

"After you left yesterday I realized that you couldn't have dealt with it so easily. It's taken a lot of soul searching for me to understand that it has to be this way. I want you too, desperately, but I want you to be in it knowing what it means, not just because it feels good at the moment."

They fell into a silence during which Lee refilled their coffees. Finally, she spoke again. "Thank you for being so understanding."

Ray shrugged. "It wouldn't be fair to you to be any other way. I just hope that it doesn't mean we can't still be friends while you work it out."

"Of course we can still be friends. I'm certain of that much."

Ray looked relieved. "Good. I was afraid things would be awkward."

Lee laughed. "Me too. I'm glad we're on the same page." She sobered. "I'm not saying I'm going to decide that it was a mistake. I'm just saying that I want to make that decision after I've had time to analyze it. I know that sounds kind of cold, but it's the only way I have to describe how I feel."

"It doesn't sound cold at all. I've known other women who've gone through what you're going through. Some of them decide they just can't deal with it. If that's what you decide, I'll accept it. There will always be a little more of a connection with you than with other people, but it doesn't mean I expect anything out of it." Ray smiled sympathetically. "I just wish I could make it easier for you."

"Thank you, Ray. Thank you for everything."

Ray let out a little laugh. "No need, but you're welcome. Are we square?"

Lee smiled, feeling a great relief about having talked. "We're square. And I didn't mind you kissing me like you did when you got here. I know you were apprehensive about it."

"I'm glad. I wouldn't do it in public."

Lee looked at her gratefully. "I know. I trust you completely, Ray. I want you to know that. If I didn't I wouldn't have let yesterday happen."

"I won't break that trust." Ray paused. "How would you

feel about going out for breakfast? I know a great little place that has the best waffles in town."

"I love waffles. Sounds like a great idea."

As they walked out the door, Lee felt a calmness that she hadn't felt ever since Ray first kissed her. If she did decide to pursue her desires, she knew Ray would be gentle enough not to scare her, would be kind enough not to expect more than she was ready to give. She was lucky that it had been Ray she had found herself drawn to.

*   *   *

"God damn it!" Ray picked up a screwdriver and threw it across the room. Jackie leaned over and looked into the outlet box.

"I'm guessing that melted wires aren't good."

"Damn straight they aren't. I'm going to have to rewire this entire wall." Ray turned and reached into the refrigerator for a beer. "Why couldn't I have found this before I bought the place? At least I'd have been prepared."

"Is it going to take long? You've only got three weeks left on your lease." Jackie leaned against the counter.

Ray cracked open her beer. "I don't know. I've been working so many hours I don't have a lot of time. I can move in without this wall working but it's going to be a pain in the ass."

"Is it safe?"

"As long as I leave the breaker off it'll be ok." Ray blew out her breath. "I'm tired of dealing with this shit. Let's go over to the bar for a couple of brews."

"Sounds fine to me. You going to invite Lee?" Jackie eyed Ray. "You haven't seen her in a couple of days."

"So?"

Jackie laughed. "So if nothing happened at the cookout why are you two avoiding each other?"

"We were barely speaking before." Ray looked away lest Jackie read her eyes.

"But you obviously made up. Did what I think happened, happen?"

"It's none of your business," Ray responded gruffly, trying to keep her promise not to reveal what *had* happened.

Jackie laughed again. "That tells me all I need to know. Obviously she's thought twice about it."

"I'm not supposed to discuss it, Jackie." Ray paused. "But since you've figured it out anyway I can't see the harm, as long as you keep your mouth shut."

Jackie looked faintly offended. "Since when have I not kept my mouth shut? So, has she thought twice about it?"

"Sort of." Ray took a long drink of her beer. "I can understand where she's coming from. It's got to be hard to realize there's a part of you that you never knew existed."

"I guess we're lucky we found out so early."

"I guess." Ray sighed. "I just wish it didn't have to be so damned hard."

"You're a good friend to feel so sympathetic," Jackie observed. "Or could it be something else?"

Startled by the question, Ray stared at her. "What? What else could it be?" Realization hit her. "I'm not in love with her, if that's what you're suggesting."

"No, I guess that was a pretty stupid idea." Jackie laughed. "It just isn't like you to be so understanding."

"Let's go to the bar," Ray growled. "I really don't want to talk about this anymore."

"Ok." Jackie tossed her beer can into the trash. "Maybe Jessie will be there. If anyone can take your mind off Lee it'll be her."

Ray considered the woman Jackie was talking about. She was gorgeous, available, and as averse to relationships as Ray was. It wouldn't be so bad to have some fun with her. They had let each other know in the past that such a thing could very well happen, and Ray thought that if it ever were to now would be a great time.

"You're a genius sometimes, Jackie."

Jackie made a fist and rubbed her knuckles again her shirt. "Thank you, thank you very much." Her Elvis impersonation wasn't very good, but Ray laughed anyway.

"Alright, genius, let's go."

As they climbed into her truck, she wondered why part of

her felt that there was something wrong with wanting to sleep with another woman besides Lee. It wasn't as though that was likely to happen again, at least any time soon, but somehow it still seemed wrong. Pushing the thought from her mind, she turned on the ignition and backed out, heading for Maddie's.

* * *

Lee waited impatiently for Louise to arrive at the club grill. She was pissed off and ready to vent. After her second glass of wine, Louise finally walked in wearing her tennis outfit. She sat down opposite Lee and signaled the waitress.

"You look ready to spit nails," Louise said as a greeting.

"I am," Lee replied tersely. She paused while Louise ordered something to drink then continued. "Did you know Robert sold the house?"

"I'd heard a rumor. So he really did?"

"Yes, God damn it."

"So why are you so pissed off? It isn't like you wanted it." Louise perused the menu. "Should I get the Monte Cristo or the tuna salad plate?"

"I don't care. Depends on whether you're on a diet again." Lee picked up a piece of bread and put too much butter on it.

"I think the salad. And soup. I wonder what it is today."

"Beef barley." Lee got impatient. "The bastard is trying to screw me over."

Louise gave her a curious look. "What do you mean?"

"I mean he sold the place for five sixty-five." Lee took drink of her wine. "That's twenty-five below even his appraisal."

"He probably wants to get this over with." Louise shrugged. "The market has been a little tenuous lately."

"He probably took the money out some other way. He sold it to John Black. I wouldn't be surprised if he's set up an offshore account. You know John is good at those tax dodges."

Louise laughed. "You're getting paranoid, Lee."

"I am *not* paranoid," Lee insisted. "I can't believe you don't see what he's trying to do."

"He hasn't complained that he had to pay your initiation fee for you to stay a member of the club."

"That was one of the first things we negotiated," Lee responded. "That and the car; those are little things compared to the house." As she thought about it, the club membership seemed more and more pointless every time she was there—which was less and less often.

Louise blew out her breath. "You said yourself you don't want half. What difference does it make if he sold the house for less than the appraisal?"

"It's the principle of the thing. And I don't know for sure I'm not going to ask for a percentage." Lee stopped the waitress and they ordered.

"I love you like a sister, but I think you might be going a little overboard with this whole thing."

Lee stared at her. "Oh, let's drop it. Maybe you're right." She thought that Louise definitely was *not* right but she wasn't in the mood for a disagreement. She wanted some sympathy and she obviously wasn't going to get it from Louise.

"I heard that you and James have stopped seeing each other." Louise made the comment off-handedly.

Lee's face flushed. "Yes."

"Why?"

"It wasn't going anywhere and I didn't want him to think it was." Lee finished her wine, not wanting to discuss James either.

"I thought so. The last couple of times I've seen you you've looked like you had a lot on your mind." Louise paused. "And yet there was something about you that made me suspect ... have you found someone else that interests you?"

Lee wasn't sure her face could turn any redder. "Of course not," she choked out. "I only went out with James to—" she cut herself off, realizing she had almost told Louise about Ray. "To convince myself I was still attractive," she finished lamely.

Louise gave her an odd look. "That isn't like you, Lee. You have more self-confidence than that. I think you're hiding something from me." She laughed. "Just as long as you haven't gotten involved with one of those lesbians."

"I haven't gotten involved with anyone—least of all a lesbian." She fought the burning of her face and tried not to feel guilty about the half-lie.

"Well, something's up. You've been acting very strangely lately."

Lee changed the subject and ate as quickly as possible, eager to get away from Louise. As much as she loved her friend, lately she had been less than understanding. *I wonder why? Don't give yourself something else to stew over.*

After dinner, Lee found herself at Maddie's. As she slid onto a barstool, she wondered how it was that when she needed to talk lately, she always seemed to end up there.

Joan came over and slapped a coaster in front of her. "You look pretty pissed off," she observed. "Wine or something stronger?"

"Bourbon and water, if you please."

After setting the drink down, Joan leaned against the counter. "Want to talk about it?"

Lee paused. "My husband is being a complete jerk." She quickly related the latest development regarding Robert. "This has finally torn it. I'm ready to file for divorce." Joan nodded sympathetically.

"I'm thinking that's the best course of action. He sounds like a real winner," she said. "You're lucky to get away from him."

"I see that more every day," Lee replied. "Him and the whole social scene. Sometimes I wonder how I ever felt at home with all that bullshit."

Joan shrugged. "You're comfortable with what you know, I guess."

"I feel comfortable here. That surprises me all the time. But I'm glad."

"Well, you certainly fit in. That's pretty good for a straight girl."

Lee blushed deeply. "Yeah. I guess so."

Joan studied her evenly. "Something else you want to talk about?"

"What else could there be?" Lee forced her voice to sound light. At least, she hoped that's how it sounded.

"Look, Lee. I'm not an idiot. I've seen how you and Ray look at each other. I've also seen how you avoid looking at each other. That tells me you're at least having second thoughts about which side of the fence to come down on." Joan gave her a stern look.

"I can't see how I could hang out here all the time and not wonder once in a while why I do."

Joan grunted. "If you say so." She started to turn away.

Lee, her mind full of Ray ever since their discussion the morning after the picnic, stopped her. "There is something between us," she admitted hastily, before she lost her nerve.

"That's obvious," Joan returned. "I'm not the only one who's noticed either. So if you think you're playing it cool you have another thing coming."

Lee groaned. "I don't want everyone to know. It isn't like we're sleeping together."

"Well, frankly kiddo, if you aren't I think you should be. If the fire between the two of you got any hotter I think you'd both implode."

"I'm not gay." Lee spoke with far more firmness than she felt.

"So you say. Are you sure about that?" Joan refilled her drink and made herself one.

"I—no, I'm not."

Joan nodded. "Well at least you aren't totally blind. Maybe you aren't, maybe you are. I can tell you one thing for almost certain, and that's that you have a major case of something more than friendship for Ray, and I've been around long enough to know that's true."

"I know." Lee sighed. "Even if I didn't want it to be true, it is. But I'm not sure I'm ready to deal with it."

"If you *were* I'd be a little worried." Joan shrugged. "At your age, you'd have to be unless you haven't been lying to yourself very well all these years."

"I must have been. I know that ... well, I know that I've never felt this way about a man."

Joan shook her head. "Have you talked about this with Ray? Because she's not the sort to get involved in something like this."

"I've talked to her," Lee said firmly. "She's been very understanding."

"Well, speak of the devil."

Lee's Awakening

Lee turned when Joan spoke and saw Ray and Jackie walking through the door. Ray caught sight of her and smiled, waving. Lee waved back. The pair sauntered over and took seats next to her. Joan pulled out two beers and set them on the bar before winking at Lee and walking off.

Lee felt strangely relieved to see Ray, and a little miffed to see that she was with Jackie. She put it out of her mind as she greeted the pair.

"How's it going?" she asked.

"Damn house is going to be the death of me," Ray growled. "I have to rewire at least half the kitchen."

"Is that going to be hard?"

"Hard enough." Ray picked up her beer. "Time consuming more than anything."

"What about you?" Jackie gave Lee a strange look. "How've you been?"

"Well, my husband is being a bastard—as usual—but other than that okay." Lee wasn't about to admit that she'd been in an emotional turmoil for four days.

"What'd he do this time," Ray asked. After Lee had explained the situation, Ray leaned over and put a hand on her shoulder. "You want us to go rough him up?"

It took a moment to realize she was joking. "He plays golf on Fridays. Maybe you could wrap a club around his neck." Lee laughed, feeling an unexpected relief to be talking to Ray. The sensation of Ray's hand on her shoulder sent a shiver through her. "It has made me decide to finalize filing for the divorce."

The way that Ray made her feel with her mere presence had contributed more to that decision than she cared to admit at that moment.

"Good for you," Jackie said with a smile. "I hope you take the son-of-a-bitch for all that he's worth."

"We were only married for five years; I doubt that I can do that. But I intend to get my fair share; that much is for certain."

The trio fell into a comfortable conversation after that, and by the time Lee left, she felt much more relaxed. Ray followed her out to her car.

"Would you like to go to karaoke tomorrow night? I want to practice."

"That sounds like fun." She shifted for a moment. "Ray ... Thank you for being such a good friend."

Ray's face showed the faintest sign of disappointment. "I'm glad I could be there," she replied after a moment's pause. "Thank you for listening to me grouse about the house."

Lee smiled. "No problem. I could help you fix it if you'd like. I'm pretty handy."

"I doubt you know anything about wiring."

"You could teach me. Or I could hand you things. Or get the beer, whatever. I'd like to learn how to do things for myself." Lee didn't want to admit that she just wanted to be near Ray. The thought was unsettling and she tried to push it away.

Ray studied her. "Ok, if you're going to be insistent about it. I'll be working on it on Saturday. Come on out around nine. Bring your bathing suit and we'll hit the pool afterwards."

"I'll be there. Where's karaoke?"

"I can pick you up if you'd like. It's at the Gator's Den." Ray shifted. "Unless you'd rather drive yourself; I know how you hate not being able to leave when you want."

Lee surprised herself with her answer. "Riding with you would be fine."

They settled on a time and then Ray leaned over and kissed her goodbye, the same gentle kiss as that Sunday morning. This time, it set Lee's insides to quivering. She forced herself not to show this and got in her car while Ray sauntered back inside.

Lee's hands shook as she started the car. *Stop behaving like a schoolgirl with a crush,* she counseled herself sternly. She still didn't know what to do about her attraction and she wasn't going to let her hormones interfere in what was a serious decision.

Still trying to convince herself of this, she put the car in gear and headed home.

*   *   *

Four hours after starting the wiring project Lee decided that Ray's job was a lot more difficult than she had suspected. There had been a great deal of cursing and not as much progress as

Ray obviously thought there should be. She finally put down her tools and turned to Lee with a look of disgust.

"Let's go swimming," she suggested gruffly.

"Sounds good to me."

Ray grabbed a beer and poured Lee a glass of wine and they went out onto the deck, where they stripped off their clothes and got into the pool in their bathing suits.

The water felt good to Lee and she floated for a long while just relaxing. Finally, she stood up and found Ray lounging against the wall watching her.

"What're you looking at," Lee asked lightly, swimming over to get her wine off the deck.

"You looked more comfortable than any human being has the right to," Ray responded. "How do you do it?"

"You just do it."

"You sound like a Nike commercial."

Lee stuck out her tongue and Ray splashed water at her. "Hey, not in the wine."

"Sorry." Ray didn't look sorry in the least. She pushed off from the wall and walked toward Lee, who felt a strange thudding in her chest.

"I need another beer, you want some more wine?"

"Sure."

Ray climbed out of the pool. "I could heat up the hot tub."

"Now that sounds nice."

An hour later, they were sitting in the hot tub. Lee was sunk up to her neck and Ray was leaned back letting the sun hit her face.

"Have you made any headway?" Ray asked suddenly, looking over at Lee with an inscrutable expression.

"Headway? Oh. Not a lot. I'll be honest; this thing with Robert has kind of taken my mind off it."

"I can understand that." Ray leaned back again.

Lee studied her. The lines of her neck and shoulders were appealing in a way that she couldn't ignore. She realized that no matter how hard she tried not to be, no matter how confused she was about the implications of it, she wanted Ray badly.

"Ray—"

"Hmm?" Ray didn't look at her.

Lee swallowed hard. "I don't know if I can stop myself from wanting you."

Ray looked at her then, her expression startled. "I'm sorry?"

"I said I still want you. But I'm also still confused. Does that make sense?"

Emotions sorted across Ray's face, finally settling into a seemingly studied calmness. Her gaze searched Lee's face as she sat up. "Some. What do you want to do about it?"

Lee didn't know how she would answer until she did. "I don't think I can control myself much longer. I've tried for a week and it hasn't worked. I know you pulled away—"

"I pulled away so you wouldn't feel pressured," Ray responded quietly. "Not because I didn't want you."

They studied each other silently for a while and then Ray floated toward her. Her hands came to rest on Lee's thighs.

"I can't help myself," Lee admitted weakly, knowing now that this was the reason she had wanted to help Ray at the house, hoping they would be alone. "If you don't kiss me I think I'm going to die."

"Are you sure?"

Lee startled herself by taking Ray's hands and pulling her between her knees. "I'm sure." She leaned forward and found Ray's lips with her own.

Ray made a sound deep in her throat as her hands turned over so that their fingers interlocked. Slowly, the kiss grew deep and inside, and when they parted Lee was breathless. Ray breathed raggedly, her gaze locked with Lee's.

"I don't want to do this if you aren't sure you're ready for what it means."

"I didn't know I was until this moment, but I am," Lee replied. "I can't deny how I feel any more. I may not be able to tell the world, but I have to tell myself. If I didn't, I'd regret it for the rest of my life."

"I can live with that." Ray kissed her again, her lips moving against Lee's with a hunger than Lee felt echoed in her own body. Their tongues reached out and danced against each other in warm wetness.

Ray released Lee's hands, her own coming to Lee's waist. She pulled Lee off the bench she was sitting on and Lee wrapped her legs around Ray's thighs. Ray leaned back against the seat on the opposite side of the Jacuzzi while her mouth continued to move against Lee's.

When her lips started to kiss down Lee's neck, Lee let out a long groan and brought her hands to Ray's sides. She slid them around Ray's back and reached to unfasten her bikini top. Ray's fingers moved to do the same and in short order they were topless. Lee leaned back and took in Ray's chest, struck anew with the beauty of her breasts, slightly pendulous with their deep pink nipples rising firm from dark brown areolas. She wanted nothing more than to feel those nipples in her mouth.

Ray's fingers closed around Lee's own nipples and Lee arched her back as Ray pinched lightly, pulling ever so gently and letting them slide between her fingers before reclaiming them. Ray's gaze was intense, her hips lifting up against Lee's center with a slow but insistent motion. Lee raised her own hands to capture Ray's nipples, and was rewarded with a shudder that ran through Ray's body. A long moan escaped her lips.

They kissed again, the backs of their hands crushed against each other as each refused to release the other's breasts. Finally, Ray pulled back and slid her hands down Lee's sides to her waist holding her as her hips began to move more firmly against Lee's center. Lee felt the hot readiness flowing from her as Ray moved against her.

"God, yes, Ray." Her voice sounded weak to her ears. Ray's lips came again to hers, hungry against her mouth. Her fingers slid between their bodies, under the waistband of Lee's bikini bottom and into Lee's hair, moving downward until they found Lee's wetness.

"Oh, Lee," Ray groaned. "God, you're wet."

"Take me," Lee begged, moving her hips to try and capture Ray's fingers. Ray rubbed against her hardened clit as her mouth moved to Lee's neck, nibbling at it. Lee's hands found Ray's shoulders where she grasped firmly, only slightly aware that she might be pressing too hard.

Ray slid her arms around Lee's waist and stood up, sitting her on the side of the hot tub. She pulled down Lee's bikini bottom and slid it off her legs, and then moved her lips down

Lee's body to claim a nipple, her hand covering the second one.

Lee groaned unintelligibly as Ray sucked the bud into her mouth, holding it between her teeth and vibrating against it with her tongue. Her hand massaged the other breast, drawing moans from Lee as she tried to draw Ray in with her legs.

Ray switched breasts, her hand now slipping between Lee's thighs again. This time she slid two fingers inside and pressed firmly against her. Lee hissed a 'yes' and lifted her hips against Ray's hand. Ray began to move against her, slowly at first and increasing in both speed and strength as Lee urged her on with her hips and her moans.

Finally, Ray began to kiss down Lee's body, her tongue drawing a lazy line to the top of her triangle. Lee held her breath as she realized what was happening, and then suddenly Ray's mouth was on her, her tongue burrowing through the hair, finding her clit, and moving against it. Lee half fell backwards, her back arching as Ray lapped at her, her fingers moving in and out in a steady rhythm.

She could barely breathe, much less speak, as Ray made long strokes with her tongue from her fingers to Lee's tip, slowly and softly then more firmly, and softening again as Lee grew more frenetic in the movement of her hips. Finally, Ray withdrew her hand and replaced it with her tongue, drawing a little cry from Lee as her fingers found Lee's breast once more. Ray's mouth turned insistent, her tongue pressing firmly against Lee's body as she slid upward again and again.

Finally, Lee could take no more. She blew into an orgasm so strong that for just a moment she felt as though she were going to black out. Then the moment passed and Ray drew more from her body than she had ever given before. After what seemed an eternity, Ray's tongue slowed and came to a firm rest against Lee's clit. When Lee's body collapsed back onto the deck, Ray kissed the insides of her thighs and moved up to lie beside her.

"Jesus Christ," Lee managed some time later, her legs still trembling. She glanced at Ray and found her grinning from ear to ear.

"I guess you like that." She let out a short laugh.

"Oh my God, yes. At least, I do now." In the back of her mind, Lee realized she had never really enjoyed being gone down on, had never responded as she had with Ray.

They lay together for a while, and then Lee found another desire surfacing. She rolled onto her side and found the tie at the top of Ray's shorts. Ray lifted her hips to allow Lee to slide them off and then lay back down with her legs slightly spread.

Lee bent her head and sucked a nipple into her mouth, relishing the sensation of Ray's skin and the movement of her body as she pressed upward against Lee's lips. She suckled at Ray's breasts for a long time, until Ray lifted her hands and pressed downward against Lee's shoulders.

Without thinking about it, Lee moved down Ray's body until she knelt between her legs. She looked down and saw the silvery wetness in Ray's hair and wanted with a sudden desperate desire to taste her.

The moment she thought it, she realized that she was afraid to follow through. Instead, she reached out her hand and wet her fingers with Ray's juice, seeking out her clit and rubbing against it. Ray's hips jerked upward. Lee rubbed against the hardened nub until Ray was groaning.

"Go inside," she begged. "Two fingers."

Lee pressed her fingers against Ray's heat, feeling the walls suck her in as she slid two fingers inside. Ray was slick and ready, moving her hips against Lee's hand with jerky motions.

Feeling a sense of power, Lee began to move against her, pressing her fingers in and pulling them out in a steady motion that Ray finally caught with her hips. Ray urged her on, telling her when to speed up and slow down, and finally clamped down on her hand with her thighs as her back arched and a strangled scream tore from her throat. When the spasms finally stopped, she allowed Lee to withdraw her hand and drew her up into her arms, tremors still running through her body.

"You learn quickly," she said after a couple of minutes, when her breathing had slowed to a normal rate.

Lee smiled. "Thank you." She burrowed against Ray's side, feeling the sun warming her body. "We seem to have a thing about water and making love."

Ray let out a laugh. "I suppose you're right. At least this time we aren't covered in sand." They lay still for a while, and then Ray sat up and looked down at her. "Are you sure you're ready for this?"

"Not for all of it," Lee admitted. "But I can't deny how I feel about having sex with you."

Ray looked at her sympathetically. "I have a feeling you're in for a bumpy ride for the next several months. But if you want to be with me for a while that's ok with me. Not that I mean be *with* me," she added hastily when Lee started to speak. "I mean sleep with me. Until you feel ready to start going out with other women."

"I was just going to say that I don't want to be tied down," Lee responded. "So thank you. I think I need to build up my confidence before I try to start dating someone. This is all so new to me."

"I can help steer you clear of the wrong women when you're ready," Ray said. "Point you toward the ones that aren't going to hurt you or try to own you."

"I guess I'm lucky to have someone like you to help me navigate this new world I'm finding myself in." Something inside Lee was sad that all there could be to their relationship was friendship and sex. She pushed the thought away with a reminder that the last thing she needed was to get involved with someone.

"I suppose we should get dressed," Ray said finally. "Jackie is liable to stop by any time to see how the project is going."

"I can imagine how she'd react if she saw how well this project is going."

Ray laughed. "She'd be tickled to prove her suspicions right."

"So you haven't told her?" Lee looked at Ray in surprise. She'd assumed that Ray told Jackie everything.

"She doesn't know the particulars, but she knows something's going on." Ray blushed slightly. "I know I promised not to tell anyone."

"I'm sure she guessed it on her own. Stacy could tell just from looking at me." Lee chuckled and then grew serious. "Even Joan knew something was going on. I guess I'm not as good at hiding as I thought I was."

"You really don't have to hide from your gay friends," Ray replied seriously. "I can understand not being ready to come out to your straight ones."

"I still don't know that I'm a lesbian." Lee's voice was a little weak. Ray gave her a stern look. "Okay, so it's ninety-nine percent certain."

"I'm going to say this one thing, Lee. If you plan on sleeping with any men, you'd better tell me now. I'm exclusive and I expect my partners to be as well, especially where that is concerned."

Lee managed a smile. "Don't worry. I don't think I'll be sleeping with any men in the near future. If ever again, and I'm leaning strongly toward the never again."

"Okay then." There was a brief lull in the conversation as they pulled their clothes back on. Ray got two more drinks and they sat on the deck chatting about what the future could hold for Lee.

Lee found the prospect of being gay a lot less daunting than she had before. And the thought of Ray showing her how it could be between women was appealing in a way she couldn't quite understand, and decided not to analyze. For now, she would just enjoy the ride.

XI.

Lee stared at the piece of paper in her hand in disbelief. She had assumed when the certified letter arrived that it was something from Robert's lawyer and had let it sit for a couple of days. Now that she had finally gotten around to opening it, part of her wished she hadn't.

She was torn as to who to call. A few months earlier, it would have automatically been Louise. But Louise had been distant recently, and Lee wasn't in a mood to listen to her talking about how she should just make up with Robert and be done with it. She hesitated only a moment longer before calling Ray's cell phone.

"Hello?"

In the background, Lee could hear the whine of power saws. "Are you still at work?"

"Oh, Lee, hi. Yeah, we're just finishing up now. What's up?"

"I don't want to bother you at work ..." Lee hesitated. "Will you meet me at Maddie's afterwards? I've gotten some bad news and I need to vent."

"Sure. I'll be off in about an hour. Hope you don't mind me sweaty and dirty."

Somehow, the thought of Ray covered with sweat made Lee shiver with excitement. She managed to keep her voice calm as she agreed and broke the connection. A few months ago, she would have worried about what outfit to wear down to the bar, but now she just went into the bedroom and changed into a blouse and a pair of shorts and slipped her feet into her sandals. The thought of talking to Ray about it calmed her considerably.

She got to the bar forty-five minutes later. Ray's truck was already parked out front and she pulled in next to it with a silent 'thank you' that she wouldn't have to repeat herself when Ray came in, knowing that she would tell Joan everything first if she'd gone in alone.

She felt like she could tell Joan everything no matter what the issue was. Joan was apparently just one of those people who were genuinely interested in others' stories. Maybe that was why she owned a bar. Of course, admitting that she'd finally taken the first step in establishing a new sexual identity was something she wasn't prepared to share with anyone, including Joan. But this was different.

Ray sat at the bar with two bottles of beer in front of her. Lee slid in beside her and gestured to Joan, who turned to pull the wine out of the refrigerator.

"Hey you." Ray sounded slightly tired, but she was smiling like there was no tomorrow.

"Hey. Thanks for meeting me."

Ray shrugged. "An excuse to see you and drink beer? I might be crazy, but I'm not stupid."

Lee laughed and pulled out her money to pay for the drink. "How was work?"

"Work. So what's got you all in a tizzy?"

Lee hesitated, still angry about the contents of the letter. "I lost my lease."

"What?" Ray turned to her with a startled expression on her face.

"I guess the owners decided to move back to Florida. They're breaking my lease. I get my deposit back with extra for moving costs but I have to be out in ninety days."

"That sucks." Ray reached over and squeezed her hand, then dropped her own back to her lap with a quick glance around to see if she'd been seen. "So what are you going to do?"

"Find a new place, I guess. I hadn't planned on moving so soon." Lee sighed and stared off into space. "And I really liked that condo. I think I'd have bought it given the chance."

"So find another one. Why haven't you bought a place already?"

Lee smiled at her. "You've obviously never been through a divorce. The last thing I need is to get tangled up in a mortgage while that's going on."

"You can always move in with me." Ray laughed. "That would be something. I don't think you could handle that much of a step-down in lifestyle."

For just a second Lee thought that it would be wonderful to move in with Ray, and then the humor of the statement sank in. She laughed as well. "My furniture wouldn't fit very well and I tend to take over the bathroom. Maybe it would be best if we just keep our own places for now."

The two looked at each other for a long moment then at the same time looked down at their drinks. There was a few moments silence before Ray spoke again. "If worse came to worse you could stay until you find a place, seriously. I have the spare bedroom."

"I appreciate the offer," Lee replied seriously. "And if worse comes to worse I might just take you up on it."

"I've gotten a couple of guys from work to help me with the damned kitchen."

It took Lee a couple of seconds to register the change in topic. "That'll help things move along, I guess."

"Yeah; I think I'll just rewire the whole thing and be done with it. If one side's gone, the other can't be far behind. I want it finished before next weekend. You are coming to the moving party, aren't you?"

"Of course! You have a party for every occasion, don't you?" Lee laughed. "You sure are an outgoing woman."

"Is there any other way to be?" Ray grinned wryly. "I like people. I like meeting new people. I always have."

Lee looked at her own reticence when it came to making new acquaintances. That she had taken to Ray so quickly was out of character for her. "Maybe you'll be a good influence on me. I tend to be shy."

"Could've fooled me."

"Will you help me look for a place?" Lee wanted to bring the topic back around to her problem. "I hate looking alone."

Louise had helped her pick out the condo she was currently living in but lately Louise had gotten to be so annoying that she didn't want to spend any more time with her than necessary and being trapped with her all day did not make Lee excited.

"Sure, if you want a Cracker viewpoint on everything. I'll be looking for whether they have a Jacuzzi or not."

Lee laughed. "I'm a Cracker too; fifth generation." She referred to the nickname given to native Floridians.

"Sixth generation here. Got you beat. Of course, my group never was particularly well off." Ray shrugged. "I suppose yours came down to buy land or something."

"As I recall they came down to buy an orange grove. That went to hell with some big freeze so they got into the grocery business." Lee was only mildly surprised that she wanted to know all about Ray's family. "What do your parents do?"

"Dad worked the railroad. Mom owns a little café outside of Ocala. She's after me to settle down." Ray laughed again. "I think she gave up on grandkids when I turned thirty-five. My brother has five kids so I suppose that's enough for her."

"My brother has three. My parents don't understand why I decided not to have children until later. I'm glad now that I waited. I'd hate to have children going through this with me." Lee stared into space. "I guess children will be out of my future entirely."

"Not necessarily," Ray replied. "I know plenty of lesbians with children."

"Sounds too complicated. I was never that keen on having them anyway."

"We're in agreement there." Ray drained her beer. "I was enough of a terror."

"I guess that leaves us footloose and fancy free," Lee said with a laugh.

"Speaking of which ..." Ray trailed off and glanced over at her. "What are you doing tonight?"

"Nothing in particular. Do you have something in mind?"

"I thought we could grab a bite to eat and see where it leads us." Ray shrugged. "Unless you have other plans."

Lee looked at her and a shiver of anticipation ran through her body. She didn't understand how the mere thought of Ray's body next to hers could send her into such a state of physical need that she was aching with desire. "I don't have other plans." Her voice sounded weak to her ears.

Ray grinned at her. "I was hoping you'd say that. Do you want me to pick you up?"

"That'll be fine." They made their plans and then parted ways after another drink. Lee went home cognizant of the fact that she might not be coming back that night and if she did, she might not be alone. Just in case, she tidied up and made the bed and then poured a glass of wine and waited for Ray to arrive.

* * *

"Hell of a party," Jackie observed, leaning against the railing next to Ray. Ray glanced at her then back at the dozen women in the pool.

"Yep; I never knew moving could go so quickly."

Jackie laughed. "Beer, barbeque and swimming? I'm surprised you only found fifteen women to help." She paused. "Speaking of women; where's Lee?"

"She's in the house." Ray gestured over her shoulder. "I think she's comparing wines with Linda."

"She looks pretty hot in that bathing suit, doesn't she?"

Ray looked at her. "Yes, she does." *And for the moment, she's all mine.* Ray felt only slightly bad for being so possessive of Lee. It was more than possessiveness; it was protectiveness. Ray didn't want anything bad to happen to Lee and she felt that their involvement was a good way to keep her safe from the local women who might not be so understanding of her position as just coming out.

"A couple of other women have noticed, Janet especially." Jackie studied her. "So fess up; is she available or isn't she? You two have been spending enough time together to make me wonder."

"You'd have to ask her," Ray growled. "But even if she is, Janet is definitely not the right woman for her."

Jackie laughed. "God, you're easy to read sometimes. If the

two of you aren't sleeping together, you might as well be."

Ray pushed off from the railing. "I need another beer." She left Jackie smirking on the deck and went inside to the kitchen. As she suspected, Lee and Linda were comparing notes on two different bottles of wine. They had obviously been sampling each. Lee was leaning her back against the counter, her sarong slipping just a bit off her waist and showing the peak of her hip.

"Ray!" Lee grinned when she saw her. "Come here and taste these and tell me which one is fruitier."

"It's this one." Linda pushed a bottle forward.

"I don't know from wine," Ray responded with a laugh, trying unsuccessfully to take her eyes off Lee's body. "All I know is I need a cold beer."

Lee pouted. "You can be so blue collar." Then she grinned and poked at Ray's side. "It's one of the things I love about you."

Startled, Ray stared at her. She realized that Lee was a little tipsy and hoped she was in control enough not to say or do anything she'd regret later.

Linda rolled her eyes. "Oh God ... save me. Even the straight girls love you, Ray. You should bottle that magnetism. You'd make a fortune off the butches world-wide."

"Shove it," Ray returned sharply, then forced her voice to be light. "I'm keeping it all for myself. I don't want competition."

Linda laughed and turned to Lee. "I still think this one is fruitier. We'll try another glass in a little while. I'd better go see what Frankie is up to before she starts hitting on someone."

After Linda had left the kitchen, Ray turned to Lee, who was studying her intently. "Are you ok?"

"I'm fine," Lee replied, reaching over to pour another glass of wine for herself. "Although with you standing so close I might have to change that position."

"You're being very flirty."

Lee shrugged. "Yes, I am. And I'm enjoying it."

Ray studied her. "Are you sure you're ok?"

"I'm fine," Lee repeated, her face drawing up. "I'm not about to kiss you in front of God and man, if that's what you're worried about."

"That wouldn't bother me, unless you didn't mean to do it.

I've done some things I didn't mean to when I've had too much to drink."

Lee's face started to twist into a scowl, and Ray thought that she had hit a little too close to home until the expression relaxed into a grin. "Is that it? Don't worry, Ray, I'm not drunk. I'm in a good mood, and I'm enjoying the party. Although I'm hoping that after everyone leaves you won't mind me kissing you. A lot."

"I won't mind," Ray laughed, relieved.

"Good." Lee pushed off from the counter and sauntered over to her. She leaned over and brushed the lightest of kisses across her lips before strolling out of the room.

Ray blew out her breath. When Lee felt comfortable, she simply oozed sensuality. It was hard not to give in to the desire to take her into her arms and kiss her as deeply as she could, to hell with everyone else. But Ray knew that the time for telling others that Lee had accepted her sexuality would only come on Lee's terms.

She had taken to expressing her desire for Ray so naturally that it was hard to believe less than three weeks before she had been running like hell from the very concept of being with a woman. Once she made up her mind, it was as if the floodgates of her passion had opened and all that pent up energy was washing over Ray like a deluge of desire.

Hardly a day had passed in the previous two weeks when there hadn't been some excuse to have sex, and Lee was most often the instigator. Ray had only seen the inside of her apartment for longer than it took to change into or out of work clothes four times in the previous nine days, and that was because she had insisted that she needed to finish packing.

She was running on about five hours sleep a night and despite the fact that her need for Lee was as desperate as Lee's apparently was for her, she was starting to wear down. She wasn't sure she remembered having so much energy at twenty-nine, but at thirty-nine, she wasn't quite up to the challenge.

Fortunately, she had taken two days off for the move, so she would have plenty of time to catch up on her sleep while Lee was at work on Monday and Tuesday.

From outside, someone yelled her name. With a contented

sigh, she grabbed a couple of beers out of the fridge and wandered back to the deck to join the party. Lee was in the pool playing water volleyball with a group of other women. Ray sat down at the patio table where she had a view of the pool and watched Lee splashing around and laughing. She seemed at home in the water.

Ray realized with a start that she seemed at home, period. She could easily imagine her sitting on the deck in the early morning, her hair tousled, reading the paper with a cup of coffee in her hand. She could imagine her doing it every morning.

Ray shook herself. She had no business imagining such things. She wasn't looking for a relationship, especially with Lee, who hadn't experienced the wide range of options available to her and couldn't possibly be looking to make an emotional commitment. Maybe she needed to back off, to take a few days away to reassert her independence. She was fond of Lee, for certain, but that was the extent of it. She didn't dare let Lee see that the thought had even raised its head for fear of scaring her off.

A shadow crossed her face and droplets of water fell on her thighs. She looked up into Lee's face, grinning at her as water ran in little rivulets down her tanned body.

"Coming in?" Lee's voice was light. "It feels great compared to the heat out here."

"I have to get the barbeque going," Ray responded somewhat weakly.

"Let Jackie do it. Come on; don't make me drip water all over you."

Ray managed a smile. "If you insist. But only for a few minutes. Then I really need to check the keg and get the fire going."

Lee reached down and caught her hand, tugging her to her feet. She moved backward, still holding onto Ray's hand until she reached the edge of the pool. With one more tug, she let go and fell backwards into the water. As she came up, Ray jumped in beside her. She may not be looking for love, but her desire for Lee burned brightly and she was more than willing to act on that as long as the brilliance lasted.

*   *   *

The stars glittered fiercely across the darkened sky as Lee rested against the seat of the hot tub looking up into the heavens. Ray was in the house getting them another round of drinks and she had time to reflect on the day. She thought Ray had seemed a little distant, as though she had a lot on her mind. But it was probably just the move.

After dinner, they had gotten into the hot tub, where they had been soaking for almost an hour, speaking little. Lee was still getting accustomed to the idea of sitting outside naked, but Ray had soothed her nerves with a soft kiss and a gentle caress down her shoulder to her arm, drawing her into the Jacuzzi.

"Do you want to go home tonight?"

Lee looked over and found Ray sitting down on one of the lounge chairs and lighting a cigar. She somehow managed to look sexy and comfortable at the same time with Lee's sarong wrapped around her waist and her bare breasts firm in the humid evening air.

"I'd rather not," she replied. "I'd rather stay with you."

Ray smiled. "I'd rather that too." She handed Lee her wine glass and picked up her beer. "I can't imagine anyone I'd rather have in my bed the first night in my new house."

"Not even Shellie?" Lee grinned. Shellie had shown up and almost made a scene when Ray didn't respond to her flirtatious behavior. She'd finally left pouting.

"Especially not Shellie." Ray stuck out her tongue quickly. "She's getting to be a nuisance."

"Well, you did throw her over for me." Lee giggled when Ray rolled her eyes and blew smoke in her direction. "OK, you threw her over and then started sleeping with me shortly thereafter."

"She doesn't know that," Ray responded archly. "Unless you'd like me to tell her."

"I'd rather you didn't."

This time is was Ray who laughed. "Don't worry."

They studied each other for the briefest of moments before

Lee stood up. She was well aware of Ray's gaze sliding down her body as she stepped out of the hot tub and reached for a towel. She wrapped it around her waist and sat down opposite Ray.

"At least we don't have to worry about screaming here." Lee grinned again.

"You mean you don't." Ray winked at her.

Lee mostly managed to stop her blush. "I can't help it. The way you touch me is …"

"I'd like to touch you like that right now."

This time the heat that shot through her wasn't in her face. "Then finish your cigar."

Ray leaned back against the lounger and bent one knee. "I think I'll make you wait a while longer."

"You're mean."

Ray grinned evilly. "Don't I know it!"

Lee reached for her wine. "You must be very excited owning your first house."

"It's my first real house, not the first time I've owned where I live." Ray puffed on her cigar. "That's how I was able to afford it."

"What do you mean?" Lee drew her brows together in confusion.

"I started out in a little trailer in a dumpy park down in Port Orange. The owners of the park decided to spruce the place up, and I was making improvements anyway, so once I was done I was able to sell for a decent profit and move into a bigger place. I kept doing that until I was able to get enough out of my last sale for the down payment on this."

Lee studied her in admiration. "That's a brilliant plan. You're smart for thinking of it. So will you sell here once you finish renovating it?"

Ray shrugged. "I don't know; I kind of fell in love with the place. I like the space to spread out. With moving so much, I haven't accumulated much stuff and at my age I'd like to just settle somewhere and maybe buy some things I've always wanted."

"I could fall in love with it too." Lee sipped at her wine. "I've never lived somewhere with land. There was barely a yard at Robert's and my house."

Ray studied her, and for a moment, Lee thought she had been misinterpreted. But then Ray laughed. "There's a trailer down the road for sale. You're about the same age I was when I started my climb."

"But you know how to do more than change the setting on a sprinkler," Lee replied. "I wouldn't know where to start."

"I could help." Ray lapsed into silence, staring out into the darkness.

"I don't think I could afford you," Lee returned lightly. "Although there would be fringe benefits."

Ray smiled thinly. "Yeah, that's true. Speaking of which, are you ready for a shower?"

Lee realized that the conversation was over. "Shouldn't we clean up?"

"It'll wait until tomorrow." Ray shrugged. "Of course, if you don't want to get wet with me ..."

"Anytime." Lee drained her wine and sat the glass on the patio table. "Will you scrub my back?"

Ray leered at her. "I'll scrub more than that."

Once in the large stand up shower, Ray showed her exactly what she meant and Lee realized just how deeply her need for Ray ran. Pinned against the wall with Ray's fingers between her legs, Lee found herself urging Ray on to more.

Ray responded by sliding three fingers into her, dropping her head with a growl to draw a nipple into her mouth. Lee's hands grasped at Ray's head, pulling her closer, as her hips strained forward against her hand. The water sluiced hotly off their bodies as Ray drew the orgasm from deep within Lee's center, thrusting against her even as she held her upright when her knees started to buckle.

Afterward, Ray drew her close and kissed her with surprising tenderness, drawing her hand to her own wet need. Lee moved against her clit with her fingers, clumsily at first, but with gaining confidence as Ray began to moan. Lee found herself biting against Ray's neck as she masturbated her, wanting to devour her very essence with the orgasm that followed. Once Ray had stopped shaking, they finished their shower and went to bed.

Lee's Awakening

Lying together, Lee waited for Ray to start seducing her again, but Ray took her into her arms and held her instead, kissing the top of her head. After a few minutes, she found Lee's mouth and began to nibble at her lips. Lee found the gentle insistence of Ray's tongue arousing in a way she hadn't felt before and opened her mouth to her, feeling the electric shocks that always came when Ray's tongue touched hers. They kissed for a long while as Ray's mouth became slowly more insistent.

Finally, they came together in the familiar fire that drew Lee in and left her screaming and shaking underneath the expert guidance of Ray's hands and mouth. She marveled once more at the intricacy of Ray's body as she returned the pleasure, and it was much later that they lay staring at the ceiling in the darkness, trying to catch their breaths.

"Damn, you learn quickly," Ray said in a rasping, ragged breath.

"I have a good teacher," Lee replied, leaning over to kiss her on the nose. Ray laughed, something close to a giggle but not quite. "I never thought I could want sex this much."

"To be honest, it's been a while since I did."

"You don't regret what's happened? I know you fought it awfully hard."

Ray rolled onto her elbow and looked down at her. "If I regretted it you wouldn't be here."

"I suppose you're right," Lee admitted. "I just worry sometimes that you're only doing this to be nice."

Ray sat up and swung her legs over the side of the bed. "I am definitely *not* doing this to be 'nice'. That isn't my style. You need to be a little more confident in yourself, Lee. You're a hell of a lover, and whoever you end up with is going to be damn lucky to have you."

Lee was afraid she had insulted her. "I wasn't suggesting it was a pity thing."

Ray stood and snagged a t-shirt. "It sounded that way. It isn't. Trust me; I wouldn't do a pity fuck for anyone, least of all you." She stared down at her for a long moment. "I'm going to smoke one more cigar; try not to hog the pillows."

Lee watched her walk out of the room then turned her gaze

back to the ceiling and blew out her breath in a frustrated sigh. She had obviously managed to insult Ray somehow. She guessed her decision to be brutally honest in their relationship would have to bring some bumps. But she didn't want any illusions that they were more than friends; she knew Ray would never tolerate it, and she wasn't ready for it.

Still, it hurt her to think that Ray might be angry with her, especially considering how close they had been ten minutes earlier. She had intended to drift off to sleep in Ray's arms, not be lying by herself hugging a pillow and wondering why she couldn't keep her mouth shut.

There was nothing to do about it now except get up and apologize, and she had a feeling that wouldn't be well received. She pulled the pillow over her head; hopefully Ray's mood would be gone in the morning and she could apologize then. For now, her body was telling her it was time to sleep.

She was barely aware when Ray returned to bed. As Ray gathered her into her arms, Lee had the vaguest notion that Ray had whispered something into her hair, but her groggy mind told her she was imagining things, especially when Ray gave her a kiss and immediately let her go, rolling onto her side. She fell back to sleep feeling strangely comforted to know that Ray's body was next to hers.

*   *   *

"Ray, can I speak to you?" Jimmy Alvarez motioned to her from the back end of his truck. With a growl, Ray joined him.

"What?"

Jimmy studied her. "How long have you been working on this crew?"

"Four years," Ray replied. "Why?"

"Well, things haven't been going as efficiently as I'd like. Since you're supposedly second man, I have to look at you for why."

Ray drew her eyebrows together. "Things have been running fine. We're ahead on our deadline."

"Not far enough ahead. The company wants us to cut more

time." Jimmy shifted. "I'm making Tom second man."

"What?" Ray stared at him. "I've been second man for two years!"

Jimmy shrugged. "You aren't getting the job done. They won't cut your pay, if that's what you're worried about."

"This is nuts. Tom has been here nine months."

"He's a better man for the job."

Ray tried to keep her temper. "Is that it? He's a man?"

"Be reasonable, Ray. My decision is final." Jimmy cocked his head. "Of course, you can always transfer to a different crew."

At that moment, Ray realized just how much her new crew boss disliked her. She also realized that Tom had come over from Martin's, where Jimmy had worked until recently. For just a moment, she wanted to throw her tool belt at him and tell him to go to hell. But she wouldn't give him the satisfaction.

"I'm not going anywhere. Tom is just going to fuck things up, and it'll be on your head."

Jimmy pursed his lips. "You aren't much of a team player, are you Ray. I'd be careful that you don't take your attitude out on the site, or you might find yourself looking for another job."

Ray's shoulders stiffened. "Are you threatening me?"

"I'm warning you. You're a decent worker. But if you can't get along you won't be working on my crew."

"Don't worry. I can get along. I've been doing it for four years. I'll be doing it long after you're gone." Ray turned and stormed off, slamming her tool belt in the back of her truck and climbing in spitting curses under her breath. She peeled out and headed toward the beach.

Sitting staring at the water for an hour didn't help her mood any and she figured she was pushing her luck by drinking another beer. The beach patrol hadn't been by in a while and she didn't want to get busted. As she put the truck in gear, she reached for her cell phone and dialed Lee, who didn't answer. After leaving a brief message, she hung up and turned her truck toward the bar.

Lisa was behind the bar when she got there, and after ordering a beer Ray rested on her elbows and chewed over the confrontation. It was obvious that Jimmy had it out for her. She might have the support of the rest of the crew, but he could do some damage if he wanted to.

"Look what the cat dragged in." Joan's voice came from behind her. "I haven't seen you in a few days."

"I've been busy," Ray replied with a slight blush.

Joan slid onto a stool next to her and signaled to her partner, who poured an old-fashioned glass of bourbon and sat it in front of her. "I can imagine what's keeping you busy. Or should I say who?"

"That's none of your business."

Joan laughed. "I seem to hear a lot of things that aren't any of my business. Did you have a fight? You seem pretty steamed."

"Trouble at work," Ray growled. "I got demoted. Damned bastard Jimmy has it out for me."

Joan frowned. "That doesn't sound good. What are you going to do?"

"I'd quit but I need to make my mortgage payments. Besides, if it got around at work that I was looking for another job I'd really be in trouble."

"Stuck between a rock and a hard place, eh?" Joan sipped her drink. "You could always go out on your own. I know you've talked about it before."

Ray sighed and ran her hand through her hair. "I don't have the money for that, not with the house. It's a nice dream, but it isn't practical."

She wished it were. She'd wanted to start her own company for years. She didn't want to do new construction or big projects, just smaller ones that she could handle alone or with one or two other crew. The idea of that kind of independence appealed to her, though at the same time it was a little scary to think she wouldn't have anything to fall back on if it failed.

They continued to chat for the better part of an hour, until Ray's cell phone rang.

"I got your message," Lee said instead of a greeting. "What happened?" Ray quickly filled her in. There was a moment of silence on the other end of the phone, and then Lee spoke again. "Why don't you come over? I'll make some dinner and you can chill out."

"OK, I'll be over in a few." Ray hung up and turned to Joan, who was giving her a knowing grin. "Oh, wipe that look off your face."

"She certainly brightened you up."

"Stuff it," Ray growled. She laid a tip on the bar and stood. "I'll see you later, Joan."

"Probably not alone," Joan replied, laughing when Ray shot her a dirty look. "Oh, get over it, Ray. She may not have come out but it isn't that hard to guess. There's only one reason for you to be spending so much time with one person and away from here."

"She's a friend."

"Right. A friend. Well, I'll see you and your friend later."

Ray growled again and left. She arrived at Lee's condo and rang the bell, realizing that she was still in her work clothes. Lee answered the door and grinned.

"All right, a sweaty woman. Come on in."

"I forgot to go home and change," Ray mumbled as she crossed the threshold.

Lee shrugged. "Take a shower. I think you have clothes here, or you can borrow some of mine."

"Thanks," Ray answered gratefully.

"I'll get you a beer when you're done, and I ordered pizza. I figured comfort food would be the best thing for this evening. I hope you like anchovies." Lee laughed when Ray grimaced. "Just kidding. Pepperoni and mushrooms, just like you like it."

"You spoil me." Ray wandered into the bathroom to shower. Once she was done, and had found a clean t-shirt and shorts that she had somehow left on a previous visit, she came back out into the living room to find an ice cold beer sitting on a coaster by the recliner she had taken to favoring and two plates of hot pizza on TV trays. Soft jazz filtered through the room.

"Sit down and relax." Lee picked up a champagne flute. "Pizza just got here so it's hot."

"Are you drinking champagne? With pizza?"

"I always drink champagne with pizza. At least at home. Would you like a glass?" Lee smiled as she took a sip of her drink and lowered the glass so that her lips were curled just above the rim.

"That's a combination I never would have guessed. Sure, I'll give it a whirl." She watched Lee stand up and smooth her slacks before crossing to the refrigerator. She returned and handed Ray a flute of champagne. Ray tasted it and took a bit of her pizza. The combination was remarkably good. "Hey, this isn't bad."

"Some Sunday we'll have to have Dom and Dominos in bed." Lee giggled.

Thinking that such a thing sounded a little too romantic, Ray shifted and took another bite of pizza. "Yeah, that sounds great."

Ever since the night of the housewarming party, part of Ray had been on pins and needles around Lee. Her words had stung with an unexpected force; Ray realized in that moment that what she felt for Lee was growing beyond friendship.

That was something dangerous, something that Lee didn't need and certainly didn't want. Ray didn't want it herself. It hadn't driven a wedge between them sexually, but emotionally Ray was spending a lot of time reeling herself in.

Lee was studying her with an odd look, so she took another swallow of champagne and sat the flute down. "I really needed something like this after today. Thanks."

"My pleasure," Lee said softly. Then she grinned. "This sure beats meeting my parents for dinner at the club."

"You shouldn't have cancelled just for me."

Lee made a dismissive gesture. "What—and sit through another lecture about how I need to grow up and realize that relationships take work and I'm not being fair to Robert? No thanks. My mother drinks and my father plays way too much golf. That's the only reason they've survived as long as they have. I've about decided that good relationships are the stuff of fairy tales; I've yet to see anyone who has one."

Ray frowned. "There's Joan and Lisa. And Stacy and Donna. And Linda and Frankie, although they've only been together a year."

"Funny." Lee laughed shortly. "I always heard lesbians had a hard time keeping relationships. Why is it they have all the strong ones?"

"I don't know." Ray shrugged. "I'm the last person to ask about that one."

"So why is that? And yes, I'm trying to distract you from this mess at work."

Ray sighed. "There was a girl, once."

Lee nodded sagely. "I figured there had to be. You run too hard and too fast just to be averse to commitment. Is this the one you told me about that night at the bar?"

Surprised that Lee remembered, Ray nodded. "I was very young, twenty-two. She was twenty-five. I caught her cheating."

"You told me. But you said something about before that. How long were you together?"

Ray looked away. "Three and a half years. She treated me more like a little sister than a lover. Only I was too in love to notice."

"Was that here? I mean, do you still run into her?"

Ray managed to laugh. "It was over fifteen years ago. I lived in Tampa then. So no, I don't see her. Thank God. Though last I heard she'd been dumped by her partner for a younger woman. Poetic justice if you ask me."

"I can't imagine anyone cheating on you. What could you find that could possibly be better?" Lee blushed suddenly and reached for her champagne.

"I'm a rogue now. I was an absolute idiot then. I drank too much, smoked too much dope, and spent too much time worrying about no one but myself. I treated her like a goddess, for sure, but the rest of my life was a mess."

"Well, you've certainly grown up nicely." Lee glanced away. "Do you want to watch a movie?"

More than willing to let the conversation die, Ray nodded. "What do you have?"

They settled on a comedy on pay-per-view and spent the next couple of hours curled up together on the couch, with Lee's head on Ray's shoulder, watching TV. After the final credits rolled, Ray stretched.

"I suppose I'd better be going." She yawned. "Thanks for taking my mind off this crap at work."

Lee studied her quietly. "I wish you wouldn't leave."

"I'm not really in the mood to fool around, Lee. I'm sorry."

"Who said anything about fooling around?" Lee looked at

the floor. "I just like the way you feel when I sleep. And I thought it might relax you."

Ray was startled. She hadn't thought Lee looked at their relationship in anything but a sexual light. "Sounds nice." The words were out before she even had time to make a conscious decision.

Lee smiled. "Good. Let me neaten up and I'll be in. Just don't hog the pillows." She winked and stood up. Ray stood as well and helped her clear the glasses and pizza box, and then wandered into the bedroom to get undressed.

As she pulled her t-shirt over her head, she realized that there was no place she would rather be than holding Lee while she slept. The implications of that thought were too much for her to process so late at night, and she pushed them away with a stern warning not to return.

Lee joined her in bed shortly thereafter and it wasn't long before both women were sound asleep, Lee nestled against Ray's side and Ray's arm protectively across Lee's chest.

XII.

The doorbell sounded insistently, dragging Lee out of a pleasant sleep. Beside her, Ray shifted and slid a leg across Lee's thighs.

"Tell them to go away," Ray mumbled.

"I can't imagine who it is," Lee replied. The doorbell sounded again and Lee came fully awake with a start, realizing what day it was. "Oh shit, it's Louise. We're supposed to go shopping this morning."

The pair flew out of bed and fell over themselves getting dressed. By the time Lee got to the front door, the bell had rung twice more.

"I was beginning to think you weren't home," Louise said as she came through the door. She pulled up short when she saw Ray. "Oh."

"Louise, this is my friend Ray. Ray, Louise." Lee hoped she wasn't blushing. Louise looked Ray up and down as though she were studying a bug and turned back to Lee.

"She's here awfully early."

Annoyed that Louise hadn't even had the decency to say hello, Lee was tempted to tell her exactly *why* Ray was there that early, but at the last moment she thought better of it. "I forgot we were going shopping. I told Ray we could go fishing this morning."

"Nice to meet you too," Ray commented, crossing her arms.

Louise looked as though she had finally seen her. "Yes." Her gaze shifted to Lee and her eyebrows drew together. "Where did you get that shirt? I wasn't aware you were a fan of Godsmack."

With a start, Lee realized she was wearing Ray's t-shirt and Ray was wearing one of hers. This time she couldn't stop the blush that raced toward her hairline. "I borrowed it from Ray. So I wouldn't get one of my blouses all messed up fishing." It was a horrible lie, but the best she could come up with on such short notice.

"I see." Louise didn't look like she believed a word Lee was saying, but she dropped the subject. "So is shopping off then?"

Lee and Ray exchanged glances and Ray tilted her head slightly toward Louise. "No, not at all. Sorry Ray, I forgot all about it," Lee said weakly.

"It's not a problem," Ray replied smoothly. "We can go tomorrow. I'll catch you later."

After the door had closed behind her, Lee took a second to regain her composure and faced Louise. "Would you like a cup of coffee?"

"That would be nice. What took you so long to answer the door?" Louise's eyes were warily curious.

"We were on the balcony." Lee walked into the kitchen area and pulled the coffee out of the freezer, hoping her answer didn't sound too lame.

"She's very rough around the edges, isn't she? And that hair. It was like she never brushes it." Ray's hair had been tousled from sleep, sticking up at all angles. Lee had thought it actually looked kind of cute.

Lee faced the counter and sighed. Without turning she said, "She's a friend of mine, Louise. Why don't you try to be a little less pompous about her? She's a very nice person."

"I'm not being pompous," Louise returned sharply.

Lee let it go and made the coffee. When they were sitting in the living area, Lee finally spoke again. "Where are we going today?"

"The usual haunts. Talbot's is having a sale. Were you really going fishing?"

Lee pursed her lips. "Yes, we were going fishing. Why else would I say we were?"

"I thought fishing grossed you out." Louise raised an eyebrow and studied her.

"Touching the fish grosses me out, not catching it. Ray promised to take care of that end of things." Lee knew she had to divert Louise's attention, and quickly. Once she got an idea in her mind, she would dig after it until she got to the truth.

"You sure are spending a lot of time with her lately. All I hear is Ray this, Ray that. If I didn't know better I'd swear you were sleeping with her."

Lee paled. "That's ridiculous." She hoped her voice sounded as strong as she was trying to make it.

Louise laughed. "Of course it is. But I'm beginning to feel like I'm being replaced as your best friend, and by a lesbian on top of it."

"Don't be silly." Lee managed to laugh as well. "We've known each other too long for that to happen." She chose to ignore the last comment. "Why don't we have lunch at the Peach Street Café?" She added, hoping to distract Louise's attention from lesbians in general, and Ray in particular.

"Sounds fine with me. Are you planning on changing?"

Lee glanced down. Somehow, the shorts and t-shirt she wore were more appealing than a blouse and slacks, but she knew she had to say yes. "Just give me a few minutes and I'll be ready."

In the bedroom, she glanced at the rumpled mess of the bed and smiled softly. Sleeping with Ray, just sleeping, had been more pleasant than anything she had experienced in years. It had been satisfying and comforting in a way she didn't expect.

In fact, the entire evening had been wonderful; just being with Ray made her feel warm and secure. The domesticity of the setting struck home; they had spent similar evenings together over the past weeks, but now it seemed terribly intimate, romantic, and Lee was startled that it didn't scare her more.

Pulling herself from what promised to be an uncomfortable train of thought, Lee finished changing and went to rejoin Louise. Maybe a day listening to her babble about their mutual friends would cure the burgeoning realization of something deeper growing between her and Ray. That was something she wasn't sure she was prepared to deal with.

*   *   *

"People are starting to talk, you know." Stacy leaned over conspiratorially. "You two have been inseparable for almost a month now."

"God, don't they have anything better to do?" Lee reached for her wine cooler and looked to see if Ray had arrived yet.

Stacy laughed. "When Ray Elliot goes a month without a girl on her arm, people are going to notice, especially when she's hanging out exclusively with a supposedly straight woman."

"I suppose it is kind of obvious. And here I am trying to play it cool."

"I don't think anyone would actually be surprised. There's a few that might be relieved Ray hasn't gone off the deep end, but for the most part it would just satisfy their curiosity."

Lee leaned back in her chair and brought the bottle to her lips. After a long swallow, she admitted, "I'm getting tired of hiding it, to be honest."

"So don't." Stacy shrugged. "It's not like it's a tough crowd. You aren't the first person in the world who's ever come out, you know."

"I know." Lee sighed. "It just feels awkward thinking about being physical with Ray in public. I mean, kissing her on the cheek is one thing."

Stacy made a noise. "Lately you've been kissing her on the lips. A friendly kiss, but on the lips anyway."

"I have? I hadn't noticed." Lee felt a blush run up her cheeks.

"Well, either way, Ray just got here. Try not to fall over your own feet getting over to see her."

Lee stuck out her tongue as she got up. She met Ray halfway between the truck and the volleyball court. Even though her initial instinct was to throw her arms around her, she settled for a discreet hug and a kiss feathered across the lips.

"I missed you last night." Ray's voice was low. "How was

your dinner party?"

"Boring," Lee replied, hooking her arm through Ray's. "I would have much rather had dinner with you."

"Well, dinner tonight then."

They walked together back to courtside, where Ray set up her camp chair and set down her cooler next to Lee's seat. She waved at Donna and Stacy before sitting down and reaching into the cooler for a beer. Lee sat back down next to her and shot Stacy a glance. Stacy smiled and winked at her. Lee smiled back and turned to Ray, and found herself wondering whether she could actually do something like kiss her in front of everyone. She wasn't at all sure she could, and that was disconcerting to her.

The first opportunity came after the first game as they were congratulating themselves on their win. Lee found herself standing in front of Ray, who was grinning at her with a daring look in her eyes. Lee started to reach out and kiss her but found that she couldn't. She settled for a bear hug and returned to her seat for something to drink. Ray followed after a minute of chatting with Jackie and another woman.

"That was some kind of hug," Ray commented as she sat down.

Lee blushed. "I had hoped to do more but I chickened out."

Ray turned her full attention to her and raised an eyebrow. "Hoped to do more what?"

"I'm tired to hiding. If I can't come out to this group then what does that say about me?"

Stacy came over, looked at the two, and then grabbed Donna and wandered off toward the other end of the court.

"There isn't some kind of deadline for coming out." Ray leaned closer to her. "You don't need to make a plan of attack for it. Stop being so analytical. If you're ready, then it'll happen."

Lee took a swallow from her wine cooler. "It's ok with you if I were to, isn't it? I mean, you don't mind if people know?"

"Hell, no." Ray leaned back and grinned. "I think I'm the luckiest woman in town. Of course, I'll have quite a lot of competition once everyone knows you're available, but I can handle that. You'll let me know when you're ready to move on." Her face suddenly went blank and she shifted her gaze out across the pasture.

Lee turned over her words. There had never been any pretense that their relationship was more than physical, and yet hearing Ray mention an end to it made Lee's heart stop for just a moment. Part of her knew she didn't want there to be an end to it, even as she knew Ray wasn't going to let emotions capture her. For an instant she reconsidered letting anyone else know that she'd made this discovery about herself, if only because it meant prolonging her relationship with Ray. But then she shook herself and told herself sternly that it wasn't fair to Ray to be thinking like that.

"Well, it's going to be quite a lot different from when I made my debut, but I suppose the result will be the same," she said rather thinly. "I hope I'm ready for what will happen next."

Ray met her gaze with an expression that for just a moment suggested she wasn't looking forward to what the end result of Lee's coming out might be either. Then the look was gone and Ray was her old self again. "You're a beautiful woman, Lee. You'll have to beat them off with a stick. But don't worry, I'll play bodyguard for you."

"I appreciate that. Of course, you're doing a very good job with my body as it is." She forced herself into an appropriate leer, at which Ray laughed. The pair finished their drinks and got up for the second game.

Lee's mind wasn't on playing, however, and her performance suffered. She was glad when it was over and she could return to her seat for something else to drink. Ray wandered over to the other side of the court where a group of women was smoking a joint, leaving Lee to stare into space and wonder at why she found it so hard to simply come out and show what she and Ray were sharing.

On the surface, it seemed obvious that she was nervous about sharing the change that had happened within her. It was like announcing something deeply intimate, and it wasn't the sort of thing she had been raised to discuss in public. She knew that no one would be offended by it, if in fact they cared one way or another at all, but she still felt uncomfortable doing it.

Something lurked beneath the surface of the convenient

explanation, however. Something that Lee was not particularly keen on revealing, even to herself. Letting others know of her relationship with Ray was the same as putting a limit on the time they would have together. Once she had come out, Ray would be expecting her to move on, to start dating other women.

They would always be friends, of course, but the physical relationship would come to an end. Lee knew she shouldn't be upset about it; after all, Ray was the first woman she had been with, and she couldn't expect to be happy without knowing what else was out there for her. But at the same time, she knew that she liked things with Ray, and she wasn't at all sure she would find anything better elsewhere.

That something emotional had started to form between them couldn't be denied. Lee didn't expect it was possible for two people to be so intimate for so long without a bond developing. But Ray had been clear that she wasn't looking for that kind of relationship, and Lee knew she wasn't either. So why did the thought of things coming to an end unsettle her so much?

Realizing that her thoughts had taken a dangerous turn away from simply letting others know that she was now one of them, Lee shook herself and forced her focus back to the matter at hand. She reached for another wine cooler and thought for the briefest of moments that joining Ray and the others for a hit might calm her down.

She hadn't smoked dope in years; it hadn't done anything for her during college and she didn't expect it to do anything now. She took a long swallow from her bottle and sought Ray out among the group on the opposite side of the court.

Ray caught her gaze and grinned. Lee grinned back, feeling all the confusion fall away. Ray's smile could do that to her, simply wash away all her frustration and leave a deeply relaxed feeling that permeated her body and made her feel all was right with the world. She stood as Ray crossed the court and joined her.

"Ready for the third game?" Ray asked, still grinning.

"Do you have any idea how cute you are when you grin?"

Ray laughed. "No, tell me."

Lee leaned over and kissed her on the nose. "I'd rather show you later."

"Promise?" Lee was vaguely aware that people had noticed what she had just done. She nodded, not trusting her voice. "Well, I can't wait for this to be over then." Ray winked at her and ruffled her hair, then let her arm drop as they continued to study each other.

"Let's play already," Mitch called a few moments later. Lee shook herself and stepped away from Ray, who rubbed her face before moving back onto the court.

It was a wild and intense game, the score see-sawing back and forth. Lee forgot all about her deliberations of earlier as she threw herself into helping win. She and Ray were in position to set and spike for each other, and when it came down to it, she set a perfect ball that Ray drove over the net for the win.

"Yeah!" Jackie yelled from the service line. "Way to go Ray!"

"Lee set it up for me," Ray replied, panting. She turned and looked at Lee with a tired grin.

"You made the point, sweetheart." Lee stepped up and wrapped her arms around Ray's waist. Without thinking, she planted a deep, hungry kiss on her lips. "Great game," she whispered in Ray's ear.

Ray stared at her when she pulled back. "You do realize what you just did?" she asked quietly.

"Oh. I did, didn't I?" Lee blushed. "Do you think anyone noticed?"

"Holy shit." The words were murmured by Kalynn, who was standing nearest the couple.

"I think they noticed." Ray grinned. "So now what?"

"I need a drink." Lee turned and started toward her chair. Ray caught up with her halfway there.

"So you kissed me. You wanted to anyway, right?"

Lee bit her lip and looked at her. "I wanted to be a little more subtle."

Ray laughed. "That was subtle. I can show you not subtle."

"Please don't." Lee looked around nervously. "I really wasn't ready ..."

"I told you you'd do it when you were ready to. Obviously you were ready to."

Lee's Awakening

Lee sat down and reached into her cooler, sensing the eyes on her and Ray. "I feel awkward."

Ray sank down beside her and took her hand. "Don't. I know it's weird at first, but really, you'll feel a lot more comfortable now that it's out in the open."

Lee looked inward; she did feel weird, but at the same time, there was a relief that she didn't have to hide anything anymore. "I guess you're right. After all, if I hadn't wanted to let everyone know I wouldn't have done it, would I?"

"I know I'm right. Look around; no one is freaking out, are they?" Lee shook her head. "Then don't worry about it."

Mitch came up and sat down next to Lee. "So, is it official finally?"

Lee blushed. "I guess it is."

"About damned time." Mitch laughed. "Ray, I didn't know you could keep a secret so well."

"Ah, shut up," Ray responded with a grin.

"Congratulations, Lee." Mitch inclined her head. "You could do a lot worse than Ray."

"It isn't like we're getting married," Ray growled, the grin fading from her face.

"Whatever." Mitch waved dismissively.

"I guess I could do a lot worse." Lee glanced over at Ray, who was looking flustered.

After another half hour of similar sentiments, Lee was ready to leave. She was uncomfortable with all the attention, and said her goodbyes and walked to her car. Ray followed her.

"Would you like me to bring some pizza over?" Ray asked quietly.

"Okay." Lee blew out her breath. "I thought you said no one would make a big deal of it."

Ray shrugged. "They didn't, really. I never said no one would say anything."

"True." Lee smiled. "I do feel better at any rate. What time will you be over?"

"About six? I'll bring clothes for work, if it's ok with you."

"Of course it is." Lee stepped forward and slid her arms around Ray's waist. "I'll stop for some champagne on the way home."

"Sounds wonderful." Ray bent over and kissed her gently. "See you in a little while."

After Lee had watched her climb into her truck and drive off, she sighed and turned to her own car. There was no hiding any more, not from their friends. But there was still a large part of her life that had to be kept in the dark; Louise and Lee's own family wouldn't be nearly as accepting. Lee realized that she was going to have to live another lie; first, she had lied that she was happy with Robert. Now she would have to lie that she wasn't happy with Ray. Life just didn't seem fair.

*   *   *

Ray stood over the bed watching Lee sleep. She was curled on her side with her face buried in a pillow. She had kicked the covers off her chest and halfway onto the floor. Ray smiled; she looked so comfortable that she hated to wake her. She had planned to have breakfast in bed, but looking at Lee, she decided to let her sleep. As she turned to go, she heard Lee move.

"Good morning." Lee's voice was groggy.

"Morning," Ray replied. "Did you sleep well?"

Lee stretched. "Mm-hmm. Did you?"

"Yes. I thought we'd have breakfast in bed today. How does that sound?"

"Divine." Lee yawned. "Can I help cook?"

Ray smiled at her. "No. Just relax. I'll have it whipped up in a jiffy." As she left the room, Lee was burrowing back into the sheets. Ray went to the kitchen and finished the meal she had started; bagels with cream cheese, fresh fruit, and bacon. She opened a bottle of champagne, made mimosas, and set up the whole thing on a large serving tray.

Lee was dozing when she returned, and woke at Ray's touch. She held the tray while Ray crawled in next to her and then took one of the champagne glasses.

"This looks good," she commented as Ray took her own glass.

"Something light to get us going for the day." Ray picked up a piece of cantaloupe and held it out for Lee take with her teeth.

"You can spoil a girl, you know that?"

Ray laughed. "Practice. Here's to finding the perfect place for you today." She held up her glass.

Lee touched it with her own. "Here's to finding any place today. I'm running out of time."

Ray leaned over and kissed her. "We'll find something."

Lee picked up a piece of bacon and fed it to her. Ray sucked at her fingers after she had taken the food, nibbling at the tips before letting them slide between her lips. Lee moaned softly. "Look out, you'll start something."

Ray leaned back against the pillows and drank from her mimosa. "And this would be a bad thing?"

Lee took a bite of bagel. "Not particularly."

They continued to tease each other as they finished eating, and once they were through Ray removed the tray to the floor before returning to Lee's side, her body telling her it was time for dessert. Lee didn't resist when she took the champagne from her hand and sat it on the bedside table, and came into her arms willingly. Ray kissed her, savoring the taste of her mouth, amazed as always that she could have such a deep want for someone.

Lee's hands moved down Ray's arms and slid around her waist, pulling her closer. She had become much more comfortable with expressing her desires in the previous weeks, and let Ray know that she was ready for more than just kisses by starting to roll over on top of her. Ray caught her and pressed her back into the bed, capturing her mouth once again as her hands went to her hips.

Lee willingly spread her legs and allowed Ray to nestle between them. Ray moved her mouth from Lee's lips to her neck and began kissing hotly down her body to capture a nipple between her teeth. Lee's breasts fascinated her; they were supple but grew firm as she was aroused, the nipples rising to erect hardness with the barest of touches from Ray's tongue. The taste of Lee's skin mesmerized her and she drew the nipple into her mouth savoring the salt of her sweat left from the previous night's lovemaking.

Lee groaned and arched her back to press against Ray's

mouth. Ray's fingers sought out the other nipple, rubbing across it before catching it between thumb and forefinger. Lee gasped as she pinched lightly, at the same time vibrating her tongue against the nipple in her mouth. She pressed her body against Lee's wetness and felt Lee's hips lift against her in return.

"Oh, God, Ray ..." Lee's voice was thick with hunger. It continued to amaze Ray how quickly Lee could become fully aroused; amazed and excited her. She knew she was already wet, and Lee had done nothing to her save trail her fingers across her breasts as she moved down Lee's body.

Of all the tastes of Lee, there was one she loved the most, and she slid further down until she was looking at the curly thatch between Lee's thighs. Lee's clit was erect and pink, her hair showing the silvery wetness of arousal. Ray kissed the insides of her thighs, teasingly blowing across her hair and grinning when Lee's hips jerked upward.

"Please." The word was uttered with a groan of hunger, and Ray reveled in the power that it gave her. She moved her head and burrowed her tongue in between Lee's lips, making a long slow upward stroke that danced off the tip of her clit with a sharp stroke. Lee groaned again and brought her hands up to the sides of Ray's head.

Ray repeated the motion, this time sucking Lee's hardened tip into her mouth, holding it lightly between her teeth as her tongue flicked at it. Lee's hips jerked again. Relishing the taste of her wetness, Ray dropped her head and began to lap at her, delving into her to taste the source of her arousal and then sliding her tongue up and across the hardness of her clit with repeated motions.

Lee tilted her hips back, making it easier for Ray to drive her tongue into the heated well before returning to lash against the rigid bud. Ray had never enjoyed going down on a woman so much; her desire to taste Lee's juices seemed unquenchable. Too quickly for her, Lee's back arched higher and she let out a strangled scream. Ray held to her as she came and then brought her down with softer strokes of her tongue, finally kissing her way back to Lee's dry, trembling mouth.

"My God you do that well," Lee breathed finally.

"I love the way you taste," Ray replied, taking her into her arms. "I can't help it."

"Well, I'm certainly glad you do."

"You should try it some time." Ray kissed her forehead. "It's amazing."

She sensed Lee blushing. "I'm sure I'll get around to it," Lee said weakly.

Ray smiled into her hair; Lee may have caught the nuances of using her fingers quickly, but she was still reticent about using her mouth anywhere but Ray's breasts.

Ray didn't want to push her, but thought it a little funny that she could enjoy something so much and not be eager to try it for herself.

"Ready for more?"

Lee pulled away and looked into her eyes. "What about you?"

"Oh, if you insist." Ray grinned wryly at her and Lee stuck out her tongue. "It shouldn't take much; just looking at you gets me so hot I can hardly stand myself."

Lee took more time with her, her lips working across Ray's breasts with what seemed like wonderment before her fingers slid between Ray's thighs and sought out her wetness. She was no longer clumsy in her movements, and Ray quickly caught her rhythm with her hips. True to her word, it wasn't long before the orgasm tore through her, leaving her trembling and panting against Lee's side.

They lay together for a while and then Ray rose and took Lee again, this time drawing the screams from her with her fingers. Afterwards, they got up and showered together, and then went out onto the deck for coffee.

Ray studied Lee over her mug; she was wearing a t-shirt and a pair of Ray's boxers, her hair still wet and her eyes bright. Ray thought she looked absolutely gorgeous. With a start, she realized she had imagined Lee sitting there almost exactly like that, although at the time it had seemed an impossible dream. But here she was, and Ray was troubled to realize that she didn't want her to be anywhere else. Not right then, not ever.

She pushed the thought away as though it were poisonous. She wasn't about to fall in love with someone, least of all Lee, who deserved to experience the wide range of opportunities now opened to her. The ten year disparity in their ages didn't help matters. There was no way Lee would ever fall in love with her, and even if she did, Ray couldn't—in good conscience—allow it to continue.

"Are you ok?" Lee's expression told Ray that her face was showing at least some of her confusion.

"I'm fine," she replied quickly. "We've had a good start to the day."

Lee stretched and grinned. "Yes, we have. I hope the rest of the day is as fruitful."

Ray took a drink of her coffee, burning her mouth. "Me too."

Lee studied her, looking for the world like she was about to say something else, and then she just smiled and picked up her own coffee cup. They chatted and drank their coffee for a while longer, until Ray had almost convinced herself that she was imagining things and that her desire for Lee was as unencumbered as it had always been; almost.

XIII.

Lee stared into her wine glass and listened to the country song playing on the jukebox. Ray wouldn't arrive for another half hour and she was getting antsy. At the end of the bar, Joan and Lisa had their heads together chatting. As Lee finished her wine, Joan came over with a refill.

"Where's your shadow?" she asked as she set a clean glass in front of Lee.

"Helping Jackie move something. She'll be here later."

"I see." Joan leaned on the counter. "How's the house-hunting going?"

Lee groaned. "Don't ask. We saw three places today and none of them was quite right. I've only got a few more weeks to find a place. At this rate, I'm going to end up in Ray's spare bedroom."

Joan studied her. "Are you sure that isn't what you're hoping?"

"What does that mean?" Lee raised an eyebrow at her.

Joan shrugged. "With the possible exception of Ray — and I reserve judgment on that account — women don't play around as long as you two have without emotions getting tangled up in things. Are you sure that hasn't happened to you?"

Lee opened her mouth to deny it but couldn't choke out the lie. "I'm beginning to wonder." She looked down at the bar. "I know it would be hard to live there as just a roommate."

"How do you think Ray would take that?"

"Not well." Lee sighed. "I might as well forget the idea ever even came up."

Joan made a noise. "So this just for fun thing has gone past that for you, eh?"

Lee nodded. "I didn't mean it to. I certainly wasn't looking to..." she trailed off and stared at the wall across the bar. She couldn't say the words, not even to herself.

Joan apparently had no qualms about it. "You've fallen in love with her, haven't you? You don't have to answer," she added when Lee raised pained eyes to her. "Seems to me you've gotten yourself into quite the mess."

"She didn't have to make it so easy," Lee said defensively.

"I'm sure she wasn't trying to," Joan returned. "Ray's lovable, but she doesn't want to be loved. I've never quite figured out why, but that's the way it is. Are you going to tell her?"

Lee studied her hands. "I suppose I should. But I don't want to ruin things. I'd rather her think I just was ready to move on."

"Do you think you could do that?"

Lee shrugged. "I don't know. I know I don't want to lose her friendship, if that's all I can have."

"And that doesn't include being a roommate?"

"It would just be so awkward." Lee fell silent and Joan cleaned the top of the bar with a towel. Finally, Lee spoke again. "And here I thought realizing I was gay was going to make my life easier."

Joan laughed. "Hardly. Welcome to the real world, kiddo. It's going to get harder before it gets easier."

"What would you do, Joan?"

"Oh, no. I'm not getting caught in that one. It's up to you what you would do, not what I would do." Joan leaned against the bar again. "Has she even offered you the spare room?"

"She did a while ago, right after I found out I had to move. But she hasn't lately. I suppose I'll just wait until the last minute and take whatever comes up." Lee rested her chin on her fist. "Of course, that doesn't solve my other problem, which I didn't really see as a problem until now."

"What's that?"

"What to do about Ray. I've just been going along like it's always going to be this way, and it can't be. I don't want to wait for her to get tired of me. But I don't want to end it either."

Joan straightened. "That's something only you can puzzle out." She topped off Lee's wine and went back to where Lisa sat at the end of the bar, leaving Lee chewing on her lower lip and trying to work her way through the unexpected maze of emotions that the conversation had brought up.

She had thought it was just about where to live, but she now saw that it was much more than that. She and Ray had been together for almost two months; something had to give one way or another soon. She had seen how long Ray's flings lasted with others; theirs was tipping way over the edge of expiration. It wasn't that Ray had shown any signs that she was getting bored, but Lee wondered if she was too naïve to see them if they were there.

She was in love with Ray. She had to admit that much to herself. She certainly hadn't planned for it to happen, but it had. She suspected she had been in love with her before realizing she was attracted to her. Love was something she wouldn't get back from Ray. Ray had at least explained why to her. Lee may not agree with the reasons but she couldn't say she didn't know them.

She tried to imagine sleeping with another woman. There were a few she had seen in the bar that turned her on, but though she could imagine having sex with them, she couldn't imagine the comfortable rhythm that her relationship with Ray had become. Perhaps in time, someone could replicate that comfort zone, but at the moment, Lee didn't want anyone to try.

Maybe it was for the best that they stop seeing one another before Ray figured out what was going on. At least Lee could salvage the friendship from it. And the hurt of not having Ray in her life in the way she wanted would serve her well down the road; it would prevent her from giving her heart away too easily the next time.

By the time Ray arrived with Jackie in tow, Lee was near tears. The sight of the dark-haired woman didn't make matters any easier but Lee took a long swallow of wine and put a brave face on. Ray loped over and planted a kiss on her lips before sliding onto the bar stool next to her.

"Hey, what's wrong? You look like someone died."

Lee forced a smile. "Nothing. I've just got a lot on my mind."

"We'll find you a place, don't worry." Ray signaled for a drink.

"I'm sure something will come up." Lee tried to look Ray in the face and couldn't. Her eyes darted around the room, settling on Jackie, who was giving her a curious look.

For the next half hour, Lee tried to concentrate on the conversation. All she succeeded in doing was driving herself half-crazy thinking about how she could have been so blind as to not see that she was falling in love. Finally, the words she had been dreading came.

"Well, like I said before, the spare room is there if you want it."

Lee's face flushed. She stared at the bar. She stared at Joan across the room. She fought desperately to think of something cool to say when all she really wanted to do was scream.

"I'll think about it," she managed, finishing her drink. "I really need to get going."

Ray looked startled and exchanged glances with Jackie. "So early? I thought—"

"I just want to go home," Lee interrupted, more forcefully than she had intended.

"Okay. I'll walk you out."

"No, that's okay. I'll call you." Lee grabbed her purse and walked as calmly as she could to the door. She was at her car before she sensed Ray behind her.

"What's going on, Lee?" Ray's voice was concerned.

Lee forced herself to face her. "Nothing. I just ..." She trailed off and studied Ray, who was looking at her with confusion. "I need some time alone."

"Did I do something?"

"No." Lee blew out her breath. "No, you didn't do anything. I just don't think ... I can't take you up on your offer. I can't ... I don't think I can do this anymore." She hadn't intended to say it, but once the words were out, she knew there was no going back.

Ray's eyebrows drew together. "What do you mean, you can't do this anymore? Do what?"

"Us. It's time to move on."

Emotions sorted rapidly across Ray's face, ending in disbelief. "What brought this on? I didn't mean anything by offering—"

Lee's reserves burst. "That's exactly it. You didn't mean anything. We don't mean anything. I can't do it anymore." As soon as she had finished she realized that she had admitted the one thing that she'd sworn to herself she never would.

"Oh, God. Lee …"

"Don't say anything. Just let me walk away with my dignity intact."

Ray blew out her breath. "Lee, don't do this. Not like this."

"How else can I do it, Ray? I can't go on like you don't mean anything to me." Lee fought the tears. "And I can't go on knowing I don't mean anything to you."

"You do mean something to me. You're one of my best friends." Ray took a step forward and Lee stepped away, crossing her arms.

"God damn it, Ray. Don't you get it? I'm in love with you."

Ray stopped dead, her face going blank. "You can't. I won't let you be."

"Well, I am. As useless as it is, I am." Lee wished she could just get in her car and leave. "And it isn't up to you to decide."

"You can't fall in love with the first woman you're with. You just think you are because it's all so new."

Lee felt anger growing underneath her distress. "I'm not a child. I know my own emotions. You sound just like Robert, telling me how I should think."

"Well, you obviously aren't thinking clearly, otherwise we wouldn't be having this conversation." Ray crossed her arms as well. "This is hardly the time or place for it."

"And when would be the time; after we've made love?" Lee felt herself beginning to shake. "Things don't automatically go the way you want them to, Ray."

"I never said they did." Ray's voice grew sharp. "Why did you have to tell me? All you had to do was tell me you wanted to move on. You didn't have to make a huge scene out of it. I guess I can't help it if you think you love me, but you didn't have to slap me in the face with it out of the blue."

"You know what? I don't think you can feel anything for someone else. All that romanticism you claim you have is just an act. All of it has been an act." Lee fumbled for her keys.

"I didn't lie," Ray retorted. "You should have said something a long time ago if you were feeling like this. We could have ended it then, and none of this would have happened."

"Fuck you, Ray." Lee managed to get her door open. She ground the ignition, finally got the car started, and spun her wheels backing out. Ray was still standing in the parking lot as she took off toward home.

*   *   *

Ray squinted in the early morning light, fighting a headache and the slight nausea that too many beers had brought on. Despite having tried her best, she hadn't succeeded in drinking the fight away, and had spent most of the night tossing and turning and wondering how things could have gone so horribly wrong.

She hadn't been very understanding, that much she knew. But Lee had blindsided her and she had reacted the way she always reacted when a woman admitted an emotional attachment to her. Given some kind of warning, she would have done things differently. But there had been no warning, only a sudden outburst of emotion.

She rolled over, missing the scent of Lee's hair and the warmth of her body. She should have guessed, should have known Lee's emotions would get tangled up in things. They had gone on too long for them not to. Ray knew she should have put an end to it weeks ago, but somehow she hadn't been able to.

She dragged herself through breakfast and sat on the deck nursing a cup of coffee and wondering just how responsible she was for what had happened. That her emotions for Lee went beyond friendship was something she couldn't deny, but she wasn't about to allow herself to call them love.

The phone rang around noon and for just a second Ray's heart leapt, thinking it might be Lee. It wasn't.

"Are you ok?" Jackie's voice was hesitant. "You took off awfully fast last night."

"I'll be alright," Ray replied.

"Have you called her?"

"No." Ray frowned. "And I don't intend to."

Jackie made a noise. "You probably should."

Ray hadn't told Jackie half of what had transpired outside the night before. As far as she knew, they had fought about Ray's offer and nothing else. "I don't think she'll talk to me."

"You're a dope, you know that? I could have told you she'd take you asking her to move in the wrong way."

"I don't want to talk about it." Ray pulled open the fridge and stared at what was left of her beer. Somehow, it didn't seem very palatable, and she settled for a bottle of water.

"Fine. Are you coming to volleyball or are you going to sulk?"

Ray didn't particularly want to risk facing Lee so soon, but she suspected she wouldn't be making an appearance at the game. At the same time, she didn't feel much like socializing. "I don't know."

"There was more to it than what you told me, wasn't there?" It wasn't a question.

"I said I don't want to talk about it."

Jackie grunted. "Fine. But if you don't show, I'm coming out there."

"Don't. I said I'd be fine." Ray grimaced and paced back to the living room. "I'll probably just do some work around the house."

"Well, if you need to talk, call me." Jackie sounded unconvinced.

"Alright." Ray hung up and stared at the fireplace. *What's there to talk about? I acted like a jerk.* The thought didn't make her feel any better. She realized she owed Lee more consideration than she'd shown her; she should have been more sensitive to her feelings.

She would call in a few days and apologize for the way she handled things, once Lee had had a chance to calm down some. Maybe they could salvage their friendship out of the mess. Ray tried to comfort herself with the thought, but as the afternoon wore on, she couldn't help but notice that friendship sounded somehow hollow after what they had shared. Once again, she put the thought away and reminded herself that she wasn't about to get caught, wasn't about to open her heart to anyone again, not even to Lee.

* * *

"We missed you at volleyball today." Stacy leaned forward, picked up her beer, and studied Lee. "I figured you and Ray were off together. I was kind of surprised when you told me you were home."

"Ray and I ... ended things. Last night." Lee blushed and looked away. "Rather, I ended things."

Stacy was silent for a long moment. "Oh."

"I didn't mean for it to happen the way it did, but it did. I'm sure she's not happy with me."

"I'm assuming you want to talk about it, otherwise you wouldn't have asked me over." Stacy bit her lip. "I didn't see it coming, that's for sure."

Lee dropped her gaze. "She asked me to move in. As a roommate," she added when Stacy drew in a startled breath. "I couldn't do it."

"That's hardly a reason to—"

"I'm in love with her." Lee forced the words out before she could stop herself. She needed to tell someone, needed some kind of support.

Stacy looked at her with sympathetic eyes. "I can't say that's a surprise, Lee. Although, to be honest I thought ..." she shook herself. "Did you tell her?"

"I didn't mean to. I meant to just end things and salvage some kind of friendship. But it didn't work out that way. She didn't ... she didn't react well, let's put it that way."

"Knowing Ray, I can imagine not. So now what?"

Lee sighed. "I don't know. It hurts, I know that much. I don't think I knew what love was until now. And knowing I've probably lost her friendship almost hurts worse."

Stacy glanced away and then back. "Maybe after some time has passed you'll get that back. I do hope this doesn't mean you're going to start avoiding us all."

"I'm not sure of a lot right now, but I'm sure I'm still a lesbian." Lee forced a laugh. "It may take me a while to lick my wounds but I'll bounce back eventually, even if it doesn't feel like it right now."

Stacy left an hour later after some much needed consoling, and Lee dragged herself into the bedroom to neaten up. She hadn't slept well, and the bed was a mess.

She started to make it before realizing that Ray had stayed over Thursday night and she hadn't washed the sheets since then. With a sigh, she stripped the bed and took the load to the washing machine. She got fresh sheets then set to tidying the rest of the room.

Going through the pile of clothes on the chair next to the dresser, she pulled out a pair of Ray's jeans and two of her t-shirts. Sinking down onto the bed, she stared at the clothing, resisting the urge to bring it to her face just to smell Ray's scent one more time. She tried to catch the tears, but she couldn't, and threw herself down across the pillows and cried until she couldn't cry any more.

*   *   *

The rain pounded down incessantly against the roof and Ray wondered just how flooded the driveway would be by the time it finished. She was accustomed to the afternoon storms brought up by the sea breeze, but this one seemed to be lasting longer than usual. Thunder crashed overhead and flashes of light showed that the storm was almost right on top of the house.

She tried to read but her mind kept dredging up memories of other thunderstorms, with Lee curled next to her side and a fire going in the fireplace, the promise of an afternoon spent making love hanging in the air. It had been four days with no contact, and Ray was beginning to feel as though a lifetime had passed since she had tasted Lee's lips.

She had made a neat pile of Lee's clothes in the spare bedroom, waiting for enough time to pass to call her and let her know she could pick them up. *If Lee will talk to me.*

At least she had gotten to lay off work early. All week had been a bear, with Jimmy finding something wrong with almost everything she did. The company had started a round of layoffs, and she was beginning to worry that he might try to engineer putting her on the list to be cut. That was the last thing she needed.

Jackie and a couple of other women were supposed to be coming over for poker that night, but Ray wondered if the storm would stop them. After a particularly loud peal of thunder, she reached for the phone.

"Quite the storm, eh?" Jackie sounded jazzed. She loved thunderstorms. She was probably on her balcony watching the light show.

"It sounds like the roof is going to come down here."

"Do you think the roads will be passable? I was looking forward to taking your money." Jackie made an 'ooo'-ing sound that suggested to Ray she had seen a particularly brilliant bolt of lightning.

"I don't know. I was looking forward to some company tonight, too." Ray reached for her beer.

"Missing Lee?"

"No, of course not," Ray growled.

Jackie blew out her breath. "Bullshit. You should call her. She's got to be over it by now."

"I still don't want to talk about it, Jackie." Actually, she did want to talk about it, but she couldn't admit to someone that there was an empty spot where Lee used to be. Especially Jackie, who would be smug with her 'I knew it'-s.

Outside, there was a brilliant flash and almost immediately the lights went out and the phone went dead. A minute later, they came back on, but the lights in the kitchen remained off. Cursing, Ray headed toward the garage to check the fuse box.

What greeted her brought an even louder curse. A large

portion of the ceiling had given way, showering sheetrock onto the floor. Water dripped from the hole, making a puddle on top of the pile. As she stared at the mess, the phone rang in the house. Automatically, she went to answer it.

"Did you hang up on me?" Jackie sounded perturbed.

"No, the power went out," Ray explained with irritation. "Part of the garage ceiling collapsed, God damn it. I must have a hell of a leak in the roof."

"You're kidding me. Is it bad?"

Ray sighed and ran her hand through her hair. "It's about eight by eight. I won't know until I can get up in the crawlspace. I'm not doing it right now, that's for sure." Outside, the storm seemed to be moving off. Ray checked the fuse box and reset the breaker for the kitchen, then went back inside and pulled a beer out of the refrigerator. "I've about had it with this damn house."

"You knew it was a fixer-upper." Jackie's voice was encouraging. "At least it isn't the whole roof."

"As far as I know. If part of it is leaking there's a good chance the whole thing needs replacing."

"Just relax. I'll make it out there somehow and bring some weed. You've been on edge all week; you need to take some time and chill out. A night of poker would do you some good."

"You're probably right. I have been a little cranky this week. It seems everything is hitting me at once; work, Lee, now the house." *Oops, didn't mean to mention her.* Ray cursed silently. Jackie was sure to pick up on what she'd said.

"Ray, I'm going to say this as your best friend. Whatever happened between you and Lee, you need to talk about it. It's eating you up, I can tell." Jackie sounded concerned.

Ray sighed again, defeated. She had to talk to someone before she went crazy. "All right, come out and I'll tell you about it. I'm going to call off the game though. All of a sudden I'm not in the mood."

"I'll head out now; the storm is slowing down. Do you want me to bring you some beer?"

"Jack Daniels if you have it."

Jackie agreed and they hung up. Ray made the phone calls to cancel the card game and waited impatiently for Jackie to arrive, afraid that she would chicken out of admitting what was going through her mind.

Jackie arrived forty minutes later, bearing a fifth of Jack Daniels and a bag of marijuana. She came in and went to look at the garage ceiling, made appropriately consoling comments, and then they went back into the living room and sat down, Ray with a strong drink and Jackie with a beer.

"All right, tell me what's been tearing you up for the last five days." Jackie started picking the seeds out of the pot. Ray hesitated, not sure she really wanted to admit what she was thinking. Finally, Jackie glared at her. "I drove all the way out here in a rain storm. 'Fess up."

"We fought over more than just me asking her to move in."

"I figured that. So what exactly did you fight about?" Jackie studied her curiously.

Ray rubbed her face wearily. "She told me she loved me."

"Oh, boy." Jackie leaned back. "What did you say to her?"

"I reacted all wrong. It was so out of left field ..."

"So you pulled the same thing you pull every time someone gets attached to you."

"Yes," Ray admitted guiltily. "I didn't have time to think."

Jackie gave her a sideways look. "And now you have."

"Yes." Ray swallowed. "There's a big hole where she was. I'd gotten used to her being around."

"Hmm; seems to me there's more than that."

"What do you mean?" Ray looked at her curiously. "I miss her. It doesn't mean I love her."

"Are you sure?" Jackie licked the joint and reached for her lighter. "I'm not the only one who thinks you do."

"Oh, for Chrissake, I don't." Something in the back of Ray's mind was disagreeing with her, and she wasn't happy to think it.

"Then what is it? You're obviously miserable."

Ray hesitated. "I'm ... not sure. I just wasn't ready for it to end."

Jackie laughed. "Ray, sometimes you're an idiot. If I were you, I'd be crawling on my hands and knees to make up with Lee. She's the best thing that's ever happened to you."

"So what if she was?" Ray took a long drink from her glass.

"I don't think I'm capable of loving someone. And she deserves better than that. She deserves better than me."

"Obviously she loves *you*."

Ray stared at the wall. "How does she know it's even love? I mean, I'm the first woman she's been with. Finding out you've been living half a life has to open a whole bunch of emotions; how do I know she isn't just assuming she's in love because she's so happy with the sex?"

"She's an adult, Ray. I think she can tell when she's in love." Jackie rolled her eyes. "You should give her some credit. She's an intelligent woman."

"I don't want her to be in love with me."

"Jesus, that isn't something you have a say over. And I don't care what you think; I think you're in love with her too." Jackie lit the joint and inhaled from it, passing it to Ray, who gratefully took it and put it to her lips.

"I am *not* in love with her," Ray insisted after letting the smoke curl from her mouth. She knew she sounded more emphatic than she felt, which made her confusion all the worse. "We had great sex and I miss it. That's all."

"Whatever you say, Ray. Just keep telling yourself that. Maybe you'll eventually even believe it."

Ray didn't respond and after a few silent minutes, the conversation turned to more mundane matters. But even as they talked, Ray's mind kept turning over what Jackie had said. She couldn't love Lee. She just couldn't. Just because her heart felt like it had been ripped from her chest didn't mean she was in love with her.

The thoughts followed her to bed. As she pulled the blankets up under her chin, she was once again aware of the painful sensation of missing Lee's body next to hers. She fell asleep trying to convince herself that the loss was purely physical. But somewhere in the back of her mind, she knew she was lying to herself.

XIV.

"You can't avoid her forever." Stacy leaned back against the couch and took a drink of her wine.

Lee swirled her glass and stared at it for a long moment. "I suppose not. But what am I going to say to her when I do see her? She's got to be pissed as hell at me."

"Not necessarily. Besides, you have clothes of hers, don't you?"

"Yes." Lee nodded. "And she has some of mine. I suppose you're right, we at least need to exchange those. But what do I say when I call her?"

Stacy shrugged. "Just arrange to meet. Do it at volleyball if you don't want to be alone with her."

Lee considered Stacy's words. Intellectually, she knew she and Ray had to come to some resolution that would allow them to be in the same room together. But emotionally she was still devastated by Ray's response. Her words had been harsh, and Lee was having trouble getting past that. Stacy studied her silently.

"We could meet up at volleyball," Lee responded slowly. "That's a nice safe place. I'm just afraid I'll burst into tears or something equally idiotic when I see her."

Stacy shook her head. "I doubt that seriously. She hurt you, but you've bounced back pretty well, I think. You'll find someone else special down the road and this will just have been one of those things."

"Right now, it still hurts. She was so cold about it."

"Ray doesn't handle emotions very well sometimes, especially when it comes to love. She'll probably apologize for being so mean when you talk to her." Stacy gestured with her wine glass. "It would be a shame for your friendship to end over this. I know what happened is a big deal, but you two got really close."

"Maybe that's why it hurts so much. I should never have told her I loved her." Lee sighed and drained her wine.

"Well you did. Now you have to get past it."

"I know." She was silent for a few moments. "I just don't want to get hurt again. What if she's as angry when I call her?"

"She won't be," Stacy promised. "I've known Ray a long time. She doesn't like being rude, she just can't handle someone being emotionally attached to her. I think you can still salvage your friendship."

"Okay, I'll call her."

"Good. Do you have more wine?"

Lee got up. "Of course. Thanks for coming over. After mediation today I needed some company and Louise was not going to be very empathetic, I had a feeling." She crossed to the kitchen and retrieved the wine bottle from the refrigerator.

"What did happen in mediation? You still haven't told me." Stacy held up her glass for Lee to refill.

"The bastard cold lied. He said his asset paperwork was estimating on the high end. He's been liquidating the stocks and hiding money, I just know he has." Lee refilled her own glass and returned the bottle to the fridge. "He also suggested that I had a mental condition and that's why I was being so persistent about it. He practically came out and called me hysterical."

They continued to discuss Robert and the process of the divorce for a while. Finally, Stacy shrugged. "I still don't know what you saw in him. He's a real prick. I've thought so all along."

"I wish you'd warned me." Lee sat back down, "although I probably wouldn't have listened. He kind of swept me off my feet with his romantic fool routine. I was stupid enough to think I was in love with him. What a joke."

"Everyone makes mistakes. He was the handsome, smitten doctor and you were wishing for romance to hit you." Stacy paused. "You don't suppose—you don't suppose that's what's happened with Ray, do you?"

Lee glared at her. "No. Ray is the last person I would have expected to fall in love with, and I certainly wasn't looking for romance when I got involved with her."

"Then why did you get involved? If I can ask," Stacy added when Lee glared at her again. "Just tell me if it isn't any of my business."

Lee shrugged helplessly. "I'm not sure. Everything was so new and I guess I wanted to feel safe while I got used to the idea of being with a woman. Ray was very kind to me in that respect."

"You could have done worse for a first relationship," Stacy admitted. "Despite how it turned out."

Lee stared into space for a moment, fighting with her emotions. True, she was angry with how things had turned out, and hurt that Ray didn't share her feelings. But the friendship they had forged was one of the strongest she had ever had, even stronger than her friendship with Louise.

The realization of this struck her with a hard blow. She had to try and regain that part of their relationship. If she failed, it would hurt twice as much. She had to just put her feelings of love away and concentrate on making Ray see that they could go back to the way things had been before.

"I'll call her," she promised quietly.

"Good. I have to be going soon. Donna will have my hide if I'm not back for dinner. She's making one of her weird Indian things again and she hates it when I'm late."

"Well, thanks again for coming over. You've made me feel a lot better." Lee smiled softly.

"My pleasure."

After Stacy had left, Lee got up and paced for several minutes, drinking her wine and trying to work up the nerve to dial Ray's number. She debated calling the house, knowing that Ray hardly ever answered that phone. She could leave a message and avoid actually talking to her. But she knew that was just wimping out on what she really needed to do and finally she picked up the phone and called Ray's cell.

"Hello, Lee." Ray's voice was tired.

"Hi. Um, I have some of your clothes here. You probably want them back." Lee spoke quickly, afraid of losing her nerve.

Ray paused. "Yes, I do. I have some of yours at the house too."

"We could exchange them at volleyball on Sunday," Lee offered.

Ray paused again. "That sounds fine. Look Lee ..." the pause was longer this time. "We probably should talk about what happened."

"I guess you're right. But not over the phone."

"On Sunday, then. I promise I won't be as short." Ray coughed.

Lee bit her lip. "On Sunday," she repeated. "I promise I won't yell."

They broke the connection and Lee sank down onto the couch, staring out the sliding glass doors at the river. The fact that Ray wanted to talk was promising. Maybe things could go back to the way they were before. *Well, not exactly the way they were.* Lee sighed. The thought of Ray still sent a shiver through her body and brought a twinge to her groin. She knew she had to get past it, but part of her didn't want to give up that feeling.

Finally, she got up and went to pour another glass of wine. There was no backing out of it now. She had three days to steel herself for the conversation, three days to figure out what to say. Whatever that was, maybe it would be enough to convince Ray that they could be friends again. Lee certainly hoped so.

*   *   *

For perhaps the fiftieth time, Ray looked toward the gate to the pasture in hopes that she would spot Lee's car. They were through with the first game and there was still no sign of her. She still wasn't sure what she would say when she did see her, but she was anxious to see her just the same. Jackie nudged her and handed her the joint that was passing around. Ray took a hit off it and passed it to Donna.

"Stop looking so antsy," Jackie instructed sternly. "She said she'd be here."

"What am I going to say to her? I was such a jerk."

"Well, an apology might be a good way to start," Jackie replied.

"I know." Ray ran her hand through her hair. "I'm not sure she'll want to hear one, though. She sounded really pissed off on the phone."

She had sounded pissed off. Pissed off and hurt. Ray had heard those emotions in women's voices before, only not to the same degree. She felt a deep sorrow for having caused that anger and pain, but she knew to have encouraged Lee would have proven more disastrous. As she thought it, she cringed. She not only had not encouraged her, she had been downright mean. She was usually short when a woman started talking emotional commitment, but never that short.

Stacy's cell phone rang. After speaking on it for a minute, she closed the phone, got up and walked toward Ray and Jackie.

"I want to talk to you, Ray."

Sighing, Ray got up and walked with her a distance away from everyone else. "What?"

"Lee will be here in a few minutes. She's really nervous about this meeting, and you'd better not do anything to upset her any more, do you hear me?" Stacy crossed her arms and gave Ray a hard look.

"I don't plan on upsetting her," Ray returned. "I just want to talk to her."

"I've known you for a long time, Ray. I never knew you could be such a jackass."

Ray grimaced. "Alright, I was a jerk. There's nothing I can do about that now."

"You'd damn well better apologize, for starters." Stacy's look grew even harder. "You were supposed to be her friend, not treat her like shit."

"This really isn't any of your business, Stacy." Ray crossed her arms as well and glowered.

"I'm making it my business. Lee is a wonderful woman and

she deserves to be treated a hell of a lot better than you did. You're just as bad as that bastard of a husband of hers."

Ray let her arms fall. "That's not fair. I lost my cool, that's all. I feel bad about it."

"Well, if you want to salvage any kind of friendship out of this mess you'd better make sure you let her know just how bad you feel. I can't believe you blew her off like that." Stacy poked Ray in the chest. "And I know she only told me half of it."

Ray sighed. "I'll let her know. I didn't mean for it to happen this way. But it's between me and her, and I'd appreciate you staying out of it."

"I'll stay out of it as long as she isn't sobbing on my shoulder."

"Fine." Ray turned.

Stacy let her walk away. She returned to her seat and pulled a fresh beer from her cooler. Jackie was looking at her with a curious expression.

"What was that all about," she asked.

"Giving me a damn lecture, like I don't already know what an ass I was."

Jackie shrugged. "Well, I hate to say it, but it sounds like you *were* an ass. She's probably just looking out for Lee. That's what friends do."

Ray cringed and looked away. *She* was supposed to be Lee's friend too, and she certainly hadn't looked out for her. She'd been downright cruel in what she'd said; she could try to justify it as being blindsided all she wanted, but she couldn't take it back. She had never wished for something more than to be able to undo those words.

"I hope I can make it right."

Jackie snorted. "Just be satisfied if you can make it a little better. You're lucky she wants to speak to you at all."

As Ray started to reply, she saw Lee's Mercedes turn into the pasture. Her heart leapt to her throat. There was no more time for planning now. She'd just have to face Lee and try to speak her heart. But she wasn't sure where her heart was. She was fond of Lee, for sure, but was she in love? She couldn't be, not after all these years of studiously avoiding any emotional entanglement. She'd just have to be gentle in explaining that.

"Don't screw this up," Jackie warned as Ray stood. "I don't think you'll get a second chance."

"Trust me, the last thing I want to do is screw this up." Ray took a long swig of her beer and started across the pasture toward where Lee was parking. They met under one of the oak trees between the two places. Lee looked as nervous as Ray felt and Ray felt a shooting pang of guilt for being the cause of the stress evident on Lee's face.

"Hello, Ray." Lee's voice was quiet. "How are you?"

Ray swallowed hard. "I've been better. I guess you have too."

Lee's pained laugh made Ray cringe. "You could say that. I have your stuff in the car."

"I wanted—I was hoping we could talk about what happened."

"You made yourself fairly clear that night." Lee studied her, her expression unreadable.

"I was an asshole," Ray responded. "I wanted to apologize."

Being so close to Lee was bringing up twinges of desire that Ray fought to ignore. She wanted nothing more than to take Lee in her arms and kiss her until everything was alright again. But Lee's body language told her contact was the last thing she wanted. Ray frowned. This was going to be harder than she thought.

"You were a complete asshole," Lee agreed firmly. "If I'd had any doubts that you felt nothing for me, you erased them."

Ray held out her hands, desperate to make Lee see that she was hurting too. "I never meant to be so rough. I don't know what possessed me to say those things. I overreacted."

"You speak your mind, Ray. I'm sure you meant everything you said."

"If I could take it back, I would. You've got to believe me. The last thing I ever wanted to do was hurt you." Ray felt a lump in her throat and told herself sternly that she was not going to cry.

"Well, you did; a lot." Lee crossed her arms.

Ray dropped her gaze. "I'm sorry doesn't even begin to express how bad I feel."

"I hope you do. I hope you feel just as bad as you made me

feel." Lee hesitated. "No, I don't. I wouldn't want anyone to feel the way I did."

Ray closed her eyes and fought the tears. She could hardly think for her sorrow at what she had done. Her next words came out of nowhere. "I was scared."

"Scared? Of what?" Lee sounded a little startled.

"Of how you make me feel." Once she had spoken the words, Ray realized they were true. Lee did scare her. She had awakened emotions that Ray thought long extinct.

Lee made a noise and Ray dared to look up at her. She looked confused and disbelieving. "And how exactly do I make you feel, Ray?"

"I'm very fond of you —"

Lee looked away as a pained expression crossed her face. "Don't you get it? I don't want you to be fond of me. Being fond of me is just as bad as feeling nothing. And I could probably have dealt with *that* if you hadn't shoved it down my throat."

Ray struggled with her emotions. Lee looked so angry, and yet at the same time so lost, that she wanted to do anything to make her feel better. But she wasn't sure how she could do that. Her heart ached with the thought that she was responsible for Lee's pain. But what could she do now save apologize and hope that someday they could move past what had happened?

"Lee, I'm so sorry ..."

Lee heaved a sigh. "You've said that. And I accept your apology. But it doesn't make it any easier. Do you have any idea how much it hurts just standing here talking to you?"

Ray hung her head. "I never meant for any of this to happen," she mumbled.

"But it did, and it's going to take me a while to get over it — to get over you."

Ray suddenly realized she didn't want Lee to get over her. She wanted Lee to be with her. Not just for fun but for real. She wasn't sure what to call the emotion but it was more than fondness. And she had ruined any chance of that happening with careless words.

"What can I say to make it better?" Ray forced herself to look into Lee's eyes.

"There's only one thing you could say that would make it any better and I know that isn't in your vocabulary. I didn't want to accept that, but now I have to." Lee let her breath out slowly. "Come on, let's get this over with." She turned and started back toward her car.

Ray knew if she let Lee walk away she would never have a chance to be more than a distant friend. And that thought was more than Ray could bear. "Lee, wait."

"There's nothing else to say, Ray." Lee spoke over her shoulder.

"Yes there is. I think ... I think I love you too." She hadn't realized she was actually going to say it until it came out of her mouth, and once it did she realized that there was a very real chance she *was* in love with her. That was the only thing to explain why she felt like she'd been torn in two since their argument.

Slowly, Lee turned back around and stared at her. "You *think* you love me?"

"Yes."

Lee laughed, although it sounded forced. "You think you love me. I'm sorry, Ray, but that isn't good enough. It's a start, but it isn't enough to make up for what you did."

"It's all I can say right now. I haven't been in love in a very long time. I've forgotten what it feels like." Ray lifted her hands pleadingly. "Give me a chance."

Lee studied her. "Come get your clothes."

Ray's shoulders sagged. She had put herself on the line and even that wasn't enough to undo the words she had spoken. "Okay."

They walked to the car without speaking. Ray got Lee's clothes out of her truck and exchanged them for her own. They studied each other for a long silent time after that.

"I have to go," Lee finally said in a soft voice.

"I understand." She didn't, but her emotions were so confused that she didn't have the energy to ask any questions.

Lee opened her car door and then hesitated. She looked back at Ray and gave her a little smile. "You decide whether you love me or not. It's all or nothing, Ray. If it's all, we can start rebuilding. If it's nothing, maybe we can work on being friends again. The choice is yours. You call me when you've figured it out."

Ray's heart hammered full force against her ribcage. Lee had opened the door to another chance. Ray didn't know for sure whether she was in love or not, but she knew she had to find out, and that meant analyzing her actions for the past six months; even longer, really. She knew she had to dredge up her feelings for Tina and decide if she was willing to open herself again to that much pain.

"I will." It was all she could say. Lee smiled once more, got in her car and drove off, leaving Ray standing there with a bursting feeling of relief. She had delivered a serious dose of pain to Lee and yet Lee was still willing to give her another chance. Ray owed it to her to search her own heart and discover to what depth she had gotten into her psyche, into her emotions, into her need. And at that moment, there was nothing in the world she wanted to do more.

*   *   *

Lee paced the living room, stopping and staring out the sliding glass doors at the river occasionally. It had taken all she had to be so firm with Ray, especially when Ray had told her she thought she loved her. Part of her, mostly her heart, had leapt at the words, ready to take anything that would mean they could resume their relationship. But the intellectual part realized that thinking something wasn't the same as making it so and almost loving was in many ways worse than not loving at all.

Ray was genuinely sorry, that much was obvious. But Lee was still hurt by what had been said, and the part of her that hurt so much wanted Ray to squirm, to feel some of the pain she had felt herself. She knew it was mean and in many ways petty, but the fact remained that she wanted to exact some kind of revenge.

Still, she had opened the door for Ray to redeem herself. She knew how much it had taken for Ray even to admit to the possibility of loving her and she hoped with all her heart that

Ray would decide that she, in fact, couldn't live without her.

As she was about to sink down onto the sofa the doorbell rang. For a brief moment, Lee thought it might be Ray, but then reason took hold of her and she went to answer it. Stacy stood in the doorway, looking apprehensive.

"May I come in?"

Lee stepped back to allow her inside. "You could have called."

"I had a feeling you wouldn't answer your phone." Stacy shifted. "I wanted to make sure you were okay."

Lee smiled. "I'm fine. You want a soda or some wine?"

"A soda sounds great. I've had enough beer for today."

Once they were sitting in the living room, Stacy leaned forward and looked softly at Lee. "How did it go? You weren't talking very long."

"She apologized." Lee glanced away. "Beyond that, I'm not entirely sure."

"She'd better have apologized or I'd kick her ass. She left right after you did and didn't say a word to anyone." Stacy looked at her glass. "I was afraid she had made things worse."

"No, she didn't. But I wasn't easy on her. I told her exactly how I felt."

Stacy drew her eyebrows together. "How did she take it? I know you're pissed off."

"I think she took it pretty well." Lee shrugged. "She didn't blow up at me like last time."

They discussed the meeting further, although Lee didn't mention that Ray had suggested she might be in love with her. That was something between her and Ray and it wasn't fair to Ray to reveal it.

Finally, Stacy gave her a stern look. "You said you'd give her another chance, didn't you?" It wasn't a question.

Lee blushed. "Yes."

"Oh, Lee. Are you sure that was a good idea? She really behaved like a jerk."

"I'm not sure," Lee admitted. "But I believe in second chances. It doesn't mean I'm willing to go back to the way things were."

Stacy frowned. "Then what does it mean?"

"It means I'm willing to move forward if she can stop being so unemotional. It means if she can't love me I want to try and be friends."

"I'm not entirely sure she knows what love means. She hasn't had a serious relationship since I've known her, and that's been over ten years. She always runs when things start to get serious." Stacy shrugged. "Of course, there's always the chance that you can change that. But I wouldn't get your hopes up."

Lee sighed. "I'm not getting my hopes up, Stacy."

"Good. I mean, there will be other women. It doesn't always happen overnight."

"You're one to talk." Lee laughed. "You've been with Donna since you were twenty-one. How many can there have been before that?"

Stacy coughed. "More than I care to discuss. But I was twenty-one and I got lucky; our relationship stuck. I thank God every day that she still loves me."

Lee contemplated her. "So what you're saying is it takes luck to find the right relationship? Don't you believe in luck on the first try?"

"Not in the lesbian world. Lesbians will move in with each other after a week. Then it's usually a year of sheer hell as things fall apart, until you finally admit you made a mistake. I'd rather you not make that same mistake." Stacy shrugged. "Of course, you're an adult. I can hardly tell you what to do."

"You're not exactly encouraging me to pursue other relationships," Lee said soberly.

"I'm just trying to be realistic. Even if she were to tell you she loved you, would you ever not have that doubt in the back of your mind because of how she acted?"

Lee looked inward, Stacy's words striking a little too close to home. It was true she wanted with all her heart for Ray to say she loved her, but she couldn't be sure she wouldn't always hold a little bit of herself back because of Ray's initial reaction. She had to wonder if it was really fair to pursue a love that had that rocky of a start. Despite her intellectual assessment of the situation, her heart kept telling her the same thing.

"I don't know. But I can't ignore how I feel."

"I'm not suggesting you do," Stacy replied firmly. "I'm just warning you that even if she does say she loves you there's always the chance that things will go sour."

Lee shrugged. "I don't think any relationship comes with a one hundred percent guarantee. But if you don't try, you can't succeed."

"That's true." Stacy contemplated her. "Maybe I'm being a little overprotective because of the divorce and you just coming out and all. I don't want you to be hurt again down the road."

Lee smiled. "Like you said, I'm a big girl. I can take my lumps, even if they hurt. Yes, I've been in a state for the last week. But that doesn't mean I want to give up."

"As long as you know what you're doing."

"I do."

Stacy finished her soda. "I shouldn't stay. I just wanted to check on you."

"Thanks. I'll call you later." They both stood up and Lee gave Stacy a hug. Stacy smiled and left.

After closing the door, Lee returned to the couch and sank down. She now realized that she was chasing a dream that didn't automatically come with a happy ending. True, she and Ray had known each other for months, but that was no guarantee that an ongoing emotional relationship would last.

Despite this, her heart kept telling her that Ray was the one that she wanted; Ray was the one that she needed. She had opened the door to something more than friendship and sex. It was now up to Ray whether or not to walk through that door. The only thing to do now was to wait.

*   *   *

Ray sat in the parking lot of the bar staring at the back door. She was hesitant to go inside, because she was there to talk to Joan and she knew it would be a difficult conversation. But Joan would shoot straight with her and Ray needed that right now. Her thoughts were still turning over her discussion with Lee, and she was no closer to a decision than she had been after Lee left. Long years of independence made it hard to imagine opening herself to another person the way that loving them would do.

It had been just over twenty-four hours since they had met in the pasture and Lee hadn't rejected her out of hand. Ray had thought of little else since then, to the point of almost electrocuting herself on the job site. Jimmy had taken obvious pleasure in confronting her about it, but even her anger toward him vanished beneath the confusing emotions that ran through her when she thought of Lee.

Ray lit a cigarillo and climbed out of her truck. She walked toward the door and paced back and forth until the cigar had burned to a stub, which she then flicked into the parking lot. With a sigh, she squared her shoulders and pulled open the door.

Joan wasn't behind the bar. Partially relieved, Ray sat down and ordered a beer. It tasted good going down, and she ordered another before scanning the room looking for Joan. The door to the office was ajar but Ray knew the unwritten rule against going in. She turned back to the bar and stared at her beer bottle, fighting the image of the first time she had seen Lee walk in the back door. She lifted the bottle to her lips and sighed before tipping it up.

"You look like someone with a lot on her mind."

Ray turned and saw Joan standing behind her. "Yeah. I was hoping I could talk to you."

Joan eyed her for a moment. "Sure. Let's sit over here." Once they were seated at a table in the corner, she leaned back in her chair and studied Ray carefully. "This has to do with Lee, doesn't it?"

Ray nodded. "I'm not sure what to do about her."

"You'll have to be more specific, Ray. I know you had a fight. I could tell from your face when you walked back in here that night. And she's hardly been in here since then."

"She told me she loved me. I didn't know what to do, so I made an ass of myself." Ray bit her lip. "She didn't speak to me for almost a week."

Joan made a noise. "I'm not surprised. Do you love her?"

"I don't know. I'm not sure what love is. I was hoping you could help me understand."

"I'm no specialist in matters of the heart." Joan laughed.

Ray shrugged. "But you have more experience than I do. How do you know you're in love?"

"Well, you want them in your life. It's not so much you can't live without them as you don't want to have to." Joan shrugged. "I knew because when Lisa went on a business trip, it was like half of me was missing."

Ray contemplated her words. True she did want Lee in her life; but in what sense? She knew she missed making love to her, and she did miss waking up next to her, but did that count as love? That was the difficult question.

"I know I miss her," she admitted, feeling at a loss to explain her emotions.

"Well, that's a start. I can give you a dozen different things you feel when you're in love, but only you can know for sure whether they mean anything to you. No one can answer those questions for you, Ray. You have to answer them on your own." Joan smiled softly. "Sometimes it's hard to accept that you want someone in your life, especially when you've been on your own for a long time."

"I've been chewing it over all day. My brain is starting to get tired."

Joan laughed again. "Don't overanalyze it Ray, just feel it. You won't know until you let yourself really do that."

Realizing that Joan wasn't going to give her any more advice, Ray nodded. "Thanks, Joan. I guess I need to stop obsessing about it."

"You're right. Now, do you want another beer?"

Ray nodded again. "I need something to take my mind off this for a while."

Two hours later, she was on the road heading toward home, and she began to turn over Joan's words. She could imagine life without Lee in it, but she didn't particularly like the image. The question was—did she dislike it enough to call it love, or was it still just sexual? It was so hard to tell where one started and the other might begin.

She thought back to her time with Tina; back then, she thought she couldn't live without her in her life, to the point that she allowed Tina to dictate a lot of things that she now realized she should never have let happen.

It was more of an obsession than anything, what she thought was that first true love, even though it didn't seem equal. And though she had been crushed to find out that Tina was cheating on her, it seemed now that it was mostly the blow to her ego and a shattering of her image of her lover as perfect instead of a heartfelt loss.

She compared her memories of Tina with the way she felt about Lee; with Lee, things were equal. They both had their own lives outside of each other, and it didn't feel like an insult when one wanted to do something by herself; yet when they were together, it seemed like the rest of the world faded into the background.

Tina had forced the world to take a back seat, had been upset when Ray didn't put her first and foremost. They had been together almost every moment when they weren't working, with Tina usually the one deciding what they would do and where they would go. At the time it had seemed like Tina was just being butch, but now that Ray had come into her own as far as being butch went she saw that it was simply controlling. No wonder she could empathize with Lee so easily about her husband. They had both been through the same thing.

Her thoughts continued to dance around Joan's words until she got home. Once she got inside, she headed to the kitchen for a soda; another beer just didn't seem right when she had such serious thoughts running through her mind. When she opened the fridge, she saw one of Lee's bottles of wine still sitting in the door. With a long sigh, she grabbed a soda can and went into the den.

She turned on the stereo, put on a Billie Holiday CD and collapsed on the sofa staring at the blank TV screen. When the phone rang an hour later, she almost didn't answer it, lost in her own thoughts. Finally, she dragged herself back to reality and reached for the handset.

"Where are you? We were supposed to meet for karaoke. The finals are next week." Jackie sounded concerned.

Ray squinted up her face. "Oh, shit. I forgot."

"Still have Lee on the brain?" Jackie coughed. "Obsessing isn't good for you."

"I'm not obsessing," Ray returned. "I have a serious decision to make."

"And where are you with that?"

"I talked to Joan. She confused me more than anything." She blew out her breath in frustration. "Why does it have to be so hard?"

"Because the result is so wonderful, I suppose."

Ray bit her upper lip. "So why aren't you in love?"

"I'm waiting for the right woman," Jackie answered soberly. "I'm tired of the eighteen month relationships; I'm getting too old for it. That doesn't mean I've given up looking. But we aren't talking about me."

"I just wish I could *know* ... could be sure."

"Do you miss her?"

"Yes." Ray leaned back. "A lot more than I'd like to admit."

"When you wake up, is your first thought that she isn't there?" Jackie's voice held a stern tone.

"Yes."

"When something happens, good or bad, do you wish you could tell her?"

Ray sighed. "Yes."

"Well, kiddo, I think the answer is right in front of your face. It's just a matter of whether you're willing to drop your walls long enough to admit it."

"I don't know ..." Ray trailed off.

Jackie grunted. "Yes, you do. It's knocking on the door. Let it in."

"I'll think about it."

"You do that. Call me tomorrow." Jackie said goodbye and hung up.

Ray blew out her breath. Was she strong enough to let Lee past her walls and into her heart? Was she already there? Finally, after what seemed an eternity, the answer came clearly and she felt a weight lifting from her shoulders.

There was only one thing to do. She picked up the phone.

XV.

Lee started when the phone rang. She glanced at the clock before picking up the handset and looking at the caller ID. Sighing, she hit the talk button.

"Hello, Ray."

Ray's voice sounded strange. "I need to see you."

Lee sighed again. "It's nine-thirty at night. What could be so important?"

"I don't want to talk about it on the phone."

"What do you want?" Lee reached for her wine.

Ray paused. "It's about Sunday."

For a moment Lee's heart leapt. But she forced herself to be calm; there was no point in getting her hopes up. Ray was just as likely to want to tell her she wasn't in love and get it over with as to be bursting to admit she was.

"Well, I'm not meeting you tonight. How about tomorrow? I can meet you at Maddie's around six-thirty." Lee tried to sound noncommittal.

"I don't want to do this in public."

That doesn't sound good. "Why not?"

Ray hesitated again, a little bit longer this time. "Please, come out to the house. Around seven?"

"Fine."

The relief was evident in Ray's voice. "Thank you."

They broke the connection and Lee stared out the sliding glass doors. The conversation had sent mixed signals to her; on the one hand, it sounded like Ray just didn't want to tell her she didn't love her in public. On the other hand, she had sounded pleading when she asked Lee to come out to the house. Pleading in a way that suggested she wasn't about to crush Lee's hopes.

Lee went to bed still chewing over the conversation, trying to get some forewarning of what was going to transpire the next day. She slept fitfully and woke wanting to get it over with. She was distracted enough at work that her boss let her go early, and so she paced her apartment until time to leave.

Ray met her at the door with an apprehensive expression. "I'm glad you came." She stepped back to allow Lee inside. "I was afraid you wouldn't."

"I said I would. I don't go back on promises."

Ray shifted uncomfortably. "Would you like a glass of wine? You left some."

"That would be nice." Lee followed her into the den and sat down on the sofa while Ray disappeared into the kitchen. After taking the wine glass that she returned with, she looked at Ray and decided she didn't want to postpone the inevitable with small talk. "Why am I here?"

"I've been doing a lot of thinking. I think I've reached a decision."

Lee blew out her breath. "I told you, Ray, thinking is as bad as not doing."

Ray studied her. "I've made a decision," she said firmly.

"And what is it?" Lee hoped her hands weren't trembling noticeably but Ray's eyes were on her face.

"I *am* fond of you, Lee. You're one of my best friends. But I wasn't sure there was anything more to it than that."

Lee fought the urge to start crying, sure what Ray's next words were going to be. "We can work on being friends again." She forced herself to sound calm.

"I don't want to be friends."

Tears formed in the corners of Lee's eyes and she blinked at them with irritation. She wouldn't break down in front of Ray. If friendship were all she could try to regain, then friendship it would have to be. "I'd hate to lose that, Ray."

Ray got up from the recliner and paced across the room. She stared at the bookshelf for a long silent moment before turning back around. "I meant I don't want to be just friends."

"I told you, I'm not going back to the way things were. I couldn't bear it."

Ray studied her and Lee forced herself to meet her gaze. "What do you think I'm saying to you, Lee?"

Startled, Lee opened her mouth, and then closed it again. Thoughts whirled through her mind as she tried to process Ray's words. "You're saying you don't love me."

To her surprise, Ray laughed. "You're way off base."

"Then tell me. Stop dancing around the subject and tell me." Lee crossed her arms.

Ray hesitated and swallowed hard. "I love you, Lee. I have for a long time. I was just too foolish to see it."

Lee froze, not certain she had word the words right. "You love me? You're sure?"

"As sure as a person can be," Ray replied solemnly. "I just hope you still love me after I've been such a jerk."

Lee stood. The two women studied each other for what seemed to Lee an eternity, and then she stepped forward until she was inches from Ray. "I still love you," she said softly.

Ray's mouth on hers set off an explosion in her body. It was as if they had never kissed before and the sensation jolted Lee's groin with the force of a lightning bolt. Ray's tongue traced a line of fire around her lips until she parted them and reached with her own to dare Ray to deepen the kiss. Ray did, and Lee breathed her in as though she were giving her life.

"God, I missed you," Ray whispered when they parted. "I've been so stupid."

Lee shushed her and kissed her again, her arms moving around Ray's waist even as Ray's lifted to her shoulders. Lee pulled the other woman against her, relishing the warmth and softness of her body. Ray's breath came hot on her skin as she kissed her way down to the joining of neck and shoulder and Lee shuddered as she nibbled her way back up. Ray found her mouth, her tongue delving into the warm darkness to dance against Lee's with abandon.

Lee desperately wanted to feel Ray's skin under her fingers and worked her t-shirt out of her jeans, slipping underneath it run her fingers along the curve of her lower back and up the plane of her spine to her shoulder blades, lifting the shirt as she went.

Ray stepped away long enough to pull it over her head. She dropped it to the floor, her mouth recapturing Lee's even as she started unbuttoning Lee's blouse. The fabric fell away, and she ran her tongue down the front of Lee's neck to the hollow and then began to kiss her way down between her breasts as she pulled the blouse open.

Once the last button had been undone, Lee shrugged the shirt off and pulled Ray back up to kiss her again. Her skin was on fire everywhere that it touched Ray's, lighting an inferno in her stomach that she knew only one thing could assuage. She groaned when Ray's fingers came to the hook on her bra, let Ray unfasten it and slide it down her arms, watching as her eyes moved over her naked breasts.

Ray reached to run her palms across Lee's nipples. Lee groaned again, and Ray smiled at her. "You have the most beautiful breasts," she said in a low voice, the same gravelly voice that had drawn Lee in the first time they met.

Lee thought to answer in a teasing tone, but words failed her as Ray's fingers closed on her hardened buds and began to roll them gently between thumb and forefinger.

"Oh, God," she gasped, arching her back to press against Ray's hands. Ray pinched her lightly, lifting her hands to pull the nipples outward. Lee could barely think through the thick arousal that spread through her body in waves of fire.

When Ray's mouth returned to hers, Lee found the strength to lift her arms and work Ray's sports bra up. Ray docilely raised her arms and allowed Lee to pull it off, and then brought her arms down around her shoulders so that the entire length of their torsos pressed together.

The sensation of Ray's skin against hers sent new tendrils of hunger snaking through her body.

When Ray stepped away again, Lee devoured her breasts with hungry eyes, her hands coming up to claim them, her fingers capturing the hardened nubs of her nipples. Ray closed her eyes and groaned, her hands sliding up Lee's arms. Her fingers tightened on Lee's shoulders as Lee rolled and pinched at her nipples the way that she knew aroused her most.

Finally, Ray reached down and took her hand. Wordlessly, they made their way to the bedroom where both women kicked off their shoes. Ray reached out to unfasten the buckle of Lee's belt. "It's been so lonely here without you."

"I was lonely too, but we don't have to be any more," Lee replied, watching as Ray's hands went to the button on her slacks. As Ray slid the fabric over her hips, Lee wondered if she had been this aroused the first time they had made love.

Now that she knew what Ray could do—what Ray *would* do—to her body, the thought of what was to come sent shockwaves of hunger through her chest and into her groin, so strong that for a moment she thought her knees would buckle. She moved to pull her underwear down, but Ray stopped her.

"Not yet," she whispered. "I just want to look at you."

Lee stepped out of her pants and stood for Ray's inspection. Ray studied her, and then reached out and lightly began to run her fingers over her skin, along the curve of her waist and hips, across her stomach, up her arms and across her torso, without touching her breasts. She seemed to be trying to memorize Lee's body. Finally, she dipped below the waistband of Lee's underwear at the hips and slowly pulled them down, gazing with undisguised hunger at what was revealed.

Once Lee was naked, Ray slid her arms around her waist, pivoted, and lowered her to the bed. She straightened and pulled her jeans and boxers off before kneeling between Lee's legs. She ran her hands across Lee's belly and down the fronts of her thighs, trailing her fingernails up the sensitive insides and brushing through her curly blonde hair. Lee jerked her hips upwards.

"You're so beautiful," Ray breathed.

Lee looked up at her, took in her dark tan and the white skin where she wore her shorts, the thick dark hair covering her center, the tautness of her belly, and the creamy white triangles that barely covered her nipples. Her full breasts hung tantalizingly with the dark rose nipples hardened and beckoning.

"You take my breath away," Lee whispered back. "I want to feel you."

Slowly, Ray leaned forward and lowered herself onto Lee's body. Her hips fit neatly between Lee's thighs, and she pressed against Lee's pubic bone with her own. Lee tilted her hips and reached down to cup Ray's bottom, pulling her more firmly against her.

Ray kissed her hotly, her fingers gripping Lee's hair not quite tightly enough to hurt. Lee responded with her hips, pressing up against Ray with a steady, slow motion. Ray's mouth moved down to her throat, trailing a line of fire with her tongue as she slid further down and captured a nipple in her mouth.

Lee's back arched and she let out a loud 'ah!' as Ray's lips closed on her nipple. Ray sucked it in, holding it lightly with her teeth as her tongue circled against it. She let it scrape through her teeth and between her lips before sucking it back in, harder this time. Lee knew she had never felt this desperate arousal, this need to have someone touch her, taste her, fill her and draw the orgasm from her with passionate energy. Her hunger for Ray transcended everything that had come before and threatened to wash her away with its power.

Ray's fingers claimed Lee's other breast, teasing the nipple as she rubbed across it with her palm, circling slowly against its hardness, her tongue now vibrating against the tip of the one she held in her mouth. Lee pulled her hands up Ray's back and pressed against the back of her head, feeding the nipple to her even as Ray sucked it in.

Ray trailed her tongue across to the other nipple, drawing it into her mouth as her hand moved down into the blonde thatch of Lee's triangle. She brushed her fingers across the hardness of Lee's clit, eliciting a jerk from her hips, and then slid down further. She insinuated one finger between Lee's lips, wetting it with the hot slickness of Lee's juices.

Lee groaned as she slowly drew her finger upwards, pressing with slightly more pressure against the hardened tip at the top of Lee's lips. She repeated the motion while her mouth continued to suck at Lee's nipple.

"God, please." Lee's voice sounded ragged to her ears. "Don't tease me."

Ray lifted her head and looked into her eyes. "I want to fuck you so hard," she said, her own voice betraying her desire.

"Yes." It was all Lee could manage, the word trailing into a hiss as Ray filled her with two fingers. She bent her head to Lee's breast again as she began to move firmly in and out of Lee's well. Lee bent her legs up and tilted her hips, gasping with pleasure when Ray added a third finger and began thrusting even harder.

Ray took her with a passionate fierceness that left Lee fighting for breath. She found herself urging Ray on, begging her to go faster, to go harder, to please make her come.

Ray complied with the first two, but kept her teetering on the edge for what seemed an eternity before sending her into a wailing free-fall of pleasure. The spasms seemed to engulf her entire body, shaking her to the core with their intensity.

Finally, Ray slowed her hand and brought her back to earth. Once she had removed her fingers, she slid up Lee's body and lay beside her, pulling her into her arms as she kissed her dry mouth with gentle, loving lips. It took several minutes for Lee to be able to speak, her body still trembling.

"You can't know how much I love you," she managed, her throat sore from screaming.

Ray smiled and kissed her nose. "I'm not sure why you do, but I sure am glad."

"No one has ever made me feel like this."

"And if I have a say, no one else will ever get the chance." Ray tightened her grip, pulling Lee closer against her. "I almost let you slip away once. It isn't a mistake I plan to make again."

They lay in silence for a while before Ray pressed her hips against Lee's thigh in a silent request. Lee turned to her and met her lips with a tenderness that hardened into a deep, hungry kiss, Lee's tongue dancing against Ray's, her lips claiming Ray's mouth with intense certainty. Lee rolled her onto her back and came on top of her, slipping between her thighs with her hips even as Ray bent her legs up.

She claimed one of Ray's breasts with her hand and the other with her mouth, her movements alternately fierce and tender. Ray groaned and rocked her hips upward. Lee bit against her nipple in the way she knew Ray liked best, drawing it up with her teeth and letting it scrape back out of her mouth before sucking it in again. Her hand rolled and twisted at the other nipple, until Ray was practically writhing beneath her. Ray's hands came to her shoulders and pressed her down her body.

Lee sat up so that she was kneeling between Ray's thighs. She slid her hand into Ray's wetness, her fingers dancing with practiced expertise in all the places that made Ray's hips jerk with pleasure. When Ray started making noises in the back of her throat, Lee went to slide into her.

"God, yes—"

Lee began to move in and out with her hand as the other began to circle against Ray's clit. As she looked down and saw the wetness covering her hand, she felt the need to do more to please Ray, something to bring her to a higher plane than she had ever gone to before.

She wasn't sure she was going to do it until she slid down the bed and burrowed between Ray's lips with her tongue. The taste was amazing, salty and thick, the juices slick against her tongue. *Oh my God, she tastes good.* She lapped upward, her tongue slipping off the tip of Ray's clit as though she were licking an ice cream cone.

This is what it's like. This is why Ray loves to taste me so much. All this time and I was missing the best part of making love to her. Lee's amazement shot through her with the bolts of intense arousal that tingled through her breasts. *I think I could do this all night.*

At first Ray went rigid, and then after a moment she relaxed back onto the mattress and spread her legs even wider, making a guttural noise of pleasure that drove Lee on to explore her with her mouth. She learned that sucking Ray's clit into her mouth and biting lightly against it made her groan in much the same way as doing the same thing to her nipple did, that filling her with her tongue made her plead for more.

She was amazed at the wetness that flowed from Ray's center, wetting her nose and chin as she tasted all of her, finally returning to her clit to make firm, deliberate strokes. Ray's hands came to the back of her head, holding her in place as her hips moved beneath her.

Lee heard her breathing grow more ragged, sensed the

tensing of her leg muscles, and took the orgasm from her with a delight she had never expected to feel from making love, relishing the knowledge that it was she who was making Ray cry out with such force, drawing every ounce of energy from her body with her mouth.

When it was over, Ray fell back limply against the bed, now trying to pull Lee up into her arms. Lee acquiesced and lay watching the irregular rise and fall of Ray's chest as she fought for breath with a sense of power at having reduced her to such a quivering mass. Finally, Ray turned her head and caught Lee's lips in a gentle kiss.

"Thank you," she whispered.

"My pleasure." Lee ran her hand up Ray's belly and smiled when she twitched. "You were right, it is amazing."

Ray groaned. "I don't think I've ever come that hard."

"I can't wait to do it to you again."

They lay in silence again for a while until Ray lifted her head and looked at the clock. "It's nine. You probably need to go."

Lee looked up at the ceiling feeling the satiation of her body and the awakening of new desire. "No. I'm thinking of calling off tomorrow morning. I have more important things to do."

Ray buried her face against Lee's shoulder and laughed. "I was thinking the same thing."

They turned to each other and began the dance again, stopping only when exhaustion overtook them and they fell asleep tangled in the sheets and each other's arms.

*   *   *

Hunger finally drove them out of bed at around noon the next day. They sat outside drinking tea and eating sandwiches and playing footsie under the table. Ray had woken to the scent of Lee's hair in her nose; the delicate scent of her hair and other things. Lee lay on her stomach with one arm thrown across Ray's chest and she woke as soon as Ray tried to move. They got up long enough call out of work and take care of their basic morning routines before returning to bed and each other's arms.

Ray couldn't remember a time when she had been happier.

240

Once she had spoken the words, the fullness of her love for Lee had come bursting through her walls like water through a dam; it washed over and overwhelmed her with its intensity, but it didn't scare her any longer. It was as though she had loved Lee all her life; she saw that she had loved her long before they became intimate. Lee had admitted the same thing to her and they had laughed about it.

"Where did your mind go? You're awfully quiet over there." Lee's voice, sultry and slow, broke into her thoughts and she shook herself and focused on her lover's face.

"I was thinking how much time I wasted trying not to love you."

Lee smiled softly. "It doesn't matter as long as you love me now."

"I do, with all my heart. I can't figure out why you picked me though. I'm just a blue collar working girl. I can't give you a Mercedes or a house on the river." Ray glanced away.

"If I was the type to fall in love with money I'd still be married." Lee's voice was stern and perhaps a little annoyed. "It was you I fell in love with, not your social status or credit limit."

Ray sighed. "I know. It's just hard to believe. It doesn't make me love you less." She tried to put the discomfort away and concentrate on the woman across from her.

"If you have any doubts, let me take you back to bed and see if I can erase them."

Ray laughed. "You can take me back to bed regardless."

"I intend to." Lee batted her eyelashes and looked coy. "I'm still getting the hang of that tongue thing."

"Anything to help you practice." Ray grinned at her.

"My heroine."

Ray grew serious and studied her. She had imagined Lee sitting there like this, had seen it once, and yet now that she knew she was in love she saw Lee in a whole new light. Lee was wearing a tank top and a pair of Ray's boxer shorts, her hair tousled. Her nipples were half hard, rising as small points through the fabric of the shirt. She looked supremely at home and Ray was struck anew with a sense that she had always been there and would always be there.

Lee's Awakening

This thought tugged at her. She had offered the spare room initially as a friend. When she had offered it again, that night when everything went to hell, she now realized she had meant it as so much more. But they hadn't spoken in a week and Lee's time was running out; Ray didn't know if she hadn't already found a new place to live.

"How has the house hunting gone?" she asked, trying to sound casual.

Lee rubbed her face. "Horrible. I took Louise three times and all she could do was nit-pick about not having marble bathroom tile or a riverfront view or a tennis court."

"I'm sorry."

"Why are you sorry? I'm the one who had to put up with her. I swear she's trying to engineer my reconciliation with Robert. And I've told her repeatedly there's no chance." Lee took a drink of her tea and looked irritated. "Some best friend she's turned into."

Ray shrugged. "Sometimes friends grow apart. You are hiding something pretty major from her."

"From her and half the people I know. I still haven't figured out how to handle that situation, thank you very much for reminding me."

Ray thought she was seriously annoyed until she saw the smile on Lee's face.

"Just take me to one of your club dances. That ought to take care of things."

Lee laughed outright. "If I had more nerve, I probably would. My mother would simply die."

"Lee ..." Ray hesitated, wondering if it was too soon to propose what she was thinking.

"Hmm?" Lee glanced up from her sandwich.

"I was wondering ... if maybe ... you'd move in here, with me." Ray tried not to blush.

Lee's face went blank for a moment. "I don't know, Ray. That's a pretty big step. I'm just getting used to having my independence."

Ray looked away. "Yeah, I guess it was jumping the gun."

"I didn't say that. I just said it's something I'd have to seriously think about."

Glad that she hadn't been rejected out of hand, Ray replied, "I wish you would. When I offered before, I really meant it; I just didn't realize it at the time."

"I promise, I will." Lee smiled gently at her. "Are we going out tonight, or do you want to stay in?"

Accepting the change in subject, Ray shrugged. "I was supposed to meet Jackie after work. I kind of ditched her night before last, so I really should go. I mean — we should go."

"Just because you love me doesn't mean you have to go everywhere with me. If you want to go out and pal around with Jackie by yourself, by all means do so." Lee shrugged as well. "I don't own you and I don't want to."

Ray didn't know how to react. She wondered if Lee was telling the truth, or if it was some attempt at gauging Ray's commitment to the relationship. Tentatively she said, "I'd rather you go with me."

Lee smiled. "I'm glad; I didn't want to spend tonight alone. But if you two have plans, I'll more than understand. Don't think you have to take me."

"You wouldn't mind?"

"I'll be honest; I'd be a little disappointed, with everything that's happened in the last twenty-four hours. But I'm not going to demand to go." Lee nibbled on a potato chip.

Ray studied her for a moment. "I'd really like you to go. I don't want to spend tonight alone either. But that's not the reason. I don't want to be apart from you for that long, not just yet. The time may come when I want to, but not right now."

"Okay, it's settled then." Lee finished her sandwich. "So what'll it be; swimming, wild sex in the hot tub, or seeing just how much further we can destroy the bed?"

Ray laughed. "I vote for bed. There's still a corner of the sheet in the right place."

Lee pushed her chair back and stood up. "Last one there has to remake it."

Ray stood also. They stared at each other for a moment and then bolted toward the door at the same time. They didn't make it to the bedroom, and Ray would later vow that she was much too old for sex on the living room floor, but at the time, it seemed the perfect thing to do.

*   *   *

Conversation all but stopped when Ray and Lee walked into the bar. Heads swiveled in their direction and after a moment's lull, the low buzz of conversation returned. Jackie, sitting next to Donna, gaped at the pair as they made their way to the bar. Ray graciously pulled out the one remaining barstool for Lee and then squeezed in between her and Jackie.

"I guess you two made up?" Jackie eyed the pair before exchanging glances with Donna.

Lee looked at Ray and smiled. "Yes, we made up."

"Thank God," Donna said firmly. "I was beginning to think I'd never see Stacy again for all the time she was spending at your place."

"I came to my senses," Ray told Jackie. "My head isn't as hard as I thought it was."

Joan walked over, gave them a grin that suggested she was expecting the reconciliation, and slapped two coasters down. Lee ordered a bourbon and water while Ray had her usual beer. Once the drinks had arrived, Jackie looked at Lee and cocked her head.

"You actually want to put up with this bitch?"

Lee laughed. "I suppose I should have my head examined, eh?"

"I have a feeling that's the only thing that isn't being examined at this point," Donna replied with a wry grin. "Knowing what I know about both of you."

"And what do you know about me?" Lee raised an eyebrow. Donna just laughed and after a moment, Lee did too.

"So what are your plans?" Jackie drained her beer and signaled for another. "Have you set a date yet?"

Ray stuck out her tongue. "I think making up is a pretty big first step. I don't want to worry about that sort of thing right now. It might give me a headache, don't you agree, Lee?"

Lee laughed again. "I still have to get divorced before I can worry about that."

Conversation died and they all looked at each other for a tense moment. Finally, Jackie broke the silence. "Did you make her crawl on her hands and knees, Lee?"

"No, but that's a tantalizing idea I should have thought of."

"Where's Stacy?" Ray looked uncomfortable all of a sudden.

Donna gestured with her hand. "Some idiotic training seminar. She might meet us later if it doesn't run over."

"I sure don't miss those," Lee said firmly. "What a waste of time and money."

Conversation turned to the ordinary and Lee spent two pleasant hours catching up, although Ray somehow seemed a little distant. After they left, Ray drove to the beach and they walked a little way away from the access and sank down at the foot of a sea wall. Both looked silently out over the ocean, barely illuminated by a new moon.

Finally, Lee spoke. "Did I say something tonight?"

"What?" Ray turned to her.

"I felt like you weren't all there. Was it something I said?"

Ray shifted in the sand and looked away. "Well, I suppose there was."

"What was it?" Lee turned so that she was facing Ray.

"You mentioned that you weren't divorced yet. It made me realize you really aren't really free, no matter what your feelings might be."

"Oh, for God's sake. You're kidding me right?" Ray shook her head. "Robert and I are separated. I'm not cheating on him." *Technically, I guess I am but ... what's a piece of paper without love or attraction?*

"I'll just feel better once that whole thing is over with."

Lee was silent for a long moment. "So will I. It isn't going to be a big problem, is it?"

Ray shook her head again. "No. It's just a wrinkle I hadn't looked at before. What if he finds out about us?"

"I'll deal with that when and if it happens." Lee leaned back on her hands and looked up at the stars. "Aren't they beautiful?"

Ray followed her gaze. "Yes. But not as beautiful as you."

Lee grinned and leaned over to kiss her on the nose. "Flattery will get you everywhere."

"I'd like nothing better than to make love to you right now."

"Despite my not being divorced?" Lee raised an eyebrow, not able to resist teasing.

"Actually, the thought of you cheating with me is kind of a turn-on." Lee wasn't certain in the darkness, but it looked like Ray was blushing. "Strange, isn't it?"

"I don't know, but don't get too fresh. Sand in uncomfortable places, remember?" Lee laughed.

Ray kissed her, a passionate but not demanding kiss. "All too well. I'll remember every moment of that day for the rest of my life."

Lee shifted and slid between her legs, leaning against her chest so that both of them faced the ocean. Ray put her arms around her and they listened to the waves breaking for a while. Finally, Lee looked over her shoulder into Ray's face.

"I like moments like this just as much as I like making love," she murmured. "It's moments like this that I know how much I love you."

Ray squeezed her. "It's moments like this that make me realize just how special you are."

Lee sighed and turned her head back to the ocean. "I'm glad you do love me."

"I love you so much it scares me," Ray responded. "But I'm willing to work through that fear, as long as you're there."

"If I were to move in, how would we work it?"

Ray considered her words. "Fifty-fifty, I guess."

Lee laughed. "I meant I like having my own space. You've already spread out into all the rooms in the house."

"I can empty one of them. We don't really need a guest room. There isn't anyone I'd want staying over as long as we're sleeping in the same bed. It might get noisy enough to be embarrassing." Ray made the sound that Lee had learned was her version of a giggle, a deep, gravelly version of one.

"I could put my furniture in storage, as long as I can have my computer and my books and a couple of special pieces."

Ray leaned forward and kissed her hair. "We can pile all

my stuff in the pasture and burn it, for all I care. I just can't imagine ever not waking up next to you again."

Lee slid forward and turned around onto her knees. "Do you really mean that?"

"Yes."

"You do realize our tastes are very different. I might tend to run over you."

Ray grinned. "I realize that. Your decorating taste is much superior to mine. By that, I mean that you have one. I'm a butch; my house could use a woman's touch. I smoke a lot of cigars and tend to leave beer bottles all over the place."

"I don't mind the cigars and you'd better pick the bottles up in the morning." Lee grinned back. "And I recycle."

"I can get used to that. I think we complement each other well." Ray leaned over and kissed her.

"I don't know how to mow a lawn."

"I love to," Ray told her. "So what are you saying, Lee? Are you saying yes?"

Lee gazed into her eyes, seeing the tentative hope in them. She wanted so much to say yes, but part of her was still shy about surrendering so much of her freedom. "I'm saying maybe."

Ray was obviously disappointed, but she smiled anyway. "Maybe I can convince you."

"You can always try."

When they got home, they had to shower to remove the sand from the most uncomfortable places. But Lee's mind was still not made up, and part of her found that unsettling.

XVI.

"You're actually moving in with Ray? The same Ray I met that morning at your condo?" Louise stared at Lee as though she had just sprouted a second head.

"Yes, that Ray. And I'm just thinking about it." Lee reached for her iced tea and wished Louise would keep her voice down. They were sitting on the outside patio of the grill at the club eating lunch. As usual, Louise was picking at a salad while Lee enjoyed something much more substantial.

"For the love of God, why?" Louise signaled for another glass of wine and turned an incredulous face to Lee.

Lee sighed. "It makes good financial sense. I don't know how long our assets are going to be tied up in this divorce and I don't want to go heavily into my savings. Besides, she and I get along very well."

"I think you're crazy." Louise poked at her salad. "You could easily afford another condo."

Lee decided that it might not have been a good idea to bring up her possible move at that particular time. Several women she knew were sitting around them and a couple had turned their heads and appeared to be listening to the conversation.

"It's my decision," she said calmly but firmly.

Louise shook her head. "Honestly, Lee. You realize people are going to talk."

"About what? You're the only one who knows Ray is a lesbian. And I would hope you aren't going around telling my friends that."

"Of course I'm not." Louise took a long swallow of her fresh glass of wine. "I wouldn't want anyone to know just how off your rocker you've gone."

Lee blew out her breath in irritation. "For the last time, I am not off my rocker. Why is it that everyone seems to think I've gone nuts?"

"Because of the way you're acting. Because we rarely see you around here. Because you haven't seen your parents in almost a month. Because you seem more interested in your lesbian friends than in us — in me," Louise finished, immediately looking as though she didn't mean to say it.

"I haven't seen my parents because every time I do, all they can talk about is Robert and reconciliation. I haven't been around here because I now work during the week. And as for my lesbian friends, they are friends first and lesbians second. And their sexuality is none of your or my business when it comes right down to it."

"Why is it I see you so rarely? Until today, I hadn't seen you for over a week." Louise shifted in her chair. "We seem to have drifted so far apart since this divorce started."

Lee studied her, wishing she could just come out and tell her that she was deliriously happy with Ray; that for once in her life she felt complete and happy. Not the false happiness of an expensive home and the 'right' friends but a real inner happiness that made it a joy to get up in the morning.

She realized that she was afraid to tell Louise, that if she were to admit her true sexuality Louise would recoil in horror. As annoyingly unsupportive as Louise had been since the divorce was filed, she was still a dear friend and Lee didn't want to lose that.

"Lee? Lee!" Louise's voice dragged her out of her thoughts. "Where did you go? You were staring into space."

"I was trying to figure out why we haven't spent a lot of time together," Lee replied lamely.

"And?"

Lee shifted uncomfortably in her chair. "I don't feel

249

completely at home here anymore. I don't like being the topic of gossip on the golf course."

"There's more gossip because you've vanished." Louise snorted. "People are beginning to wonder if you're having some kind of breakdown."

"Well, I'm not." Lee picked up her fork. She was determined to finish her meal before it got cold and Louise was distracting her.

"Hmph." Louise gave her a look that suggested she wasn't certain. After a pause, she spoke again. "Lee, I have to ask you something. I'm only asking as your best friend, and I'm not sure I want to know the answer, but I have to ask anyway. Have you gotten involved with this woman?"

Lee almost choked on the bite of food she had just taken. She covered her shock with a long drink of tea. "I'm not even going to dignify that with an answer," she replied, with more strength than she felt. It was the only answer she could come up that wasn't a lie and wasn't admitting the truth.

The relief was evident on Louise's face, telling Lee she was assuming the answer was no. "Thank God. I would hate to think someone had taken advantage of your confusion at the divorce, especially some lesbian."

"And you think I'm so confused and vulnerable because of the divorce that I couldn't make a rational decision on my own? If I was involved with Ray it would be my choice, not some seduction." Lee emphasized the word 'if' with a little too much strength for her own comfort.

"That isn't what I meant," Louise said quickly, though Lee knew it was exactly what she meant. "I just meant that you might not be thinking completely clearly."

Lee rolled her eyes and fought the urge to reach out and slap some sense into her best friend. "It has been over six months since Robert and I separated. Just how broken up do you think I am about it? I'm the one who filed for divorce, remember?"

Louise was silent for a moment. "I'm just not sure what I'd do if you were to get involved with a woman. It's so wrong."

Lee colored. "Why is it wrong? Love is love."

"Oh, you don't believe that any more than I do. It's one thing to be friends with a lesbian, but to completely approve of their relationships? Not even you are that understanding."

For just a moment, Lee thought she was going to explode. She forced herself to be calm as she responded, "I don't see anything wrong with a lesbian relationship. You're being very shallow, Louise."

Louise's next words convinced Lee that if she ever were to tell her about her involvement with Ray it would be the end of their friendship. "Well, I know I would never be friends with someone who sleeps with other women. It's disgusting."

Lee made a show of looking at her watch while counting to ten. She pushed her plate away and stood. "I forgot I have an appointment. Thanks for having lunch with me."

Louise looked a little confused, but nodded. "I wish we could do it more often."

"Me too," Lee lied, wanting nothing more than to escape from the woman she had thought understood her better than anyone else.

The realization that Louise was one of the most homophobic people Lee had ever met stung deep within her heart. She left the club and got into her car fighting the urge to speed out of the parking lot. Once she was on the public road, she forcibly relaxed the death grip she had on the steering wheel and hit the button on her Bluetooth to call Ray.

"What's up, sweetheart?" Lee could hear the wind behind Ray's voice. She and Jackie had gone fishing that morning and Lee surmised they were still there.

"I just left the club. I'm so furious I can hardly see straight."

Ray's tone changed. "You want me to come home? What happened?"

"Louise is an ass," Lee growled. "I never realized what a bitch she was until just now."

"I'll meet you at home." Ray said something away from the mouthpiece, to Jackie, Lee assumed. "We'll leave in a few minutes."

"Why don't I meet you there? I need something to relax me." Lee turned north toward High Bridge, the park beside the drawbridge that Ray favored for a fishing spot.

"Well, you know where we are. Would you bring another

twelve-pack of beer?"

"Of course." Lee saw a Quick Mart coming up and slowed down. "I'll be there in a few minutes."

As she climbed out of the car, she realized that she would rather be fishing with Ray than playing golf with Louise. Contemplating how complete the change in her life had been since Donna's birthday party, she bought the beer and a four-pack of wine coolers and headed back north to meet up with Ray.

*   *   *

Ray slammed her truck door and stormed into the house carrying what was left of the six-pack she had bought after leaving work. Lee looked up from a magazine as she stalked into the living room cracking open a can. For just a moment, Ray imagined that she was there because she lived there but then realized she'd let herself in with the key Ray had given her; they were supposed to go out that night and Lee was to be the designated driver.

"What's got you so riled up?"

Ray collapsed on the couch mindless of her dirty work clothes and took a long swallow of beer. "I got laid off."

Lee closed the magazine and turned to face her. "What?"

"The whole crew did. They say it's temporary, but they don't know how long we'll be out of work." Ray's face showed her anger clearly. "I'm so pissed off I could spit nails. This couldn't have happened at a worse time."

"Why do you say that?" Lee reached out and touched her hand. Ray welcomed the gesture, but it did nothing to calm her anger.

"I need a new roof. Do you have any idea how much that's going to cost me?"

Lee studied her for a moment. "Do you have to do it right now? Couldn't you wait until you get called back to work?"

"Not unless I want the entire garage ceiling to collapse on me. There are spots over the den that're starting to leak too." Ray stood up and paced toward the fireplace, trying to calm herself. "I'm beginning to think I'm in over my head with this house. Maybe I should sell it."

Lee made a noise. "I don't think you should. You seem so happy here."

"Well, right now I'm not happy." Ray drained half her beer and sat the can on the mantle. "The thought of sinking that much money into this place isn't sitting well with me."

Lee got up, walked over, and slid her arms around Ray's waist. "You're angry about work. Once you calm down some you'll realize everything will be okay."

"You do realize I'm covered in sweat and sawdust."

Lee pressed herself closer against Ray's body and sought out her lips. "You have no idea how much you turn me on when you come home from work," she whispered into Ray's ear a little while later.

"God, you make it hard to be angry." Ray tried not to smile and failed. She was still angry as hell, but Lee's nearness was quickly draining that emotion from her body.

Lee stepped back and kissed her on the nose. "Let's take a shower."

"I'm still pissed off, Lee. I'm not in the mood for fooling around." Ray rubbed her face. "Just let me clean up and cool off."

"Okay." Lee shrugged. "You do that and I'll put some dinner on. I went shopping for you today. When I'm not here you seem to think you can exist on ramen noodles and white bread." She had just gotten back from a four-day trip to New York with Louise and two of their friends. She hadn't wanted to go, but she had promised months ago, and Ray had waited impatiently for her return.

"And peanut butter. Don't forget the peanut butter."

Lee smacked her on the ass. "Go shower."

"Yes, Ma'am." Ray loped off toward the bathroom, pulling her t-shirt over her head as she went. The shower was hot and relaxing, and it gave Ray some time to think a little more rationally than she had been. By the time she got out, she had begun to formulate a possible answer to her work problems.

Lee looked up from the stove when Ray returned to the kitchen. "You look a little better." She lifted the lid on a pot and stirred its contents.

"What's for dinner?"

"Spaghetti with vodka sauce. I can throw some meatballs in if you like. I bought some frozen." Lee replaced the lid and turned to pull a beer out of the refrigerator. She handed it to Ray and then retrieved an open bottle of wine and topped off the glass next to the stove. "Garlic bread and a tossed salad. Cheesecake for dessert."

"Yum." Ray opened the beer and leaned against the counter. "What would you think if I started looking for another job?"

Lee studied her for a long moment. "That sounds like a good idea. You certainly seem miserable at this one."

"If they find out they won't call me back in. I'd be totally out of work."

Lee shrugged. "With your experience I can't imagine you having trouble finding another company."

Ray considered her words. "It's a risk. I don't like the idea of losing a job without having a new one, especially with the work that needs done here."

"I know how hard it is to dip into savings. I could ..." Lee trailed off and stared at the wall for a moment. "I could loan you the money."

Startled, it took Ray a moment to process her comment. She tried to pick her response carefully. "Thanks for the offer, but I don't want your money. I promised myself when we got involved that your finances would be your own. You have so much more money than I do, and I don't want you thinking I'm taking advantage of that."

Lee pursed her lips. "I don't think that. I was just trying to make it easier for you to make a decision."

"I didn't mean to piss you off."

Lee sighed and then shrugged. "I'm not pissed off. I just wish you would realize that I'm in this for the long haul, and that means I want to pull my fair share, which includes contributing to the house."

"Really, I appreciate your offering, but I'm used to doing things on my own. It's really hard for me to consider taking a loan from my girlfriend." Ray bit her lip. "It might be different if you lived here, but still, not that kind of money."

"I might be living here soon. I just need some time to make a decision." Lee studied her. "I guess I'm stepping over the line by offering. I know you're still getting used to this whole situation."

Ray closed her eyes for a moment, trying not to let the words hurt. "I don't look at us as a situation, Lee. You haven't moved in because you value your independence. Well I value mine as well, and taking money from you just doesn't feel right."

The two women looked at each other for a long silent moment, and then Lee sighed again. "I can't blame you for that." She turned and reached for the box of spaghetti that sat on the counter. "So, how many other companies are there for you to look at?"

"I don't know, five or six that are big enough for me to have a chance at getting in." Ray tipped her beer can and let the liquid slide down her throat. It tasted damn good, and she welcomed the taste after such an exasperating day.

"I know I'd hire you." Lee cocked her head and looked contemplative for a second. "Why not go out on your own?"

Ray laughed. "You're kidding, right? Do you realize what's involved in starting a company?" She pushed down the sadness that rose as she realized such a thing just wasn't possible.

"It was just an idea."

"It's not that it's a bad one," Ray responded quickly. "It's just a little unrealistic right now. Like you said, I shouldn't have too much trouble finding another company to work for."

Lee picked up her wine. "Then relax. Everything will work out for the best, I'm sure."

"Sit in the hot tub with me later?" Ray lifted her eyebrows and tried to look inviting.

"Depends on whether we'll just be sitting," Lee replied coyly. "Otherwise I might just go home and unpack."

Ray growled playfully. "I've got something for you to unpack."

"Then let's get dinner out of the way and discuss the issue further." Lee winked.

Feeling much less worried than she had when she came home, Ray grinned. "Deal."

After dinner, sitting in the hot tub, Lee made the last of her anger disappear in a rush of pleasure that surprised her with its intensity and later, as they nestled together in bed, Ray stared at the ceiling and thanked God that something as good as Lee had come into her life. To hell with work; she could find another job. Having Lee beside her made the risks seem unimportant.

*   *   *

Lee flipped through a magazine and waited for her attorney to come out of his office. She was slightly bored, having been sitting there for over half an hour. She had refused an offer of soda twice and was wishing she had brought something other than her divorce paperwork to read.

"Ms. Compton?"

Lee looked up into the eyes of one of the most beautiful women she had ever seen. She was tall, with chestnut brown hair that curled down her shoulders and eyes that seemed like they had been scooped up out of the bluest water in the Gulf of Mexico. After the initial shock of realizing she found the woman sexy, she recognized her from the club.

"Yes?" Lee found her throat dry.

"I'm Melissa Barnhart, Donald's associate? He was called into court unexpectedly and he asked me to go over the papers with you."

"Oh, okay. Please, call me Lee."

Melissa gave her a smile that sent a tiny shock through Lee's body and stepped back to allow Lee to stand. *What is going on? Why is this woman making me feel like this?* Lee followed her to her office and sat down in the chair Melissa gestured to, uncomfortably aware of the gold chain that glittered in the V of her blouse just above a pair of voluptuous breasts.

They discussed the papers that Donald Wilson had drawn up for her for a few minutes, and then Melissa met her eyes and gave her another secret smile. "Haven't I seen you somewhere before?" she asked.

Lee shook herself from a study of the lines of Melissa's lips. "Probably at the club; I've seen you there."

Melissa cocked her head and kept her gaze. "No, somewhere else I think." She ran her hand through her hair before flipping it back over her shoulder. Lee immediately noticed the small triangle-shaped earring she wore. It was a vibrant pink.

Oh my God, she's flirting with me. The realization sent a jolt of arousal through Lee's body. Immediately she felt both embarrassment and discomfort. She shouldn't be turned on by another woman; she was in love with Ray. "I can't imagine where," she said weakly.

Melissa was silent for a long moment as she studied Lee. Lee felt the uncomfortable tingling of her nipples heightening the longer Melissa looked at her. She averted her gaze and hoped she would go back to the paperwork.

"Do you do karaoke?"

The question was unexpected and Lee responded before thinking. "Sometimes."

"That's where I've seen you." Melissa's tone changed, dropping into a purr that sent a shiver through Lee even as she fought to get her body back under control.

She met Melissa's gaze again and realized with a start that she had seen her at Maddie's. The confirmation that she was a lesbian did nothing to assuage the growing heat in her stomach. *Get yourself under control, Lee.* She swallowed and looked away again.

"I think I've seen you there too," she managed to choke out.

Melissa made a noise and grinned. "So we both know where, then."

"Yes."

"No wonder you want a divorce." Melissa glanced at the papers in front of her. "Too bad I couldn't take this case over from Donald. I'd enjoy working with you on it."

"Oh." Lee swallowed hard. No matter how hard she tried, she couldn't seem to shut off the pulsing waves of hunger that washed over her. She felt guilty about it, but she couldn't deny it.

She remembered Ray telling her that she might regret not experiencing the diversity of women that were out there and this moment seemed to be one of those times, though her response was entirely physical.

"Maybe we could talk about it over dinner?" Melissa's voice dropped back into the same purr.

Lee's face flamed. "I—I'm w—with someone," she stuttered.

Melissa's expression never changed. "That's too bad. Is it serious?"

"Yes." The question finally allowed Lee to get herself back under control. It was serious, and no matter how much she might find her body lusting after the woman across the desk from her, it was Ray who held her heart.

"Mmm. I'd like to meet her. She must be something."

"She is." Lee breathed in deeply and blew back out. "She does karaoke too."

Melissa cocked her head. "Then I might know her. What's her name?"

"Ray Elliot." Lee watched the expressions sort across Melissa's face, settling finally into a look that told Lee she knew Ray's reputation well. It suggested she might even know it firsthand. The thought was disquieting and Lee pushed it away.

"Well then, I'll have to congratulate Ray the next time I see her." Her voice told Lee that she held out little hope for the relationship lasting and that it pleased her. Lee's irritation flared. *How dare she make an assumption like that?*

"Can we get back to the paperwork?" Her voice was controlled, and she saw that Melissa had caught the tone in it. She was immediately professional again.

Half an hour later Lee was able to make her escape. As she sat in her car, she pondered Melissa and how she had thrown her into such a state as she had. When Lee left, Melissa held her hand for a few moments longer than Lee thought necessary for a handshake, her eyes suggesting that she was as taken with Lee as Lee was with her; at least, as physically taken as Lee was.

As hard as she tried to ignore it, she knew that sitting across the desk from Melissa had her turned on. She'd been flirted with at the bar plenty of times in the past months, but no one had caused a reaction like this.

Lee shook herself. *Of course, a beautiful woman is going to turn me on, especially when she starts flirting with me. It had to happen eventually. I certainly don't have to do anything about it.* The fact that she had even thought the last part made her very uncomfortable. She was in love with Ray. She had been in love with Ray for quite some time, and Ray loved her. They had a fabulous sex life and there was absolutely no reason for her to doubt that their relationship would last. But if, for some reason it didn't, Melissa was just the sort of woman Lee knew she could find very interesting. *Don't even think it. You're an idiot for even entertaining the thought of Ray leaving.*

Then again, Melissa had seemed more than a little forward, and her reaction to hearing that Ray was her lover suggested she had no qualms about continuing to flirt seriously with a woman even if she was unavailable. This hadn't been the joking flirtation that Lee and her friends engaged in at volleyball; this was a serious, intentional come on. And Lee was ashamed of herself for not immediately finding it totally inappropriate.

She finally put the car in gear. She needed some time alone to deal with what had happened and her reaction to it. She certainly could never tell Ray about it; she could only imagine how she'd respond, and the thought of pissing Ray off that seriously wasn't a pleasant one.

Lee blew out her breath; if Melissa could make her feel this way, what would she do when another woman did? Would she eventually want to taste the lips of someone other than Ray? She couldn't imagine that her love for Ray would ever fade enough to consider leaving, but the thoughts persisted. There were too many hard questions. Lee tried to clear her mind and headed for home.

* * *

"Good morning, sleepyhead."

Lee opened her eyes fully to find Ray leaning against the doorway with a bottle of champagne in one hand and a pair of flutes by the stems in the other. She had been drowsing for a while and wondered how long Ray had been standing there waiting for her to awake enough to talk to.

"Morning." She yawned. "What time is it?"

"Breakfast time." Ray grinned. "Happy birthday."

Lee groaned. "Thirty. I can't believe it."

"Wait 'til you're staring forty in the face." Ray laughed. "Have some champagne." She walked toward the bed and put the glasses down on the bedside table. She poured a glass and handed it to Lee, who took it gratefully.

"This sure beats the last few years. I spent last year alone and the year before that Robert got up early to play golf. I didn't see him until two o'clock and then he got called to the hospital."

Ray made a face. "Seems time to actually celebrate." She poured herself a glass and crawled into bed beside Lee, planting a kiss on her lips as she went.

"You really are a romantic, you know that?" Lee smiled and sipped the champagne. "No orange juice?"

"Don't tell anyone I'm a romantic. I don't want to ruin my image. And no, no orange juice. Today you get the best straight up." Ray tipped her glass back and took a not-so-tiny swallow.

Lee glanced over at the bottle sitting on the table next to her and saw the green label. "You bought Dom?" She felt a pang of guilt that Ray had spent so much money.

"You think I'd buy the cheap stuff? It isn't every day you hit thirty. Besides, what better way to spend my winnings?"

Ray's third place finish in the karaoke contest had netted her seven hundred dollars. She swore it was the love song she had chosen that had tipped the scales in her favor, and was insistent on spending it on Lee, despite Lee's equal insistence that Ray splurge on something for herself. Obviously, Ray had gotten her way.

Lee laughed. "Knowing you, there's caviar for the eggs."

Ray looked innocent. "Isn't the Dom enough for you?"

Her face told Lee that she was right. She shook her head and smiled. "You can't lie for shit."

"You do like them poached, right?" Ray reached out a hand and trailed her fingers up Lee's stomach. As always, Lee felt a tingling in her nipples.

"After all this time you can't remember how I like my eggs? I'm shocked."

Ray stuck out her tongue. "Just for that you don't get your present."

"I promise I'll be a good girl." Lee grinned.

After a glass of champagne, Ray got up and left the room, returning with a bed tray. Lee had to laugh when she sat it down; there was enough food on it for two people. "I hope you're hungry."

Lee looked at the plate. Ray had made poached eggs, which were indeed topped with caviar, toast that looked like sourdough, bacon *and* sausage, and a bowl of grits with butter melting on top. There was a tall glass of orange juice and a cup of black coffee. A small cup held strawberry jelly, Lee's favorite.

"My God, do you really think I can eat all this? Where's your plate?"

Ray smiled. "I ate already. This is your morning. I intend to wait on you hand and foot."

Lee picked up her knife and fork. "You spoil me."

"That's the idea," Ray replied, sitting on the end of the bed. "We can't be together tonight, so I made breakfast special."

Lee groaned. "You had to remind me about tonight." She was to have her annual dinner at the club with her parents, her brother, and his wife, and she was looking forward to it about as much as she would a root canal.

"Sorry. Just forget about it. For now it's just you and me and a bottle of champagne."

"And caviar. Don't forget that." Lee smiled and cut into her egg.

"There's more. I didn't know how much you'd want this early." Ray reclined across the foot of the bed, leaning on her elbow.

"All of it, of course. I'll share, if you like." She batted her

261

eyelashes and Ray laughed.

"If you insist."

They continued to banter back and forth while Lee ate. Once she was done and Ray had cleared the tray away, Lee welcomed her back into bed with a kiss.

"Now, if you're waiting on me hand and foot, I know what I want next." She grinned.

Ray rolled over and put one hand on each side of her waist, looking down into her face. "And what is that?"

For an answer, Lee wrapped her arms around Ray's shoulders and pulled her down. There was a mutual groan as their bodies met, their lips finding each other's in a kiss at once familiar and new. Their tongues met and danced together as their hips began to move against one another's.

Lee spread her legs and allowed Ray to nestle in between, her hands sliding down her body to run across the small of her back and then down the cheeks of her ass. Ray pressed forward against her and Lee made a sound deep in her throat.

Ray lifted away, supporting her weight on her forearms. Her eyes searched Lee's as a secret smile wreathed her lips. When Lee opened her mouth to speak, Ray bent her head and captured her mouth.

"Don't talk," she whispered when she lifted her head. Her hips moved with excruciating slowness against Lee's center as she kissed her again.

As deliberate as Ray's movements were, Lee was still frozen beneath her, feeling the buzzing of energy growing within her with each gentle thrust. Ray arched her back and captured a nipple between her teeth, drawing it into her mouth and suckling against it with the same slow rhythm as her hips. Her hands caressed Lee's sides and arms, stopping her each time she tried to lift them. She switched nipples and covered the wet one with a hand, massaging it gently.

Lee thought she was going to die if Ray didn't touch her soon, but she didn't dare speak for fear of breaking the spell of Ray's movements. Finally, after what felt like an eternity, Ray slid a hand between their bodies and wet her fingers with Lee's arousal. With the same deliberate slowness, she worked her middle finger between Lee's lips and found the source of the wetness, making long slow strokes between center and clit. Lee lifted her hips against Ray's fingers, trying not to groan with pleasure.

Ray slid her fingers down and pressed two inside Lee's heat. Her in and out motion was mirrored by the thrusting of her hips, pressing Lee against the mattress. Slowly, she increased the speed of her movements and Lee lifted her hips against her hand, certain she was going to explode at any moment.

"Don't scream," Ray instructed as her hand reached a rhythm that Lee knew would push her over the edge in minutes. Lee bent her knees up and allowed Ray to fill her fully, and gave herself to the sensations that spiraled out through her body with greater intensity than she had ever experienced when she finally came.

She barely had time to come down from the orgasm before Ray was sliding down her body, spreading her lips with her fingers and seeking out her clit with her tongue. Her hands slid under Lee's legs and wrapped around her, her fingers now pressing against the sensitive skin of her inner thighs as she lapped slowly at Lee's hardened bud, flicking at it at the end of each stroke. Lee gasped each time, and Ray finally made a sound that was obviously telling her to stop. She swallowed her groans as Ray continued to move against her, finally sucking her clit into her mouth and vibrating her tongue against it. Her hand slid upward and captured Lee's nipple, and she drew an even stronger orgasm from her body that left Lee shaking all over.

When it was over, Ray climbed beside her and took her in her arms. Lee buried her face against her neck and fought for breath. Ray held her until she could move again, then pulled back and looked down into her face.

"Oh. My. God." Lee stared up at her in amazement.

Ray smiled softly. "Did you like that?"

"Oh my God," Lee repeated. She moved her hands to find Ray's nipples, but Ray stopped her.

"Not yet. Let's just lay here for a little while."

They lay in silence for several minutes until finally Lee looked over into Ray's face and saw to her surprise that there seemed to be tears in Ray's eyes. "Are you ok?" she asked in concern.

Ray blinked. "Yeah. I'm fine. I haven't done it like that in a while. I forgot how powerful it is."

"Powerful is one word for it." Lee reached up to caress Ray's cheek. "Thank you for sharing it with me."

"My pleasure," Ray responded distantly. Then she shook herself and gave Lee a familiar grin. "Now, shall I give you an excuse to practice your screaming?"

"What about you?"

Ray rolled on top of her. "There'll be plenty of time for me later."

Lee's response was lost in the passionate kiss that Ray gave her.

XVII.

Lee and Ray had another bottle of champagne at Lee's condo later that day while Lee tried to catch up on all the messages she had received wishing her a happy thirtieth. She started a load of laundry, stripping the clothes she had on and throwing Ray's in as well. They walked around the condo naked, making lewd comments about one another and teasingly touching.

Finally, all the flirting came to a head as Lee pushed Ray down onto the couch and spread her legs, kneeling between her thighs with her face buried deep against Ray's folds while Ray lifted against her and groaned words that even a lover couldn't quite understand.

When they were done, they lay together on the couch, caressing and touching with familiar comfort.

"What a great birthday," Lee finally said. "Even dinner with my parents can't ruin this day."

Ray kissed her on the nose. "You deserve a great birthday."

Just as Lee was about to respond, the doorbell rang. "What the hell ...?" Lee stared at the door, trying to figure out who would be coming over at two in the afternoon.

"Don't answer it. They'll go away." Ray ran her fingers up Lee's back.

"You think I'm going to? We're both buck-ass naked."

Ray laughed. "It certainly would give whoever it is a shock."

Lee's Awakening

The doorbell rang again, this time for several seconds as though someone were holding the button down. Irritated, Lee sat up. "Who the hell could it be?"

Before Ray could answer, a voice called through the door. "Lee? Lee, open the door. I know you're in there, I saw your car."

"Oh my God, it's Louise." Lee's eyes widened as she looked down at Ray. "She won't go away until I answer her."

They flew up and dashed to the laundry room. The load of clothes was only half-dry. Ray gave her a panicked look. "I don't think I have anything over here."

"You can wear a pair of my jeans. I have one of your t-shirts somewhere." Feeling panic sinking in, Lee pushed into the bedroom and rummaged frantically through her dresser. The doorbell kept ringing and Louise kept shouting, sounding angrier and angrier.

Finally dressed, Lee went to answer it while Ray hid in the bedroom. Louise pushed past her into the condo with an exasperated look on her face.

"It's about damned time. Where have you been?"

"I was asleep," Lee lied, avoiding kissing Louise's cheek as she realized her face was still covered with Ray's scent.

"At two in the afternoon on your birthday? That might explain why you weren't here last night or this morning." Louise glared at her. "Did you forget I always take you to breakfast on your birthday? We've only been doing it for ten years."

Lee realized she had indeed forgotten in the passion of the previous night. "I ... ah—" she cast around for an excuse and failed. "I had a little too much to drink last night." A moment later, she added, "How do you know I wasn't here?"

"Other than the six phone calls you didn't answer and the fact that your car wasn't here at eleven?" Louise crossed her arms. "What's going on, Lee?"

"Why were you here at eleven?" Lee drew her eyebrows together.

"I drove by after the play." She didn't say why she had driven by, just gave Lee a stern look. "So what's the deal?"

"I was ... busy."

Louise snorted. "With who?"

"That's none of your business," Lee replied with more firmness than she felt. Her head was spinning. This was threatening to get out of control very quickly. "As long as you're here, do you want something to drink?"

"A glass of wine would be nice." Louise walked over to the sliding glass doors and looked out over the river while Lee went to the kitchen for a pair of wine glasses. "Who is he?"

Startled by the question, Lee spilled wine across the countertop. Hoping Louise wouldn't notice, she finished pouring and rejoined her friend, handing her the glass.

"There is no he," she answered, weakly but truthfully.

"Well, someone obviously kept you out all night. Did you have fun?"

Lee swallowed hard. "Yes, I had fun. And it's still none of your business."

"Robert sent you flowers. They must be with one of your neighbors. I thought it very sweet of him, considering." Louise took a sip of her wine and stared back out the window.

"I don't want him sending me flowers," Lee growled. "I want him to realize it's over."

Louise gave her an odd look. "So it's really over?"

"My God; I've been saying that for months."

"I never really believed you." Louise glanced away. "I thought you'd change your mind."

Lee rolled her eyes. "Trust me, I won't change my mind."

Louise turned and walked to the couch. Lee held her breath, hoping no signs of what had happened there just half an hour before remained. Louise sank down and put her glass on the coffee table. Lee realized that the two champagne flutes were still sitting there. Louise looked at them and then looked at her.

"What's the real reason it took you so long to answer the door?"

For a moment, Lee wished Ray could just climb out the window; on the second floor that was hardly practical and besides, she'd never do it. Lee didn't really want her to, but she didn't like the alternative any better. "I was getting dressed," she said quietly.

Louise made a noise and stared at the ceiling for a minute.

"It doesn't take five minutes to put on a pair of jeans and a blouse, Lee. You aren't even wearing a bra."

Guiltily, Lee realized that in the rush, she'd forgotten to put one on. "You woke me up."

Louise stared directly at her. "Bullshit."

"What, you think I have a man hiding in my bedroom? Be serious."

"To be honest, I don't know who to think is in your bedroom." Louise kept staring at her, unblinking. "I haven't been able to guess who was in your bedroom in quite some time."

Lee's knees went weak. *She can't possibly have figured it out.* "What do you mean?"

"Not wanting to spend time at the club I can almost see. But spending all your time with a group of lesbians and ignoring everyone else—even your own family—is kind of hard to explain away. I want the truth, Lee. Who's in the bedroom?" Louise crossed her arms and leaned back against the couch.

"No one." Lee's voice sounded weak even to her own ears.

Louise stood up. "If you won't tell me, I'll look for myself."

"Don't you dare!" Lee's anger flared. "You have no right to go snooping around my house. This isn't any of your business."

"When my best friend would rather spend time with someone like Ray than with me, I have to assume there's a reason for it. And I'm not talking about making new friends." Louise took a step toward the bedroom. "Who is it?"

Lee's anger exploded. "Do you really want to know? Do you really want an honest answer to that question? Are you ready to hear it?"

Louise looked at her with a flat expression. "I'm pretty sure I already know the answer. I just want to hear it from you."

Lee's voice shook as she answered, not from fear but from anger. "I'm a lesbian. Is that what you want to hear?" She raised her voice. "Ray, come out here." The bedroom door opened and Ray slowly stepped into the living room, looking very nervous. "There. That's who was in my bedroom, Louise. She's been in my bedroom for months. And it's better with her than it ever was with Robert."

Louise's face showed shock and Lee realized she'd been

fishing, that she hadn't been at all sure of the answer. It took her friend almost a minute to respond. "I can't believe it." Her voice wavered. "I didn't think it was true."

"Well, it is true, and if you tell a soul I'll never forgive you, Louise. No one needs to know my personal business."

Louise returned to the couch and sank down, obviously still in shock. "You lied to me."

"I never lied. I let you believe what you wanted from what I said." Lee walked over and slid her arm around Ray's waist. "I'm happy. I feel complete. That's all that should matter."

"It most certainly isn't all that matters." Louise was getting over her shock obviously, and her voice grew stronger as she spoke. "How long have you known this? How long have you been living a lie? I suppose James was just a cover so no one would get suspicious. I suppose this is the real reason for the divorce."

Lee blew out her breath violently. "No, it isn't. It confirmed it, but it didn't cause it."

"I never would have thought … I thought I knew you."

"People change, Louise. People grow. I've found out something that lets me feel good about myself. What's wrong with that?"

Louise stood, the lines of her body mirroring her words. "It's disgusting. How could you—it's repulsive."

"It's not disgusting. It's perfectly normal. I haven't changed. I'm still the same person I was a year ago." Lee knew that Louise's mind was still spinning, but that she was regaining her self-control. She was starting to act the way she had acted during their last conversation. She knew what was coming even before Louise spoke.

"It's disgusting," Louise repeated. "I can only imagine how your parents would react. And you have the nerve to play tennis at the club and act like you're one of us, when in fact you're anything but."

"You think I'm the only lesbian who belongs to the club? You're deluding yourself if you think I am." Lee raised her voice. "And if you tell my parents I'll never forgive you."

"You think I want to be the one to break their hearts? My God, I thought you were my friend."

"I *am* your friend, Louise." Lee started to say more, but Louise picked up her purse.

"Not anymore. You just keep to your perverted friends and stay away from me. I'll be civil, but don't expect me to be more than that." She started toward the door.

"Louise, don't do this."

Her hand on the doorknob, Louise looked back at her. "I'm not the one who should be sorry, Lee." With that, she was gone, the door slamming behind her.

Lee and Ray stood there for the space of several minutes just staring at the door. Finally, Ray turned to her. "That went real well."

Lee strode to the couch and picked up her wine glass. After a healthy swallow, she let out a loud growl. "God damn it! Why did she have to be so nosy?"

Ray sighed and ran a hand through her hair. "Coming out is usually not pleasant. That was actually fairly mild."

Lee collapsed onto the couch. "Oh my God. She's going to tell everyone."

"Maybe not. Something tells me she doesn't want her name associated with the L-word."

"This is ridiculous. We've been best friends for twenty years. How can she just turn her back like that?" Lee ran her hand across her face. "I never thought she was that shallow."

Ray joined her, squeezing her leg as she sat down. "It's possible she'll come around once she's had time to adjust to the idea."

Lee grunted. "That's about as likely as me getting back with Robert. Once she makes up her mind, she doesn't change it."

"I'm sorry."

Lee turned and looked at her, drawing her eyebrows together. "For what?"

"For what just happened. I'm not sorry about you being a lesbian. I'm sorry that you have to go through this. It isn't going to get any easier until everyone knows. I was just hoping your friends would figure it out gradually. People react better that way." Ray leaned over and kissed her softly. "And I'm sorry it happened on your birthday. Is there anything I can do?"

"Just hold me. Hold me tight and tell me it will be ok." Lee leaned against her, drawing comfort from her heat and her closeness.

"It will be ok, Lee. Eventually, it will be ok." Ray enveloped her in her arms and buried her face in her hair. Lee sagged and allowed Ray to hold her up.

She realized she didn't even want to cry about losing Louise as a friend. She was so angry at Louise's reaction that she wanted nothing more than to walk away with her head held high, knowing that it was Louise who was losing out. And that's what she intended to do.

*   *   *

Ray sat at the bar with Jackie nursing a Jack Daniels and coke, wondering how Lee's dinner was going. The bar was filling up and Callie was setting up her karaoke equipment. Ray wanted to sing, but it was preferable to spend the evening with Lee instead.

"Things seem to be going well." Jackie's voice broke into her thoughts.

"For the most part," Ray responded. "She came out to her friend Louise today. That was an unpleasant experience."

Jackie grimaced. "On her birthday? Ouch. Why did she do that?"

"Louise forced the issue. I would have given anything for it not to have happened that way, but it did and now she's suffering through dinner with her parents on top of it."

"Hell of a way to spend your thirtieth birthday." Jackie shook her head and picked up her drink. "I don't remember mine too well, but at least I had a good time."

Ray grinned. "Well, she had a good time this morning. I spoiled her rotten."

"There you go, acting like you're smitten again. I swear you two are positively disgusting sometimes; you make me want to tell you to get a room every time I see you." Jackie laughed.

The conversation continued for a while longer, until someone came up behind Ray and ordered a drink.

"Long time no see, Ray."

Ray turned to see Melissa Barnhart standing just behind her. With an inward groan, she forced a smile. "Hi, Mel."

Melissa returned the smile. "No one's called me that in a while. I hear you have a new girlfriend."

Remembering how their relationship had ended, Ray was instantly on guard. "Yes. You probably don't know her."

"Lee Compton. She's a client at my firm. She says it's serious; I suppose you'll be moving on soon, knowing that. It's too bad; she's a good looking woman."

"It is serious," Ray growled.

Melissa's face suggested she didn't believe her. "Well, congratulations then. She was in my office the other day; she's very friendly, isn't she?"

"She can be," Ray replied cautiously.

Melissa's reputation was slightly different from Ray's. She had moved in on more than one woman in a committed relationship, and her looks and sensuality usually elicited more than a casual response from women she'd decided she liked.

She'd broken up more than one relationship and cheated with God knew how many other women, and Ray was worried that she'd set her sights on Lee; knowing that Lee had never been with anyone but her made her worry even more.

"I thought her attorney was a man. Donald something or other."

Melissa shrugged. "I might be taking it over. Donald is very busy with a criminal case right now."

"Keep your hands to yourself," Ray warned.

Melissa blinked innocently. "I can't imagine what you mean."

"I mean that I know you. You won't get anywhere with Lee, so don't even try."

"I won't. It's not my fault if women decide I'm better than their girlfriends. Knowing you, if she's really that committed I can't imagine that would be the case with Lee." Melissa gave her a smile.

Ray didn't trust her for one minute, but she knew she was telling the technical truth. That's how Melissa had avoided getting the crap beat out of her by the angry partner of someone she'd lured away. They always admitted they'd made the first move. Ray wasn't sure how she did it, but that's the way it was. It made her feel better knowing that Lee's commitment was strong enough to survive what Ray had done to her; Melissa wasn't really much of a threat considering that.

"She's that committed," Ray affirmed. "And she's not an idiot."

"That's obvious. I'm honestly glad for you, Ray. It's nice to see you settling down."

You mean because it leaves you more women to seduce. Ray knew how Melissa operated. It had been a mutual seduction between them, but it hadn't lasted long. Melissa apparently didn't know the word monogamy, and Ray wasn't about to continue the relationship for more than a couple of weeks. "Thanks."

"Will Lee be here tonight?"

"I doubt it. It's her birthday and she's at dinner with her parents."

Melissa's face showed disappointment. "Too bad. Are you singing tonight?"

"No. I plan on heading home soon; Lee should be finishing up at the club." Ray couldn't resist grinning suggestively, just to see the annoyance on Melissa's face. She didn't like failing when she wanted a woman, and Ray knew she didn't have a chance with Lee.

Melissa didn't look as annoyed as Ray expected. "I'm sure you have a wonderful birthday present for her. Well then, I'll leave you to finish your drink. Nice to see you. You too, Jackie."

Jackie just grunted and narrowed her eyes at her. Not looking offended in the least, Melissa picked up her drink and vanished into the crowd.

"What the hell was *that* all about?" Jackie looked after her with her eyebrows drawn together.

"Melissa being Melissa." Ray shrugged. "I'm sure knowing Lee is with me makes her an attractive target. But I'm not particularly worried about it." She was, in fact, a little worried about it. She'd been worried for some time that Lee might be curious about other women.

She didn't think she'd cheat intentionally, but she might get caught up in something she wasn't expecting if Melissa started working her charms. If Melissa could get to first base with her, it would mean that Lee wasn't as certain that their relationship would last as Ray hoped she was.

The thought that Lee even might be tempted by another woman didn't sit well with her. She trusted Lee, but she *was* the only woman Lee had been with. She would have to warn her about Melissa; forewarned was forearmed.

"Don't be worried. Lee is so unbelievably in love with you it's disgusting."

Ray forced a laugh and picked up her drink. "I almost wish Melissa would try. It would be fun to see her totally rejected for a change."

"Melissa only picks women she knows are wavering. She may be a jerk, but most relationships she busts up were on their last breaths anyway." Jackie shrugged. "I think she was just trying to get a rise out of you."

Ray sought Melissa out through the crowd. She was sitting at a table with another woman, leaning in with very suggestive body language. Melissa really was no threat, and Ray felt bad for thinking she might be. She took a long swallow of her drink.

"To hell with her."

Jackie raised her glass. "Here's to that."

As they drank, the inkling of a doubt raised itself once more in Ray's mind. With a growl, she pushed Melissa from her thoughts and concentrated on how she and Lee would spend the rest of her birthday; knowing Lee's passion, she would quickly erase any doubts.

*   *   *

Lee escaped from her parents as soon as possible after dinner. Even on her birthday, the topic of discussion had included Robert—although Lee's recent distance was also brought up. As she was leaving she phoned Ray, who agreed to meet her at Maddie's for a few drinks.

When she walked into the bar, Ray was sitting at a table with Jackie, Jackie's current paramour, Stacy and Donna. Lee went to the bar and ordered a drink before joining them.

"I hope it's OK," Ray said. "They were all here so I thought we could do a little party for you tonight, to help cleanse you of parent germs."

Lee laughed. "That sounds like a great idea. As usual, all they wanted to talk about was Robert and how I seem to have dropped off the face of the planet. I wish they'd get a clue that I'm over the country club scene."

"Well, we'll help you forget it." Stacy shot her a wry grin. "It's tradition around here for everyone to buy you a shot of tequila."

"Oh—God, no." Lee blushed and looked helplessly at Ray, hoping she could communicate her problem without Ray bringing it up verbally. "Tequila is not the best drink for me. Can't we make it something else?"

"I don't know," Ray replied. "I kind of like the idea of how you act after a few."

Lee stuck out her tongue. "I don't think you'd like it if it happened in public."

"Oh. Then we can do something else." Ray thought quickly; she certainly would *not* like that to happen in public. "How about Goldschlager?"

"Hmmm. How many do I have to do?"

"Five." Ray shrugged. "That or butterscotch schnapps. I know you like that."

Lee considered her options. "I think I'll take the schnapps. Five shots of Goldschlager seems like it won't feel good tomorrow morning."

Ray grinned. "Alrighty then. Schnapps it is."

An hour and a half later, after the fifth shot and a rum and Coke, Lee was starting to feel several shades past tipsy. She finally got up to use the restroom, realizing she was sliding dangerously close to being way too drunk for what she'd hoped to end her evening with. She checked her watch; ten-thirty. It was about time to go home.

As she came back out of the bathroom, she ran into Melissa Barnhart. Melissa gave her a winning grin.

"Well, surprise to see you here," she said in the purring voice that had made Lee so weak in the knees in her office. "I hear it's your birthday."

"Yes." The same tingling attraction that Lee had felt before started to rise through her body, heightened by the amount of alcohol she had consumed.

She went to move past Melissa, wanting to put distance between them. Ray had mentioned Melissa's presence and warned her to beware of her flirting. Lee felt guilty about not mentioning her reaction to Melissa earlier in the week, but she thought it was neither the time nor place to discuss it, and she had not expected to meet up with her alone.

"Donald is very busy with a criminal case right now; I may be taking over the details of yours." Melissa studied her from under her eyelids, her smile turning secretive in an instant.

Lee's nerves jangled with the energy that the smile sent through her. *Damn it, stop! This woman is nothing but trouble.* "Well, that's nice," she managed, wanting nothing more than to decline the change in attorneys.

Melissa took a step forward, and Lee took a step back. Melissa's smile grew. "I see that Ray has said something to you about me. She does get jealous easily."

"What would she have to be jealous about?" Lee queried, hoping Melissa hadn't noticed how she had affected Lee at their first meeting and mentioned it to Ray.

Melissa stepped forward again and Lee again stepped back, feeling the wall behind her; Melissa had her trapped and the only way out of the situation was to push past her. Lee started to do so, but Melissa wouldn't move.

"I know you found me interesting the other day. I could see it in your eyes. You know I find you interesting."

A blush raced up Lee's face, the burning heat of it only deepening her concern about how the situation was going. *She's going to get the wrong idea ...* "And you know I'm with Ray."

Melissa shrugged. "She's your first, isn't she?"

"Yes." Lee swallowed. "And she's going to be my last."

"Really." Melissa laughed, a sound that heightened Lee's nervousness. "I don't know many women who can resist finding out what else is available, eventually."

Despite her growing concern that Melissa was drunk, she

realized that she still hadn't forcibly pushed past her and a sense of dangerous curiosity persisted. "I don't need to. I have everything I want already. I really should get back to the table."

Melissa put one hand on the wall next to Lee's shoulder, blocking her escape. "Not until I wish you a happy birthday."

As she realized just *how* drunk Melissa really was, the brunette stepped forward and pressed Lee into the wall with her body, her mouth seeking out Lee's in a surprisingly sensual kiss.

Lee's mind froze along with her body and she closed her eyes, but out of shock not hunger. Melissa's mouth moved against hers, her tongue pushing its way past her lips and claiming her.

Oh my God, what do I do now?

Ray glanced in the direction of the bathroom and turned to Stacy. "She's been in there an awfully long time. I'd better go check and make sure she isn't sick."

"I'll go with you." Jackie stood up. "I need to pee anyway."

The two women made their way to the hallway leading to the bathrooms. As they came around the corner, Ray froze. Melissa and Lee were in a tight embrace, Melissa's mouth hungrily devouring Lee's. Lee had her eyes closed, her body moving against Melissa's in an unmistakable motion.

Jackie pulled up short too and stared at the couple before glancing over at Ray. "Ray—"

"God damn it!" Ray spun and almost ran toward the back door.

Lee's senses returned to her almost immediately and she brought her hands up and pushed Melissa away firmly. Melissa stepped back and stared at her.

"What the hell do you think you're doing?" Lee's voice shook with anger.

"If it didn't turn you on you would have stopped me sooner.

277

Obviously, Ray isn't enough for you."

Lee reacted without thinking, bringing her hand up and slapping Melissa hard across the cheek. "How dare you make an assumption like that? And how dare you kiss me in the first place?" As she spoke, she glanced over toward the main bar. Her heart sank as she saw Jackie standing rooted in place, staring directly at them.

Melissa obviously saw her too. "Now what are you going to do?" she asked, crossing her arms.

Jesus, could this get any worse? "The question is what are you going to do? Jackie obviously saw the whole thing. When I tell Ray what you did she won't be happy."

"If she believes you. Even with Jackie backing you up, Ray might not. She's stubborn that way." Melissa stepped back when Lee started to raise her hand again.

"Are you intentionally trying to ruin my relationship? What did I—or Ray for that matter—ever do to you?" Lee let her hand drop. Slapping Melissa again wouldn't serve any purpose.

For a moment, Melissa's face hardened. "She did plenty," she answered strongly. Then she closed her eyes and made a noise that might have been a sigh. "Look, maybe I shouldn't have done it. But you did let me."

"I couldn't believe you were doing it," Lee responded. "And you're damn right you shouldn't have done it."

Melissa opened her mouth to say something, then turned and walked away, leaving Lee and Jackie staring at each other. Lee took a step in her direction, saw clearly her expression, and couldn't bear to face her. Holding back tears of anger, she pulled open the door of the restroom and ran inside, locking herself in one of the stalls. She leaned her head against the door, feeling the cold metal.

What if Ray finds out? What if she doesn't believe me? Any thought that another woman might hold more for her than Ray had vanished the moment Melissa kissed her. The more she thought about it, the more afraid she became of what the repercussions might be. Her emotions finally overwhelmed her and she started to cry.

* * *

Ray threw open the back door and half fell outside. She grabbed onto the railing and tried to control her breathing. "God damn it," she repeated to the air.

Everything she thought she knew about Lee collapsed into a pile of disappointment. True, she was extremely tipsy, but it was obvious she was very much enjoying the kiss. Her hands had been on Melissa's sides, moving up toward her breasts, her hips pushing forward as Melissa pressed her into the wall. Melissa's hands were at her shoulders, pulling her closer.

Ray closed her eyes. She had allowed herself to love Lee, and now Lee had shattered her heart into a million pieces. What turned the knife even more was that couple was in the same spot where Ray herself had almost kissed Lee so many months before.

She pulled out her cigar case by instinct and put one to her lips, lighting it with trembling hands. She would go in and confront both of them, demand to find out if this was the first time it had happened or whether Lee had been lying to her for a while. The morning and afternoon had seemed so passionate, but now Ray wondered if Lee were trying to convince her or herself that she still loved her, that it was all to cover for her attraction to Melissa.

The fact that it was Melissa made things even worse; she had been so firm with her that Lee couldn't be tempted when it was possible Melissa already knew she could be. Lee had made a fool of her, and Melissa had too. *How can I survive this?*

Ray drew on the cigar and coughed as she inhaled too deeply. She had allowed herself to feel things she hadn't felt since Tina, and now Lee had done exactly what Tina had, only now that Ray was older and her love ran more deeply, the pain was more intense than it had ever been.

The door opened behind her and Ray spun, ready to lay into Lee if she had dared to come looking for her. When she saw it was Jackie, she sagged against the railing.

"Ray ... calm down." Jackie stepped toward her and Ray tensed.

"Calm down? After what I just saw you want me to calm

down?" Ray's voice rose with each word.

"Yes. It wasn't what you think."

Ray drew on her cigar angrily. "What else could it have been? You saw them. Lee was grinding against her with intent."

"She wasn't. She was trying to push her away." Jackie raised her hands. "I'm telling you, she didn't mean it."

"Bullshit. She must have seen you and put on an act." Ray's hands clenched on the railing. "I'm going to go in there and find out how long this has been going on. Did you know anything about it?"

"I'm telling you, it wasn't an act. She was trying to get away."

Ray narrowed her eyes, angry that Jackie was sticking up for Lee. "Melissa doesn't kiss women first. You know that. Stop trying to blow this off."

"You need to get your shit straight before you go barging in there and make a complete ass of yourself. Don't you trust Lee any more than that?" Jackie crossed her arms and gave Ray a stern look.

"Then I'll just leave. I can't look Lee in the face and act like nothing happened."

"I doubt she knows you saw her; she'll wonder where the hell you went. You can't just vanish." Jackie blew out her breath. "Talk to her when you calm down. You have to give her a chance to explain. It wasn't an act; she really didn't want Melissa kissing her."

Ray pushed off from the railing and walked across the concrete pad to the wall. "I suppose she told you that."

"She saw me, but she didn't talk to me. She pushed Melissa away and slapped the shit out of her, and ran into the bathroom. Melissa slunk by me with a look like she knew she was in trouble. She left right away. As far as I know, Lee's still in the bathroom." Jackie's voice grew soft. "Come on, Ray, you can't throw away all that trust without hearing Lee's side of it. You love her, and she loves you. She would never do something like this intentionally."

Ray stared at her, her words sinking in, but only slightly. Maybe it wasn't intentional, but it had happened and Ray wouldn't be easily convinced that what she saw was anything other than she thought it was. *Maybe it was just a drunken mistake.* Regardless, it showed that Lee could be tempted, that she really did wonder what it could be like with another woman.

"I'll come back inside. I'll even go home with her. But only because it's her birthday and I don't want to confront her until I've had time to cool off and she's had time to sober up. Besides, the last thing I really want is a huge fight in front of everyone. Too many people would be laughing at me for being such an idiot."

"Promise me you won't bring it up until you've had time to calm down. You need to approach this with a level head. I'm telling you, it wasn't what you think." Jackie stepped toward the door. "Come on. At least pretend you're ok."

"Alright. But don't expect me to stay long. If we saw her other people could have too." Ray turned and smacked her hand against the wall with enough force that it stung. "God damn it, why did this have to happen?"

"Jesus Christ, Ray, you can be so fucking blind sometimes. But I can see telling you the truth isn't going to do any good, so you just do what you have to do to get out of here without causing a scene and swear to me you won't bring it up for a couple of days." Jackie pulled open the door. "I know you; it'll take you that long to calm down."

Ray followed her, spotting Lee sitting at the table looking towards her. The guilt was written all over her face, but Ray forced herself to pretend she hadn't noticed. Despite everything, she owed it to Lee not to discuss it until she had a rational plan for what to say. With a growl, she followed Jackie into the bar.

After fifteen tense minutes, Lee finally suggested leaving, citing the stress of the day and a desire to get some sleep. They stood in the parking lot studying each other for a while before Lee quietly said she wanted to go to her own condo that night. Ray, thankful she didn't have to pretend to be enjoying sex later, didn't try to change her mind and they parted ways with the barest of kisses good night.

As Ray climbed into her truck her mind insisted on replaying the moment when she had come around the corner and seen Lee and Melissa together. She couldn't help but wonder if Lee was going home to be with Melissa for a different kind of birthday present. For just a moment, she considered following Lee home to see who showed up, but she realized she didn't want to know if her suspicions were true. Her heart tore into a thousand pieces once again and she dropped her head against the steering wheel and cried.

XVIII.

Lee paced back and forth on the deck of Stacy's house waiting for her friend to return with coffee. The sun was still low in the sky and Lee was tired; she hadn't slept at all well the previous night, between Ray's absence and thoughts of what had happened with Melissa.

She had been so nervous when Ray returned from smoking with Jackie, certain that Jackie had told her what happened. But besides seeming tired, Ray hadn't acted like she knew anything. She did seem preoccupied, but at that point, Lee was drunk enough that she wasn't paying a whole lot of attention to anything except deciding whether she should ask someone to drive her home or call a cab.

Stacy came out the French doors with two mugs of coffee and handed one to Lee before sinking down into one of the chairs by the patio table. "Ok, what's going on?"

"I feel like my life is falling apart. Like I've hit thirty and now everything is going to hell."

Stacy blew across her coffee and considered her over the rim of the mug. "Just because you had to come out to Louise? She was always a pompous bitch anyway."

"Not just because of that." Lee sat down opposite Stacy and leaned on her elbows, sipping from her mug carefully so as not to burn her mouth. "There was last night."

"What about it?" Stacy sat her mug down and looked confused. "You were tipsy, Ray was tired—which doesn't surprise me considering how you two have been going at it—and you'd had to deal with your parents. That seems like a fairly normal evening."

Lee hesitated, not certain she wanted to admit what had happened. But she had to tell someone, had to get some advice on how to go about telling Ray without Ray losing her mind. She wished the whole episode had never happened, but it had, and she worried that she might not have pushed Melissa away as quickly as she could have, that for just a second she had enjoyed Melissa's mouth on hers.

But the feeling had quickly vanished as she realized there was no emotion behind it, that Melissa wasn't even trying to seduce her. There was some other reason for kissing her, something Lee knew had to do with Ray, but couldn't puzzle out.

"Stop staring into space." Stacy's voice pulled her back to reality. "What happened last night?"

Lee bit her lip. "Do you know Melissa Barnhart?"

"Yes." Stacy drew out the word and looked like the name was distasteful.

"She works at the same law firm as my attorney. I met her the other day when I went in to go over some paperwork. She's very attractive."

Stacy gave her an odd look. "Yes, she is. And she knows it. Why?"

"What happened between her and Ray that they so obviously hate each other?" Lee sipped at her coffee again to hide her discomfort.

"I'm not entirely sure." Stacy shrugged. "For a while, maybe five years ago, they were nearly best friends. They were even involved with each other for a couple of weeks. Not long— Melissa has a roving eye and Ray didn't like it."

"That doesn't seem like enough to hate someone."

Stacy cleared her throat. "A few years ago, so I've heard, Ray kept Melissa from breaking up a relationship. I heard Melissa was in love with one of the women, and Ray wasn't about to let her destroy a six-year partnership over it."

"It seems like that isn't the sort of thing that happens one-sidedly. The woman must have been having doubts about her relationship to start with."

"There are more ways to break up a relationship than seduction," Stacy pointed out quietly. "Anyway, I guess Melissa was head over heels for this woman and was furious with Ray for keeping her from getting what she wanted. I don't know what else happened, but they've hated each other ever since."

Lee considered her words, wondering if Melissa hated Ray enough to stage what happened knowing that Ray would find out. "Well, I didn't know all that when I met Melissa. I ... she's very attractive."

"You already said that." Stacy looked at her sternly. "There's something more."

"She came on to me at the office. I told her about Ray and she still came on to me. And I have to admit ..." Lee trailed off, not sure how to word what she had felt.

Stacy rubbed the back of her neck and seemed to be considering something. "A lot of women think she's hot," she finally commented quietly.

"She kinda turned me on. I don't know why, and I certainly didn't plan to do anything about it, but she did."

"I see." Stacy studied her for a long time before she sighed and picked up her mug again. She took a long sip before continuing. "You have to realize you're going to get that feeling about women other than Ray. You'd be weird if you didn't. But what makes you different from Melissa is you don't do anything about it. Or are you wondering whether you jumped into something too quickly with Ray?"

"No," Lee replied hastily. "I'm sure I made the right choice with Ray. But I couldn't help but wonder ... what it would be like with another woman."

Stacy laughed. "That's what has you in such a tizzy? If you don't occasionally wonder that, you're crazy. Hell, I still wonder that occasionally."

"There's more." Lee swallowed. "You know Melissa was there last night."

"Yes, I saw her. She and Ray shot darts at each other a

285

couple of times."

"She cornered me in the hall. I didn't try as hard as I should have to get away from her." Lee blushed. "I should have just pushed past her and walked away. Ray had warned me about her flirting."

Stacy looked at her levelly. "What happened?"

"She kissed me."

Stacy made a startled sound. "She kissed you? Melissa kissed *you*. Melissa doesn't kiss women first. Everyone knows that. She gets her kicks from making women so crazy they kiss her."

"I know that now," Lee said with a pained expression on her face. "That's what made what happened next even worse."

"You didn't kiss her back, did you?"

"God, no. As soon as I realized what was happened I pushed her away. And then I slapped her. But Jackie saw the whole thing." Lee hung her head. "I'm afraid she told Ray about it. I'm afraid she's going to tell Ray about it. I don't know how to tell Ray about it, and I know I have to."

Stacy studied her for a long silent moment. "You have a knack for getting yourself into some serious messes, you know that?"

"What do I do?" Lee asked pleadingly. "Ray is going to lose her mind."

"Well, I have to admit this isn't the sort of thing she'd take calmly. But surely Jackie will back you up that you weren't expecting it and you obviously didn't want it to happen."

Lee chewed on her upper lip. "Ray's been hurt before. I don't want her to think I'm going to hurt her again, because I'm not. If anything, what happened reaffirmed how much I love her and want to be with her; just her."

"Well, the longer you wait to tell her, the worse it will be. Have you talked to her this morning?" Stacy took another drink of her coffee.

"No. She didn't answer her house phone or her cell phone. She's probably fishing or down at the beach with Jackie and Linda. The waves looked pretty nice when I drove up A1A."

"It seems to me the only thing to do is straight up tell her. She may get pissed off for a while, but better you tell her than

Jackie. Or anyone else who saw you and maybe didn't see the ending of it." Stacy ran her hand through her hair. "I hope you read Melissa the riot act."

"Pretty much. She wasn't as cocky when she left as she was when she started the whole thing." Lee stared off into the back yard. "But I don't know what she's said to anyone, if she's said anything. She seems like the type to talk about things like that."

"She is. That's why you need to tell Ray as soon as possible." Stacy studied her. "If she doesn't already know."

The two lapsed into silence for several minutes, drinking their coffee. Finally, Lee put her mug down and got up. "We agreed to meet at volleyball. I'll talk to her after that."

"I wouldn't do it in public."

"I don't intend to. But we always go back to her house to shower and have dinner." Lee glanced away again. "Something tells me that's all that'll happen tonight after I talk to her. I guess I should expect a few days of tension between us."

"Better to expect it and be surprised than not to and be devastated." Stacy looked at her sympathetically. "I wouldn't want to be in your shoes, kiddo. But being up front about it is the only way to get past it."

Lee sighed. "You're right. Thanks for the advice. I was really at a loss."

"Any time."

When Lee left, she was both relieved and terrified of what was to come. But she knew she had to do it. If their relationship was to last, Ray needed to know the things that went through Lee's mind, even the things she would prefer not to reveal. Things might be rocky for a while, but postponing it might do so much damage that they couldn't recover. And that was the last thing Lee wanted.

*   *   *

Ray had calmed down considerably by the time she got to volleyball. After a fitful night's sleep, she had come to the realization that she was being unfair to Lee to assume the worst.

Lee's Awakening

Jackie wouldn't lie to her, and it seemed unlikely that Lee would actually stage something to throw her off. But what she had seen still haunted her. It didn't matter what Jackie said; she was certain that Lee had been enjoying what was happening, at least when Ray came around the corner.

Lee had been very tipsy. If Ray hadn't been so angry, she wouldn't have let her drive home. But even being tipsy, it hurt that she could enjoy kissing another woman as much as she obviously had. That she couldn't just come out and tell her hurt even more.

It suggested that Lee had less trust in her than she had thought. Ray's own trust had been damaged; she wasn't sure she wouldn't always have the fear in the back of her mind that Lee might find greener pastures.

Lee was there already, and the two exchanged a kiss that seemed less heartfelt than it could have. Ray was both relieved and saddened to see that Lee's eyes were as tired as hers. They sat together and made small talk, neither seeming to want to bring up the previous night. Finally, Lee turned and asked her if she could come over after they left. Ray agreed reluctantly, still not sure if she had the nerve to confront her.

The moment came too soon. They were sitting on the deck, Ray with a beer and Lee with a bottle of water. Tension hung uneasily in the air. Lee broke the silence in a voice that suggested she was as nervous as Ray.

"I need to tell you something."

Ray bit her lip. "What's that?"

"Please don't freak out on me. I don't think I could take that right now." Lee shifted uncomfortably in her chair.

"I'll try not to," Ray responded, hoping that her worst fears weren't about to be realized.

Lee paused for a long second. "Something happened last night, with Melissa Barnhart." She paused again and Ray waited for her to continue. "She kissed me."

"I know," Ray said quietly.

"I figured Jackie had told you. But if she hadn't, I wanted to before someone else did."

"She didn't have to tell me. I saw you myself."

"Oh, God," Lee groaned. "I hope you saw all of it."

"I saw enough to hurt." Ray looked away. "From what I saw, you weren't fighting too hard." She felt the anger rising and tried to force it back down. Nothing good would come from screaming.

Lee flushed and opened her mouth, but nothing came out. Ray looked at her, waiting for what she would say, hoping that it wouldn't be the words she dreaded hearing.

Finally, Lee was able to talk. Her voice wavered as she said, "Then you hardly saw anything. I can't deny I was so shocked that for a few seconds I didn't do anything, but I did fight back once my brain kicked in."

"So what does it mean?" Ray rolled her beer bottle between her palms. "How much did you enjoy it?"

Lee drew in a deep breath. "I didn't. Not once I realized what was happening."

Ray narrowed her eyes, realizing she hadn't exactly answered the question. "How long did that take?"

"About three seconds." Lee met her gaze steadily. "And then I slapped her."

"That's what Jackie told me." Ray paused, searching for the words that would keep her from dredging up the anger of the previous night. "Melissa doesn't make a move on a woman who hasn't expressed at least some interest."

"But I didn't!" Lee exclaimed. "I'd only met her once before, at the law firm."

"You must have shown something to her, otherwise she never would have done what she did."

Lee hung her head. Her next words were a long time in coming. "I found her attractive. But I didn't let it show. At least, I thought I didn't."

Ray looked away, disconcerted by the admission. Lee had found someone else attractive, obviously in more than just a casual way. The thought bothered her; if it happened once, it could happen again, and this time maybe the temptation would be too much.

"Please, Ray. Say something."

"Is this the first time, or has it happened before?" Ray ran her hand through her hair and pushed at the feelings of hurt that were starting to fill her stomach. "How attractive?"

"It's the first time." Lee paused and seemed to be struggling with her words. "I found her very attractive; unsettlingly so." Her voice was quiet. "I'm sorry."

Ray sighed. "I should have expected it. I was a fool for thinking it wouldn't happen." She had trusted Lee so completely that she had allowed herself to imagine that she would be the only one Lee would ever look at in that light. Now that trust was broken, and Ray wondered where it left her, left them.

"I didn't want it to. I was ashamed of myself. But it happened, and ..." she trailed off and swallowed hard.

Ray closed her eyes against the sharp pain in her heart. "God, did it have to be Melissa?"

"I'm sorry. I'm so sorry. I wish it had never happened; I wish I'd never met her." Lee's voice wavered again and when Ray looked at her, there were tears in her eyes.

"But you did meet her, and it did happen. Do you have any idea how much that hurts?"

Lee didn't answer her, just looked away and blinked several times before bringing her hand up and wiping quickly at her eyes.

Ray felt torn; part of her wanted to take Lee in her arms and comfort her, but part of her was still angry and unsure of whether Lee was telling her the whole truth.

After a long moment of silence, she finally spoke. "I believe you that you didn't start it. But I'm having trouble with the rest of it. I want to, but ... after everything that's happened ... I don't know what I'd do if you left me. Part of me wants to protect myself against that happening." She paused and looked away. "And part of my trust is gone."

Lee started crying then. "I'm not going to leave you. I love you."

"And I love you. I'm not going to break up with you over this, but I need some time to process what's happened. I have to pull back."

"Ray, please." Lee's face showed her anguish, but Ray refused to be moved by it; it would take more than tears to regain the trust she had felt. "Please, don't do this."

"I'm sorry, Lee. It's the way it has to be. Not for long maybe, but for a while." Ray tried to fight her own tears. "I've opened my heart to you. And no matter how it happened, I'm hurt and I'm confused. I don't want to shut down; I want to keep loving you. I just need to deal with this by myself."

Lee sniffled. "That's it then."

"It isn't that I don't want to see you. But I can't ... I can't sleep with you until I sort this out." Lee started crying again. Ray fought against getting up, but finally she did and went around the table, leaned over and wrapped her arms around Lee's chest from behind. She dropped a quick kiss in her hair. "I'm sorry, Lee. I still love you."

"I understand your position," Lee choked out. "But it still hurts. You're punishing me for something I didn't start."

"I'm sorry," she repeated.

Lee pushed Ray's arms away and stood up, tears still running down her cheeks. "I have to go. I can't listen to any more right now."

Ray stepped back and let her gather her purse. She tried to kiss Lee's cheek, but Lee pulled away. "I'll call you later."

"I might not answer," Lee replied. "I guess I need some time to process this all myself."

Ray swallowed hard. "I don't want to break up over this."

"Neither do I. But I think we need to take a breather and reassess our commitment. If you're going to pull back over something like this, how can I know you aren't going to pull back again? How do I know you aren't going to try and control me like Robert did?"

Hurt, Ray bit her lip. "I don't want to control you."

Lee closed her eyes for a long second. "I just need to think about it."

"Ok. You call me when you're ready. I don't want to not see you."

"I'm not sure I *can* see you for a few days." Lee shouldered her purse. "But I still love you." With that, she walked down the steps and through the yard, disappearing around the corner of the house. Ray heard her car accelerating down the driveway and dropped her head. She refused to feel in the wrong about what had happened. It was Lee who had broken the trust. She would just have to deal with that.

* * *

By Wednesday afternoon, Lee's mood hadn't improved. She'd gone through alternating periods of anger and sadness, blaming herself, blaming Ray, blaming the world for being so unfair. Then at tennis that morning, she'd had to suffer through Louise's glares and refusal to speak to her. She called off work and went home, poured a glass of tea and sat on the balcony staring out over the water.

She missed Ray's presence, but she was still angry with her; angry and hurt. One of the first things she had done Monday morning was call her lawyer and tell him she did not want Melissa working on her case. He seemed confused but acceded to her wishes. It was the only thing positive she had been able to do.

She'd finally gotten past the tears and now only a simmering anger remained. Anger that Ray hadn't been more understanding, that she had assumed Lee wasn't telling her the whole truth when in fact she had been brutally honest. Anger that something she hadn't even started had caused such a rift between them. She wanted nothing more than to face Ray and demand an apology, but she knew it would serve no purpose other than making things worse.

Deep inside she knew too, that both of them would have to bend in order to get through it. Lee wasn't sure how she could bend, because she had already put all her cards on the table, but if it was necessary, she would figure out a way.

She had another glass of tea and continued to contemplate the discussion and Ray's reaction. About five, the phone rang. Tempted not to answer, she finally went inside and picked up the handset.

"I'm glad you're home," Robert said shortly.

Lee groaned inwardly. "What do you want, Robert?"

"I've had new papers drawn up and sent to your lawyer. You're going to drop your claim on my assets and settle for a lower alimony."

"What? Are you insane?" Lee drew her eyebrows together

in confusion. "I'll do no such thing."

His voice was almost gleeful. "I think you will, unless you want me to tell your parents what I've learned."

Uh-oh. Lee had a good idea what he was talking about, but still she asked, "And what's that?"

"Louise told me everything. I'm sure your parents would just love to know their daughter is a dyke. So tell me, how many women did you cheat on me with?"

"None. I never cheated on you, Robert." Lee felt the veins in her neck pulsating. "And you had better not dare tell my parents anything."

He laughed. "There's only one way to stop me."

"You will not blackmail me."

"I'll give you a few days to think about it, Lee. You know once I tell your parents I won't have any problem telling everyone else. You'll be through at the club." He laughed again. "And here I thought I could win you back. I never had you in the first place. You lied to me from the get go. What was your reason for marrying me; was I your cover?" He didn't sound upset about it, more amused.

"I did not lie to you. I didn't realize I was a lesbian until after I left you." Lee crossed the kitchen and poured a glass of wine.

"I don't think anyone would believe that, Lee. So not only are you going to be thought of as the dyke, you'll be thought of as the cheating dyke."

If Lee hadn't already been angry about Ray, she might have started crying at the thought of her parents finding out from Robert that she was gay. As it was, her anger turned on him with force. "I knew you were an asshole, I just didn't realize how much of one. How dare you try to force me to do something by threatening to out me."

"It isn't a threat. It's a very real promise unless you agree to my terms. I'll give you until Monday to make up your mind."

"Go to hell." Lee disconnected and slammed the handset down on the counter. "Son-of-a-bitch!" she screamed.

After a moment, the impact of his threat sank in and she felt her stomach turn. She didn't particularly care about her social life at the club, but her relationship with her parents was tenuous enough without throwing her sexuality into the mix.

She picked up her wine glass and collapsed onto the couch. On top of everything else that had happened that week, she now had to face the very real possibility of being outed to her parents.

She retrieved the handset and wondered if Stacy was home. She didn't realize she was dialing Ray's cell phone until it started to ring. Ray sounded tired when she answered it.

"How're you doing?" she queried.

"I've been a lot better. I'm still mad at you, but I need you."

Ray made a noise. "I'm still kinda mad at you too. But I've been miserable since Sunday. We've got to get past this."

Lee ran her hand through her hair. "I know. Look, Ray ... is there any chance you can come by here tonight? I really need someone to talk to."

There was a long pause. "OK, I'll be over in a little while. What are we talking about?"

"Robert. He's threatening to out me to my parents."

"The bastard." Ray's voice was venomous. "I'll get changed and be right over."

"Thank you. I—I do love you, Ray." Lee bit her lower lip.

"And I love you. I'll be there as soon as I can."

Lee was pacing the room by the time the doorbell rang. She opened it and stepped back to allow Ray to come inside. "Thank you for coming."

"Of course I came. You're my girlfriend. Just because we're having a problem doesn't mean I don't want to be there for you."

Lee sighed and sank down on the couch. Ray sat in the recliner and leaned forward. "I just don't know what to do," Lee said quietly. "My parents would lose their minds if they found out I was gay."

"I'm assuming Robert wants something to keep his mouth shut." Ray gazed at her.

"Yes." Lee nodded and blew out her breath. "He wants me to sign divorce papers that from the sounds of it give me nothing."

"That's bullshit," Ray growled. "You aren't going to do it, are you?"

"I don't know," Lee responded miserably. "But being outed

294

isn't exactly my idea of fun.   God, I can't believe Louise told him."

Ray snorted.   "She did it because she's a pompous bitch. Why don't you tell them yourself, before Robert can?"

Lee considered her words, wondering if she had the courage to tell her parents, wondering if they would ever speak to her again once they knew.   "I don't know if I can."

"Better to hear it from you than from him."

"True," Lee admitted, "but I don't know if I have the nerve to do it."

Ray studied her for a long silent moment.   Finally, she spoke. "I'll be there for you.   If you want, I'll go with you."

"If I decide to do it, I'd want you to go with me.   I'm almost positive I couldn't do it on my own.   Of course, they will probably make a guess when they see you."   Lee laughed.   It felt good to, after so many days of being miserable.

"Not exactly subtle, am I?"   Ray grinned at her.   Lee shook her head.   "Well take me or leave me, I love their daughter and I don't plan on going anywhere."

Lee's eyes searched Ray's face.   "Are you sure about that?"

"Yes."   Ray shrugged.   "I'm still hurt, but I'm not going anywhere."

"I'm hurt too.   I was totally honest with you and you acted like I was lying.   You didn't even consider that I might be beating myself up over what happened."

"I'm sorry for the way I handled it."   Ray spoke quietly, clearly regretful.   "It was just that much worse because it was Melissa, and when you said you'd enjoyed part of it — even for a second … I lost my cool.   The fact that you told me should have meant more."

"I can't help that I saw her in that light.   I tried not to, but I couldn't help it.   That doesn't mean I want to sleep with her, or with anyone else.   In fact, that kiss convinced me I *don't* want to sleep with anyone else.   I'm in love with you.   But I am human and I am going to find other women attractive occasionally.   It isn't fair for you to get so upset about that."

Ray chewed on her lower lip for a few seconds.   "You're right.   My pride was hurt and I reacted poorly.   It's still going to take me some time to get over it completely, but I shouldn't have pushed you so far away."

"No, you shouldn't have." Lee studied her and she blushed. "But I'm willing to let it go if you are."

"I can try." Ray bit her lip again when Lee rolled her eyes. "OK, I'm willing to let it go."

"So we can kiss and make up?"

"Yes." Ray stood up and stepped over to the couch, sitting down next to Lee. The pair studied one another for a moment, and then met in a mutual kiss. It was soft and tender; growing in heat the longer it lasted. Lee felt all her anger drain away as her tongue danced against Ray's, replaced by the raw want Ray brought out in her. When they finally parted, Lee took Ray's hand and led her to the bedroom.

They stripped each other, caressing and kissing skin as it was revealed. Once naked, they fell together on the bed in a tight embrace that quickly turned into something more. They made love slowly, bringing each other to heights of pleasure that left them trembling and gasping for air. Afterwards, they lay together against the pillows looking into one another's eyes.

"I missed you," Ray whispered. "You have no idea how much I missed you."

Lee kissed her nose. "I missed you too. Let's make this our last fight."

"Works for me."

They lay for a while longer, and then Lee turned to Ray and began running her fingertips over her chest, brushing across her nipples with a light touch, trailing down her belly to the curve of her hip, and then back up. As her palm circled over Ray's nipple, Ray let out a soft moan.

"I love your body." Lee moved her hand to the other breast. "I love the taste of you, all the different tastes." She bent her head and ran her tongue around the nipple she had just been playing with. Ray moaned louder.

Lee slid down the bed and between Ray's thighs. Ray bent her legs up and groaned when Lee ran her tongue ran up the inside of one thigh and down the other. After a moment's pause, she leaned in and slid her tongue between Ray's lips, making a long, languid upward stroke that ended with a flick across her clit. Ray's hips jerked. Smiling, Lee repeated the motion, and then settled down and began to move in earnest, bringing her lover to a writhing orgasm as she cried out her pleasure. Finally, Ray gathered her into her arms and held her.

Lee nestled against her and kissed her shoulder. "How can anyone think this is wrong?"

"I don't know."

After a while of just caressing one another, they got up, showered and ordered pizza. Later, completely sated, they fell asleep tangled together in a mess of sheets and comforter.

XIX.

"Are you sure you want to do this?"

They were sitting in Lee's car in the driveway of her parents' house. After agonizing for two days, Lee had decided that the only thing she could do was to tell her parents before Robert did. She had called to ensure that they would be home, and now was trying to work up the nerve to go into the house.

Ray studied her. "Are you sure?" she asked again.

Lee swallowed. "Not really. But I have to."

"I'll be there. No matter what happens, I'll be right there." Ray leaned over and kissed her softly. "Ready?"

"Yes," Lee replied with a sigh. The two got out of the car and walked up to the kitchen door. Her mother was inside unloading the dishwasher.

"Lee!" She frowned when she saw Ray. "Who's this?"

"This is Ray."

"Nice to meet you, Ray." To Lee, she said, "I thought you needed to talk to us."

"I do."

Ellen frowned and glanced at Ray again. After an obvious effort, she smiled. "Well, would you like something to drink?"

"Wine, please. Ray, do you want a glass? There won't be any beer." Lee resisted the urge to squeeze Ray's hand, seeing the discomfort on her face.

"Sure."

Once they had their drinks, Ellen led the way into the family room, where Lee's father sat in his easy chair watching the television. He turned it off when they came in and gave Ray a startled look very similar to the one Ellen had.

"John, this is Ray — Lee's friend."

"It's a pleasure, sir." Ray stepped forward and extended her hand. He stared at it for a second before shaking it. They all sat down and made small talk for the better part of fifteen minutes, until Lee's father cleared his throat and turned to her.

"So, your mother tells me you needed to talk to us." His eyes kept sliding to Ray, but his face was impassive.

For a second, they all looked at each other. Finally, Lee was able to speak. "I know you two want me to reconcile with Robert. It isn't going to happen."

"Why not?" Ellen looked curious. "I mean, as I said before, you went from happy to unhappy so quickly."

"And I told you, because he's a controlling bastard. But that's not the whole reason I won't reconcile with him, at least not now."

Ellen and John exchanged glances. "What do you mean, not now?" John leaned forward.

Lee swallowed. *I can't believe I'm doing this.* "I've met someone else. Someone who means more to me than Robert ever did. I realized I was living half a life before they came into it." She glanced at Ray, who gave her a little smile.

Her parents looked at Ray again. "Do we know him?" Ellen's voice sounded strange, slightly higher pitched than normal.

Lee swallowed again and forced the words out. "It isn't a him."

"Pardon me?" Ellen cocked her head and stared at her daughter.

"I said, it isn't a him. Mom, Dad ... I'm a lesbian."

Silence reigned for several seconds as Ellen and John looked at each other. Lee held her breath, waiting for the explosion.

Finally, Ellen sighed heavily. "That's not a complete surprise, Lee."

"I assume this is her?" John gestured toward Ray, who

flushed slightly.

"Yes. And why isn't it a surprise?" Lee furrowed her brow and looked at her mother quizzically. *If Robert told them, why aren't they angrier?*

"We've thought for a long time that you might be. That's why we were so excited when you married Robert. And why we've fought so hard to keep you together." Ellen's voice wavered.

"How long?"

"Since high school," her father replied gruffly. "The signs were there then. Your mother was convinced you wouldn't ever marry." He turned his attention to Ray. "How old are you?"

"Thirty-nine." Ray sounded a little nervous.

"And what do you do?"

"I'm an electrician."

John considered this while Ellen kept staring at Lee. "How long has this been going on? Before the separation?"

"Of course not!" Lee exclaimed. "Do you honestly think I'd cheat? We've been seeing each other for about four months."

There was another silence, which was broken when Ellen stood up. "Would anyone like another drink? I think I need another drink." Everyone demurred and she vanished into the kitchen.

Lee's father was silent while she was gone, studying Ray intently. Ray, for her part, kept glancing at Lee with an expression that suggested she wanted nothing more than to get out of there.

When Ellen returned, she sank back down and drew in a deep breath. "Are you sure? I mean … has this happened before?"

"No, Mom. And yes, I'm sure. Without going into details … I'm sure." She looked between her parents. "Why aren't you freaking out?"

"Would you like us to?" John made a noise. "We've had plenty of time to reconcile ourselves to the possibility; although I thought after all these years with Robert you might have fooled us."

"How could you possibly have suspected when I was in high school? I didn't suspect until seven months ago."

"Oh, several things, Lee. You were very athletic, you rarely dated, you idolized strong women ..." Ellen trailed off and looked at Ray. "I guess you still do."

Lee watched Ray turn bright pink. "Mother!"

"Is it serious?" John shifted in his seat.

"Yes, it's very serious," Lee responded.

"What do you have to say?" he asked, turning his attention to Ray. "Is it serious enough to alienate my daughter from everyone she knows?"

Ray bit her lip. "Mr. Compton ... I love Lee. I don't want to see her hurt in any way. It was her choice to become involved with me; she knew the ramifications."

"I don't care about my social reputation any more, Dad," Lee interjected. "Those people aren't real. I have friends now who accept me for who I am, not how much money I have."

Ellen looked hurt. "That's an unfair thing to say."

"Why did you decide to tell us anyway? Why now?"

Lee coughed. "Robert found out. He threatened to tell you unless I signed the divorce papers he drew up. I'd have gotten nothing."

"So how long were you planning on hiding this from us?"

"I didn't know how you'd handle it," Lee admitted. "I thought you'd take it badly. I thought you'd be angry. I never expected you to take this so calmly."

"We don't have to understand it or agree with it, Lee. But you're our daughter, so we do have to accept it." He turned to Ray. "If you hurt her you'll answer to me."

"I don't intend to hurt her," Ray replied firmly.

"What are your plans now?" Ellen still sounded a little faint. "Do you intend to—what do they call it—come out to everyone else?"

"I don't know," Lee answered honestly. "I'm sure Robert will tell everyone he knows once he realizes he can't blackmail me and I'm certain Louise will back him up."

"Louise? She's your best friend."

"Not anymore." Lee looked away and frowned. "She wants nothing to do with me."

"You're going to alienate a lot of your friends," Ellen commented. "You've picked a pretty hard road."

Lee blew out her breath loudly. "I didn't *pick* anything, Mom. I just woke up to what was there all along."

"You aren't going to get a crew cut and tattoos, are you?"

Lee had to laugh at the serious expression on her mother's face and the way she was looking dubiously at Ray. "No, I'm not. And there's nothing wrong with crew cuts or tattoos. I happen to think Ray's hair is cute. And her tattoos."

Ray turned pink again. "Lee!" she exclaimed under her breath.

"No offense, Ray, but you're very ... not what I'd expect my daughter to be involved with."

"The word is butch," Ray supplied.

Her mother colored slightly. "Yes. Well. Butch, then."

"She works for a living too," Lee added firmly. "And I don't care if you approve or not. I'm in love with her."

John spread his hands. "It's your life, Lee. You have to understand, it's going to take some time for your mother and I to adjust to this new you. You can't blame us for being confused."

"I don't. But I won't tolerate you putting Ray down."

"It wasn't meant as an insult," Ellen replied somewhat archly.

"I didn't take it as one." Ray looked at Lee. "Really, Lee, it's ok."

"I'm going to move in with her."

Her parents exchanged glances. "If that's what you want to do," Ellen said carefully.

"It is." Lee stood up. "Thank you for listening to me, and thanks for not flipping out."

"We love you, dear. We just want you to be happy."

"I am." They exchanged goodbyes and left.

On the way home, Ray was strangely quiet. Finally, Lee glanced over at her and found her gazing out the window with a lost look on her face. "What's the matter? I hope my mother didn't upset you."

"No, she didn't," Ray responded absently. "I'm just thinking about something you said."

"What's that?"

Ray turned and studied her intently. "You said you were

going to move in with me."

"Yes, I did." Lee waited for the stoplight before meeting her gaze. "If you still want me to."

"Of course I do! I just thought ... with everything that's happened ... maybe you'd want more time on your own." Ray blushed.

"Another condo would just be a place to store my belongings. I don't want to wake up without you anymore."

"Then you won't." Ray grinned. "Should we start moving your clothes tonight?"

"Why don't we start right now?" Lee turned the car toward her condo.

"Deal."

* * *

Ray slipped out of bed, pulled on a t-shirt and her boxers, and padded quietly to the bathroom, leaving Lee curled up under the covers snoring lightly. From there she went into the kitchen and started a pot of coffee. They had slept in, having stayed up late to put away the three suitcases of clothes that Lee had brought from her condo, but now Ray was wide awake and ready to start the day. She knew Lee, however; she would sleep for another hour if allowed to.

Taking a cup of coffee, she wandered out onto the deck and sat down. She was still in shock that Lee had finally agreed they should live together, but it was a welcome shock. Everything seemed to be falling into place; Lee's parents had accepted her coming out with more grace than either of them had expected, she had agreed to move in, and the house was finally shaping up into what Ray had hoped it would be when she bought it.

Robert could still out Lee to her friends in the country club set, but Lee didn't seem particularly concerned about that. Ray wondered if she truly didn't care, or if she was just putting a brave face on something that seemed likely to happen. Lee had changed a lot since the first time they made love.

She had blossomed into a self-confident woman at ease with her sexuality and unwilling to live a lie just to make others happy. That she had so unflinchingly claimed Ray as her own to her parents calmed what lingering uncertainty she'd had that the relationship might not be as strong as she hoped. Ray was certain she'd have told her parents the truth sooner rather than later had the issue not been forced. She was proud of her.

The only thing still hanging over Ray's head was work. She had contacted several contracting companies, but still had no solid offers. In the back of her mind, she knew that if word got back to Baylight, she'd be permanently laid off, but she also knew she had to get out. Even taking a cut in pay didn't sound so horrible next to having to put up with Jimmy sniping at everything she did. And with Lee paying half the bills for the house, she could afford to continue making improvements without the extra income.

Ray glanced up when she heard the screen door open. Lee wandered out holding a coffee mug and looking sleepy. Her hair was still tousled and she had only pulled on a pair of sleep pants before coming out. Ray smiled; another thing Lee had taken to quickly was not wearing a top around the house, even outside.

"Good morning, sweetheart." Lee yawned.

"Morning. Nice out, isn't it?"

"Mmhmm." Lee sat down next to her and squinted across the pasture. "Have you been up long?"

"About an hour. What's on your agenda for today?" Ray leaned over and kissed her. As usual, it took more than several seconds for them to part.

"Getting boxes and starting to pack. I'll have to sort out what's going into storage and what's coming here."

"Well, any of your furniture is going to be nicer than mine. I'd rather get rid of mine, or put it in the barn, and use yours." Ray finished her coffee and stood. "I'll be right back."

She went inside and poured another cup. Glancing at her cell phone, she noticed that there were messages and realized she hadn't checked it the night before. Wondering if Jackie had called to find out how things had gone, she grabbed the phone and dialed her voice mail.

The message was terse and to the point. Jimmy's voice held a note of triumph that made Ray's blood boil. She hit erase before he was even done, slammed the phone down, and stalked outside.

Lee turned as she stomped across the deck. "What's the matter?"

"Mother-fucking son-of-a-bitch!"

"Alrighty then. Care to elaborate?"

Ray collapsed into her chair. "The bastard fired me."

"What? Why?" Lee drew her eyebrows together.

"I didn't listen to all of it, but the short version is a round of permanent layoffs. I knew looking for another job would bite me in the ass." She put her head in her hands. Just fifteen minutes before she'd been thinking how their life was coming together. Now hers was crashing down around her. She'd known it might happen, but she didn't really believe it would.

"Can't you go over his head? Surely you could talk to the owner."

Ray laughed shortly. "He's the one who would have had to approve it. Now I'm totally screwed."

"No you aren't," Lee responded quietly. "I can help out until you find another job."

Ray pulled herself to her feet and walked over to the railing, facing away from Lee so she wouldn't see the tears of anger in her eyes. "I told you before; I don't want your money."

"And you also told me it would be different if I lived here. Which I do now." Lee's voice was even and calm. "I'm sure you'll find something soon, but until then let me help."

"I don't know, Lee." Ray groaned. "My pride won't let me."

"Oh, for God's sake. It isn't like it's going to break me."

Ray spun, her eyes sparking. "Don't remind me how much more money you have than me!"

Lee looked taken aback. "That wasn't what I was trying to do."

"I'm sorry. I'm just so angry right now." Ray forced herself to breathe. She couldn't take her frustration and anger out on Lee. It wasn't fair.

"Then we'll discuss it when you aren't angry." Lee picked up her coffee mug.

Ray studied her for a long silent moment before returning to her chair and sitting back down. "Do you want some breakfast?"

"Something light." Lee shrugged. "Toast and fruit maybe."

"I have cantaloupe."

"That sounds good. Would you like me to fix it?" Lee blew across her coffee and took a sip before looking into Ray's eyes.

Ray saw the warmth and love in Lee's face and felt it wash away some of the anger. The frustration remained, but she felt much calmer than she had a few minutes before.

"No, I'll get it."

In the kitchen, Ray leaned against the counter and closed her eyes, wishing that there was an easy answer to the situation, but there wasn't. She couldn't pull a job out of thin air, and despite her years of experience the fact that she hadn't gotten more than a vague promise to look into putting her on a payroll told her she was in for an uphill battle.

She couldn't let Lee support her; her pride wouldn't allow that, and she didn't want Lee thinking she was taking advantage of her for having money. She would just have to live on her savings until she could find something. With a sigh, she turned to fixing breakfast.

*   *   *

Ray and Lee arrived at Maddie's at a little past eight. The parking lot was half-full, and when they pushed through the door, the main room was already growing smoky and the jukebox was playing some hip-hop song. They made their way to the bar and ordered drinks, then sat down and looked at each other.

"What time did they say they'd be here again?" Lee sipped at her wine and checked her watch.

"Eight-thirty, give or take half an hour." Ray waved at Joan, who sat on the opposite side of the bar talking to Lisa then turned her attention to her beer.

"We'll be lucky to see them by nine. Why is it you're so prompt and no one else we know is?"

Ray shrugged. "Couldn't tell you. What's the problem; don't want to spend an hour alone with me?"

Lee pushed at her playfully. "You're a shit."

"But I'm your shit." Ray kissed her.

Lee thought that Ray seemed in a much better mood than she had that morning. It pleased her; she wanted to celebrate foiling Robert's plans and her parents' relatively calm acceptance of her announcement without worrying that Ray might still be sulking. Of course, the beer she had drunk during the afternoon might have helped lift her spirits. She'd had enough sense to let Lee drive, and Lee expected her to enjoy the freedom of a designated driver.

Jackie joined them at eight-fifteen, to Lee's surprise, and Donna and Stacy arrived half an hour later. They moved to a table and Lee had to repeat the story of coming out to her parents that she had told Jackie.

"You're a lucky bitch, you know that?" Stacy grumbled when she had finished. "My parents didn't speak to me for a year after I told them."

"I only talk to mine at Christmas," Jackie added. "I found out my grandmother had died six months after it happened."

Donna just laughed. "Leave it to the rich kid's parents to shrug and say they expected it."

"I am *not* the rich kid," Lee retorted. "And I can't believe they thought I was gay in high school."

"Hell, I *told* my parents in high school," Donna responded. "They just didn't believe me until I brought Stacy home."

"That was a day I'll remember forever," Stacy said. "I had a mullet and thought I was so butch. They just looked at Donna and asked why she didn't bring home a girl."

Lee tried to picture Stacy as butch as Ray. Since she'd known her, she'd always worn her hair in a ponytail and dressed in casual and mostly feminine clothes. The image of her with a mullet and a bad attitude was so amusing she had to laugh.

"So, where are your tattoos?" she asked with a giggle.

Stacy raised an eyebrow. "Somewhere you'll never see, that's for sure."

"She has this abstract yin-yang made with two bent triangles on her—"

"Donna!" Stacy cut her partner off with a glare.

Lee laughed again. It felt good to be so relaxed again after the hell she and Ray and been through recently. She glanced at Ray. "There's that one tattoo on the inside of your thigh ..." she trailed off when Ray shot her a similar glare.

Everyone laughed then. The jovial mood continued for the next hour, until Lee happened to look toward the door and saw Melissa coming in. "Shit," she muttered.

"What?" Ray followed her gaze. "God damned bitch." Her fists clenched on the table.

"Ray, calm down." Lee reached out and covered one fist with her hand.

"Give me one reason not to go pound the shit out of her," Ray snarled back.

"It's over. Forget it."

"Someone needs to knock some decency into her." Ray pulled her hand out from under Lee's and picked up her beer.

"Don't let her ruin our night." Lee's gaze searched Ray's face.

The other three women all looked at each other nervously as Ray met her gaze with a defiant look. It slowly melted away as Lee continued studying her. "You're right. She isn't worth it."

The relief at the table was palpable. "Thank God," Donna murmured.

Lee looked again and Melissa had vanished into the crowd. She turned her attention to a story that Jackie was telling about Ray, pushing all thought of Melissa from her mind. Ray was right; she wasn't worth it.

* * *

Ray was coming back from the bathroom when she saw Melissa again. Or rather, she almost ran into her. Melissa pulled back and looked both startled and nervous at the same time.

"Well, look what crawled in," Ray observed in her most venomous voice.

"Ray! I've been hoping to see you." Melissa sounded almost frightened.

"What for, trying to twist the knife a little more? What the hell were you thinking?"

Melissa swallowed hard. "I'd rather just forget it happened. I was very drunk."

"Drunk is no excuse. You know that." Ray narrowed her eyes and remembered her promise to Lee that she wouldn't lash out.

"Look, I'm sorry. I stepped over the line and I shouldn't have."

"And I know why you did. It was five years ago, Melissa. Get over it." Ray crossed her arms and gave Melissa a hard stare.

Melissa dropped her eyes. "I'd like to apologize to Lee."

"That would be up to her," Ray responded. "I'm fairly certain she doesn't want to talk to you after what you pulled."

"I know you're angry —"

"The only reason I'm not taking you outside to beat the crap out of you is that I promised Lee I wouldn't."

Melissa sighed. "I want to make it up to her."

"And how exactly do you think you could do that? You intentionally tried to ruin our relationship." Ray held back from slapping Melissa across the face. "That's low, even for you. How did you time it to make sure I'd see?"

Melissa gave her a startled stare. "You saw us?"

"Don't give me that bullshit innocent routine. I know you too well."

"I swear I didn't know you'd seen it. I knew Jackie was there but ..." she trailed off when Ray raised an eyebrow and glared at her. "I swear. I was just trying ... I don't even know what I was trying to do."

Ray tried to remember what she had ever seen in Melissa, why they had been such good friends. All she could see now was a conniving, vicious woman. A woman who wouldn't let something as minor as Lee's feelings interfere with an attempt to exact revenge on Ray for having some kind of morals five years ago.

"If you want to apologize to Lee, come and do it. But I won't let you talk to her alone. I don't trust you as far as I can throw you." Ray snorted. "If that far."

Melissa bit her lip. "Fine. I have something to tell her, to try and make things up at least a little bit."

"What's that?"

Melissa finally seemed to regain some of her composure. She lifted her head and looked Ray in the eye squarely. "That's between her and me. I won't tell you before I do her."

"You'd better not be trying to pull something." Ray gave her another hard look.

"I'm not."

Ray uncrossed her arms and gestured toward the table, and then followed as Melissa started toward it.

Lee looked up from her drink and saw with a start that Ray was returning with Melissa. The other three women at the table were exchanging similarly confused looks. Melissa reached the table first, and Ray stepped up beside her with a fierce look on her face.

"Melissa has something to say to you."

Melissa glanced at her, then at Lee. "I'd really rather do this in private," she mumbled.

"You didn't mind God and man knowing before."

"Fine." Melissa turned her attention to Lee. "I want to apologize. What I did was completely inappropriate. I was very drunk but" — she gave Ray a quick look — "that's no excuse. I want to make it up to you."

Lee pursed her lips. "And how exactly to you think you can do that? Do you realize what I went through because of you?"

Melissa's eyes shifted nervously. "I looked into your case."

"I told Donald I didn't want you anywhere near it." Lee felt her pulse quicken. "You had no right."

"Well, I did. And I made a few phone calls, called in a few favors. Donald should have done that months ago. You wouldn't have had to go through so much."

Lee drew her eyebrows together in confusion. "What do you mean?" Despite herself, she was curious where Melissa was going.

"I don't know who yet —"

"Oh, for God's sake. Spit it out." Lee's patience wore thin. "If you have something to tell me, do it. Otherwise, you can just slink back to where you came from."

Melissa drew in a breath and put on the professional face Lee had first seen at her office. "Robert is having an affair. He has been for some time, apparently."

Shocked, Lee could only stare at her for a long moment. "*What?*"

"Your husband is sleeping with someone else. He has been for at least three years."

"First, don't ever refer to him as my husband again. Second, how do you know this?" Lee's mind was spinning with disbelief. Robert barely had time to spend with her; how could he possibly have found time for a mistress?

"We occasionally use private detectives. I had one look into Robert. It only took him a few days of poking around to find out. Robert has an apartment near the hospital. The manager there says that when she sees him, he's always with the same brunette, and they are obviously more than just friends." Melissa coughed. "Like I said—I don't know who it is yet, but I should by Wednesday."

"Holy crap," Stacy murmured.

"How did he have time? He was always getting paged to the hospital—" Lee cut herself off as the answer became obvious. How many of those pages hadn't been from the hospital at all?

"You can nail him to the wall with this." Melissa spoke firmly. "He'll be lucky to be able to afford that apartment when Donald is through with him."

"I have to admit, Melissa, this is a pretty good start toward making things right," Ray said in a slightly awed voice.

"I may be a bitch Ray, but it serves me well in divorce law. I know what to look for."

"Of that I have no doubt," Ray returned snidely. Melissa twitched. "But this time it's worked in Lee's favor."

Lee automatically picked up her glass and took a long swallow of wine. "Three years?"

"As far as we know. That's how long he's had the apartment." Melissa shifted. "I left two messages on your machine trying to get you to call me back. I guess you erased them."

"I haven't checked my messages in a couple of days," Lee commented absently as her mind turned over what Melissa had told her. "Robert had the nerve to threaten to out me when he's been having an affair for most of our marriage? What a bastard."

"It does take a certain amount of gall," Jackie said calmly.

"I know this doesn't make up for what happened, Lee. But it's all I could do to try." Melissa hesitated. "I'll call you on Wednesday when I get the final report, if that's OK."

Lee could only nod and watch as Melissa walked off, disappearing into the crowd. For almost a minute, everyone just stared at each other. Finally, Donna started laughing. After a moment, Lee joined her. The other three looked at them as though they'd lost their minds.

"What's so funny?" Ray looked completely confused.

"This. The whole thing." Lee wiped at the tears laughing had brought to her eyes. "Mister High and Mighty being brought to his knees."

"And Melissa, of all people, being the one to put it out in the open," Donna added with a giggle.

"That is pretty weird," Ray acknowledged slowly. "It's out of character for her. I didn't think she was capable of being sorry."

"What difference does it make? If Robert outs Lee, she can out him," Jackie pointed out.

"I can hardly wait for Wednesday," Donna added. "This is better than a soap opera."

Lee narrowed her eyes. "Ok, it's funny, but not that funny. This is my life, not some soap opera."

"Sorry." Donna smothered another giggle.

"It's probably someone he works with," Stacy commented.

"We'll find out soon enough," Ray replied.

For the rest of the evening, conversation kept coming back to Melissa's news. When the group finally split up to go home, everyone had agreed that the most likely suspect for Robert's mistress was one of the nurses from the hospital.

Ray and Lee were fairly silent on the way home, Ray's hand caressing Lee's thigh as she drove. Only once they had crawled into bed did they talk about it again.

"I really don't believe it." Lee cuddled up against Ray's side. "It's not like I ever really loved him, and I have no idea why I'm so pissed off about it. But I am."

"You're probably pissed off because he had you on a short leash while he was doing as he pleased." Ray paused and seemed embarrassed. "That might not be the best way to put it."

Lee nuzzled against her neck. "No, that sounds about right. I do wonder who it is, though."

Ray put an arm under her shoulders and pulled her closer. "I guess we'll find out soon enough. It should ease your mind though. Now you really don't have to sign those ridiculous papers."

"And he accused *me* of cheating," Lee grumbled with a yawn. "He has more nerve than Melissa."

"Don't give him another thought." Ray turned her head to kiss Lee's hair. Lee lifted her face and met her second kiss with her mouth. Ray's seduction ensured that Robert was erased completely from Lee's mind, and she fell asleep with Ray's scent in her nose and her thoughts full of her love for the woman beside her.

XX.

Lee and Ray sat curled up on the sofa watching the fireplace flicker. Naked underneath the quilt they shared, Ray caressed Lee's thigh absently while Lee's head rested against her shoulder. It had been a quiet Monday, as Lee had taken the day off to talk to movers about putting Ray's furniture in storage and bringing hers to the house, while Ray had finished putting up sheetrock on one wall of the garage.

They had been silent for some time, enjoying each other's presence, when Ray finally shifted and spoke. "Shouldn't Robert be calling?"

Lee giggled. "He's probably scratching his head trying to figure out why I haven't called him. Or he's leaving messages on the machine at the condo; I expect he'll try six or seven times before he calls my cell phone."

"What are you going to tell him?"

Lee smiled and kissed her on the neck. "To go to hell."

"I mean, about the affair, silly." Ray ran her fingers into the hair at Lee's triangle and pulled slightly. Lee jumped.

"Ouch!"

"That didn't hurt and you know it," Ray laughed. "So, what are you going to say about the affair?"

"Nothing at the moment; I want to know who the woman is before I blast him out of the water."

Ray fell silent for a few moments. "Are you going to let him out you to everyone without at least threatening him with what you know?"

"I don't really care if he outs me." Lee shrugged. "Those people aren't really my friends if they can't deal with it."

"I don't think I could be so cavalier," Ray said quietly.

Lee grinned into her shoulder. "I'm pretty surprised I am."

"Do you really think Melissa will find out who it is?"

Lee sat up and looked into Ray's face. "I don't know. I have a suspicion that once Melissa gets something she wants in her mind, she doesn't let it go until she gets it."

"That's Melissa," Ray agreed. "Still, I'd want him to suffer wondering if I'd tell on him."

"Oh, he'll suffer." Lee smiled sweetly. "He'll suffer a lot."

"What do you have in mind?" Ray looked at her curiously. "What's going on in that brain of yours?"

"I haven't decided yet, but his humiliation will be quite thorough."

Ray laughed. "It kind of turns me on to see you plotting so deviously."

Lee lifted her hand and found one of Ray's breasts. "How turned on?"

Ray groaned and pushed her back onto the couch. Fifteen minutes later, Lee's cell phone rang, pulling them apart from serious foreplay.

"I'll bet that's him," Lee said, breathing heavily.

Ray pinched her nipple. "Let it ring."

"No, I want to get this over with. He'll be calling all night if I don't." Lee got up and retrieved her phone off the sofa table. Glancing at the screen, she nodded. "It's him."

"All right. But don't forget how wet I am."

Lee grinned and hit the talk button. "Robert."

"Where the hell are you? I've been by your house twice today and called you a half dozen times."

"Obviously, I'm not home." Lee rolled her eyes and Ray smothered a laugh.

Robert made an irritated noise. "Obviously. Have you come to your senses and decided to sign the papers, or should my next call be to your parents?"

315

Lee's Awakening

Lee contemplated how best to answer him. "If you call my parents, you'll look like an idiot."

"By the time I'm through, they'll believe me." His voice was assured.

"I'm sure they will," Lee agreed, "considering they already know."

There was a long silence on the other end of the phone. Finally, Robert growled, "Your friends don't."

"Robert, don't you get it? I don't care who knows."

"It'll ruin your reputation."

Lee knew he was trying to bluster.

"So? I have plenty of friends who accept me for who I am." Lee reached over and ran her fingers down the side of Ray's face. Ray turned her head and caught two of her fingers in her mouth, sucking gently on them.

There was another pause. "Oh, I get it. You're pretending you don't care so I won't bother saying anything. It won't work."

Lee laughed. "Go ahead. I'll tell you what. Ray and I will meet you on Wednesday night at the club buffet and you can announce it to the entire room. Won't that be nice for you?"

Ray made a startled noise and dropped Lee's fingers, looking up at her with a confused expression. "What?" Her voice was quiet but concerned.

Robert echoed the word. "You don't have the nerve to bring your lover to the club," he stated firmly.

"The hell I don't! We'll be there at seven-thirty."

"That is worth waiting for. But if you don't show up, I'll tell everyone anyway."

"Oh, we'll be there." Lee broke the connection and put the phone down before turning to look into Ray's shocked face. "What?"

"Are you insane?" Ray's eyes were wide. "I can't go to your club."

Lee shrugged. "Why not? I'm a member, you're my girlfriend."

Ray sputtered for a minute. "Look at me! It's bad enough you're going to get outed without me there looking like the stereotypical dyke."

"I'm not worried about it," Lee said laughingly. "It'll do them some good to be shaken up a bit. Besides, there's nothing wrong with the way you look."

Ray lifted her arm to show the tribal tattoo running around her bicep. "Um, excuse me, but I think this is going to be noticeable."

"So wear long sleeves if you're worried about it. I'm not." Lee sobered and looked at her. "I guess I shouldn't have done that without asking you. I'm sorry. He just pisses me off so much with his Holier-than-Thou attitude."

Ray sighed heavily and studied her. "It's ok. I'm just not sure it's such a great idea." She paused. "What exactly is the club buffet anyway?"

"Wednesday and Sunday nights there's a buffet in the ballroom. There are usually sixty or seventy people there. I know most of them. There's dancing after dinner, that sort of thing. The food is fabulous."

"Oh, well, if the food is fabulous then how can I refuse?"

"You can't. Your femme is demanding your presence." Lee batted her eyelashes. "If you want me to be your femme."

"Damn straight you're my femme," Ray rumbled. She paused and cocked her head. "Well, my semi-femme. I still don't like you in makeup. You won't wear any to the club, will you?"

"Not if you don't want me to. That in and of itself will convince people Robert is telling the truth." Lee laughed. "Even without you there."

Ray suddenly looked hesitant. "You don't want me there *because* I'm so butch, do you?"

Lee's eyebrows drew together and she looked quizzically at her lover. "Why would you ask that?"

"I'm hard to mistake for anything but a lesbian. You aren't planning to drag me into the middle of anything, are you?"

For a split second, Lee was angry that Ray would even think such a thing. Then the anger passed and she realized that Ray was nervous about going. "I want you to go because you're my girlfriend and I want your moral support. If you'd really rather not, I can go alone."

Ray considered her. "No. You told Robert we'd both be

there, and we will. But I'm not femming up just because it's the country club."

"Don't. You have a wonderful suit that looks fabulous on you. Wear that. The linen one."

"OK. I'm in. I think you're crazy, but I'm in." Ray smiled. "After all, your parents didn't pass out when they met me."

"I think they just waited until we left to break out the hard liquor," Lee responded with a grin. "But you'll grow on them."

"God, I can't believe I'm agreeing to this."

"Here, let me help make it easier for you." Lee slid over the arm of the sofa and onto Ray's chest. They lay stomach to stomach with Lee's face very close to Ray's. "Do you want me to attack you here, or in bed?"

"Come here, you little debutante vixen," Ray growled, grabbing her around the waist. "I'm going to show you some down home cracker loving."

"Help me—oh, help me," Lee gasped with false fear. Ray grinned before kissing her firmly. By the time they got to the bedroom, all they could think of was sleep.

*   *   *

Ray heard Steve's truck pulling into the driveway. He'd called and promised he would be there in five minutes, and he was right on time. In short order, he came through the garage door holding up a twelve-pack of beer.

"Howdy, stranger!" Ray put down her hammer and went to give him a bear hug.

"How's life treating you?" Steve ruffled her hair. "I brought liquid courage."

Ray laughed. "Come on, you aren't afraid of a little carpentry work, are you?"

"Terrifies me," Steve said with a perfectly straight face. "I'm afraid a wall is going to fall on me."

"You're a mess." Ray reached for her own beer. "Thanks for helping me get this ceiling fixed."

Steve stepped all the way into the garage and examined the hole where the sheetrock had collapsed. He whistled.

"Damn. Must've been a hell of a leak."

"Tell me about it. Let me throw that beer in the fridge."

Steve handed it over and walked with Ray to the kitchen door. She called for Lee as she pushed it open; the blonde came around the corner shortly after Ray had made room in the refrigerator for Steve's twelve-pack.

"Hi, Steve." Lee grinned. "Here to keep Ray in line with this repair work?"

"Ma'am." Steve had taken to calling her that after Ray explained Lee's debutante status to him. As always, Lee looked vaguely annoyed. "I can't let this young-un out of my sight for two weeks without her knocking holes in things."

"Smart ass. Do you mind if Steve stays for dinner, sweetheart? Maybe we can turn him on to champagne and pizza."

"Champagne, ugh." Steve made a face. "Stuff makes my head spin."

Lee laughed. "Then pizza yes, champagne no. Just let me know when you want me to call it in and you can go pick it up."

"Why don't you go so Steve and I can get rude and crude while you're gone?"

"Yes Ma'am. Don't want to be cussin' around such a genteel lady as yourself." Steve pretended to spit on the floor and hiked up his jeans.

"Steve, you're an ass," Lee replied archly. "Ray, you can go get the pizza. I'm unpacking. And stop calling me Ma'am!"

Both Ray and Steve burst out into laughter. Lee glared at them before spinning and marching back toward the bedroom she had claimed as an office. Ray waited until she was gone to hand Steve a beer. "She loves you and you know it."

"Ah, but it's a hard kind of love." Steve winked. "Come on, let's tackle this bitch."

Four hours, several beers and a lot of cursing later, Steve, Ray and Lee sat on the back deck enjoying a rare day of 80's weather. A demolished pizza sat in the middle of the table and beer cans were piled on the deck. Lee was drinking her usual wine and looking between the two with a look that could only be interpreted as bemusement.

"I'm telling you Ray, when I said I was looking forward to being a handyman I sure didn't know what I was talking about." Steve lit a cigarette.

Ray puffed on her cigar and blew the smoke into the air. "At least you're working."

"Yeah, I heard about you getting fired."

"Permanently laid off due to work slowdown," Ray muttered with distaste. "What a bullshit excuse."

Steve blew smoke rings. "You'll land a job. Just give it time to blow over."

"Yeah, right." Ray didn't really believe him. She had a suspicion he didn't either and was just saying it to cheer her up. "I'd stand a better chance as a handyman like you."

"Well, why not?" Steve shrugged. "Dyke for hire. Dyketricity. The Wiring Dyke." He laughed when Ray stuck out her tongue at him. She shot Lee a glare when she saw her stifling a giggle.

"How about dyke shoves a boot up your ass," she growled. "And you stop laughing, Lee."

"I can't help it." Tears of laughter came to her eyes. She snickered again and then bit her lip and gave Ray an innocent look. "Why couldn't you be a handywoman?"

"I know electrical. That's it. Sure, I can knock things together ok, but not well enough to charge for them. Too bad we couldn't go into business together, Steve. Steve & Ray, electrical contractors; no job too small." Ray laughed at the silliness of her comment.

"And where would you suggest we get the money to get that little enterprise off the ground?" Steve chuckled.

"What kind of money would you make on something like that?" Lee sounded only vaguely interested as she toyed with her wineglass.

"Depends on how big we were. Four or five guys on a crew, we could tackle decent sized jobs ... pretty good money to be had." Steve shrugged. "Of course, you have to mortgage your ass to get the bond and the insurance and all the equipment and shit, and there's all that damned paperwork."

"Besides, Steve doesn't want to work full time any more,

right Steve?" Ray flipped a bottle cap at him.

"I could be tempted," he answered wryly. "Dangle the job in front of me and I just might bite. Like I said, handyman work isn't all it's cracked up to be."

"What if I loaned you the money?" Lee's voice was quiet but firm.

Ray and Steve exchanged glances and burst out laughing at the same time.

"Good one, Lee," Ray gasped when she could talk again. "I won't let you help me fix the roof, and you think I'm going to borrow start-up money from you?"

Lee shrugged and smiled, though Ray thought, oddly, that it wasn't from humor. "I suppose you're right. I'll just buy you a Hummer instead. After all, my boi toy deserves boy toys."

Ray's laugh died off even as Steve's got louder. "I don't want a Hummer."

"Don't worry, I was joking." Lee stuck her tongue out.

Ray got the impression that she really wasn't, but she let the thought pass and the conversation turned to other matters.

That night as they got ready for bed, Ray turned to Lee, who was just crawling under the covers. "What you said earlier, about your boi toy. Did you mean that?"

Lee looked a little startled. "Why?"

"Because I hope I'm more than a toy."

Lee pursed her lips. "Oh, for God's sake, Ray. After all we've been through you're worried about *that*? Of course, you're more than a toy. I love you. I want to spend the rest of my life with you. You most certainly are not a toy."

Ray smiled. "Ok then, answer this. Were you serious about loaning us start-up money?"

"Yes." Lee looked at her evenly. "And I think you're an idiot for not accepting."

Ray's eyes sparked. "An idiot? I've told you a dozen times; I don't want your money."

"I'm not giving it to you. I'm investing it in you. Call me a silent partner if you want; I know you dream of owning your own company. I have the capital to make that happen, or at least get it started. Why are you so stubborn?" Lee pulled her knees up to her chin and wrapped her arms around her legs, studying Ray intently.

"I want to start my own company with my own money," Ray insisted sharply, angry that Lee was bringing the subject up right before bed. A moment later, she realized she had been the one to bring it up and wished she hadn't.

Lee blew out her breath. "Nobody starts a business without a loan. Not a business of any size. If I invest in you, I take my repayment out of profits. I'm not going to sink that kind of money into something just because I love you and want to help. I believe you really are that good, and you say Steve is better than you are. I trust you."

Ray sank down on the side of the bed as Lee's words penetrated her thoughts. "So what you're saying is you want to go into business *with* us."

"Yes. I put up the capital, you two put up the expertise. It's not an uncommon arrangement."

"I'll have to think about it." Ray crawled beside her. "And I have to talk to Steve. But—" she looked into Lee's eyes and melted, just as she knew she eventually would. "As long as you're an equal partner ... I suppose ..."

Lee grabbed her and pulled her down onto the bed, tickling her mercilessly. "Just say yes, you stubborn cow!"

Trying to fend her off, Ray finally surrendered. "Yes!"

Lee released her and sank back against the pillows. "God, that was hard. I can't imagine what I'll have to go through to convince you to put in a tennis court." She laughed when Ray rose up and gave her an incredulous stare, ready to launch into another battle. "You're too easy to bait, precious."

"I'll get you for that," Ray growled.

Lee raised her arms over her head and looked at her with a come-hither expression. "Promise?"

* * *

Lee sat nervously in the reception room staring at her watch. Ray and Steve were down at the licensing office finding out what they had to do to get registered as contractors. Ray had told her to come to meet Melissa alone, saying she trusted her and that Melissa would have to be professional at the office. Even so, she was uncomfortable with the thought of being alone in a room with the woman.

"Lee." Melissa's voice suggested she was looking forward to the meeting about as much as Lee was. "Are you ready?"

"Yes." Lee stood up and followed Melissa into her office, sinking down into the same chair she had taken when they first met. Melissa also sat down and opened a folder on her desk.

"First of all, I'm glad I could do something to help you out." Melissa's voice was quiet.

Lee bit her upper lip. "Look, Melissa. I hardly know you. Ray obviously dislikes you—" she paused when Melissa snorted. "But the only thing I have to judge you on is what happened. And that wasn't a very good impression."

Melissa's jaw tightened and she looked at the ceiling for a long moment before slowly exhaling. "I understand that. I … I have a drinking problem. It's one of the reasons Ray hates me so much. I've done some very nasty things to people when I was drunk. What happened last week … I'd had way too much, and when I saw Ray, I somehow got it into my head to try and hurt her through you." There was a long pause during which Lee looked at her steadily and Melissa's eyes darted around the room. "Like I said, I'm not a very nice person when I'm drinking."

Lee considered her words. "I forgive you," she replied finally. "But I don't think we will ever be friends."

Melissa hung her head. "I'm not surprised. What happened was a real wake-up call for me. Not only was it unfair to you, it came too close to damaging my professional reputation for my liking."

Lee glanced away, uncomfortable with the feelings of sympathy she felt toward Melissa. "Let's just talk about Robert."

Melissa seemed relieved. "I've got the final report from the PI here. He got lucky; apparently, Robert has been spending almost every Saturday night at his apartment, and he staked the place out. He got these pictures of the mystery brunette." She slid a photograph forward. "I recognize her from the club. Do you know her?"

Lee looked down and felt the blood drain from her face. For a long second, she couldn't breathe—much less speak. She looked back up at Melissa, who was staring at her with a concerned expression.

"Please tell me this is some kind of joke. Please tell me this is some idea you've cooked up."

Melissa looked hurt. "Of course not!" She paused. "I take it you know her."

Lee closed her eyes, hoping against hope that when she opened them again, the woman in the photo would be someone else. It wasn't. "Yes," she confirmed in a low, angry voice.

"Who is she?"

Lee met her gaze steadily. "Louise Wiley; until a week ago, she was my best friend."

* * *

Lee pulled the Mercedes into a convenient parking space and turned to Ray, who was looking around nervously. "Relax, sweetheart. It's just going to be a huge confrontation destroying the reputations of all involved."

"That's what worries me," Ray replied quietly. "I don't want to have to hit your ex-husband."

"He'd probably collapse in a heap and sue you," Lee said. "So don't hit him."

She was still fuming over Louise's deceit; Robert had pissed her off, but Louise ... that was a whole other level of anger. Ray had finally calmed her down enough to think coherently though she still had moments of rage that threatened to overwhelm her. She kept trying to think of a punishment strong enough for what Louise and Robert had done, but kept failing.

"Do I look alright?" Ray was obviously trying to distract her, but Lee looked anyway.

Ray was wearing a brown linen pantsuit with a jacket that hung off her frame in a way that highlighted every curve of her body without being form-fitting. Underneath, she wore one of Lee's silk blouses. She had done her hair as usual, spiked on top, but had run a brush through so the spikes were uniform instead of at all angles.

When Lee had first seen her, she'd thought she was going to have to throw her onto the bed and ravish her. She still hadn't put that thought out of her head, but now it lingered behind the more intense thoughts of ruining Robert and the bitch who had called herself a friend.

"You look fine." Lee opened her door. "Let's go. I'm sure Robert will be prompt."

When the pair walked into the ballroom, several heads turned in their direction. Lee deduced from the way those people leaned together and started whispering that Robert hadn't kept his mouth completely shut. She walked up to the hostess stand and waited for the waitress to take them to their table. Ray stood beside her, shifting nervously from foot to foot. Finally, Lee reached out and took her wrist, squeezing reassuringly. Ray looked at her and smiled.

The only open small table was near the center of the room. When they were seated, she looked around for people she knew. She could name at least half those present; some twenty were friends of hers. These came over for the usual round of air kisses and introductions, though not one of the women seemed to understand Lee's meaning when she called Ray her girlfriend.

She did not see Robert or Louise. After ordering drinks, she and Ray went through the buffet line and sat back down. "Better eat now," Lee warned. "I don't think we'll have much chance once Robert arrives."

"I'm so nervous I don't know if I *can* eat," Ray whispered. "Are you sure this is a good idea?"

Lee reached out and touched her hand. "I know this is going to be tough, but I love you and we'll survive."

They managed to get about halfway through their meal before Lee saw Robert walk in. Louise and her husband were right behind him. Lee couldn't resist smiling. She didn't care that it was a mean thing to do; she was going to enjoy confronting Robert and his mistress.

The three were seated together at a table in the corner and Lee waited for Robert's gaze to find her. It did, and he immediately leaned in to speak to Louise, who also turned and stared in their direction.

Robert spent half an hour at the table eating, continually shooting dirty looks across the room at Lee as she and Ray finished their meals. Finally, as they sat back down with dessert, he approached.

"I honestly didn't think you'd come," he said in a low voice. "Do you really enjoy being humiliated that much?"

"Frankly, Robert, I wouldn't be the one you should be worried about." Lee smiled sweetly at him.

"When I'm done you won't be able to show your face in this club ever again." Robert's voice was deadly calm.

Lee looked at him levelly. "You really should think twice about what you're doing. You might not like the consequences."

"I'm going to destroy you."

Lee laughed. "Nothing you say can destroy me, Robert. By the way, you haven't met my girlfriend. Ray, this is my weasel of an ex-husband."

"So, this is the dyke, eh?" His voice was loud enough to be heard at nearby tables, and Lee saw heads swivel in their direction. "Jesus, Lee; could you have picked anyone more masculine?"

Out of the corner of her eye, Lee saw Ray redden, but Lee herself remained calm and spoke as loudly as he had. "I tried that, remember? But as it turns out, he was only half a man to begin with."

Robert paused. "So this is what you left me for. That's pitiful, Lee." His voice got a little louder.

Lee stood up and took a deep breath, realizing what she was about to do. By this time, half the room was staring in their direction and conversation had all but ceased.

"What exactly are you talking about, Robert? I didn't leave you for anybody. But what I found is a thousand times better than you ever were. Oh, Louise! Why don't you come over here? You're the one who so kindly filled Robert in on what's going on. Let's make sure we get it all straight."

Louise whispered to her husband and stood up, walking slowly towards them with a nervous expression on her face.

When she drew up next to Robert, she and Lee exchanged looks.

"Have you lost your mind, Lee?" Her voice wavered.

"You're a lying, pathetic bitch!" Lee drew back her hand to slap Louise across the face, but hesitated. *She's not worth it.*

"What the hell are you doing?" Robert roared. By this time, anyone who wasn't watching them had to be either deaf or dead.

"I'm thanking Louise for her honesty and support over the years," Lee returned venomously, lowering her hand.

Louise looked stunned. Lee watched as her husband leapt from his seat and started striding their way. "How dare you!" Louise's voice shook.

"How dare I?" Lee's voice rose and grew even angrier. She fought to keep herself under control, wanting nothing more than to punch Louise in the nose. "How dare *I?* How dare *you!*"

"You've completely lost your mind," Robert snarled. "Completely and totally lost it."

David Wiley reached the group, but before he could speak, Lee stepped up to Robert and glared at him with every ounce of hostility she could muster.

"You son-of-a-bitch." Robert stared at her. "You really had me believing that so-in-love bullshit you were dishing out. You missed your calling; you should have been an actor."

"Don't talk to me about faking love," Robert returned angrily. "I didn't get married hiding the fact that I was—"

"Was what, Robert?" Lee interrupted him, her voice scathing. "A lesbian? I only wish I'd known that then; it would have saved five miserable years with you. I may never have loved you, but at least I was faithful. You got married hiding the fact that you were sleeping with my best friend!"

There was a stunned silence. Robert looked at Louise. Louise looked at her husband. David stared at Lee. Ray sat there quietly, her arms crossed, watching them. Finally, Louise reached out and slapped Lee hard across the cheek. Instantly, Ray was on her feet.

"Don't touch her again," she growled.

"How dare you accuse us of such a thing!" Louise's voice shook, but Lee knew it was from fear, not anger. "I've done nothing but try to keep the two of you together — "

Lee narrowed her eyes. "I couldn't figure that out at first, but now ... you were afraid your dirty little secret would get out, weren't you?"

"You and your dyke girlfriend walk in here and think you can accuse us of something when you're the one who's been living a lie?"

Lee looked squarely at Robert, who was standing with a look of shock on his face, his jaw hanging slack. "You have an apartment near the hospital," she announced loudly. "You have for three years. You and Louise meet there every Saturday night."

"You don't know what you're talking about," Robert sputtered. "Don't try and change the subject. You're in the wrong here."

"Because I'm gay?" Lee lowered her voice, knowing that anyone in the room who couldn't still hear her would be told what she'd said moments after she said it. "What, Robert," she continued when he stared at her, "you didn't think I could admit it?" She looked around, seeing the faces turned towards them, seeing her friends' shocked expressions. "Guess what, everyone, I'm a lesbian. And I'm not at all ashamed of that fact." She turned back to Robert. "As opposed to you."

"I am not having an affair with Louise!"

Lee shook her head and laughed. "I've seen the pictures, you idiot. They're in my car; should I go get them and pass them around so everyone can decide if I'm imagining things?"

Robert turned on Ray, his eyes narrowed. "You did this to her. You made her change. You slunk in and ruined my marriage!"

"Buddy, I think you've proven you're more than capable of doing that yourself," Ray responded calmly, glancing at Lee. "I didn't meet Lee until after she'd left you, but I can tell you I'm damn glad she did."

"How can you choose this ... this woman over me?" Robert's voice cracked.

"I love her," Lee answered firmly, noticing several people turning away from them. "I love her more than I've ever loved someone in my life. But at least I'm honest enough to admit it. I don't care if no one in this room ever speaks to me again. I see no reason to hide what I'm doing. Obviously, you can't say the same."

David grabbed Louise by the arm and pulled her close. They spoke in low voices for almost a minute, and then David pushed her away, turned and strode off angrily. Louise looked helplessly at Robert, who glared back at her accusingly.

"Do you love her, Robert? If you do, say it now. I dare you." Lee crossed her arms. "Or do you even know what love is?"

"Robert, please. It's out in the open now." Louise's eyes searched Robert's face.

Robert turned his glare on Lee, who glared back unflinchingly. Just as she was about to turn and tell Ray it was time to leave, he reached out and caught a handful of her blouse. Yanking her close to him, he whispered venomously, "You'll pay dearly for this, Lee."

"No, Robert, you will; in more ways than one."

She wasn't expecting the fist that smashed into her face. As she collapsed, she had quick vivid image of several men smothering Robert, pulling him back as he screamed and cursed. Then she hit the edge of the table and blackness overtook her.

When she came to, she was on the floor with Ray's arms cradled around her. A friend of Robert's was taking her pulse and another was holding something wet to her head. There was a ring of people around, but all she could focus on was Ray.

"Lee? Lee, focus over here." Robert's doctor friend was waving a finger at her. She blinked several times and finally brought the digit into focus. He seemed pleased.

"Ray."

Ray tightened her arms. "I'm right here, sweetheart."

"I think I hit my head." Lee became aware of a throbbing pain just behind her left ear, where the pressure from the rag was, and a wet sensation on her face as something dripped across her lips. When she tasted it, she realized it was blood.

"You did," the second man attending her said, reaching for a napkin to hand her. She put it up to stem her nosebleed. "A good solid whack, too. We're waiting for the EMTs to get here."

Lee blinked again, her vision blurring for a moment. "He hit me!"

"Yes, he did," Ray answered quietly. "I didn't see it coming until it was too late."

"My nose hurts."

The doctor bent over and gently touched her on the bridge of her nose. She yelped. "Hmm, might be broken." He glanced up at someone. "Are the police here yet?"

"Not yet," a voice she couldn't identify replied. "But he's just sitting in the lobby staring at the floor. John and Ted won't take their eyes off him."

"Is this the first time he's hit you?" the second man asked.

Lee nodded, wincing at the pain. "Ray ... you didn't hit him back, did you?"

Ray smiled. "No, Lee, I didn't hit him."

Lee managed to laugh. "Good. I don't want to have to bail you out of jail."

The second man moved the rag from behind her ear and Lee turned her head to see him dunking a napkin into a water glass. The water was red. He reapplied pressure and smiled down at her. "You're ok."

"You're going to be ok, Lee." Ray's voice wavered. "I could have killed him."

"God, I love you." Lee didn't care who heard her. The smile that lit Ray's face held her attention and everyone else faded into the background.

Ray bent and lightly kissed her. "I love you too," she whispered.

Then the EMTs and the police were there, and Lee lost track of what was going on in the flurry of activity. She was cognizant of being loaded into an ambulance and of Ray climbing in beside her, holding her hand. After that, there was only a blur and the sound of Ray's voice talking to her in soothing tones.

*   *   *

Ray slept fitfully in the chair beside Lee's bed that night, having declined her invitation to crawl in despite the IVs.

Every time Lee stirred, she came instantly awake, and when the nurses came to check on her she would follow them into the hall to make sure that everything was OK. Finally, one of them threatened her with a sedative and she returned to Lee's side and forced herself to sleep again.

Lee was released the next morning and Ray took her home and put her to bed, ignoring her arguments that she was fine. Her first phone call after making sure that Lee was comfortable was to Jackie. Her cell phone had rung several times during the previous evening, but she had been too distracted answer.

"What the hell happened?" Jackie voice was concerned. "I called you about a dozen times."

"The bastard hit her," Ray replied, her anger at what had happened rising again. "She cracked her head when she went down. We spent last night at the hospital."

There was a long silence. "I hope they hauled his ass off to jail," Jackie finally growled. "Is she OK?"

"They say she's fine. I've got her in bed now, just to make sure."

"Is there anything I can do?" From her tone, Ray could tell that Jackie was angry. "Like go down and beat the crap out of him?"

"No, I'm sure he'll be suffering enough before it's all over." Ray managed to laugh. "I can't imagine it will help his reputation to have cold-cocked his wife in public."

"Well, if there's anything I can do just let me know."

Ray agreed and they hung up. As she suspected, within half an hour her phone was ringing off the hook. After repeating her story to six or seven of their friends, she turned off the ringer on the house phone and shut off her cell.

She went to check on Lee and found her sound asleep on her side, the covers pulled up under her chin. She returned to the living room and collapsed across the couch, letting her anger at Robert flow through her. Part of her wished she had tackled him and beat the ever-loving shit out of him, even though she knew it was the wrong thing to do.

When he punched Lee, all Ray could do was try and break her fall, and she hadn't even succeeded in that. She had been terrified when she saw Lee's head bounce off the edge of the table and saw the blood when she hit the floor—blood streaming from her nose and spreading from behind her head with sickening speed.

No one had moved to stop her when she threw herself to her knees, but when she tried to pick Lee up a man caught her arm and said not to move her. She was only vaguely aware of the others pulling Robert away as he screamed and cursed at them, of Louise's shocked expression before she turned and pushed her way through the crowd.

Lee was unconscious for what seemed like an eternity but was more likely only a couple of minutes as a man who identified himself as a doctor knelt beside her and another man pressed a cloth napkin to her head to stop the bleeding. The stunned silence seemed to last almost as long, and there was a palpable sense of relief from the crowd when Lee finally stirred and opened her eyes. As she started to come around, the doctor allowed Ray to slide her arms under Lee's shoulders and lift her into her lap.

After that, things became a blur. Only when the doctor at the hospital said that Lee would be fine did things slow back to their normal pace. Somehow, she had avoided a broken nose, but a mild concussion would leave her with a hell of a headache for a few days.

If Ray had felt any doubts of her love for Lee, they would have been erased in those few minutes when she lay unconscious. Her anger toward Robert started to fade as she realized he had done himself far worse damage than he had done Lee. Lee would recover; Ray somehow doubted that Robert would be as fortunate.

*   *   *

Lee finally got tired of Ray relaying messages from friends who had either been at the club or who had heard about what happened and called to insist that they stood by her and applauded her bravery. From the other comments they made about Louise and Robert, Lee gathered that the reputations of both had been damaged far worse than hers—Robert's especially.

Apparently, though affairs among members of the club were hardly uncommon, this was the first time someone had actually gotten punched in the face at dinner over one. The fact that Robert was a doctor made things doubly worse.

Ray kept feeding her chicken soup and crackers until she had to remind her that these were things you gave someone with a cold—at which point she tried toast. Lee finally requested pizza, which they ate with Ray perched on the edge of the mattress watching her intently as if she was going to choke. Every night, Ray crawled into bed beside her and kissed her, rubbing her belly but not going any further before nestling down and going to sleep.

Finally, after four days of this, Lee had had enough. She got out of bed and walked to the kitchen, where Ray was fixing breakfast.

Ray turned and jumped. "Jesus, you scared me! Why are you out of bed?"

"I hit my head, Ray. I don't need to stay in bed for a week. I'm tired of being in bed."

"But the doctor told me you needed to rest."

Lee laughed. "I think he meant for twenty-four hours, dearest."

Ray coughed. "Sorry. I'm being overprotective, aren't I?"

"A little." Lee grinned at her. "Forget breakfast. Come back to bed."

Once they were comfortably ensconced under the covers, Lee turned to Ray and kissed her. Ray responded gingerly, at which point Lee poked her in the ribs.

"Ow! What was that for?"

"Kiss me, damn it! I didn't go through all this for you to be scared to touch me."

Ray studied her before bending her head and kissing her again. Lee drew her in with her lips, her arms coming around Ray's shoulders, pulling her down. They made love gently, Ray guiding her to a brilliant explosion of light and pleasure before they lay together and stared at the ceiling, their breaths coming raggedly.

"I love you, Lee." Ray's voice was soft. "I don't know what I'd have done if he'd really hurt you."

"And I love you. Let's rest for a few minutes and then you can show me how much you love me. I expect to be shown several times; I have four days to make up for."

A few minutes later, Ray did.

* * *

"He's not even trying to negotiate." Donald shuffled the papers on the table in front of him. "I think he'll give you anything to drop the charges."

"It was never really about the money. If I don't drop the charges, what will happen?" Lee looked over at Ray, who smiled at her reassuringly.

Donald explained it all; including that Robert's privileges at the hospital had been revoked pending the outcome. After he was done, he paused and looked at her.

"He's done so much damage to his reputation that I'm not sure he could dig himself out of the situation even if he gave you everything," he commented quietly. "He certainly shocked a lot of people. Louise isn't in any better of a boat herself. Once they found out she's the one that told him you were a lesbian, most of her friends dropped her like a rock. They may not approve of you, but they approve of what happened less."

"I have to admit that from the social invitations I've been getting, people either don't care or they're doing their damnedest to distance themselves from Robert." Lee laughed. "I'm sure once the shock wears off, they'll think better of associating with me. Not that I care."

Donald splayed his hands and shrugged. "I think a lot of that depends on how vindictive you want to be. Right now they're looking at you as the mostly innocent victim." He paused and looked at Ray. "Although to be honest, I wouldn't suggest bringing her to the club anytime soon. No offense, Ray."

"That isn't a problem for me," Ray replied. "Golf and

tennis aren't really my bag anyway."

Lee looked off into space for a few seconds. She had been vindictive enough as it was. Her original intentions had been overshadowed by Robert's reaction, and Louise had been caught in the aftermath. She had never intended it to escalate this far, but it had and now it was mostly out of her hands. She chewed on her lower lip.

"I don't want him to get away with it," she said firmly, "but I don't want to completely ruin him either. I don't want to look like I'm just after the money, and I'm afraid that's how it will appear if I accept his offer. What do you suggest, Donald?"

Donald cleared his throat. "My job is to get you the best settlement that I can," he reminded her. "But if it really isn't about the money, then I suggest you up your original request to forty percent and require him to take anger management in order for you to drop the charges."

"Let me think about it for a few days and I'll get back to you." Lee stood and Ray did as well. They exchanged goodbyes and walked to the truck in silence. Finally, as they were pulling out, Lee turned to Ray. "What do you think I should do?"

Ray shrugged. "It's really up to you. I'm still so mad at him I'd like to see him fry, but I know that's being unreasonable."

Lee rubbed her temples. "All I really wanted to do was embarrass him. I can't believe it's gone this far. And Louise … she's really gotten caught in the fallout. I feel a little bad about that."

"It's out of your hands now, sweetheart. I think the best thing to do at this point is take Donald's advice." Ray slid a hand on to Lee's thigh and squeezed gently.

"I suppose you're right." Lee sighed. She turned and stared out the window for a while. Her head was starting to hurt. Finally, she looked back at Ray and managed a smile. "I'm tired of thinking about it. It seems to me the decision's been made. Let's grab something to eat."

"It's a little early — but what about the Crab Shack?"

"It's never too early for that," Lee laughed. "Then we can

swing by and see how things are going at the shop."

"Steve's like a kid at Christmas. I think he'd buy every tool known to man if he didn't have a budget. Once we're ready to open up, most of the crew from Baylight is coming over. We can't pay as much, but I guess Jimmy is just being an asshole and they're all sick of it." Ray grinned. "Steve's got some good connections. We'll have as much work as we can handle as soon as we're ready. Of course, you're helping too."

Lee smiled lightly. "I may be a silent partner, but I do know a couple of contractors who are willing to give you a chance. I suppose all in all things are going really well for us."

"I suppose they are. I'll tell you what—forget eating. I can think of something I'd much rather be doing and I know the perfect spot for it. There's water but no sand, and I have a blanket in the back. We could pick up some champagne ..."

"In broad daylight?"

They pulled up to a stoplight and Ray leaned over and kissed her firmly. "Why not?"

"You're a goof, you know that?" Lee kissed her back quickly before the light changed.

"Is that a yes?"

"Of course it's a yes."

With a broad grin, Ray headed towards the park.

www.ingramcontent.com/pod-product-compliance
Lightning Source LLC
Chambersburg PA
CBHW070204260626
47160CB00002B/442